NORA and .....

...bits and... ANON

NORA  and ......

a novel by
Peter Whitehead

[signature: Whitehead]

Brookside Press

Published by Brookside Press,
26a Shepherds Hill, London N6 5AH
Distributed by John Walsh, Kettering Books,
14 Horsemarket, Kettering NN16 0DQ
Tel: (0536) 84987

British Library publication data is available
on application to The Library

ISBN 0 85173 012 4

Copyright © 1990 by Peter Whitehead

First printed 1990

Printed in England

for Andrew

Grateful acknowledgement is made for permission to reprint from the following:

'Telepathy' by Jacques Derrida, *The Oxford Literary Review, Volume Ten*, Department of English, The University, Southampton. 'Totem and Taboo' Sigmund Freud. Copyright 1950. Translated by James Strachey. Published by Routledge and Kegan Paul Ltd. 'Spillway' by Djuna Barnes. First published 1962. Published by Faber and Faber Ltd. 'The Life and Work of Sigmund Freud' by Ernest Jones. Published by Penguin Books. 'The Ten Principal Upanishads' Translated by Shree Purohit Swami and W. B. Yeats. 1937. Faber and Faber Ltd. 'Nadja' by André Breton. Copyright 1960. Grove Press Inc. 'Thalassa' by Sandor Ferenczi. Published 1968 by W. W. Norton and Company Inc. Translated by Henry Alden Bunker, M.D. 'Lilith' by George Macdonald. Published by Ballantine Books Ltd. 'The Notebook of Malte Laurids Brigge' by Rainer Maria Rilke. 1959. Published by The Hogarth Press London. 'The Moonstone' by Wilkie Collins. Published by J. M. Dent and Sons. 'The Confessions of an English Opium-Eater' by Thomas de Quincey, Penguin Books Ltd. 'Steppenwolf' by Herman Hesse. Penguin Books Ltd.

'..... "the theme of telepathy is in essence alien to psycho-analysis"..... You remember, one day I told you; you are my daughter and I have no daughter..... I have a foreign body in my head, you remember..... As for Ferenczi and his daughter, and the "experiments" which he apparently carried out with them, there'd be so much to say.'

              'Telepathy' by Jacques Derrida
              The Oxford Literary Review

Part One

One

'Have you heard the news? All hell let loose! The police have gone crazy, attacked the Sorbonne and arrested the student leaders on the pretext of three broken chairs! Carted them off in Black Marias. Now the university is surrounded by an army of CRS and they'll be bringing in tanks next! All for a gang of students demanding reforms in their time-tables and hung up on a bunch of peasants in the jungles of Vietnam. Now they're martyrs, thanks to the police, and even more students are camped behind barricades singing revolutionary songs, or flinging themselves at the police like badly equipped Vietcong, armed with broken traffic signs and getting beaten up in the name of liberation - the liberation of a university! Have we all gone mad? Or is it a movie and the publicity got out of hand?'

'So I heard,' said Raymond, coldly. 'Not as bad as all that I'm quite sure. The newspapers exaggerating as usual. You see why I don't read them!'

'No such luck my friend! A bunch of students take up politics, and why not, and the police panic and now there are barricades all over Boul-Mich. Piles of burnt out cars and junk everywhere. They're tearing up the cobblestones, singing rock-'n'-roll and even making a shot at the Marseillaise. Someone will be killed soon. And then? God knows! It looks like the Nazi occupation all over again.'

'Yes, so I heard,' Raymond said again, even more coldly. He had heard rumours of the troubles escalating. But he was used to Jean-Pierre exaggerating everything - typical French! There were more important things to think about than a bunch of anarchist students and their solidarity with the Vietnamese.

Raymond was standing at the window, gazing intently at the laboratory garden. Inside the high stone wall, the neat flower-gardens were laid out in geometrical patterns, resembling an Italian Renaissance print. It couldn't be more simple. Inside the wall the plants could thrive, safe and protected from the ravages of city life outside. It was the most essential of all natural structures. Without the cell wall there could be no life of any kind. Walls to keep things out, and keep things in. The good and the bad, the right and the wrong. Everything singular and separate and alone and alive was defined by those walls. There was no freedom to live, to be a living creature, without them.

But he was wondering, for the thousandth time that week, how the lymphocyte cells recognised the invading organisms, how they knew what was alien, foreign, unwanted, unnecessary, how they knew only to attack those creatures that were a real danger to the body and its structural harmony. Instinctively, they formed an impenetrable wall around the invading organisms and killed them off. The biggest mystery of all though, was why they didn't attack the body itself. He had decided that every cell in the body must have its own badge.

'Makes me want to be a student again,' Jean-Pierre continued. He was accustomed to talking to Raymond knowing he wasn't listening. He was practising for later at his favourite Bar. 'I always loved a fight, especially someone in uniform! Mind you, when I was a soldier. Wow! Why do girls always fall for men in uniforms? God knows why I took up micro-biology!' With a despairing sigh of resignation, he returned his eye to the lens of the microscope, adding, with the best English accent he could muster, 'Back I must go, alas, to the world of the otherwise invisible and all its mysterious beauty!'

'Quite!' said Raymond, hoping he'd be silent now for a while.

The door opened and a pretty face peered inside. 'Hey you guys, you wanna drink? It's my biirrthdaaay! Mind you, all Paris is celebrating the pagan rites of spring it seems, so why not me? I'm ready to be sacrificed to any cause!'

'Kerpow! You bet, Beverly! Et tu, Raymond?' Jean-Pierre sang out, leaping up from his work bench. 'Ah, les sang-froid Anglais! Come on Raymond, even you can't refuse a pretty girl on her birrrrthdaaaaay?' Jean-Pierre insisted. He always enjoyed a chance to taunt Raymond for his seriousness.

'No of course, I'll share a drink, if it's her birthday,' Raymond replied reluctantly.

'Wow! Er, your'e rooom or maan?' Beverly added coquetishly, her Texan accent - as Jean-Pierre had wise-cracked more than once - as broad as her hips.

Raymond looked sharply at Jean-Pierre. He looked guilty and

replied hurriedly, 'Er..... In yours Beverly. We'll be there in a flash.'

Raymond had caught them making love on the laboratory floor some nights before, stoned out of their minds, and had not spoken civilly to either of them since.

★

Raymond worked late that evening, as he usually did, battling with the complexities of the human immune system, enjoying the peace and quiet after everyone else had gone. But on the way home, before taking the local Metro to his poky two-roomed flat near the Bastille, he decided to pass by the Sorbonne and see what was really happening. It couldn't be as bad as all that. The University quarter wasn't far out of his way from the Institute Pasteur. Half way there, he stopped for a beer in a café, surprised to hear people arguing passionately, so passionately he hardly heard the words they were using. But he recognised 'Merde, merde, merde alors, c'est pas vrai!' Nothing unusual really. The French were always like that. They'd fight over the price of bread.

But when he approached closer to the scene of devastation, he was shocked. None of the garbled reports had prepared him for the real thing. It was far worse than he could have imagined.

Police were everywhere, their cars alive with menace with their frantic circling blue lights, and sirens screaming. They were blocking most of the streets to the university. Lined up behind them were rows of sinister looking buses. Ambulances were vainly pushing their way through the other helpless traffic, jammed and tangled in every street. Groups of students were dashing about, singing or screaming abuse or both. A couple of cars were full of journalists with the inevitable television cameras. They were ecstatically waving arms and showing badges as they tried to push through the chaos. Raymond stopped some students who were clearly leaving, to ask what was happening. Much to his surprise, one of them snarled, 'Fuck off, bloody Americans!' He told them indignantly he was English and they became more friendly, but warned him to keep out of the Sorbonne area. 'It's getting nasty - No student jokes any longer! It's not à 'La Chinoise', my friend. It's *for the reality!*' a young girl said, articulating the last phrase emphatically, obviously proud of her English.

Raymond had seen Godard's film 'La Chinoise' some months before, in one of the many small cinemas near the Sorbonne. In fact he associated the area with the cinema rather than the university. Since arriving in Paris in 1966, he had seen all the Godard films, having fallen head-over-heels for Anna Karina in 'Le Petit Soldat'. He was continually surprised to be the only person in the world to see Godard as a total Romantic, like himself, in love with the intangible beauty of women, before and above everything else - ideas coming a dull second. But he had not imagined when seeing 'La Chinoise', alas without Anna Karina, that Godard was being so amazingly clairvoyant, miraculously foretelling the events that were suddenly, dramatically unfolding before his eyes - the students in active revolt against the might of the State and occupying the University. If Godard was not clairvoyant then he was responsible. Raymond had considered the film to be 'mere fantasy', rather naive and dull, an opinion he was hastily needing to revise.

Suddenly, he and a group of other would-be audience of the exciting, unexpected spectacle were roughly pushed back by an aggressive bunch of police, down the street towards Place Odéon. Even there, at that distance away from the centre of the action, the commotion amongst the crowd, a mixture of euphoria and rage, was so tangible and frightening, Raymond decided to do the wise thing and escape from the scene immediately. But he was going down the steps into the Métro, when a group of students charged up and scornfully knocked him out of the way, swearing at him, something that might have been, 'bourgeois pig', but he wasn't sure. He was surprised how radiant and gay they all looked, flushed with expectation and urgency, heedless of danger as they surged off on their way to the front lines - to wage war. He resented being so instantly excluded, so instantly recognised as not being one of them. Probably the blazer and umbrella. Suddenly he felt guilty he was not participating.

Impulsively he abandoned his umbrella against the metal railings, took out a black beret he always kept crunched in his pocket in case he needed to look French, and headed off after the students. It had to be more exciting than 'La Chinoise' he told himself, thrusting through the chaotic crowd, determined to reach the hub of the action around the Sorbonne.

It wasn't easy to reach even the Boulevard St. Michel, but finally he found a small side street he could slip through, and was quite startled to find himself close behind a group of students hastily building a barricade. A couple of cars had been thrust together and were being covered with splintered advertising material torn from nearby walls and a Tabac kiosk. He recognised a fragment of the life-size poster for 'Les Folies-Bergère'. It was strange to see the pink stockings and white frilly knickers kicking up over the bonnet of a Renault Quatre, as if the luscious creature was enjoying a quick bang before things got worse. Two students nearby were frantically using scaffold poles to dig near the trees, loosening the cobblestones. Why had he not expected the confrontation to be so passionate? He was astonished he'd so successfully blocked the images from his mind, preferring the easy way out, to think the French were as usual blowing something up out of all proportion. He was clearly quite immune to such images, to imagining such violent anarchy actually on the streets. Not now, here, today, Paris, 1968. Where had all this energy come from so suddenly?

He reached the main Boulevard in time to see another phalanx of police advancing up the street behind riot shields, and he nervously slipped into a doorway to hide and keep out of trouble. Further down the street were rows of armoured police cars looking like tanks behind the advancing police. A wave of students stormed down the main boulevard towards them, throwing whatever they could lay their hands on. The police advanced steadily and the students were forced back, but this clearly didn't matter to them — gaining ground was irrelevant - it was the ecstasy of the thrusting and screaming and hurling that mattered and after every retreat, they thrust forward again, until more students came sweeping down the street from behind as if from nowhere, and Raymond couldn't believe his eyes when he saw the pitched battle between the uniformed police and the scruffy people's army of students. But he felt nauseated suddenly, when something seemed to click in his mind and he was able to stop looking, and see, to know that the blows were real blows, and the staggering students were really being brutally beaten.

He looked round, deciding he must escape, and saw he was hiding near an emergency exit door of the Luxembourg Cinema. He couldn't understand why the cinema seemed to be still open. He didn't know the violence had only spilled over from the university precincts into the neighbouring streets earlier that evening. He crept round towards the foyer and was amazed to see the woman in the ticket-booth calmly looking out from behind her window, knitting. Maybe she had left her glasses at home. He wondered what she must be thinking - obviously it was a film about one of those wars that people never stopped making films about. He asked her what film was showing, to make conversation. Apart from being over eighty and clearly almost blind, she was definitely confused. 'A nouvelle-vague film. 'La Benéfice du Doute!' When he asked for more details, she said it was a play by Wilhelm Shakers-pierre about the Vietnam war.....

Curious to learn more about the Bard's remarkable, hitherto undocumented divinatory powers, Raymond looked for a poster to find out more details. He discovered the film was about a theatre play called 'US' performed by the Royal Shakespeare Company in London, a semi-documentary film examining the wider question of protest and the vietnam war, made by an English film-director whose name he didn't recognise. The main 'still' was the well-known photograph of the Buddhist monk burning himself to death in the main square of Saigon.

Raymond remembered that Ingmar Bergman had used the actual film of the event at the beginning of his film 'Persona' - in the opening asylum scenes. The sequence was seen on a Television screen by the woman, an actress, who had 'dried up ' - gone silent in the middle of a rehearsal for Elektra, as if she had forgotten her lines - but in fact, the silence was by choice and she'd not spoken since.

Suddenly it dawned on Raymond how weird it all was. From what he'd picked up casually about the student protests, they were predictably about American Imperialism in Vietnam. But now the students were being *really* beaten up for the cause. Why were they prepared to go this far? A few marches yes, a few sit-ins. But not flinging themselves at armed police. It made no sense at all. Was it really about identifying with the Vietnamese, a vicarious love of the oppressed? Or was it not more complex, tapping hate rather than love, an identification with the war-machine causing the conflict?

The police were getting closer. Suddenly they fired tear gas, and one of the canisters landed in the foyer of the cinema. The old lady screamed and went down, gasping, out of sight, disappearing behind the ticket machines. At last she'd got the message. The modern cinema was becoming too realistic for words.....

Raymond clamped his beret over his mouth like a gask mask and headed up the street. He'd not had so much fun for a long time. It really was a film come true. He found a doorway in deep shadow in which to hide, and he slipped into the darkness, but he couldn't avoid wondering if a black cat would come into the shadows and give him away..... except this was Paris, not the war-torn Vienna of 'The Third Man'. But he wasn't selecting images. They were selecting him. Raymond knew he was a typical child of his time, all his dreams and fantasies peopled by images of films and many of them were war films. His was the generation for whom war had been painfully close, but never real, as young hands clutched the edge of worn seats. And yet at that age such distinctions were almost meaningless, real or not real, especially on the deeper level, where instincts were still being tamed and moulded. It was too easy to say they were 'only films'..... they were shaping the soul.

Now though, he was becoming more and more disturbed by his mounting feelings of fascination, although from this distance, he was not able to see the actual brutality. It was more like a slow-motion ballet. But the scene was more profoundly unnerving because it wasn't the expected 'war', a huge war that wars ought to be and always would be from now onwards, post-the-cinema. The action was only seen happening 'here and there' - it was a kind of sporadic warfare in clusters that one imagined happened when two tribes were fighting at the edge of their jungle territories, or in the medieval battles in so many 'period' films - any minute he'd see Laurence Olivier on horseback! It was unnerving because it refused to be real as much as he tried to make it real - and he knew that just beyond the outer membrane of the seething battles, life was carrying on quite normally. He could walk a hundred yards and leave the quartier and have a coffee in a pavement café and there would be merely argument, albeit passionate, perhaps discussion about the sounds of it all - the sound-track - 'Ah! It's spilled into Rue le Prince!' - 'No, it's the other way!' Or he could pick up a whore on the next street corner and they'd go to one of the nearby seedy hotels, and from the window he might look down at the fighting as it surged momentarily up their street, and imagine the scene captured by a master etcher in the classic style, recalling images of the storming of the Bastille..... But not now, here and now. But that was the problem. There was something archetypal, un-modern about it all which made him profoundly nervous - not the danger that seemed far away still, nor the implication of it all that had not yet really dawned on him, but its subtle unreality meant it was happening on the level of the unconscious. Maybe that was why it was actually happening. To tap something at that level and make it conscious..... Time would tell.

He was now starting to feel something else - a mysterious, tangible force trying to draw him into the action - and he felt really scared - no longer able to experience it objectively. Now he could feel some inner barrier becoming obscure - dissolving - it was harder suddenly to keep reality at a safe distance.

He made a conscious effort and managed to force the images to recede and become mere images on the screen again of the film he was vicariously watching. He'd not realized until now, quite so sharply, just how many of his experiences and their accompanying emotions, were contained, walled in by the reality of the cinema. Now he was being forced to expect something more drastic to happen, more violent and destructive and therefore exciting. The next scene. That is how it worked. Narrative. Each scene more exciting or you were being cheated. He felt guilty, knowing he was already hoping to see some real terror! He knew it was a failure in himself not to feel anything authentic at that moment, as the people directly involved with the action were experiencing. Or were they? Were they also being duped into living out someone else's scenario? Were they like him, cocooned in swathes of images, unable to know it was 'for the reality', as the young French girl had said?

It was all becoming so confusing, he decided he must leave immediately, before he did something he might regret, plunging into the fray to make it tangible to his own body and senses. He set off down the hill, but reaching the cinema he saw a small gathering of people in front of it, from which he was astonished to see the old lady from the kiosk emerge, but carried on a blood-stained stretcher, spluttering and suffocating from the effects of the tear gas fumes. Just as he was thinking he ought to offer to help with his medical expertise, the inner doors swung open and the audience emerged, slowly, rubbing eyes, yawning and then clutching throats, gasping at the tear gas still lingering on the torn air, already staggering as if from a dentist's surgery after a brief period of anaesthesia. Raymond watched them with fascination, dazed and confused, trying to adjust their eyes to the new images, still numbed by the cinema's pseudo-hypnotic power. They stood still for some time, pillars of salt, refusing to believe the new collage-montage. When they'd gone into the cinema, there had been some scuffles further up the street, out of sight. Now, it had ruptured into real violence and the tide of action had swept down and engulfed the cinema. The students were now frantically digging up cobble-stones and screaming for Robespierre. The comfort of cinematic illusion had gone. The projector lamp had failed. History was now being enacted in front of their reluctant eyes.

Raymond knew he must go home. If he got more involved, wanting to or not, he'd end up doing something silly and losing his position at the laboratory. It wasn't so much cowardice, or lack of nerve. He was getting really hungry! But he still couldn't drag himself away, fascinated by the way the students formed into small 'groupuscules', and stood their ground, and despite the vicious, impersonal, uniform power of the helmeted police, armed with all their riot gear, the students managed to defy them, pushing them back by hurling a few blunt cobblestones and more important, sharp, well-aimed verbal abuse. The euphoria was energised by the words they could hurl at their uniformed brothers..... insulting them as pigs and puppets of their masters. This was no longer about solidarity with Vietnam or the Third World. It was about State Imperialism, repression here at home in the very structure of the shared society. And at last here was proof! Images! At last 'they' were unwittingly showing their true face..... their true colours. A black wall of faceless faces. Fascism. Self versus self. And the words and images to make it fully conscious were flowing, now that the dam had burst.

Raymond still couldn't move though and was starting to panic. He was disturbed by the obscure feelings of recognition, of familiarity suddenly welling up inside him for reasons he couldn't immediately explain. It was not merely images remembered from old movies after all. That was the easy interpretation. He was starting to become emotional, and could feel the tangible, almost magnetic pull towards the primal scene. He didn't want to be involved. A voyeur, yes, perhaps, but no more than that. A spectator. But, no involvement! Let them fight. He must keep himself safe with the images still on the surface - although they were tapping deeper memories, calling up ghosts he didn't want to be haunted by. But the force pulling him, sucking him into the action was getting stronger and stronger with every minute that passed and he knew he must get out - fast. Before it was too late. It was not his kind of scene at all. Why hadn't he gone home and watched it on television like most of everyone else?

At last he made the decision. The hypnotic thread snapped. He was off home.

He was scurrying down a side road off the main Boulevard when he suddenly found himself trapped. A group of police appeared from a small alley and were surging towards him, thrusting back a group of students still trying to hurl cobblestones. But at the moment the police seemed capable of engaging the students and crushing them, unexpectedly, as if they'd lost their nerve, or had become considerate, which seemed unlikely, they stopped - ordered to retreat by an officer behind them, shouting through a megaphone, his voice hideously metallic and impersonal. The students hurled abuse and shouts of triumph and followed them back down the street chanting slogans..... 'Down with the CRS! Down with the Nazis! Down with the SS!' Then they danced and sang 'Dessous les pavés la plage', over and over again as they linked arms and performed an improvised jig in a circle, mocking the police for their retreat.

Raymond's immediate thought, and he knew it was inappropriate and unfair, was to remember the end of term romps at *his* university - Cambridge - protesting the price of beer or the scarcity of Swedish and French au-pair girls. He felt ashamed of the thought and was starting to hate himself for his inability to interpret anything calmly any longer. In future he'd stay with the cinema for his dreams and excitements.

But suddenly he noticed a small creature huddled against a wall, a heap of helpless limbs, like a crab or jelly fish left behind by receding sea water..... an organism still barely alive in the flotsam. Cautiously he went closer, scared that the figure wasn't moving. It seemed quite dead. He gently pulled back the folds of a black coat that had twisted around it like a half sloughed-skin, filthy and torn from the fighting, and he saw a young, dark-haired girl, apparently unconscious, her head covered in blood. He tried to prop her up against the wall but she slumped down again, moaning. He didn't know why but he noticed she was wearing a tight black cat-suit. It seemed an inappropriate outfit to wage war in. Over it was only the thin black raincoat. He called for help to two students passing nearby. They looked down at her dispassionately. 'Take your woman to a doctor, friend, NOT to the hospital! There are fascists there too. They will arrest her. Take her home and then get your local doctor!!' They had presumed she belonged to him. Or was it mere words, 'Prenez votre femme'?

He knelt down next to her and gently parted her hair, but couldn't see the wound for the tangled mess of hair and blood. She moaned again and tried to open her eyes, but couldn't regain consciousness. In fragmented German, which he could barely understand, mixed with some French, he decided she was murmuring 'Enough, enough, please take me home', before she passed out completely.

He lifted her up, relieved to find she was quite light. He hobbled down towards Place Odéon, her body limp and draped over his shoulder. He was astonished that everyone ignored them. Someone even said 'Bonsoir', almost casually. Obviously it had become a commonplace sight, a young woman being carried home, damaged after the fight, going back to think again..... to talk all night of revolution, and dream, enjoying the wounds. Proud of the scars.

But when Raymond reached the main Boulevard St. Germain, a taxi stopped for them, and the driver insisted on helping them, shouting it was 'Free! Free! Nothing to pay!' Once they were in the car, his arms waving towards a hidden 'Them' as if 'They' were hovering in the electric sky in front of them, he enthusiastically explained he was sympathetic towards the students and was proud that at last someone had got the guts to stand up and DO something about 'Them!'..... and even get hurt for it. 'Now the police have physically attacked and beaten the students, all the workers will join them. You'll see! Not to share their ideas necessarily! But because the State has shown its true self! Fascism! Repression! Nazi pigs!' Raymond was amazed at his passion. He was frothing with rage.....

★

They arrived at Raymond's address and the driver adamantly refused any payment, even saying he'd go and find a doctor if one was needed, but Raymond said he could cope, being a medical man himself.

The young woman was still barely conscious, muttering broken sounds only barely resembling words, when he squeezed her into the narrow lift and took her to the top floor. There, his small flat was located, squeezed into a space the size and shape of a few contorted cupboards beneath the leaded roof. Servant quarters for a certain Dr. Caligari who might have lived on one of the spacious floors beneath, before taking a wrong step somewhere along the line.

Raymond laid the young woman on the bed and eased off her long black leather boots, while she moaned and mumbled more fragments in German, French and now, some English, as if she sensed the presence of his English posters and books. Raymond wasn't sure if she was in pain or was hallucinating. Her slurred words made him think she might be on drugs of some kind. He wondered if he ought to ring a doctor, but he decided he knew enough medicine himself to cope with a blow on the head and simple concussion. He took water and a sponge and started to gently wash away the caked blood in her jet black hair. He managed eventually to part the hair enough to see a long gash, which was quite deep. It might need stitches. He could do that himself if necessary. He had a bent needle and some cat-gut he had used to make himself an eye-piece for his microscope when Jean-Pierre had lost the rubber one.

With warm water he cleaned the wound and then bathed it

with antiseptic cream, while she continued to groan and moan fragments of German and smatterings of French. She said 'mer' a few times but he didn't know if it was meant to mean the sea or mother or some word in German he didn't know - or was half-way to 'merde'. He wondered if he ought to ring a doctor after all. What if she died in the night? But he didn't want to. He was enjoying the adventure too much. If, when she woke up, she needed one, he would take her to one of his friends from the Institute, heeding the warnings of the students not to take her to a hospital where she might get picked up by the police.

He made himself a cup of good English tea and looked at her. He didn't know why, but he knew immediately she was Jewish. Normally he didn't notice such things. Her face was too much covered with blood for him to be sure she was pretty, but he felt sure she was. Very gently, and tenderly, he took off her raincoat and wrapped her with blankets. After a few minutes, when she had become warm, she curled up, bringing her knees to her chin, as if in the womb. Almost immediately she seemed to relax and started to sleep soundly, breathing slowly and deeply. He saw her eyelids flickering rapidly, like a film that has jumped a sprocket in a projector. She was dreaming.

He found a sleeping-bag he kept for guests and laid it out on the couch. There was some cheese and ham in his desk-top fridge and he made a sandwich with some hard, unfriendly bread, washing it down with a can of beer. It was all so unreal. He gazed fondly at the lithe creature, so unexpectedly curled up on his bed like a squirrel, wondering at the speed with which she had been precipitated into his life. He said out loud, as if speaking to her. 'Why me? I just went to watch!'

Moving quietly not to awaken her, he crept out and took the lift to the ground floor to collect his mail. There were two letters, one from California which he knew contained a paper written by another Immunologist, and a letter from Jane, which he had hoped might be there. He doubted if she would have approved of the impulsive way he had brought the girl back to his flat. Not that she would ever know.

Upstairs he read her letter eagerly, feeling guilty for some obscure reason..... wishful thinking probably.

'Dearest Raymond,

Is April in Paris as romantic as they say? Can't be as beautiful as Kerula, alas - Oh, if only I could describe the magic of the spring here. Impossible - After all, I came here to escape from words, so even in writing to you I must try not to lapse, to spend time groping in my mind for metaphors for beauty - suffice it to say, the earth has bloomed - the birds have made their nests. Everything nourishes.

I'm sorry it has been so long since I wrote. Was it really two months? It is not because I do not think of you. But my vow of silence has started to tap its real significance. It is not simply that all of us in the Ashram must be silent. That is easy to deal with eventually. But I start to hear myself again, the child in me is speaking again, because I have no-one to listen to but myself, and it becomes harder and harder even to write to you, the only person I want to write to at all. Even though I do not speak these words out loud to you, I am speaking them inside my head, so it seems like speaking.

My vow of silence has at last engulfed me, broken me off from the external world, the surfaces, and permeated into the inner rivers of my blood. I start to discover the true, deep peace I came here to find. The world of words and images seems very far away from me now - and don't take this as a judgment that you are still in it! I miss you deeply.

I dance for two hours in the morning and two in the afternoon. Imagine how strange it is to dance to music that I am not allowed to hear, that I have to imagine, that has to be part of the way the air moves around me, the sound of the wind - the sound of crickets in the evening. I danced for an hour the other night. I needed an external music! Such a jerky, staccatto little dance - infinitely small moves to the music - a symphony of cricket chirps! Was I cheating? Someone has told me of a small lake near here where at night the sound of the frogs, mating, can be heard hundreds of yards away. Don't know what dance and abandon I will make of that! I am almost ready to snap.....

After my period of silence, my teacher will allow me to learn classical Indian music - Ragas and such. The other night I dreamt I danced with myself, outside of myself, with an astral image of myself, as if I was on a stage and someone

was projecting a film of myself dancing. One day I will make a film of birds, flying, and I will dance with that - and it will be very erotic. I don't know why.
Je t'aime - terriblement. With love. J. xxxxxxxxxxx
P.S. I try to write other things, but too many dots appear. They are taking over! Spaces. Pauses. Doubts. Moments of reflection. I don't know yet what it means!'

Raymond put the letter in his desk, in a file marked 'J'.

The girl was snoring.................clusters of small grunts, but then sharp complaints, interrupting dreams.

He wondered why she had been so determined to fight the police, even to the point of being injured. She seemed so frail!

He searched in her raincoat pockets, hoping to find her identification papers. But nothing like that emerged.....

In one pocket he found a white handkerchief with perfect impressions of her lips in bright crimson lipstick, or someone else's lips, a pair of dirty black tights rolled into a ball, the keys to a Citröen car, and a crumpled coloured postcard reproduction of 'The Wrathful Deities from The Tibetan Book of the Dead', on which was written, 'Every woman loves a fascist! Be careful, be-ware, be-wary. My love. A. P.S. M. called. Perhaps for Maso-anarchist?' On another small piece of crumpled paper, 'M. wants to see you desperately. I advise you stay away. They are planning something desperate. A.'

In the other pocket he found a strange wooden object, wrapped in a black silk handkerchief. It was quite old. The polished wood was worn in parts and its surface was scarred. He couldn't fathom out what it was. A string was attached to one end. The other end was pointed and was marked with a geometrical pattern of angular waves. He held it in his fingers by the string and swung it in the air, backwards and forwards, like a pendulum. He guessed it was a 'primitive object', by which he meant it was something once used by natives..... possibly in some kind of primitive rite. Either that, or it was something to do with measuring. Perhaps it was a weight. He put it back in her pocket. He was surprised she had no identification papers. If she had been arrested, there would have been serious trouble without them.

He spent the evening reading the scientific paper from California about 'Helper Cells' - those cells that seemed to instigate the protective behaviour of the lymphocytes. Then he fiddled around with some results from his day's work, trying to see a pattern in a collage of apparently random results. He always worked for a few hours in the evening. He was determined to become one of the world's important Immunologists.

But he was finding it difficult to concentrate. He was too aware of the girl's breathing, which seemed at times to be too faint and too slow. But he was also too aware of his own heartbeats, which were too loud and too fast. He knew his blood temperature was up, as it would be when it went into attack-mode against invading organisms. Or unwanted ideas. Funny how the body often reacted as if it was being attacked by organisms when it was merely being threatened by unwelcome ideas! Or the unexpected tension of rescuing a poor frail young woman from the clutches of the CRS..... perhaps saving her from worse injury. Possessed now by her absence..... she being unconscious still. Elsewhere. Absente.

He couldn't stop thinking about her, the person 'residing in the body' he had plucked from the street. What would she be like when she returned to herself? He was sure she was German. He was longing for her to wake up, even though it was better for her to sleep as long as possible, to give her immune system more time to deal with her wound.

He drank another beer and suddenly felt very tired. He had worked that morning from seven o'clock. The girl seemed to have no intention of waking up, so he took off his trousers and slipped into the sleeping bag. He lay in the darkness for some time, imagining all kinds of 'girl' that might be attached to the physical presence breathing on his bed. As Rimbaud said, 'La vrai vie est absente'......But then he felt guilty and thought instead of Jane, practising her dancing to the 'music' of the frogs. How different he imagined they were, these two women who had spoken to him tonight..... in their different ways! Quite soon, with an image of Jane dancing in his mind, naked in the night near a dark pool full of frogs, their bulging and lustful faces looking like a chorus of the Wrathful Deities, he fell asleep.

★

All night, Raymond slept badly. Images from the day's events and other images, deeper, involuted memories, resonated with each other and crystallised into sharp-edged, piercing dreams, confusing past and present, hope and despair. All night he seemed to be trying to be somewhere else. The dreams seemed mostly to be projected against dark walls in dank sombre rooms, or in blitzed buildings behind ghetto walls, where uniformed men stood in rows like dead statues, broken columns, colonnades of ruined temples, and women in black with faces covered in torn veils were fading into the shadows between them, leaving traces of words written on the crumbling walls, in blood..... and he a child, looking for someone.....

As he was waking, writhing and battling to escape his own mind as if it was the worst thing that had ever happened to him, knowing even inside the space of dream that the dreams were not his, a different dream, more tangible, finally surfaced to dominate his eddying consciousness. He was with a group of people, prisoners of some kind, building a wall. The job was exhausting and repetitive and the wall stretched as far as the eye could see. It was proof of some scientific theorem about infinity and so the work could never end, in order to prove it. Something about 'One to the power infinity' which didn't make sense. He was shovelling gravel and his hands were bleeding. He was struggling to become awake in order to escape the work. After much rising and falling along waves of conflicting feelings and meaning, he seemed at last to be escaping the grey, brittle images, and dragging himself back to awakened consciousness, to his tiny flat, which in comparison would seem warm and cosy. But he could still feel blood oozing out of the ends of his swollen fingers.

Suddenly he remembered the young woman and the thought of her instantly wiped his mind clean of the dreams and he sat up sharply, nearly falling off the couch in excitement at the prospect of seeing her again. He looked quickly towards the bed to see if she was awake, or still curled up and sleeping like a baby. Or even dead.

For a moment he seemed to be somewhere else. But then he felt his throat going taut. She wasn't there! At least not on the bed. Perhaps she was still there but invisible. He listened so intently, he would have heard the mouse breathing under the floorboards. But she had gone. He was scared by the intensity of the desolation that flooded into him. He thought of trying to sleep again, to return to the harrowing space of the dreams, which would have been more bearable. He nearly wept with frustration and disappointment, reminded of the last scenes of Godard's 'A Bout de Souffle' when the girl had betrayed, which had hurt unexpectedly and lingered for some time. He preferred happy endings. But almost in a trance, as if still caught by the ambience of his dreams, he started to search for her, quite irrationally, hoping to find her hiding in a cupboard, under a chair or at least in the toilet. But she had gone. She'd crept out like a cat, silently, in the night.

Then he found her note on his desk. He was surprised to see it was written in English.

'Dear Doctor Faulkner, Thankyou for helping me. I took one of your visiting cards - So I can telephone you! I remember everything, yet I remember nothing. Maybe that is how it always is. Always on two planes. It just seems more lucid - sharper at the moment, now that I have a hole in my head! Like Apollinaire, shot by a Nazi bullet in the war! 'Blessé à la tête, trepané sous le chloroforme', wasn't it?
Thanks again.
Nora.'

He saw his wallet, still open, from where she'd taken the card, and he fingered it, fearing the worst - and instinctively he counted his money. It was all there. Then he felt guilty for his uncharitable thoughts. After all, he'd looked through her pockets!

He went for his customary breakfast in the Café de la Paix, in the nearby square. He was surprised the newspaper stories about the events of the night before seemed so oblique, vague, confused. He guessed it must be deliberate. But most of all he was thinking of his own story, feeling sad, even betrayed, by a mere slip of a girl. All he knew was her name. She could at least have stayed for breakfast.

★

At the laboratory, he tried to work, but he wasn't concentrating sharply enough. Nothing was lucid. Perhaps he too needed a hole in his head! Jean-Pierre asked him why he hadn't shaved that morning. He hadn't noticed.

He couldn't get her face out of his mind, framed by the mask of blood. He wanted to see her smiling. He wanted to see her teeth. He wanted to see her dancing. He couldn't bare seeing her always limp and bedraggled. He wanted to hear her voice on the telephone, cheerful and confident. See her fully alive, not crushed and wounded..... or so it seemed.....

He heard Jean-Pierre joking on the phone with Beverly about their night together, and it irritated him. He had seen Beverly as a bad influence, guaranteed to disrupt the harmony of the laboratory, the first moment she waltzed through the door, wearing a scarlet blouse, too tight for her over-optimistic breasts, and a purple silk scarf advertising a shop in Dallas. 'Hi there folks. I''''Aaaaam Beverly!' His lymphocytes would have loved to have surrounded her and dissolved her away. He hated 'loud' people in general, but especially loud women.

Just before lunch he was called unexpectedly to the office of his boss, Professor Bardot - no relation to Brigitte, alas - to discuss finance he'd requested for some expensive new equipment he needed. He was surprised to learn his request had been promptly accepted. 'It seems you have been immediately approved by the Powers-that-be! People are more and more interested in the Human Immune System now we start to unravel its mysteries, especially in the States. You are onto a winner here Docteur Faulken...eur!' But even this good news couldn't cheer him up.

He was too nervous to work, so went to a café to think things over. He glanced at more newspapers. They seemed to be playing the story down. Either that or words on a page were inevitably pale in comparsion to the real thing. Maybe he'd been privileged to be there. There was little talk of the worst violence, the direct confrontation in the streets - mere 'isolated incidents'. Brief mention of the confused ideologies involved. Someone 'on the left' was claiming already that 'May 1968' would become one of the great chapters in modern history. There were no photographs of the barricades. He'd hoped to find interviews with the occupying students. It seemed the 'anarchy' had been triggered off by a petrol bomb thrown through the window of the TWA Airlines Office in Place de L'Opéra. Prior to that it had all been peaceful student committees and debates and only talk of further peaceful protest. Not fighting in the streets and blatant police repression and brutality.

That afternoon his concentration was so poor he read 'scientific papers' rather than work on his experiments. Why didn't she phone, as she promised? Jean-Pierre was irritating him beyond words, talking about women in general, although it was obviously Beverly he was referring to without mentioning her name. Finally Raymond snarled at him, 'Why don't you bring that Texan whore in here and fuck her on the floor, I'd like to watch again!'

Jean-Pierre shrugged, muttering 'Les Anglais, Les Anglais!'

'You're a racist!' snapped Raymond.

Jean-Pierre laughed but became serious, almost vicious. 'So are the cold blooded English my dear friend! Against everyone, especially women!' Then he stormed out, saying he'd not be seen again that afternoon and Raymond could stuff his lymphocytes up his arse.

Raymond was relieved to be alone and delighted to see him go. That's what he'd wanted all along. But then he felt guilty and wondered why he hadn't made it easier and told Jean-Pierre to take the day off. He'd have been off like a shot! Now it had become nasty. It was not often they admitted so openly what they thought of each other. But Raymond was upset most of all because he knew it wasn't true. Not him! He adored women!

★

That evening Raymond ventured towards the Sorbonne area again, but was turned back by police, who'd successfully blocked off the whole area. He was amazed to see barricades actually burning in the distance. But there were so many police cars and ambulances and noise and tear gas, he was pleased to go home immediately.

In the evening he wrote a letter to Jane, telling her the students were in revolt, and all hell was let loose. People were calling it 'revolution' - whatever that could mean in this day and age. He told her about the slogan, 'Dessous les pavés la plage', which he knew she would like. One of her 'problems' had been to find a way to control 'those oceanic feelings' that rose in her so often, threatening to engulf her. For that reason she'd gone to India, where they seemed to be able to 'believe in the authenticity of such experiences' - part of their cultural heritage, dealing with the intangible, and especially the oceanic..... He was missing her desperately, disappointed their letters were getting further and further apart in time. He wished she'd agreed to marry him before she left, instead of promising it would be the first thing they would do after her return.

He felt really lonely. He watched television. There were some brief news flashes - 'a problem with some extremist, anarchist groups, inciting the students'. So this was the Media's message. Playing it cool on the subject..... But maybe he wanted it to be more than it was? There was some unconscious reason to enjoy imagining all hell let loose, at the first signs..... at the first images. But it still seemed mysteriously unreal - as if etched on old grey paper - even though he'd seen it at first hand. He wondered if maybe the Media were right. Perhaps it was just a bunch of crazy students and it was only his own naive romanticism that made him want to believe it was something more..... a collective stand against the unseen 'cruel authority of the state', a phrase he remembered from somewhere.

But if he was honest with himself, such problems never gave him much trouble, ideologically or physically. He saw himself as a normal person who accepted the flaws in the system. All systems were flawed, even those in nature. In certain conditions the human body failed. So it was with the body politic..... Hell was a disease that provoked dreams and had its own set of identifying images.....

He decided he must try to work. It was his only escape from worrying. He studied some electron-microscope photographs he had just received from scientists in Cambridge, showing newly discovered cell antigens whose function was still not understood, although it was known they were part of the immune system's extremely sophisticated and complicated defence strategy - that invisible wall of cells that united so harmoniously, always ready to pounce on unwanted intruders. But he couldn't concentrate. Instead, he was wondering if Nora had taken one of the cards with his home telephone number written on the back - for special people! Suddenly he guessed the truth. She would not call! Why should she bother? She'd be too busy building barricades and fighting the police, or she'd crawled off home to forget it all and get her wounded head sorted out.

He slept even less that night. The following day he worked even more superficially. The following night he couldn't sleep at all, and had to take sleeping pills, which he hated doing. He had decided by now that she wasn't his type at all, anyway.....

The following evening he accepted a dinner invitation with some science colleagues, to talk 'shop', but most of the talk was about the student revolt. 'The Sorbonne has virtually become a ghetto, surrounded by a wall of police. I might say - a ghetto of the privileged!' someone pronounced indignantly. Raymond could sense their resentment towards the students.

One of the scientists from New York's Columbia University told horrific stories of the previous month's student occupation of that university campus, which had gone on for more than a week. There, the students were also protesting the Vietnam War, but more precisely the Physics department's CIA finance for the design of specific technology for the war. The students had been joined eventually by all the leading 'Lefties' of New York. The occupation had been 'busted' very violently by the police. As far as the scientist was concerned - 'With justification. It was them or the University! And now, look, escalation. It's happening everywhere!'

Raymond was bored - he was thinking too much about Nora. Why did he want her to telephone so much, when he knew so little about her? He'd not even seen her face properly! And most of his memories of her were unpleasant - the image of her crumpled up in the doorway, the way she fell so limply into his arms, the gash in her head, the dirty black stockings, the curious little wooden object that smacked of black magic, the way her eyelids jerked and flickered wildly when she was dreaming, the way she had left so stealthily and worst of all, the written words he'd found in her pocket, suggesting she was actually one of the militants - an anarchist. He'd probably not like her at all when they met, if ever they did. She was probably 'into everything'..... which had never been his style, if he was to be truthful with himself. He'd always felt out of everything..... everything that smacked of abandon.

★

Late in the morning the following day, while he was arguing with Jean-Pierre about the trigger mechanism and the remarkable speed with which the marauding lymphocytes moved into action once the alien bacteria were detected, she rang, from a phone-box.

'May I speak with Dr. Faulkner please?' Her English was unexpectedly elegant and correct, only lightly coloured with a German accent.

Raymond was shaking. 'Hello Nora! Yes. It's me! It IS Dr. Faulkner speaking. How are you?'

'Fine.................. except for a lousy head-ache!'

'I'm not surprised. Did you see a doctor?'

'Er..... Yes..... a friend of my father. It's not deep.'

'I know. I made sure of that.'

'It was very kind of you to go to so much trouble!'

'It was very easy. It was a pleasure!'

There was a moment of awkward silence, before she continued, 'Why don't I take you out for lunch? My way of saying thankyou!'

He couldn't believe his ears. It had not occured to him that such a mere slip of a girl would offer to take him out to lunch on her student grant - although he was pleased enough to accept, without further questions. 'Why..... er..... yes of course. I'd love to have lunch. But on one condition. I insist we share. Two students together!'

She laughed. She could tell he felt awkward. She enjoyed embarrassing men about money and who should pay for a shared meal, especially at a first meeting. To embarrass him more she said, 'No, I insist! It's on me! But I must go now..... see you one o'clock prompt at Brassérie Lipp. I'll reserve the best table. Bye!' And she had gone. Again.

Raymond knew Brassérie Lipp was the most expensive and fashionable restaurant in the Latin Quarter. He couldn't even afford to eat there on his modest research grant. Some revolutionary! She was even more a mystery than he had dared to imagine.

★

When he arrived, a little early, she was already there, standing in front of the door, smiling a delightful, cheeky smile. 'What a pity! It's full. And my favourite waiter isn't here to arrange a table! Let's have a sandwich somewhere quiet instead!' Raymond was much relieved.

She was wearing her black raincoat over a black blouse, black skirt, black stockings and black shoes, and was wearing a black scarf and a black beret. Either she was colour blind or her favourite song was 'Paint it Black'. Even her eyes were heavily circled with black khol, and they were the most beautiful eyes he had ever seen in his life. Her eyelids were heavy, half-closing her eyes, which were unexpectedly, pale blue. Bright crimson lipstick emphasised the paleness of her skin..... 'Comme la mort'..... thought Raymond. She was almost as tall as him, but gave the impression of being smaller, being so sinewy and slim. She moved exactly like a cat.

'Sorry I teased you about Lipp. I heard you lose your breath when I said I'd take you to lunch! But I insist on buying the sandwiches. And the wine. I'm quite rich you know!'

She strode off and he followed her almost meekly. She exuded so much confidence, he found it hard to remember her as he had found her..... so weak and helpless.

She took him to a small café, where she was immediately recognised and welcomed warmly, and they were quickly given a quiet table in the corner. 'You see. I do have my own café. I even have credit here!'

They looked at menus, but chose sandwiches and mixed salad, and a carafe of red wine. It was one of Raymond's principles never to drink wine at lunchtime. He could never work afterwards.

'Red wine?' she asked.

'Er..... yes..... I'd love some!'

She was looking at him coolly, he thought, until he noticed her eyes were smiling, suggesting curiosity and a certain warmth. She had a strong face, almost boyish. 'Where did you find me?'

'In a doorway just down from the Luxemburg cinema.'

'The last thing I remember was looking round at my friends. I had run forward. I saw a pavé coming straight at me. I was wounded by my own tribe! Ironic isn't it. I dodged a thousand white batons and got floored by an accomplice! That's life isn't it! What do you call them? Oh yes - cobblestones? Yes? Coming straight at my head. It was too late to duck!' She smiled wanly, putting her hand to her head. She winced, showing it still hurt.

After a moment's silence, being puzzled, Raymond asked her, 'How is it you speak such fluent English?'

'Do I? Thanks for the compliment! But no great achievement. I was sent to boarding school in England!' She looked down, sadly, at her fingers. 'You probably know. Sent at the wrong time to the wrong place for the wrong reasons. Parents are so good at these kinds of things. You see my father was a psychoanalyst. He knew all the answers. He just got the questions wrong.' She smiled cynically.

Raymond nodded as if to agree. 'But now you study in Paris?'

She looked down, avoiding his gaze. 'No..... I don't study..... not any more..... except at home. I'm not a student any longer..... I gave it up. I just pass the time.'

'Doing nothing at all?'

'No. Just waiting!'

'For what?'

'What is there worth waiting for? Shall I be dramatic and say, the end of the world?' She laughed. 'You know the scenario, the film script, in glorious technicolour! The Apocalypse? Best public relations job ever done, apart from selling the image of hell.' But she smiled, to let him know she was almost certainly joking.

'It's not as bad as that, surely?' Raymond insisted. 'But if so, how long have we got to wait?'

She smiled very knowingly. 'Being clairvoyant as I am - not exactly a witch - I know exactly when it will happen. But being a woman too - alas, a mere woman - I can't reveal the secret to a mere man I have only just met, even though he rescued me in such embarrassing circumstances. Maybe when I know you better!' She laughed again, giving the impression she was mocking him gently.

The wine and sandwiches arrived. 'And you..... Heerrr Docteur Faulkneurrrre..... what do you do at the Pasteur Institute?' She was now mimicking Marlene Dietrich, her eyes even more hooded, almost disdainful.

'I'm doing research on the human immune system. Do you

know what that means?'

'Kind of..... Does it need to be researched?' she asked, rather vaguely.

'Why of course! We need to know how it works surely? And why it fails sometimes.'

'Yes I suppose so. It sounds *very* interesting,' she said somewhat coldly. She drank her wine, gazing into his eyes piercingly. He had not expected he'd feel so uncomfortable with her, not imagined she would be so sure of herself.

After a short awkward silence, he asked, 'You live in Paris?'

'No actually. I live in a very large, unfriendly, but beautiful house, fifty miles outside of Paris in the countryside. It is lovely there. Idyllic. I inherited the house when my father died a year ago. I live there with a girl-friend.'

He didn't know what to say. 'Er..... I'm sorry.....'

'About my father? Don't be. He was really quite old. He had lived his life. In a curious way he wanted to die. At least, he always told me he was ready for it.'

She was looking straight at him, still smiling, enjoying his discomfort.

'Your mother?'

'Died when I was almost thirteen.'

Now, he couldn't think of anything more to say, but she remained silent, appearing to be quite without emotion, or curiosity. She could even be bored. Eventually he decided to change the subject, if possible. 'Why were you with the students attacking the police?'

She put her glass down slowly and started to eat her sandwich, as if pondering the question carefully. 'Attacking? Weren't we defending ourselves?' But before he could answer, indifferent to his opinion, she continued. 'I could be all cocky like the others and say because of the passionate ideas I suffer from. Or I could say because of my idealism, because I'm an intellectual idealist, even though I'm an emotional anarchist. The truth, however..... was quite different. It was probably .... boredom. And along came something to get angry about. I like getting angry about ideas, don't you?'

Raymond felt sure now that she was lying, trying to hide something, or enjoying mocking him. 'No. Not me. Not angry. I like to get excited about ideas, even screwed up by them, furious with them. I spend most of my life trying to grapple with elusive, unfriendly ideas, but I am not an angry person. Why are you?'

She answered instantly, which surprised him. 'Because I am young..... and silly..... and bored..... and yet perceptive or cynical enough to know that if everything carries on as it is, it will get worse and worse and will inevitably end up with some kind of holocaust again. People can only take so much repression. They escape it by repressing someone else, even more fiercely. But that is very abstract, I know. It's not easy at this time to be objective. But why was I fighting? The truth? I was being hypocritical. I feel quite ashamed now thinking about it. But the truth, and its a privilege I tell it, I don't often. I was being hypocritical. After all, I am lucky enough to have a house to live in and a modest income and a devoted friend. I am quite happy really, but apparently quite miserable at the same time! Empty. Sad. But that is no reason to fight! But to use Freud's words, I'm aware that Eros has been killed again, quite openly, by his immortal adversary, Thanatos. It seems to me so obvious that everything is hopelessly off course, the human mind is exiled from nature, exiled from the human body. So I see these events from my point of view, that it's the beginning of the end. I just wait. Like everyone waited in 1937 and 1938......knowing something was going to happen, but hoping it might not. So the films of the time tell us. Waiting as if nothing was happening, trying to be normal. Unconsciously though everyone knew there was disaster ahead. I feel that now. Maybe I'm someone who sees the worst side of things. Really I'm quite worried about the future. Not the next few years maybe, but it's not too far off. It will be really all hell let loose. They're just practising in Vietnam. Once in a while I get angry and let off steam. I couldn't resist the moment, when so many others were revealing the same feelings. I joined in, almost without thinking. It was quite spontaneous.'

Raymond felt even more uneasy. It was her cool tone, her way of looking at her fingers rather than him, and talking as if she was giving a lecture, or repeating one. And he felt sure she was lying, perhaps deliberately trying to put him off the scent. Suddenly he blurted out, 'Ah..... I get it now. You're a typical politician. You talk and talk and reveal nothing! It is all a mask.

You are really a political activist and don't want me to know. What makes you think I am not an activist too?'

'If I am not one, why should I think you are?' she answered sharply, smiling her all-knowing smile again.

He couldn't answer that one, so he stopped gazing intently at her, and looked casually at the people at the bar. Then they ate their sandwiches and drank their wine and for some time, he couldn't really look her in the face. The last thing he wanted was a high-powered dialogue about anarchist politics and the imminent end of the world. So he remained silent. Maybe it was all a mistake.....

'Do you like Paris?' she asked eventually, obviously to make conversation. She felt sorry for him looking so miserable.

He brightened up. 'Why.....er.....yes of course. It is my home now, or I like to think so. At least I don't feel a stranger here any longer. I like my work and where I work, which helps. I like the cafés, the wine, the bread, the coffee. The pretty girls!'

She also perked up. 'Yes it *is* full of pretty girls isn't it? Quite amazing. Where do they all come from? It's not easy being a girl here, with so much competition. I ought to go back to England if I want to be noticed!'

They both laughed.

'Do you have a girl-friend here.....or maybe a wife back in England? Or both?' she asked suddenly, almost coldly.

He felt awkward replying, and she noticed it immediately. 'I have a girl-friend.....of long standing. She has gone to India for two years to study in an Ashram there, while I do temporary research here in Paris.'

'Good for her! What was she doing before?'

'Biochemistry.'

'Rather a big change, no?'

'Yes indeed! She will never be a biochemist. She woke up one morning and announced, 'You'll never believe this but I am giving it all up. It's not too late. I'm going to study to be a dancer.' And that was it. Bang. Finished. Within three months she was on her way to India.'

She looked at him searchingly. She knew there was something wrong. She could detect the sorrow in his voice he wasn't able to hide. He already knew, unconsciously, he had lost her forever, but would never admit it. Suddenly she felt quite sorry for him.

He seemed to be too gentle and kind, almost naive, to be so deceptively abandoned.....

The waiter interrupted them, telling Nora that a young lady was on the phone for her. Raymond noticed she seemed very surprised, even alarmed. She excused herself and left the table.

He was feeling confused and disappointed. Although she was being friendly enough, he felt she was judging everything he said. He was grateful she had decided to see him, but he felt so uneasy talking to her, so aware of her gaze, he felt he wouldn't want to see her again, even though she was very beautiful in a cool, classical kind of way..... she had a Pre-Raphaelite look about her, and something of the Middle East. Having decided she was too..... too calculating, too thoughtful..... he felt relieved, and laughed at himself for having become so romantic about her. He wondered why it had happened. Probably because he had found her so wounded, in such dramatic circumstances.

She was away for almost fifteen minutes, by which time he had almost worked out how he could make an ingenious experiment to fool the T-Lymphocytes into thinking there was an invasion of bacteria, by damaging the alien cell wall with a relatively harmless virus, but with a similar RNA..... breaking down the invisible wall that seemed to exist between the various cells and sub-cells. Altering the means of recognition, which must be in the cell walls somewhere. The badge of identity.

When Nora returned, Raymond saw immediately that she was upset. She was looking really miserable. Her face had lost some of its colour. Now it appeared almost grey again..... 'Please please forgive me for being away so long..... so rude of me..... but the most awful thing has happened. My God, how boring!'

She sat down and drank her wine, tapping her fingers on the table. Raymond decided not to ask what had happened. She would tell him eventually, and meanwhile he had become excited by her again. She was looking utterly radiant, despite the lack of colour - it was her eyes flashing - with rage possibly - reminding him of a black and white 'still' from a film..... he couldn't remember which one. One of his mental collection. She was tense - with anger or frustration. She looked at him almost fiercely, almost passionately, waiting for him to ask her what had happened. She was irritated when he didn't. He noticed how exotic she looked now. She looked like Cleopatra..... perhaps she'd mislaid a valued asp.

'I can see I am having to pay for my naive curiosity for the so-called revolution!' she murmured, with obvious bitterness.

'You *were* dressed like a cat, if I remember rightly?' he said, provocatively. 'And we know what it was that killed the cat!'

She seemed amused by his observation. It helped her to be less angry. 'Yes..... that's probably why I love cats so much! Too much! I was always too curious about all the wrong things. I went to see the fighting because I was curious - didn't I? - nothing else! And that was unforgivable. It served me right I was hit on the head. Though at the time, I was surprised how much hate was ready to come out. Wham!..... just like that. Strange isn't it? It was the crowd, the dangerous pull of the crowd, sucking you in, and down, like the spring tide - and all a bunch of lunatics! Beware of the crowd. Cats are wiser. They always hunt alone! I went with the current didn't I, into very troubled waters, where I didn't belong. And you found me, wounded on the beach!'

Raymond was pleased. She was on the defensive now, almost apologising. He sensed she might even be lying, trying to make him think it was spontaneous. Nothing planned. 'Don't be hard on yourself. I went there from curiosity too, and I wonder how many other people joined in for the same wrong reasons, and ended up with broken heads! We will never know, because people will never admit the truth......Wars must be like that too, alas,' he added, quietly.

She nodded. 'Yes you are right. Wars depend on crowds, not individuals. That's what my father always said. But it is easily said. Didn't the Nazi war criminals use it as their defence?'

'Yes. 'Only obeying orders'. Just one face in the crowd!'

They were silent for a few minutes, sipping wine. Then to herself more than to him, she murmured, 'Car il y a tant de choses que vous ne me laisseriez pas dire..... Ayez pitié doe moi..... Apollinaire! But *that* is not what I am talking about. Far from it. Alas, I have problems much closer home. I just spoke to Anna, my girl-friend. This is very ironic I suppose. She got back yesterday from a tour. She's a dancer. The house has been burgled in our absence. They took the TV and the usual obvious things. That doesn't matter much. But they ransacked my father's study. There is nothing there of value. He was an old man, only a poor psycho-analyst. Not all that well known. In his study are only papers and books and letters and so on. All his life's work in fact. Since his death I have been working to put it all in order, to make it into an Archive for a Psycho-Analytical Association in Austria. Apparently the thieves turned it upside down. Why on earth would they do that, to the papers of a dead man?'

'Well, perhaps they didn't know your father was dead. They were probably looking for something valuable. Something hidden. A hidden safe perhaps. And people like that always resent such places, a library..... books..... ideas..... it symbolises everything they can never possess, even by stealing. It's the only thing they can't steal. Ideas! So they destroy the objects that embody them.'

Her eyes narrowed. She looked at him almost fondly. 'You are absolutely right. Very perceptive Herr Docteur! Very good. But I am hurt and angry nevertheless, because it was my father's study, his private, sacred place. I had kept it intact. It seems unfair for someone to have invaded it. You know what I mean?'

'Yes..... My father died when I was young too and I still have his watch and his books. That is 'sacred' I suppose. Belonging to the dead. To ghosts!'

'Yes. We attach death to something and make it sacred..... and love some times, which doesn't say much for love does it. Gosh. I do seem to load you with problems don't I? First you find me bleeding to death. Well, almost, and now I am all miserable because my house has been attacked. I knew I ought to have sold it. I ought to have nothing to do with objects. It's not me at all really. I intended to sell everything, but I can only do it when I have sorted out my father's papers. And that is taking time.'

'But can *you* do it? Alone? Don't you need an expert, another psycho-analyst for example?' he asked.

She looked away. 'I have to do it. My father was very unconventional in his ways and ideas. Very. He upset most of his colleagues over the years. He became more and more embittered as time went by. In his last years he was very isolated, rejected by the psycho-analytical fraternity. Mostly because he had dared to challenge some of Freud's most sacred beliefs. My father was trained by someone very close to Freud, on the fringe of the inner circle. Until he rebelled. I can't find anyone who was prepared to listen to him in his last years.'

She paused and Raymond nodded as if he understood. Probably she was right to do it herself.

She continued, 'You see..... he was writing a book..... his only real book, apart from hundreds of papers..... in which he was going to reveal his most original, radical new theories. Ironically, he died before he could finish it. He had hesitated for years to come out and tell the truth. He had very special ideas about sex. I am trying to put the book together now, from his notes and manuscript. After that, only then I could find someone to help me to put it into its final shape, to be published. I told you I work at home. That is what I have been doing for some time. When my father died, I left university immediately. I was too miserable to work. I wanted to sell the house, but then I got interested in my father's book, and decided to finish it. I was the only person who could do it, who could *complete* his life. Then I could sell the house and live somewhere remote and beautiful..... the desert..... India or Tibet.'

She was looking more and more miserable. Raymond wanted so much to help her, to rescue her again from her new plight. He noticed how sensual her lips were, how elegant her long fingers, how tantalisingly blue were her eyes against her translucent skin, under the heavy, dark eyebrows. She made him think of a piece of amber containing an insect. He knew it wasn't very flattering but the image had slipped into his mind when he was trying to decide what colour her skin was, and it somehow connected with their discussion about the sacred...... 'Don't worry, you can easily sort out the mess. Papers thrown all over the place always look like all hell let loose. They will only have stolen silly things like pens and silver ink-wells. It always looks worse than it is. I am sure it is not too bad.'

There was a slight hint of tears in her eyes. She took off her beret and rubbed her head and Raymond was alarmed to see blood on the ends of her fingers. 'I thought you said you'd seen a doctor!'

She looked away. 'I've been too busy. I was lying. I cleaned it up. I was shouting on the phone..... shaking my head..... I have opened the wound perhaps.'

'Let me look!' Raymond stood up and parted her hair gently. He could see the wound had not been touched and was already going septic. She had done nothing at all with it. He was furious. 'You fool Nora! Do you WANT to be sick? Because you neglected it, it's now seriously infected. What good was it trying to help you, if you won't help yourself? What the hell have you been doing for two days? More fighting I suppose. Tearing up the cobblestones and achieving nothing!'

'Do you want the truth?'

'Yes!'

'Well, yes, I did get myself involved again. It's very exciting tearing up those cobblestones and giving them to the men to throw. Alas! Even though you know you'll increase the repression with every one that goes. I'm not dumb. I was trying to change myself, not the State. But the rest of the time..... you'll not believe it. I daren't really admit it. I've been looking for my car! I can't remember where I left it. Aren't I silly? I've been so dizzy I suppose. Either that or the police have towed it away. I rang them and they are not talking about cars at all. They said it was probably part of a barricade somewhere. But! In it is my handbag with all my papers..... and those aren't legal. I'm not really legal in this country at all, but it's too complicated to explain. I don't care about the car, really. But I need my papers urgently. Fake or not, they are useful! I am in a bit of a mess!'

She had become the helpless girl again, and Raymond wanted to put his arms round her and reassure her. Her heavy eyelids were drooping even more now, like an early Florentine Madonna looking down at the mysterious baby in her arms. He wanted to fold her up in his arms again and take her back to his flat, tuck her up in bed..... and make love to her..... even if the concussion had taken over and she was barely conscious.

'Where do you think you left your car?'

'Near the Luxemburg Gardens.'

'Well that not's difficult. Let's go and look! But after I have bathed your head and sorted it out.'

He looked at his watch. Jean-Pierre would still be at lunch!

'Come on..... let's go!' he said. 'NOW!'

'But we must pay,' she said, limply, amazed at his sudden confidence.

He called the waiter and paid, while she looked down at her

feet. 'My money was in my car and my cheque book and everything, and since the chaos, the banks are very wary. Apart from being scared of thieves, they might be nationalised!'

He laughed and she laughed too. He was delighted. He much preferred to be in control. He liked paying, if it brought him some power.

They took a taxi to his laboratory, and he was pleased no-one was about. He bathed her wound. It was already looking really nasty. He insisted on cutting some of her hair. He put a plaster over the wound. She looked at herself in the mirror and winced. 'Seeing my hair look so awful is more painful than the pain!' she said, but then smiled, and thanked him for caring.

She was fascinated by the piles of electron-microscope photographs on his desk. 'But they are beautiful. I'd no idea! They would make fantastic paintings. Can I borrow them? I do some painting in my spare time too.'

He was reluctant to give them to her, until it dawned on him, she would then have to give them back..... later..... which meant he would be sure to see her again! So he sorted out some poor ones and duplicates, keeping the important ones, and put them into an envelope. He was always pedantic about his work. It was sacred too, after all.

She looked at them, fascinated, fingering them as if they were precious objects. 'You must tell me what they are all about. They do look terribly sinister, just like my morbid drawings!'

He explained they were photographs of viruses and bacteria mostly, but also some of the body's own cells that resembled them closely. He showed her how the white corpuscles or lymphocytes formed barriers around the bacteria and killed them off, mostly by starving them of the nourishment they needed to survive.

'Gosh! How weird. You mean, just like miniature ghettos?' she murmured.

He insisted on getting a taxi to the Luxembourg gardens, because she was still too weak to walk any distance, but the driver would only take them to within a quarter of a mile of the place. It was too near the action. 'C'est la guerre, pas le cinema!'

He asked her where she thought she had left her car. She pointed, and they walked towards the corner of the gardens. She said she was feeling dizzy and asked if she could take his arm, and it glowed where she held it. When they reached the corner and she pointed to the small street where she had left her car, there was no sign of it.

'Have you tried the other corner?'

'No! I *know* it was this one! I always park here. It has been stolen, and as the police said, it's probably part of a barricade by now. Ironic isn't it!'

'Are you sure it wasn't the other corner?' Raymond insisted. 'Was it at night or day when you parked it?'

She thought for some time. 'It was at night.'

'Let's look at the other corner.'

'There's absolutely no point! I *know* it was *this* corner!'

But he insisted. So she patronisingly agreed to go with him. They saw a young couple huddled under a tree. The boy was obviously quite hurt, Raymond realized, half hidden under a raincoat. His arm was broken. The girl said he'd been beaten up by the police. She was frightened. The boy was barely coherent. They said they were waiting for help which was on its way. At all cost they could not go to a doctor or a hospital.

Raymond felt desolate. He asked Nora if it was really that bad. She laughed. 'You fool. Didn't you see it with your own eyes? You were there! Or did you turn a blind eye, too? It is far worse than you can imagine. What do you expect? Polite repression? They have controlled us with lies and mystification for years, and when that failed, they use brute force. Brute force provokes brute force, so it spirals. The one with the most force will win. When they bring in the army, it will be over. You will see. I didn't study Hegel, Lenin and Marx for nothing!'

'You see! I told you, you are an activist. I was right!' Raymond said triumphantly.

'Okay you were right. I am an activist. I shot two policemen. It was me who threw the first petrol bomb. I enjoyed every minute of it. It was one helluva turn-on!' she said, but then winced and held her head. And that silenced him.

They reached the other corner of the gardens and immediately found her car, parked very badly on the edge of the road. In peace-time it would have been towed away within minutes. And that silenced her.

She insisted on driving him back to the Institute, before driving herself home, but after four hundred yards and three near-misses, nearly killing them both, he offered to drive. 'My head hurts so much I can't see straight,' she said in defence.

He turned on her sharply. 'What do you think you are doing? How can you cope in this state? You are hurt. Don't be stupid! What are you trying to prove? You can't drive anywhere, least of all fifty miles into the country.'

'But I have to go home Raymond. Anna leaves tomorrow morning. The house has been burgled. What else can I do? I am alone!' She put her head in her hands. 'What a fucking nightmare! Why the hell did I join the others at the last minute? All along I knew I should be a voyeur and merely watch!'

He put an arm round her gently, and she relaxed against him.

'I'm sorry Raymond. Aren't I a bore and a nuisance. You have been very patient. Thankyou.' She closed her eyes and they rested together without moving for what seemed an eternity to Raymond. He looked at her hair. It was so shiny. She must have washed it recently, without caring for the wound! He could feel her breasts against his chest. He told himself it was lucky she was not in his apartment. He would have given her no chance to resist. Once would have been better than never.

It suddenly dawned on him what he must do. *He* would drive her home! He needed a break from his work and there was talk of Paris grinding to a halt anyway. He could leave his lymphocytes a few days. The electricity had been cut a few times already.

'Listen Nora..... I have some work to finish this afternoon. I can tie that up quickly enough. I can take a couple of days off, now, if I want them. This evening..... you have no choice..... I am going to drive you back home. No arguing!'

She turned and looked at him. She would have preferred perhaps to say no. But she had been almost asleep. Her eyes were nearly closed. She was weaker than she wanted to admit. She had lost a lot of blood. Her lips were quivering. 'You are such a gentleman Raymond. Do you really mean it?'

'Of course!'

She put her head back on his chest. 'I admit it. I feel really ill. I have no choice. I accept. My house is beautiful. You can stay there a few days and enjoy the countryside. Paris is falling to pieces anyway. Good riddance. Cities were designed only to breed disease, and wipe out the poor. The pox. Or to keep the whores all in one place. Baudelaire! Except I exaggerate. You know what he said about crowds? The desire to join them is purely erotic. Forgive me if I quote. She seemed to be going into a trance, or passing out..... but she was determined to render the appropriate quote..... She spoke in a different voice.....

> '"My intoxication in 1848. What was it? The taste for revenge. The natural pleasure in destruction. To take one's pleasure in the crowd is an art. And only the artist can indulge in the debauch of vitality at the expense of the human race. What men can love is so slight, so restricted, and so weak, compared to this inneffable orgy, this sacred prostitution of the soul that abandons itself completely..... to the crowd..... to the unexpected which reveals itself in the passing stranger."

Not bad eh? But I know it because it's my favourite quote.'

He was amazed. 'Very good,' he said, genuinely impressed, although he'd not precisely followed the argument. He'd been too fascinated by her mouth as she enunciated the words and worried whether she was about to pass out completely.....

But she carried on, her voice slurred. 'The passing stranger! Wasn't that you? But listen. It can only get worse. It will do you no good to stay in the city. Paris is sick now - a ghetto. Either that or it will recover and become worse. Come to the country. Escape. And you will enjoy yourself..... I am a good cook. I have a doctor there. The city has no doctors for itself, only police. He can help me..... er..... Baudelaire also said,

> "We all have the republican spirit in our veins, like syphilis in our bones - we are democratized and venerealized."

Er..... you were my passing stranger! Without a uniform, but Thankyou!' And she seemed to lose consciousness..... or was finally hallucinating.

He drove the car to his laboratory, left her for a moment, and brought a blanket down to her and some strong pain-killing pills and anti-biotics. He insisted she took the medicine, although she clearly didn't want to. She seemed only half-conscious. 'Ugh..... drugs..... I hate drugs.' But then she said she could sleep happily enough in the car, waiting for him while he finished his work. 'I'll be safe here like in a cocoon. Then we can go! Bye!' She passed out.

From time to time he checked on her. She was sleeping soundly, curled up like a kitten on the back seat. He kept the keys in his pocket, so she couldn't escape. He was determined not to let her out of his clutches again.

★ ★ ★

Two

During their journey, Nora still seemed drowzy and confused and gave many wrong directions, so it took them more than three hours to reach her house, an hour longer than it should have done. By the time they arrived, Raymond had revealed so many things about himself he'd have preferred not to, he was feeling quite empty and drained. Nora, however, had disclosed few things about herself, that either weren't true, or were nothing of real importance. She was feeling quite whole and unthreatened, all her veils intact. They were getting to know each other.

She had asked him, 'Why Immunology, of all weird things!'. He tried to explain but she kept interrupting. 'But that can't be the reason! .... Never! .... You don't know the truth about yourself at all! You only *think* you do! ..... There must be a reason why you are so concerned with defence systems!' She forced him to repeat many of the details of his sudden 'conversion', after wanting to be a surgeon for most of his training years, as if she was sure he'd made a profound mistake. It seemed to worry her, having to think about such a physical mechanism defending the body ..... as if she'd have preferred it to be all in the mind .....

Whenever he asked her a question, she found a way to turn it inside out, so it appeared to be a question he was really asking about himself, and it was always too late by the time he realized the subterfuge, because they were on the next question, or in the next town, circumnavigating the winding streets. He had never met a girl who was so 'political', so evasive, so conscious and secretive in everything she said. But he found her fascinating for this very reason .....

She said she was disturbed by the complexities of the body's immune system, because it only needed one of the individual particles to get out of step with the others ...... It intrigued her and provoked strange associations. Some of the phrases he used to justify his obsession - which is what she said it was, she could tell from the way he was so defensive about it - reminded her of the way her father used to talk, when he was trying to prove his work was 'scientific', for the sake of his reputation. 'Knowing it wasn't! He was very unsystematic. It was all instinct. That is why he was so successful. He was utterly romantic really, but would never admit it! Except secretly ..... to no-one else of course ..... only to me!'

Each time Raymond became more aggressive and tried to make her talk more fully about herself, she became dizzy again and appeared to drift. On the few occasions she appeared to answer his question, giving an apparently clear and lucid answer, it was not to the question he'd asked. She would then apologise for being so unclear, or 'woolly', but giving no hint she was deliberately evading the real question. Raymond knew that women could be furiously evasive on first meeting them, so he wasn't too worried. It was their prerogative to remain mysterious. Later she would be more revealing. But he felt she was being too defensive at times, and there must be a reason. He wondered if her apparent confidence was recently contrived, a defence against the loss of her father. She was probably lonely. But she had no intention of telling him anything more than the bare minimum, and often he was sure she was probably not actually telling lies, but definitely avoiding the truth .....

However, she winced each time he braked too sharply, so he knew she wasn't lying about the pain from her wound. That was quite real. He tried to drive as carefully as possible.

About two hours out of Paris, it started to rain heavily and it was difficult driving on the twisting and badly lit country roads. They didn't talk at all for the last ten miles or so, except when Nora gave erratic directions, and once or twice he recognised the same crossroads, but didn't complain. He'd almost given up hope of ever getting there, when finally she pointed to an imposing stone arch at the side of the road, framing two ornate, metal gates. 'Home!' She told him to wait, while she opened them. 'I'll do it! You'll lose the keys or something ..... it's far too complicated! These are the front gates too ......' He tried to argue but she seemed quite certain he'd mess it up somehow ..... 'My father could never get it right either!' she said finally.

She found the keys in her bag and staggered towards the gates, caught in the eerie rain-lashed cones of light from the headlights. She fumbled for some time before a gate opened. There seemed to be two locks. She pushed one of the heavy gates and indicated he could drive through the open half. It was a tight fit as he squeezed through the narrow space. Once inside she climbed back into the car, after locking the gates behind it. By now she was soaked. 'At least it will save me the pain of cleaning my wound!' she said, mischievously. He drove two hundred yards through high trees before the house came into sight. For some unknown reason he felt suddenly very excited, almost as if he recognised the house. It was a tall stone country mansion with a steeply sloping grey slated roof with turrets on each corner. A house in the style of a chateau. They were quite common. He had seen such a house a hundred times in French films. But in the rain, and illuminated only by the car lights, it looked stark and mysterious. Almost ominous, more like a set for a German Expressionist film. He was feeling quite apprehensive, but nevertheless he felt he might be staying there a while. It was 'right' somehow. Familiar. But maybe that was more wishful thinking.

Nora ordered him to stay in the car while she opened the front door, went inside, and turned on the light over the front porch. She waved and he followed her inside, carrying the bag of clothes and books he had managed to pack at the laboratory. Often he worked late into the night, sleeping on two chairs, so he kept a few bits and pieces there to make himself comfortable.

Nora had expected her girlfriend to be at the house, and she was upset to find the house so cold and empty. Scornfully, almost bitterly, she blurted out, 'Anna should be here. If she had one streak of decency in her, she damn well would be. But as usual she'll be with some man or other. Probably her new director. I don't know why I put up with her. Probably because she never brings them back here. But that's *only* because I don't allow it! I really must find myself a new girl-friend. She keeps me company so rarely I'd be better off with a labrador. Mind you, that would keep my cats away. I'd hate that!'

To Raymond's surprise she suddenly whistled a piercing wolf whistle, and two cats came scampering into the hallway. They were the most beautiful cats Raymond had ever seen. They didn't look like ordinary cats at all. They were the colour and shape of miniature lions. Normally he never noticed cats. 'Are they wild?' he asked, not knowing why such an idea came to him so quickly.

She laughed. 'They are Abyssinian Mountain cats. The only species of natural wild cat that can be tamed - if only partially. It is appropriate they are creatures from a land of the great Abyss! Some part of them always remains untameable. Like us, living perilously on the brink of the unconscious!'

'They're beautiful.....' Raymond murmured. 'So lithe, so sensual!'

'I don't need to feed them. Only symbolic meals, to show I love them. They prefer to hunt for themselves. They only say hello when I arrive. They hear the car and come inside the house. Half an hour later they are off again..... hunting.'

She knelt down and they came close to her. She caressed them proudly, not patronisingly or sentimentally, not mewing and coying. She was poised and serene. Raymond remembered a miniature painting he'd once seen of a Mughal princess with two hunting leopards at her feet, in a tent at night, on a mountain slope in Kafiristan..... listening to a Pathan poet recite a verse, probably about the beauty of gardens and women..... in that order of importance..... or the unpredictability of avalanches. Behind them was an ominous cliff that seemed about to fall and engulf them. It was at that moment he realized how beautiful Nora was. She was not obviously sensuous. Her eyes and mouth were sensual when she smiled but she was beautiful. Serene. Her beauty suggested something distant and untouchable, but nevertheless very precious. Her profile might have been drawn by a Persian calligrapher for the cover of Layla and Majnoun..... one of Jane's favourite books.

'Strange isn't it. They only come to make sure it is me. They show me just a moment's affection, a mere sign, and then they leave. In the morning I find their presents in the kitchen. Baby pigeons..... voles..... snakes. All kinds of things. But when they know I am here to stay a while..... the presents disappear. I love them passionately..... whatever that might mean..... Mere words I suppose. Their love for me is very cool and mature. But they are so perfect. So clean. So sure of their ability and *right* to kill..... ruthless and unflinching, a part of nature, expressing its certainty..... as we, strangers in the world of nature, are not! All we express, with our conscious

cruelty, is our uncertainty. Our insecurity in the natural world, now that we have to live by the harsh rules of rationality......'
She was gazing at them wistfully, talking to them more than him. 'Adrift on the surface of things with no roots in the feminine, no claws in the flesh any longer......'

Suddenly she realized she was talking to herself and stood up quickly, but too quickly and winced again, clutching her head. 'Ouch!..... You see what talking does to you! Enough. I will show you to your room Herr Docteur. We ought to sleep. I'll get you a drink. What would you like..... whisky..... a beer..... tea? Yes, of course, tea! You are an Englishman..... and..... I might add, according to the legend, a real gentleman too! It was so kind of you to drive me here. I will bring you a POT of tea..... of Darjeeling..... my favourite. Because of that, it is the only one I have in the house!'

But now she was too tired to wait for a reply, and looked ready to faint, so he picked up his bag and she took the hint. He followed her up the massive polished wooden staircase, which would not have looked amiss in a Beverly Hills mansion. On the first floor, along a small corridor, she opened the door of his room, in which he was astonished to see a huge Baroque mahogany four-poster bed. 'The guest room Sir! Sorry about the pretentious bed, but that was not my idea,' she said coldly. 'But you see it has a nice desk - Louis XIV of course - where you can work. My father had excellent taste in some things. He was once a poor man. Very poor. From the ghetto. Psycho-analysis made him rich, so he made the most of it and collected beautiful things. I will show you his Russian icons. They were fortunately in the bank at the time of the robbery. There was really nothing here worth stealing. Not even me! Especially me!' This seemed to amuse her greatly.

She kissed him fondly on the cheek, in a matter-of-fact way, as if he was now part of the family. On the way to the door she said quietly, 'See you for breakfast Herr Docteur!' He wondered about the Darjeeling tea, but it never arrived. He didn't mind. He was very tired himself and fell asleep immediately, having found the bathroom for himself.

★

The following morning, while waking, images from a dream were still haunting him. He was sleeping in a weird, elaborately decorated tent, with four walls and a carved pole in the centre. Outside, there were snow capped mountains. It was a long time ago, during the time of the Pathan poet Krushal Khan Khattack, whose poems he knew quite well and liked. Jane had often read them to him before she went to India. He was awoken in the dream by a black jaguar. The beautiful animal crept into his tent and after the initial pang of terror, he noticed it seemed to be exhausted from hunting. It let drop a small dead animal on the carpet. Then it started biting the wooden pole in the centre, as if it was sharpening its teeth..... utterly oblivious of his presence. He hardly dared to breathe, he was so scared. Suddenly the tent fell on top of them and the animal ran away...... When he woke up he was tied in knots in the sheets. So much for the sublime significance of dreams, he thought to himself as he was recovering his composure.

He still felt very tired, but he was excited and curious about his new surroundings. He dragged himself out of bed and opened the heavy velvet curtains over the tall windows opening onto a small balcony, and was astonished to see the extent and magnificence of the garden. It was a mass of bushes in flower, between tall, majestic trees..... some he could recognise, like Lebanese Cedars, massive Plane trees and tall slim Cypresses. It seemed impeccably tidy and neat. At the bottom of a sloping lawn was a small lake, its surface roughed by a strong wind, speckled with bobbing birds..... various kinds of ducks and a pair of black swans. He thought he recognized a pair of Merganzers, with chicks. There were four weeping willow trees at the edge of the water, deliberately planted in a square surrounding the curved lake, their long fingers dipping beneath the surface.....

He looked at his watch. It was not yet six oclock. He closed the curtains and went back to bed and with difficulty, managed to fall asleep again..... after wondering where Nora was sleeping, and if her walls were decorated with black silk, and if her sheets were black with crimson flowers on their borders and if she wore a black lace nightdress.....

★

Later, he was awoken by Nora's knock on the door. He called to her to come in. 'Ah . . . . . Herr Docteur! A little bit late, but here is the pot of tea I promised you!' She was dressed in black as usual, but wearing a red shiffon scarf around her neck. Her hair was loose and untidy, almost concealing her beauty. She seemed relaxed, and was smiling mischievously, obviously amused by his presence in her house.

She said she hoped he'd slept well. After saying how comfortable he'd been, he asked her about her head wound. She said it seemed better, but he ought to look at it later. She sat on the edge of the bed as he drank his tea. Then he noticed she had been crying. Her eyes were glistening, tinged at the edges with the hint of red that betrayed the recent tears, and seemed even larger than he had remembered them. He didn't feel he had the right to ask her why . . . . . but she knew he had noticed.

After a long pause, she said almost casually, 'You can stay a couple of days . . . . . or so . . . . . can't you? It is very peaceful here.'

He wanted to tell her he could happily stay there forever! Even though she was still so distant, so remote. But he felt he already knew her very well, and he could be quite happy, waiting. It might take a long time to reach her, but he would persist, however long it might take.

'Well, yes I can, for a few days . . . . . if you persuade me . . . . . until I am sure you are well, physically . . . . . and you are fed up with me!'

She smiled. 'The country air will do you good. And in Paris, all hell is let loose. I heard it on the radio. The whole city is going on strike. There are still battles in the streets. It's the *last* place to be! The University authorities still won't talk to the students. It's insane of course. Madness. It might really blow up into something bad. They treated us like sheep for too long, teaching us to live a permanent sleep and be happy with trivialities. The soft-sell with the rubbish of modern life! Now the sheep have become wolves, and the State has cowered and failed. Always they were the predators. Now it's us for a while. But not for long. It can only get worse. You are better here, breathing the healthy air. Because there is nothing *at all* we can do about it, now that the action has started. Let others fight. Look what happened to me. I got my head broken the first night! I always knew I'd be a lousy anarchist. So be sensible and stay here. If you want to let off steam, you can take my father's guns and shoot some ducks. There are hundreds of wild ones on the lake, being a nuisance to the residents!'

He was surprised by her suggestion. 'Don't worry about that. I hate that kind of thing. Me, shooting? Goodness me, I am happy just to walk and climb trees. Anyway, how would I know which ducks were visitors and which ones resident?'

She laughed. 'It's easy Herr Docteur! The way they swim on the water. I can show you. It's easy.'

'Do you *want* me to shoot the ducks?' he asked, amazed by her insistence.

'No. Not really. But you are a man . . . . . so I supposed you would need to.'

He pondered this for some time, sipping his tea. He'd never liked shooting. She was not looking at him. She was looking towards the windows.

'Did your father shoot a lot?' he asked eventually.

'Yes . . . . . he liked shooting. But for the pot only. He'd only kill if it was something that could be eaten. That is how you recognize a poor man. The rich kill for fun. He'd kill vermin of course.'

There was an awkward silence. 'What did your cats bring you this morning?'

'Half a dozen small ducklings, barely two weeks old. Tragic! I fed them to the crows. It's sad, but I cannot teach them, can I? I wish they would learn which were the unwelcome visitors!'

She turned quickly and looked at him. Her tone was suddenly serious. Almost a different voice, with more accent. 'I spoke to Anna. She was sorry not to be here last night. She wasn't expecting me! She is coming to lunch, so you will meet her. But . . . . . I shouldn't tell you really. There is some other, very bad news . . . . . very bad indeed.'

She looked away and said nothing. She was wanting him to ask about it, to be responsible for forcing her to reveal the bad news. Otherwise she wouldn't or couldn't. He presumed it was about the robbery. 'Has something valuable been stolen?'

'Yes! Exactly! The most valuable thing of all. The *only* thing of real value!' she said, almost eagerly.

He couldn't imagine what it might be. Perhaps one of the

Russian Icons not in the bank. He knew they could be very valuable. Some silver perhaps. Jewelry of her mother's. It was clear from the house and its furnishings, they were very wealthy. 'Tell me. I don't know. What is it?'

'My father's manuscript. The entire book.......... everything I needed for my work!'

Raymond didn't know what to say or how to react. Such an idea hadn't dawned on him at all.....

'It wasn't a simple burglary, a normal break-in, as Anna said. They made it look like it. No. It was a deliberate theft. They have taken the entire manuscript, his work and mine. But the worst thing is I know who it is, but even so, there is nothing I can do about it! She's too clever. I never thought she would stoop to this! The bitch!'

She was still looking towards the window. But then she lay down on the bed resting her head on his feet under the bedclothes. He could feel her body shaking with anger.

'Who is she? Why on earth did she want it so much?'

'There's only one person who would do such a thing. The woman who is the subject..... the woman whose analysis is the subject of the book!' Nora turned to look at him. She sat up on an elbow. 'You see the book was a brilliant case-history. A beautiful piece of detective work. A perfect elucidation of a particular woman's mind..... and even more important, her sexual fantasies. It is the most perfect book of its kind. It reveals precisely how the female mind works. Some might say, how it needs to lie in face of unbearable, unimaginable reality! Running away into fantasy..... and how some of the most horrific things of reality are our collective fantasies unleashed. It was a very tender book, very frank and utterly harrowing. Most of all it was about the rift between the masculine and feminine ..... which rips society apart. The rift in which invisible walls and barricades are built. The only person to want the book suppressed, alas, was her!'

'Couldn't it be published with different names? Isn't that what usually happens?'

'Of course it could. Why not! No-one of the general public could have known it was her. But it was not that really. She simply didn't want it to exist! She is a woman! Its mere existence would threaten her continuously. She didn't want the truth known. Some truths all women must keep secret, she would say. But it was my father's argument that such self-repression was as dangerous as repression from outside. If not more dangerous. But she didn't want my father . . . . . even in his death . . . . . to get the credit for curing her!'

'She doesn't sound very cured if she could be so unfair, or act so irrationally. To break in and steal the manuscript,' he said quietly.

Nora smiled. She went to the window. 'You don't know women Raymond. She *was* cured. Cured enough to become herself . . . . . her real self . . . . . her true self, which is the one she most wanted to be. However ruthless that might be! She became herself alright . . . . . and now she has won! She has proved the principle of evolution has she not? She was always a survivor. I don't begrudge her that. She survived horrors we cannot imagine. You see, she was in the Warsaw Ghetto. A mere child. At least a young woman. One of the few to survive. But it is much more complicated. Her story has many facets. Not merely survival. She has no right to suppress the truth. Her story should be given to the world, especially to the world of women, generously, in all its nakedness and shame. All its guilt. I'll tell you about it later. Shall we go for a walk, before it rains? It is sunny now, but it will rain about eleven o'clock. See you downstairs for breakfast. I unfroze some croissants last night. They are as good as new!'

★

After breakfast, they walked in the garden for more than an hour. Proudly, she took him to almost every tree . . . . . as if each one was a special person. She described the various flowering bushes, their scientific names, where they'd come from and when they blossomed. She showed him the rock gardens and small meadowed glades inside clusters of the tall trees. She pulled back branches in bushes and hedgerows to reveal bird's nests still occupied. She knew every one. He was amazed at the extent of her knowledge, and said so. 'Every little girl has a magic garden. This was mine - I was privileged, because it was quite real! When I grew up I learnt all the names, which took away most of the magic of course, but not all. I am lucky.

Because I am rooted here, I can still recall the mystery when I want to. Except it gets harder as I grow up! If I try hard enough - it's like meditation - I can make everything 'la vie en rose' again..... or should I say, en rose en rose en rose. Most of all I loved the willow trees. I don't know why, not merely because they make me sad.' She pointed out the resident ducks and the visitors. There were subtle differences in the way they swam on the surface of the water. He suspected she might be exaggerating - it seemed too easy - but not wanting to offend her, he said he could see the difference too..... and she smiled with pleasure. He was not sure whether her pleasure derived from admiring his newly acquired skill, or her power to persuade him to lie, in order to please her. It didn't matter. He loved to see her smile. That was a different kind of truth, complete in itself.

Later, after making coffee in the huge wood-panelled kitchen, she reluctantly allowed him to examine her wound. She had worn her beret while walking in the garden, 'To protect my raw, exposed brain from being ravished by the elements!'

He was horrified. The wound was much worse than the day before. 'Are you taking the antibiotics I gave you?' he asked, angrily. She seemed hurt at his gruff voice.

'Of course. What do you think I am, a fool? I want it to get better. I am doing everything you asked me to..... Herr Docteur!! It's not my fault if my body is so slow to react.'

He made her boil water and they sat at the table while it cooled. He needed to cool off too. He hated people taking medicine for granted. He needed to let off steam, so he walked round the kitchen, making sure she could see how angry he was. The kitchen was so big and lofty it resembled those in houses in the Middle Ages. He imagined himself sitting at the head of the long, oak, refectory table, listening to the complaints of the serfs, as he dished out benevolence and advice.

He bathed the wound and it hurt her. It was swollen and inflamed. He insisted on cutting off more hair which she resented bitterly, before he dressed it with antiseptic cream. 'If it's not better tomorrow, I'll have to change to different antibiotics. These are not working. It might be advisable to get it stitched, although it doesn't seem that deep, but I can't tell while it's suppurating. It should have started to heal by now, with the antibiotics. But I'm not a real doctor you know!'

She seemed utterly miserable, and sat with her head in her hands. She admitted it really hurt. It had kept her awake most of the night. She asked if he had any stronger pain-killing pills. When he said he hadn't, she murmured..... softly......'Anna will get me some. She gets me everything.' She seemed dizzy again. Touching the wound had made her more conscious of it and it hurt more. She suggested he went to his room and worked. She wanted to be alone to recover, and meanwhile she could prepare lunch.....

★

He worked in his room, reading scientific papers, occasionally looking out of the window at the idyllic scene. There wasn't another building in sight. He could have been anywhere. Sometimes it was nice being nowhere in particular, but with someone in particular, however provoking.....

Some time later, he heard Anna arrive in a car, and soon after he could hear them in the kitchen, chattering away in German. He had expected to hear them arguing, but they were laughing and giggling, apparently very happy to see each other. One of them started playing a piano, and when the music suddenly changed to a song by Marlene Dietrich, he heard Anna singing it in German. She had a smooth, seductive voice. It aroused him, just listening to it. He decided it was time to join them.

He found them in the drawing room, Nora still playing, Anna still singing. They didn't see him, so he watched, fascinated, half hidden in the curtains near the door.

Anna was not as tall as Nora, but she was striking looking, and had that indefinable theatrical quality of 'presence'. It was the way she was half draped over the piano, as if in a night-club, and the flamboyant guestures towards Nora as she sang. It was her long, straight blonde hair, cut very straight beneath her shoulders. It was the way Nora seemed to be in her power, following her, phrasing the music to her movements, her timing. It was the way she was dressed. Tight faded-blue jeans, tied with an outrageously vulgar man's tie, all stripes, and her low-cut white frilly lace blouse with huge red roses and hearts sewn on it haphazardously, by hand. It was her figure, which reminded Raymond either of a voluptuous Vargas pin-up he had kept hidden for years inside the back cover of one of his physiology text books, an image entitled 'Silk Stockings' from a 1956 Esquire Magazine, or an earlier painting called 'Fleurs du Mal', which was later used for a Miriam Hopkins epic called 'Song of Songs', a copy of which he had kept inside the book 'Experimental Reactions in Rheumatic diseases'. As a teenager he'd been an avid collector of Vargas images. Until he saw Anna naked, he would not know which of the images she recalled to his mind..... and fingers.

He tapped on the door and they both looked round sharply, having forgotten there was a man in the house. Nora stood up and waved to him to come forward. 'Anna..... This is the man who saved my life! Herr Docteur Raymond..... er.....' She had forgotten his surname! She spoke in a more exaggerated German accent than before. Anna shook his hand and smiled awkwardly and turned to Nora and said something in German. Nora translated. 'She's sorry she can't speak English, but she understands quite a lot. She says thankyou for saving me from a fate worse than death. Getting caught!'

Raymond didn't find Anna particularly pretty. She had a full mouth and a nice smile and large, pretty eyes, but her face was too long and her nose seemed too hard. He thought she was in her late twenties, and had the air of an out-of-work actress. She was too obviously sexy. Tarty. In fact she was altogether too hard looking, and she was looking at him with so much suspicion, he felt sure he would not get on with her, even if he could speak her language. But she was very sexy.....

'Lunch!' Nora declared, grabbing Anna roughly around the waist, before leading her out of the room towards the kitchen. 'Pizzas I'm afraid. This afternoon we must go shopping in the car Raymond, unless you prefer pizzas every day! The freezer is full of them.' Anna laughed, so he knew she could understand. But Nora had prepared a very pleasant lunch, with lots of side-dishes, salads and cheeses and patés and some nice red wine.

But the conversation seemed awkward to Raymond, although it was confusing, the words having to be constantly translated. He asked Anna what she was rehearsing, knowing from Nora she was 'about to go on tour'. Nora translated. She was dancing in an experimental, avant-guarde production of a ballet based on the 'Tibetan Book of the Dead'. They would later perform it at a Dance Festival at Aix-en-Provence, after a short preview in Paris. The music was mostly chanting by Tibetan Monks. The ballet had a political message about Vietnam. The person whose death was being 'celebrated' was the Monk who had burned himself to death in Saigon, to protest the continuance of war in Vietnam. And as the text was about Re-incarnation, it was really about a soul who did *not* want to be reincarnated, who was resisting a return into the dimensions of matter.....

It all sounded too esoteric for Raymond and he said so. So Anna said curtly, in English. 'In that case I shut up!'

Nora laughed. 'She doesn't mean it quite like that! She means she doesn't want to talk about it if you don't understand it!'

Anna nodded. She spoke some more in German and Nora translated.

'She doesn't expect a scientist to understand these things!' Nora pulled a face at Raymond hoping to make him smile instead of be offended. So he smiled, but as patronisingly as he could, adding that he was used to being put down by 'artistes', but he didn't care. Water off a duck's back, he was so used to it. He didn't say, from Jane.....

After a pause he said, 'I know India and Pakistan a little. I don't know much about Tibet or Buddhism. But I went to India some years ago, to a conference, and stayed on and travelled round. I went up to the North West Frontier in Pakistan. I had a friend in the consulate who got me to places normally out of bounds. It was fascinating, and I read what I could about it. People like Krushal Khan Khattack and Babur..... beautiful stuff. Such a mixture of extremes. Romanticism. Sensuality. The love of making war. So I am not *entirely* a philistine!' he said pointedly. He was showing off, but hoped it wasn't too obvious.

Nora, sensing trouble, translated as carefully as possible. Slowly. Anna smiled, and said she loved India too. Once she had done a South Indian Temple Dance after studying for six months with a teacher. Very sexy, if you knew the language.

Then the two girls smiled at him as if to indicate it was the end of the cultural exchange, and Nora apologised, saying Anna had to leave early, so there were a lot of things they *had* to talk about. Please excuse them if they spoke German in his presence.

He continued with his meal, grateful he didn't have to talk. He wanted to watch them anyway. They were a spiky pair. He tried to pick out the few words he knew in the ocean of sounds that mostly meant nothing to him..... watching their faces surrepticiously, trying to work out what they were talking about from the emotion they seemed to indicate by intonation. It was like being a child again, before the strange polyphonic music of speech becomes intelligible because it can be broken up into words - blocks, like small cobblestones in a street. Hewn and squared and functional. It reminded him suddenly of listening to Wagner's sung speech. He wondered if he should mention he adored Wagner, especially the Liebestod! He then thought better of it. But the more they talked, the more he could imagine the music of 'Das Rheingold' in the background..... and he saw Anna, naked, one of the Rhine maidens swimming in the river..... More wishful thinking, but he was enjoying himself immensely. Now that Anna was more relaxed, she appeared even more sensual..... so much in contrast to Nora. She would have made a better swan. Even a black one.

He pondered the strange events that had led him so abruptly into the life of this rich young woman, who fascinated him, and her girlfriend, whom he didn't like very much, so far, although he knew he'd not be able to resist her, given half a chance.....

★

Anna left in mid-afternoon. But before that, it had started to rain during lunch, as Nora had forecast, so he was not able to walk in the garden, which he wanted to do. So he played the piano, loudly, to make sure the girls could hear him. A few Chopin waltzes to loosen his fingers. A Brahms waltz. A piano version of a Wagner overture, and then he relaxed, and played what he enjoyed playing, a kind of kitsch pseudo-jazz. It consisted of a few jazz standards decked out with some modest improvisations, the kind of music he had heard in the ballroom restaurant in Blackpool when he was barely a teenager, taking tea with his mother and an aunt, when he had first probably decided to learn the piano..... if only to fill in the spaces, the silences, the background..... He might be a stuffy scientist, but there was another side to him if they bothered to listen.....

He heard Anna leave and he waited, hoping Nora would come to him. He heard her standing at the door, so he did a couple of fast runs to show off, and then turned and smiled at her. 'I didn't know you played the piano as well as Liberace!' she said with a mocking smile. 'I will teach you some German songs..... and we can play duets.'

He pulled a long face - hardly Liberace! She proposed tea in the kitchen. He followed her there and sat down at the table. 'What do you think of Anna?' Before he could answer, she added, 'Sexy isn't she?'

He knew immediately the conversation was going to be awkward, and somehow he couldn't win. If he lied, she would mock him for not being man enough to appreciate a sexy woman. If he told the truth, she'd put him down for being superficial - even cheap. The put-down was implied in the way she intonated the question. He wanted to say, 'Yes or no, either way, it's irrelevant. It is YOU I want!' But he knew she would have scorned the remark, or become embarrassed. It was not time yet. He weighed his words carefully. 'Being sexy has little to do with appearance you know. Being really sexy that is! I don't go for the obvious. I never did. I happen to believe that authentic 'desire' is much more profound..... much more complicated. Not obvious or easy at all.'

She was quite taken aback. She had expected him to be on the defensive, but he was really on the attack, and she knew it. There was more to him than she'd suspected.

She countered. 'You know what Baudelaire wrote?' He shook his head. 'Falling in love with intelligent women is the pederast's pastime! So, I say, beware. Better go for the obvious. It is much safer..... and much more fun!'

He nodded. She might be right! He tapped his fingers on the table, while she continued making tea. 'Is she a good actress, or dancer, or whatever she is?'

Nora laughed. 'What you meant to ask was, is she a good fuck? I don't know!' She laughed even more when he looked embarrassed. 'As for acting, she always gets the funniest parts. Always the dumb blonde, the pin-up, even when she is dancing. God knows what she is doing in the Tibetan Book of the Dead. I asked her. She looked really sad. 'I'm one of the Wrathful Deities. I embody lust!'

Raymond laughed. 'Poor thing!' he said, sarcastically.

Nora continued. 'Yes, poor child. She can't win. I told her if she didn't seduce her director every time she might get chosen for something more spiritual. Behind the facade she is a lamb. But she is always in a mess. She understands *nothing* of what is happening to her. She fascinates me. She is just 'there', always available. You're right. A child! Polymorphous perversity personified. If she is alone in a room with a man, she just assumes she *has* to make love to him and starts to take her clothes off. I tell her it is not always necessary. She even did it with my solicitor! He was on the phone. When he stopped talking, she was down to a transparent leotard, crotchless French knickers and silk-stockings. He told me later, a strange idea had flashed into his mind. He thought he was at the Munich Opera, and one of the Rhine maidens had washed up on the beach! He said it was every German's fantasy! What can a man do? Refuse? I'm sure I got charged for the overtime. She told me later. 'I felt so sorry for him!' What can I do, but love her? How can I try and protect her? Be with her all the time?'

'I hope she doesn't feel sorry for me. Or maybe I do!' Raymond replied, looking straight at her, to see how she would react. She winced a little. She saw he noticed it, so she put her hand on her head. 'Damn my head!' she said.

'I doubt if I would have the strength to refuse!' he continued, deliberately embarrassing her now. She looked away, and fussed with a few kitchen things. He was thinking fast..... it was not going to be easy to make love to Nora, but he would succeed one day..... if he was patient. Meanwhile, to seduce her might require a kind of blackmail..... maybe with Anna.

'Where is she rehearsing?' he asked, knowing Anna was probably the last thing Nora wanted to talk about now.

'Paris! Where else rehearse the Tibetan Book of the Dead? On a beach in St.Tropez? Between children digging in the sand?' She tried to make her answer sound petulant and bitter but it didn't really work. She knew he was taunting her and she should not have risen to it. But she was pleased he was like that. She hated men who were passive and allowed her to walk over them. She was surprised he seemed so strong and sure of himself. She was beginning to feel secure with him, beginning to like him more and more. And trust him.

He was trying to imagine the troupe of dancers on the beach. It was such a provocative, curious image. He saw the children digging in the sand and making sand castles. He could imagine Anna, half naked, depicting lust, just washed up on the beach, leaping about, shedding veils like jelly fish. He couldn't work out why Nora had chosen such a strange image. It certainly wasn't funny. Or even a good contrast with Paris.

'Why St. Tropez?' he asked her coolly, still enjoying the fact he was talking about Anna and her sexuality.

Nora looked at him coldly, but then smiled. 'Sorry. I admit it! It was a silly answer. I was off guard. I've no idea why I said it. I was being jealous! Just like a woman. It was the first thing that came into my silly head. I love Anna for the way she is. I think she is fun. Sexy. Why on earth should I not think everyone else feels the same?'

'They will. Don't you find her sexy?' he asked quickly.

She almost looked furious, but she looked away. 'Yes I do. But I am a woman first! I'll tell you the truth. I'd be disappointed if you didn't find her sexy. I do too . . . . . but in my intellectual way! Like Baudelaire!' She laughed. 'Poor Anna! She would think we were nuts talking about her like this! And she'd be right! Let's change the subject. Why don't you go and shoot a duck for dinner?'

'It's raining!'

'Are you afraid of the rain?' she asked coyly.

'I told you . . . . I don't like shooting.'

'Would you mind trapping them with a huge net?'

'I wouldn't mind that so much.'

'So it is the gun you don't like?'

'Yes . . . . . probably . . . . . I haven't thought about it.'

Then she laughed again, but winced, holding her head. 'There are no guns here. I threw them all in the lake. I was only joking. I hate people who like shooting. I am very very relieved. I was just testing you. You passed the test. I will feel relaxed now with you walking around my garden, knowing you don't want to shoot everything and kill it! Just the idea of it, I hate. The lust for it in someone else. Like most other men, especially the French! They shoot everything that moves. I didn't want you to even *feel* you wanted to! By the way, I don't know the difference between the visiting ducks and the residents either. I was joking. Testing you. They are all the same once they are in my garden. All of them are welcome. Sometimes you see one of the residents chasing the others off. They can be quite nasty and territorial. But I was joking really..... Have some tea. Best Darjeeling. Thank God for the British Empire! They raped the girls and the land but they produced some good brews! Not forgetting the opium!'

After drinking their tea in silence - she'd regretted mentioning the opium - she asked him if he'd like to see her father's study. It was clearly important he should see it. He said he'd love to.

It was the main room on the first floor, with a wide balcony overlooking the lake. It was exactly as Raymond had imagined it, wall to wall bookshelves, stuffed with papers and files and books. The bookshelves were built into the room, in the same style as the room, classical Georgian, with each shelf carved with decorative details and edged with a fringe of coloured leather. Raymond had not seen so many books since his college library.....

Nora stepped into the room carefully ahead of him, and spun round as he came in, stopping him. This startled Raymond. It was as if she wanted to catch the expression on his face at the first moment he saw the room. She was looking so hard at him, he wondered if she saw him as the thief, returning to the scene of the crime. Once she seemed satisfied with his expression, she turned away, to enter her father's inner sanctum ahead of him..... her head held high, as if she was an officiating priestess. She turned in front of the huge desk. 'I tidied everything up. When I first saw it, it was in a terrible mess. All hell let loose.'

'How did they get in the house?' he asked her.

She looked away quickly again and answered awkwardly, 'They smashed a small rear window in the basement. Anna was very good about that. She got it fixed immediately. I've ordered some metal grilles. You can't be too sure nowadays, even though it's now too late. She got what she came for, what she wanted so desperately.'

Nora was looking at him strangely. He felt uncomfortable. He felt sure she was still testing him all the time. She took a photograph from the drawer of the desk and handed it to him. 'My father, when he was quite young, with some of his psycho-analytical colleagues. Do you know who they are?'

There were four people in the photograph. 'Well I recognize Freud of course. Who wouldn't! And I think I recognize your father. He was very handsome. He has your serenity, your seriousness..... something around the eyes!' She looked away. She didn't like him to see she enjoyed his compliments. He continued. 'I don't know the others. I never knew much about the world of psycho-analysis. No more than the average science student. And who couldn't avoid knowing some of the superficial facts and ideas, these days?'

'You never studied it seriously?' she asked him, as if she was horrifed that he hadn't.

'Well of course not. I am a pure scientist! An immunologist! I am not interested in speculations about the structure of the mind. I would have preferred Jung anyway, from what little I know of it.'

She seemed really surprised and pleased. She chuckled. 'Good! Very good indeed! I agree exactly!' she added eagerly. She was obviously quite excited. She went to the window and pointed, immediately exclaiming, 'Come quickly..... Look. There is a heron on the lake. Come quickly.'

The heron was standing near the water's edge, silhouetted black against the light. Suddenly its head and beak darted forward into the water. Nora drew the air slowly and loudly through her teeth and it made a soothing sound, as if someone was stroking the base of her spine, or her thighs, and she was enjoying it. 'He got it! Look. He caught one of my fish!' She stayed watching the bird excitedly, as it flicked the fish around in its beak until it was into position to swallow it. With one gulp the wretched fish was sucked into the oblivion of its belly. 'Voila! La sagesse de la nature! In all its cruel beauty! What are you? Raymond? The hunter..... or would you rather be a fish?' she asked excitedly.

'I never saw myself as a hunter Nora. I think you see me wrongly. Nor as a fish. Isn't it possible to be neither? Why must everything be in those extreme terms?' he asked her almost accusingly.

She sat down in a chair opposite her father's desk. 'Sit down. You are right! Sit in his chair! Let me see you there.'

He did so. She placed the photograph in front of him. 'The

other young man is Wilhelm Tausk. He challenged Freud. He was the lover of Lou Andreas Salomé. One of them. That made Freud jealous. Freud was a father to him, then rejected him because he had ideas of his own and he committed suicide. I don't know who the other man is. My father would never tell me. I'm sure it is Ferenczi. You can hardly see his face. He was my father's great hero. All his life. But my father is very handsome isn't he? Very Jewish looking though, you must admit! So am I. No? But fortunately I have my mother's somewhat gypsy nose! But he was very handsome. He had terrible problems with his women patients. They always fell in love with him. He would mutter all the time that it was transference. You know what that is?' Raymond nodded. 'But of course it was nothing of the sort. They simply fell in love with him! If they had met him anywhere else they would have flung themselves at him. Why not in the privacy of his study, talking to him about their sexual fantasies? How naive can you get? How dumb! It was a big problem. They wanted to be fucked by him, not talked to, endlessly. Still, that was the rule. I wonder how he managed to deal with it. He must have had a will of iron.....'

She was sitting back in the leather chair, staring Raymond straight in the eye. 'Why do I feel I know you so well already?' she asked.

'Maybe because I was so open with you - so transparent! Because I told you so much about myself, so innocently and unwittingly in the car coming here. Because I never lie! I don't need to lie about myself!' he said, pointedly. He was feeling very confident in her father's chair.

She laughed. 'Like me? Just like me! You are right. I tell terrible lies all the time! But I have some excuses. I am a German girl, and Jewish, living illegally in France. My mother died when I was young, and now my father has died and I am alone. And I am a woman of property! Almost rich. Do you think I should be honest about myself? Don't you think it's necessary and wise for me to be on the defensive all the time?'

'Yes. I suppose so. Just like your father, in a way, always having to be on the defensive?'

She was very surprised by his comparison. She didn't like it much. Then she thought about it. 'I see you make connections,

Herr Docteur. Associations on the vertical as well as the horizontal. Is that the scientist in you? Or the romantic?'

'I don't know. It is the man!' he said confidently.

She paused for a while. She was amazed how sure of himself he was becoming. But she was pleased. 'Tell me, Herr Docteur, have you loved many women? No! Let me ask it differently. You are an attractive man. Anna said she thought you looked just a bit too English, but nevertheless quite manly. I know you have experienced many women. Who hasn't these liberated days! You talk to me in such a way that I know you have. The way you carried me back to your flat like a bird that had fallen out of a nest. That showed certainty. But have you ever really loved a woman, so that it hurt, so that you really suffered for it, so that you prayed to be rid of her, that she would go away, that she would die, to free you of your longing..... that can never be fulfilled, because whatever you do with her body, her soul will elude you?'

He was astonished at the intensity of her question. It took him a while to get it into perspective. The truth was he had never loved a woman like that, though he probably longed to. His love for Jane had been the most important experience in his life with a woman, but it had always been under control, so it had not inspired him. He knew exactly what Nora meant..... if only from films he had seen!

'No. I have never loved a woman that much. I am a lucky kind of romantic. I never found someone I loved enough to torture me. Should I have done?'

She paused before replying. 'Yes. You are lucky. Avoid it like the plague. But I thought I saw a wound in you somewhere, in your spirit. I don't know why. I thought you had suffered something lost. Don't ask me why. Perhaps it is me, at the moment, I have lost so much, that I want to see it in everyone else. I am sorry. You don't mind my asking these things do you? It's a habit. After all, I am the daughter of a brilliant psychoanalyst. What else can I be but my father's daughter? Above all, I AM my father's daughter!'

Suddenly Raymond remembered a film he had once seen, when he was about fifteen, after which he'd been in love with Jennifer Jones for so long afterwards, he almost broke down. 'I did once love someone like that. I once fell in love with Jennifer

Jones in a film!' he said, laughing at himself good-humouredly. 'When I was too young or thought I was. Her body *and* soul eluded me!' But Nora looked serious......

'But that's an important issue! What archetypes did young men fall in love with before there was the cinema? Pictures in books? Do you think they spent hours in the library peering at etchings and copies of Rubens and Raphael, finding out who to fall in love with? Or going to the museum? They didn't have so many museums in those days, did they? Images were not so easily accessible. It must have been so much easier to grow up, when the first person you loved was the girl next door. Unless of course it happened to be your sister you discovered you loved, which so often happened. Incest was the only threat. Now, these awful boring days of superficiality and image and media saturation, people have too much choice. God how I hate it. Such lack of vision and soul. A million women. All photographs. All of them unreal and unwinnable! It must have done something, deep down, to men's need for confidence..... collectively. No? What museums of images compose men and women's unconscious these days, breeding potential violence! Very dangerous! It started in the nineteenth century. Even earlier. Etchings. All those images of heaven and hell, longing to be let loose! To become unrepressed! What a mess we have become, raped by so many images!'

Raymond realized suddenly that Nora always talked like this, thought like this, probably dreamt like this, and it disturbed him. It must be so tiring, he thought, always analysing, analysing, trying to see associations and analogies in everything, to everything, always convinced that the surface was a betrayal and only what was hidden was the truth. She was indeed her father's daughter and it was a terrible burden. She had inherited his type of mind presumably..... his way of thinking..... never taking a single word or image for its face value. He felt sorry for her. He sensed her loneliness and he wanted to do something about it. But he felt he couldn't. She was too far away. He was symbolically sitting in her father's chair, in the seat of power, but she was the one with the power because she could lie..... say anything to provoke him, to make him think, wonder, worry, but never tell him the truth, never tell him what he wanted to know about her. The truth about her feelings, which she hardly knew herself. And without such knowledge, he probably knew, he would never know how to penetrate her defences . . . . . and touch her where she was vulnerable and real.

She seemed to sense what he was thinking. 'Didn't I tell you what Baudelaire said? Beware of women who think. I think too much. Talk too much. Analyse too much! Analyse, analyse, analyse. It's never easy. I wish I could be like Anna. She never had a single profound or truly worrying thought in her life. She is like my cats. I dress up to appear like a cat because I am not like them at all. It is wishful thinking. I dream I am a cat sometimes! But Anna IS the cat. Which is why she is here too! She is out there hunting. She has a smell about her that attracts the males and she is always available. I'm never available. She goes down on her knees at the first growl . . . . . '

Suddenly he asked her, aggressively, 'Have you Nora, ever loved a man . . . . . so longingly that it hurt? To quote, etcetera?'

She answered instantly. 'Apart from my father? Good God! No . . . . . no-one!' She sat back in the chair and smiled. 'But what I enjoy, superficially of course, about you Raymond, is your obvious Aryan good looks, with the inevitable blue eyes . . . . . your long quiff of straight fair hair that keeps falling over your eyes. Because in no way at all, are you like my father! In every way physically the opposite. And that means I can feel comfortable with you. You see? I am honest now. Do you prefer it? Do you like the truth?'

He didn't know what to say. She stood up and laughed. 'I keep thinking you are one of the patients I am talking to while you are waiting to see my father. I did that often. Probing them. Torturing them, with innocent questions. Like that psycho-analyst's joke. You know the one? 'What's your problem shorty?' You are probably the most straight-forward man in the world. Are you?'

He was still shaken by what she'd been saying, but he answered as confidently as he could. 'Yes . . . . . I'm probably a normal kind of guy. I'm quite happy most of the time, trundling along with my work. Quite together as they say. In fact I'm fascinated by my work. Obsessed as you said! What else? I like Paris. I am quite happy to be alone most of the time. I like listening to jazz! I don't need people like others do. I go to the cinema when I'm lonely. I'm a film freak which might be a sign of some psychological disease! If not before then afterwards! I've never been a swinger though! I'm a bit 'Out of time' as the song goes! You are right. I am quite lucky. I am reasonably happy. I hope that doesn't worry you?' he said smiling.

She pulled a face to mock him. 'Yes, of course it worries me. I'd prefer you to be a raving psychotic, out to destroy the world in one catastrophic, vulgar apocalyptic fit..... or sneakily waiting for a time to rape me. Then I could deal with you. I can't deal with you being so relaxed. So normal and in control. Here I am, the frustrated anarchist, and you're the smug scientist, penetrating the sacred world of the body so you can be all magician, curing people! Here I am, split and falling apart, going out of my skull with anger and grief and despair, for a very intangible reason, and I need something, someone, something REAL to smash!' Suddenly she stood up, took the photograph and flung it against the wall. It smashed into pieces behind Raymond's head. He didn't flinch. He hadn't expected her aggression to be so blatant and so sudden, but when he thought about it, he'd been unconsciously expecting her to break down or let fly for some time. He knew she was perched on the side of a volcano. That is why she fascinated him so much.

She sat down again. 'Sous les pavés..... la plage! Great! I feel better now,' she said calmly. But she put her hand to her head. 'Fuck it! I think I've opened up the wound again!' She smiled. 'I can't win at the moment, can I?'

Without a word he went to her to look at the wound. 'No. It's alright. Not too bad. No change. Just awful!' She looked desperate. 'But seriously. Just relax. I am here and I will look after you. I am happy to stay a couple of days. Stop worrying about me. I will help you if I can. It was our destiny to meet after all, so let's not make a drama out of it.' And he kissed her a very light kiss on the forehead from behind and she looked down, a few light tears in her eyes.

'Thankyou Raymond. If you could stay a few days please, it would be a great help. I will be eternally grateful. It has been a shock. First the fucking riots. Then stuck behind the barricades. Then my head. Most of all, the theft of my father's book. His text and mine. All my work. What on earth am I going to do? You see..... everything else is irrelevant. Why I am crying is because of the theft. You see I have to do something about it.

There is only one thing I *can* do.....'

'Go after the people, the woman, and get it back!' he said. 'I will help you. Why the hell don't we steal it back?'

She looked surprised. 'Well, that would be fun! Meet crime with crime. Story of my life, but don't quote me! But I have no idea where she lives. That is not what I meant. She deliberately cut off contact a long time ago. But..... we could work on that possibility, if you want to. I can start making enquiries. In my father's papers there might be a mention of her relatives or other contacts. We might find her. But..... I have another idea. Much more strange. Perhaps the answer to the whole problem ..... which you may not like!'

'Go on..... What?'

'I could go into a trance..... I'm used to it..... cut myself off from the world..... lock myself in this room..... go into a trance and write it all down..... word for word..... as best as I can remember it! Here and now..... before I forget it. I was amazed, last night in bed, I discovered I could remember whole chunks of it. It is all still there in my mind..... hovering..... like a falcon hovering over a field..... and if I pounce now, before it goes, I could retrieve most of it, maybe three quarters of it, which would be enough surely! For a start. I can remember the essence of it of course..... the heart of it..... it is engraved on my mind like a recurring dream. I feel I am half asleep. This wound makes me feel drowsy. I feel as if the whole memory is a kind of dream..... and because I am dizzy and drowsy, almost hypnotised at times, I might have access to it. My reason has been breached! In a week or so I might forget everything. It will all be erased by the light of day. Now I feel I want to sleep all day, and come in here at night and write and write and write, while it is still in my mind. I feel I must give birth to it now, because this is the only time I will ever have..... ever..... to save my father's work.'

Raymond felt almost petrified. As she was talking, he could see she was already in a trance. She had become radiant. She was seeing visions. For the first time he saw her as whole and really wholesomely beautiful. Even the features on her face had seemed to change, soften and become round and sensual. It was no longer just her eyes. It was her whole face, her whole body.

He gazed at her in astonishment, almost in a trance himself.

There was so much strength in her now, willpower, determination. Her eyes were still blazing, not looking at him at all, incandescent with excitement and vision. He could see Joan of Arc like that, explaining her voices, knowing they were real..... the only reality! He was overcome with emotion. He wanted to take her in his arms, he desired to share her intensity so much. He felt close to her powerful love, and he was amazed at his own excitement. Before he could stop himself, he stood up, went to her and put his arms around her, laid his head gently onto hers..... avoiding the wound..... 'Nora..... you are right and I will help you. You can't do it alone. I will help you. I will telephone the laboratory and say I am ill. I have a virus. I will stay here until it is done. You've GOT to do it. How long do you think it will it take?'

She looked up at him, delighted. 'I knew you would say that. I knew you'd stay and help. Ever since yesterday when I first decided on it!' she said proudly. So..... she had been planning it all along! But he didn't mind. He felt curiously privileged. He knew the sincerity of her vision. Nothing would stop her doing what she wanted to do, *had* to do, and he felt he had to help her. Somehow it had become his destiny too. One step into the so-called revolution, and look what he had found..... a crazy girl who was hell bent on justifying her dead father's life. It had a curious irony about it. It didn't make much common sense. But he wanted to do it. That was enough.

'How long will it take, do you think?'

'I don't know. A couple of weeks..... three......four..... ten. If I just scribble and scribble, just let it all come out randomly, in no order, flooding out, I just feel it is all there ready to burst out, I feel I could write fifty pages a day. I used to do that when I was a student. I had a fantastic capacity to work. But most of all I have to get it started, get launched into something. That is the hardest thing of all, making the first move. The deflowering!'

'Why don't you just speak it? Don't write it. Speak it..... do it all onto tape?' he asked suddenly.

She was looking at him with amazement. 'Of course! What a fool I am. I never thought of that. Utterly brilliant! Of course..... I will get into a trance and just let it all come out. I don't have a recorder, can you help me to get one? I have the money. There is a town five miles away, with a music shop. Anna is always buying records there. Shall we go......Now! Now? Yes, now. I can't wait. Tomorrow might be too late.'

★

They didn't speak in the car. She seemed to be already in her trance, or at least holding her thoughts back, not to pollute them with mere reality. When she saw the shop, she blurted out, 'We will buy fifty tapes! And I will do it. Yes. Sod it! I'm going to do it! Teach her a fucking lesson once and for all!'

Nora showed him she had plenty of money in her purse. 'For everything else too!' They bought a tape recorder, a microphone and tapes. They also bought lots of food from the market and Raymond was excited. 'This is going to be fun. A great trip. Just like a holiday!'

They arrived back at the house and the cats appeared again. 'They don't realize I'm staying yet!' she said, fondling them roughly.

She made some tea. 'But what are you going to do, while I work?'

'I've just been thinking about it. I have a brilliant idea. I'll drive back to Paris and get my paperwork. I have a long report I need to complete. It is months late already. Also I have a hundred papers of other people's work I've not had time to read. I'll bring it all back here. I'll tell them a relative is ill, but I can use the time to do all the theoretical work. It is quite feasible. I can work here too. I like working at night. We can work in parallel. In fact you're doing me a great favour! I need continuity and peace too. A chance to opt out of the world for a while. The laboratory and the people in it were starting to get on my nerves and I was close to doing something regrettable.'

She was obviously pleased. 'Anna will be back in a few days. Wait 'til I tell her, she *will* be surprised. But she will understand. It might be hard for her with you and me sleeping all day, out of phase with her, but we'll think of something. Mostly she is away anyway. How exciting!' She drew the air between her teeth in a long drawn out guesture of hate. 'And what sweet revenge! I'll show her! She was never one of us!'

★ ★ ★

Three

Raymond went to Paris early the following day, by train, promising to return later in the day - if the chaos in Paris permitted.

But the previous evening, he had taught Nora to use the tape recorder, which they set up in her father's study. They had practised a couple of takes, Nora reading awkwardly into the machine, apprehensive of the phallic microphone, as if it was a monster that lived only on words, sucking them up at every opportunity. She read some paragraphs from Ferenczi's 'Thalassa', after explaining the title was the Greek word for the sea - about regression to the sea in dreams and sexuality, 'To get into the mood! My favourite book to read when I'm depressed - I daren't think why! Just now it seems appropriate.'

But she promptly became depressed, almost catatonic, and Raymond wasn't sure how to get her out of it. After a number of suggestions, he said she could read some of her father's work - out loud if necessary. This prompted her to snap out of the trance, and she agreed to read some of his notebooks, in silence, to herself. She gave Raymond some of her father's 'Papers' to read, to show him what a lucid mind her father possessed, and to become acquainted with the 'jargon of psycho-analysis'. She sat down in her father's chair and started to read, with intense concentration, ignoring Raymond completely. Suddenly though, she whooped with excitement, jumped up and started to dance wildly, until she howled with pain and put her hand on her head. But she was still able to fling her arms round Raymond and kiss him on the forehead.

She'd found a structural outline of the case-history in the notebook, that she'd completely forgotten about, outlining the order and content of the sections of the text. 'I have the bare bones. Now I only need to flesh it out!' she said, triumphantly. From then on, she was in a good mood, saying how funny it seemed..... while Paris was burning..... they were entombed in her father's study reading about other people's crazed minds!

Raymond saw the funny side of it too. He'd always liked to be unpredictable.

After a while she was serious again. 'Of course we're all crazy. Our minds are structured badly. One side out of touch with the other. You wouldn't design one of your machines, would you, in which one half didn't know what the other half was doing! No wonder so many people can't fathom things out. Reason out of touch with intuition, and both out of touch with the passionate needs of the body! My father said most of his patients weren't sick at all. They were the children of parents who had failed to cope, which wasn't surprising. We forget now that all of them had seen one or two world wars! His patients were just too sensitive. They knew unacceptable truths. They'd opted out and refused to cope with a world they despised and knew was wrong. That is why there will be more wars and so-called revolutions. You can't cope with modern society and its lust for the objective without cutting yourself off even more from everything natural . . . . . and so you become crazy. Don't you?' But she was talking to herself, slurring the words as if she was a little bit drunk, and didn't look up, so Raymond said nothing. She gazed vaguely in his direction, her eyes glazed. 'It is the feminine we are all out of touch with of course! Men and women. My father knew that, and so did Ferenczi. Freud was wrong trying to prop up the patriarchy and make his patients toe the party line,' she murmured, her head bowed again, over the notebook.

After working together for an hour or so, and Raymond thinking he might not be there, really, she stopped and suggested dinner. She was still dreamy, but was looking so beautiful with it, Raymond didn't complain. They drank too much wine, and started to giggle, laughing at the foolhardiness of fighting in the streets . . . . . against a brutal army of robots . . . . . but feeling guilty about it as they said it, which made them joke and giggle even more.

They became serious again, and she told him her father's notebooks and personal diary had been in a safe, which the thieves hadn't found. It was only the working manuscript that had been on the table with all her own notes. 'Longer than the manuscript!' But now she was happy. She would 'spill out' the text in 'one long stream of consciousness monologue'. After that she could revise it, over weeks or months, however long it took. Raymond promised to help her at least through the initial period, which would be the most harrowing, psychologically.....

He was tired from the wine and the excitement and went to bed before her, intending to leave early in the morning. He heard her speaking German into the recorder while he was trying to sleep..... But he was becoming unsure of himself. Nora was treating him so much like a brother, taking him for granted as a mere presence to refer to, and showing not the smallest sign of awareness of his presence, as a man, that he felt sad..... deciding she would never be available to him. She was absent, out of touch with her body, switched off. At least to him. Maybe she had a boyfriend somewhere.....

But wasn't there always Anna? All that was needed with her, if Nora was to be believed, was to be left alone in a room with her! It might be like Berlin between the wars..... with no future and everything falling apart and little else to do, or so it seemed at that moment to Raymond, recalling some of the films of the period. Now, presumably, it was much the same with Anna..... hopefully.

*

Raymond arrived in Paris and went straight to his flat. In the afternoon he confronted Jean-Pierre with the news of his impending 'leave of absence'. Jean-Pierre seemed quite annoyed. He'd met a sexy little Vietnamese nurse who adored Americans, but couldn't tell the difference between an American and an English accent. She'd set her heart, and more of her anatomy, on meeting him. She was lonely and bored and needed cheering up. She also hoped to get a job as an assistant in the laboratory, as it would pay better than nursing. 'And we should do what we can for the victims of the war, shouldn't we?' he said, insinuating that if Raymond refused, he was a shit. 'And she is an excellent cook, if you like Vietnamese food, which I do!' Jean-Pierre was fond of Raymond really - just too English! - and would like to see him unwind and become less serious. He'd told Beverly, 'He even reads poetry. I found a copy of 'The Poems of Krushal Khan Kattack' on the shelf next to 'Serum and Synovial Fluid

Proteins in Rheumatoid Arthritis'. That was almost the last straw.

Raymond, not wishing to appear too unmanly and unenthusiastic, said he was only going away for ten days at the most. 'So maybe later if she's still around! And I adore Vietnamese spring rolls!' But he insisted he had two weeks of leave due, and it was best he took it immediately . . . . . as Paris was getting more and more difficult every day with the threat of a national strike, even civil war! Wasn't there talk of de Gaulle, who was conveniently 'absent', bringing in the army?

Most of all, Raymond explained, he was going to be working, completing his important paper on the 'Virus mimicking behaviour of Antigen B6'. He felt sure Jean-Pierre was really quite pleased he was going away. He and Beverly could keep the linoleum floor polished. They could screw at Jean-Pierre's flat but there must be something about the ambience of the lab that turned them on. Maybe Jean-Pierre believed in the 'Two Cultures', and was doing his best to bring the two together. 'But of course! Science on the one hand, and Sex on the other!' had always been his theory on that particular subject.

In the evening, Raymond managed to catch a train back to the country and took a taxi to the house. He had the keys for the front gates, and walked up the drive with difficulty, carrying two heavy bags full of clothes and books. He rang the bell on the front door and Nora let him in, kissing him absent-mindedly on the cheek, looking away quickly.

He could see immediately she had been crying. She looked weak and distressed. But she had prepared him a meal in the kitchen, with another bottle of good red wine from the cellar. Immediately they sat down to eat.

He made no mention that she had been crying. He tried to make conversation, telling her some of the gossip about the 'events'. It was far worse than the radio and TV were admitting, he told her. Impatiently she said, 'I know, I know. My friends called me during the day. It's becoming quite unreal, even to them, and they are hardened realists. Or so I thought. They talk about it too as if its a movie. It's so hard to believe they have accomplished so much, so soon. But the students won't call for an election, because they say they don't believe in them, so it looks as if it might be anarchy for a while, then civil war perhaps, if it gets out of hand. If the police lose their nerve. They've forgotten how to be good fascists. They've had it too soft for a while! But, who would have thought it, all of it provoked by an American war - not even ours any longer - in the far-away jungles of Vietnam and a bunch of students wanting to re-organise their studies in Nanterre. It doesn't make sense. I wonder what the truth is really..... behind it all. Maybe we will never know. Just the subtle repression of everyday life becoming too much. The shooting of Rudi Dutschke obviously didn't help. Yesterday, someone tried to ridicule Daniel Cohn-Bendit by accusing him of being 'a German Jew'. Do you know what the students answered to that?'

'Er..... Who is Cohn-Bendit?' he asked her, feeling awkward he didn't know.

'The principal student leader in France, ironically enough. He is German! They defused the insult by saying, 'We are all German Jews!' That was pretty good. So you see, even I am not excluded after all! Even if I'm an illegal immigrant! Everything is so weird, so interconnected and yet random at the same time. Everything is paradox at the deeper level of course. Like the unconscious. I'd like to think the revolution, so called, was coherent, but it's not. All fragments. Just like a lot of amoeba floating in the sea, subject to waves which are too big to fathom out and get in proportion, but they appear to be going in one direction, but are merely reacting to the magnetism of the moon! Just like we women. So they say! Victims of forces beyond our control.' Again she seemed to be dizzy. Her words were slurring more and more.

She put her hand on her head and winced.

'How is your head?' he asked, genuinely worried again.

'Not bad. Getting better, I'm sure. With your pills!'

'Good! What did you do all day?'

'Practised..... for the performance of the monologue.'

'How did it go?'

'Very badly. I am far too self-conscious.'

'But you can't expect it to be easy from the first word. It will take days to get into the swing of it. Then it will all come flowing back to you.....'

'Maybe. I was crying all day though, mostly from frustration. Yesterday..... at night..... in bed, it seemed to be all 'there', but when I become too conscious, too clear, it fades away. How can I manage to re-produce it in my sleep? Maybe one day in the future, they'll put electrodes on your brain and record the waves of your dreams and transform them into speech. One day they will! Ferenczi would have liked that. He was a great believer in the cosmic waves that govern the body . . . . . and of nature . . . . . seeing them not just as symbols of the emotions and the mind, but real forces. Tangible and real. He was my favourite of all those voyagers who drifted on the unknown seas of consciousness, looking for islands of form and meaning. Makes me want to cry again!'

He shook his head and told her not to be so complicated, so demanding of herself, so crazy. She must calm down.

'But I am being very sensible and serious! It is all there in my mind. I am just frustrated. There is a block. I know it won't come out! Barriers. You might even say a barricade!'

'You will find a way. Just keep trying. Listen to music. Play the piano. Go for a walk. Dance . . . . . and suddenly the words will come. You are just trying too hard. Frontal attacks are no good, on ideas. You must go sideways, be sneaky, do flanking attacks. You have to stalk them . . . . . like your cats when they are hunting. They shift around like shadows, completely invisible. Make yourself invisible, and the ideas will appear in your mind. Just relax. You are too tense. Can't you ever relax?'

She seemed angry. 'Very clever Herr Docteur. When you want to be you are very lucid! But you know I can't. Damn it. I can't even fool you can I? I can never relax. I never relaxed in my life. Never . . . . . which is why I was so happy working on my father's book. It was such a complicated task . . . . . so demanding . . . . . it meant I could be working on it all the time, frantically. It focused me. But then suddenly. Bang. Gone. I was cheated. Such a build up . . . . . to be let down so badly. If we ever find that woman, I will kill her this time, she has caused my father and I so much suffering.'

'Was she just as difficult while your father was alive?'

'Yes . . . . . very.'

'Why . . . . . when he cured her?'

'I told you. She was quite mad when she came to him. He made her able to survive. But she became paranoid about my father's 'proof' as she called it. You see, she became a practising psycho-analyst herself for a while. That often happened in those days with intelligent patients. And she had very different ideas to my father about the essential premise of Freud's work. At that time he was stuck with Freud and his circle. She was particularly aggressive about the Seduction Theory as it is called, and his so-called abandonment of it. But I won't start that again. My head aches. And I must not talk about it, must I? Doing so, dissipates valuable energy. I ought not to talk about it with you. Ever! I ought to keep it to myself. I can talk about it when it is all on the tapes. Afterwards. Then we can get them typed. Then your opinion will be very helpful, very useful. I will need an objective viewpoint . . . . . another eye . . . . . another mind to shape it, structure it, make it into a book. You would be perfect for that, I know. I sense it. I trust you. You are calm. This book is terrifying, orgiastic in a way, such a harrowing, explicit story. You see, when the woman was a little girl, she was . . . . . she was . . . . . No! I shouldn't tell you this. Not yet. Should I?'

'Go on . . . . .' he said softly.

'Well . . . . . She was in the Warsaw Ghetto. Not many survived, as I'm sure you know. She only did so because her father bartered her . . . . . for freedom. Sold her if you like - an expression she used at first - so they could both survive.' She looked him straight in the eyes.

He was taken aback, but not too shocked. He had been expecting something like that . . . . . he wasn't sure why.

'This doesn't explain why she hated your father so much.'

'It wasn't simply a matter of hate. Fear mostly. She was cured. She was grateful. Eventually she led a normal life. But of course, she didn't want to be reminded of her past. Everyone, everyone in the world would prefer to forget such things, surely? Although that is repression of course! We push the hell-on-earth down into our unconscious. But later it will shake loose and re-surface, causing unforeseen problems. More irrational behaviour. My father wanted to publish his case-history of her cure. He said she ought to rise above the personal story because it was a profound story of her time. Our time. Part of our collective unconscious. The recent past we have inherited. Especially its images! We are all sons and daughters of the holocaust, whether we like it or not. It is always there even when we try to forget it. Even more so when we try to forget it, but the images refuse to go away. Her story was a particularly poignant one, but it was a heroic sacrifice. What is life compared to virginity? She saved her father and herself by selling the most valuable part of her body, her integrity as a girl. The collective 'truth' of the story was the background, the war. The two are always related. The private myth, a part of the collective myth. Something like that. It is a very moving story!'

'Don't tell me any more! Go upstairs. Just imagine I am in your father's chair. Close your eyes, and talk as if you are telling the whole story to me! Go! Now is the moment to start!'

She looked surprised. She kissed him on the cheek, saying nothing. On the way through the door she muttered. 'Very good Herr Docteur. I am your trusting and obedient servant.'

★

That night he tried to work in his room. From time to time he passed her door and heard her speaking German into the recorder. Sometimes he heard snatches in English, which seemed to be instructions for the general structure. But he didn't want to be caught eavesdropping so he didn't listen for long. She was still talking when he tried to sleep. But he was frustrated. He was thinking of the Vietnamese nurse he was missing. Maybe he should have stayed the night in Paris. Then he thought of Anna. Then he thought of Nora, who was the cause of it all. Then he thought of Jane, who might or might not come back into his life. Finally he fell asleep . . . . . not managing to avoid all kinds of fantasies. All of them fusing into one . . . . .

Later in the night he was awoken sharply, by a nightmare. He was an alien cell invading an amorphous body. He was exhausted, finding it difficult to penetrate it. Finally he was inside the body, floating in a beautiful pool of water, inside a cavern. Several girls were swimming there but they didn't seem to see him. They were Sirens, or water spirits, barely dressed in long diaphanous costumes that seemed like skin or wings, softened in the warm water. All at once they saw him. Too late he realized they were T-lymphocytes and they encircled him and each one, at the same moment, attached themselves to him with their mouths. Where they touched his skin it stung and he knew his body membrane was being dissolved by a kind of acid from their mouths. He tried to shake them off but they were stuck on him like jelly-fish and he felt the blood draining from his body into their bodies. At the moment he became a dry, empty husk, he woke up..... laughing. Or crying. He wasn't quite sure. He could see how funny it was.....

But it took him some time before he could sleep again. It was the first time he had dreamt of his work in such an obvious, though sensual way! He could remember the feeling of pleasure when he finally entered into the huge body and he longed to recapture the sensation as he lay in the huge four-poster bed, wishing he had the courage to go to Nora, but knowing it was the last thing in the world he must do. One day..... however long it took..... he told himself again..... she would come to him. Maybe. But he had to be patient and wait, however hard it would be.....

★

He woke up late in the morning, almost lunchtime. In the kitchen was a note from Nora telling him she had gone to sleep at dawn and would not wake until two oclock, but the work was going well. 'I just closed my eyes and started talking and it all flooded out!'

It was a beautiful day, so he walked in the garden. He made himself some sandwiches for lunch. He tried to work in his room but couldn't concentrate.

She was excited and happy when she woke up and announced to him that it was all going to be alright after all. Now, it was only a question of keeping up the momentum. She asked him if he'd managed to work and he told her he was getting started. He didn't want to tell her the truth, that he was as blocked as she had been!

In the afternoon they went into town and did some shopping. Nora left him in a café, where he drank coffee, ate croissants, tartine and cheese and read the newspapers. He was feeling very happy within himself, he wasn't sure why.

Nora joined him, loaded with food, insisting she paid for it all. That is why she had left him alone!

In the late afternoon he spent some time in the garden. It was so peaceful he fell asleep for a while on the grass bank, under the weeping willow tree.

Later Nora cooked a delicious dinner. He could tell she was really trying and obviously enjoying it. It was her way of repaying him. Over the meal, she made him talk about his past, his former girl-friends and eventually she made him talk more about Jane. He was reluctant to do so, but the wine was smooth and from a good chateau and the right year and at the perfect temperature. But she didn't seem very attentive. He told her about his dream and she laughed. While he was telling it, he remembered another part of it. Somehow the police and the students had become part of the same 'body' and all the police in their steel helmets were part of the immune system and she laughed even more. 'Too obvious. Too literal. Not a dream at all. Quite real. That was a memory afterwards! Next they'll be putting massive doses of anti-biotics in the student's beer and killing them all off!'

But he seemed offended by her amusement.

She continued. 'Is that what happens when you are a scientist? You start to see the whole world in your own symbols, your own signs?'

'I don't'..... he said slowly. 'My dreams do! And I am not responsible for those!'

'Oh! Aren't you? Touché then!' she said, raising her eye-brows.

He added quickly. 'But isn't that what the artist does, and the poet? He has his system of symbols and he interprets as much as he can of the world in those terms?'

'You are very wise Herr Docteur,' she said smiling. 'I didn't know scientists were so broad in their viewpoint.'

'They aren't' he replied. 'I am one in a million. I am just an accidental mutation, which is probably why, instead of being a good scientist doing my experiments, I gave it all up at the mere drop of a hat, and am relaxing in the country, while Paris falls apart, trying to work but not hard enough really, with a beautiful girl as my sole companion.'

She looked away. She still wished he'd not make compliments. He also knew it was a mistake. He carried on though. 'And two beautiful cats and a beautiful garden as well.'

They didn't talk for a while. Then she asked him. 'Are you sure you won't be bored?'

'Yes, I'm sure I will be! But as soon as I am bored I will go. That's a promise. Stop worrying about whether I am bored. I am 32 years of age and quite capable of knowing what I want, when and how. I am enjoying the peace and quiet. I am proud I am helping you with your father's book. So shut-up about it! Just relax. Why don't we play the piano?'

She jumped up, excited at the idea, and relieved to escape the conversation which was becoming treacherous. They tried to play duets, but they weren't a resounding success, so she offered to teach him some German folk songs. She wasn't happy with the result, so she put a record on of the real thing. Then she became sentimental..... and to his surprise, asked him to dance.

For a long time they danced together, to the slow sentimental songs, primly, like an old couple celebrating their diamond wedding anniversary, with everything behind them, all passion spent. Not for a second did Raymond push himself too close to her, nor did she indicate he should narrow the space between them.

Then abruptly, she left him, saying she had to work. Inspiration was welling up in her. But her sudden departure left him feeling empty and desolate. He played the piano alone, quietly, mostly sad jazz-blues, longing for her, desperately. Should he pounce? No..... he knew it would spoil everything. He must hold back, play it her way, or he would lose everything.

★

For two more days they followed the same pattern, almost without variation, working and sleeping late, walking in the garden in the afternoon, dinner, and then dancing for a while. She had a stack of German songs and sometimes, she told him what the words meant. When she danced she closed her eyes and he could see she was far far way..... in a trance. But if he could give her that, the confidence to let go and drift off and dream, it was something valuable, he knew. He felt profound pleasure holding her in his arms at a tender distance away..... as she swayed like a branch of a weeping willow tree. Once they danced a tango and she almost went too far and broke the strange code of detachment that had sprung up between them. Then at the moment she knew he couldn't bear it..... she left him, and went upstairs again to her work.

★

The following morning, probably about ten oclock, he was in bed, sleeping, dreaming again...... moaning, groaning, tossing and turning in his sleep, dreaming of the cavernous underground pool again and the luscious, nubile girls in white diaphanous robes. He was trying to hide behind a rock, because he knew there was something devious going on and he had to plan a strategy to avoid being seen..... something like that.

He wasn't sure how it happened, or why it happened so effortously, but he awoke, thrashing about, heaving and pushing ..... making love to Anna. She had slipped into his bed, naked, and taken advantage of that curious and unexplained feature of 'REM', Rapid-Eye-Movement sleep..... dreaming sleep..... the undreamed, the real, accompanying erection. When he realized what was happening it was too late to resist, not that he would have wanted to anyway. After all, he didn't mind her nose being a little too straight, and her being rather too tarty for comfort. She was astride him, his penis firmly inside her and they made love like two animals that had met by accident in a forest glade under the moon and the time was right..... without saying a single word, until they were utterly spent and fell asleep in each other's arms.

★

He woke up reluctantly and with a sudden flush of embarrassment when Nora came into the room with a tray of tea. Anna stayed 'asleep' under the bedclothes. There were two cups on the tray, but Nora said nothing and left the room. Slowly Anna emerged from the sheets and smiled at him. She looked gorgeous. Not 'hard' at all. Where had he got that image from? She was all soft and voluptuous and utterly childish. She sat up and poured the tea for them both. After the tea he wanted her again, but she put her finger on her mouth. She let him kiss her breast. 'Later,' she said, and got out of bed, leaving him panting. She opened the curtains and he saw her body silhouetted against the window. He still wasn't sure which of his two favourite pin-ups she had reminded him of. It didn't matter any longer. He was even prepared to admit he might have made a mistake, and remembered her from a film he had once seen, or a girl in a Soho strip club he frequented in the old days. All he wanted to know was, how long was 'later' and what was Nora going to say or do about it?

Anna left after their shared tea. Naked. All smiles.

He stayed in his room and worked for a while, afraid to confront Nora. Unexpectedly he was feeling like working, and decided he didn't want to face either of the girls. He'd had an exciting new idea about how experimental models of Rubella virus infection could be used to test the behaviour of one of the newly discovered antigens.

He could hear the two girls laughing and being very jolly together. He longed to know what they were saying. If only he'd learned German as an extra subject, instead of Serology!

*

Raymond worked in his room until the middle of the afternoon, working well. Eventually he decided to look for the girls and found them having a picnic on the edge of the lake, under one of the willow trees. As he approached them, he felt self-conscious, wondering how they would react to him.

The way they were sitting on the edge of the bank seemed unexpectedly familiar. Suddenly he made the association. Although Anna was fully clothed, in his mind's eye she was still totally naked . . . . . as he now prefered to think of her. He was remembering the Manet painting he'd seen in the Louvre some weeks before. 'Ah . . . . . Le dejeuner sur l'herbe!' Anna missed the joke and looked guilty, but Nora gazed at her, puzzled only for a moment, until she understood Raymond's reference, laughed delightedly and much to his surprise, gave him a hug and a kiss. She paused, looking at the water, and Raymond sensed she was trying to think of a similar image or phrase. 'Absolutely right Herr Docteur. We see what we don't see! And vice versa. She may be clothed, but we see her naked! "Denn alles Fleisch es ist wie Gras . . . . ."'

He frowned, not understanding her reference. 'Er . . . . . ?'

Nora smiled. 'Well, my image was a bit oblique, I admit, and not as apt as yours. But it wasn't bad. From the bible, and Brahms's Requiem . . . . . "Behold all flesh is as the grass"!'

Most of all, he was relieved she seemed so relaxed and unbothered about finding Anna in his bed. He sat down on the grass, next to the spread-tablecloth. Anna poured him a glass of wine and he helped himself to a sandwich. Bourgeois life wasn't so bad after all.

Nora apologised for having to speak German - some important things - and carried on talking to Anna. He heard many mentions of the days of the week, of Munich and Vienna, about ballet and the theatre. He was starting to learn German. He hoped he would continue to need it.

However, Anna hardly looked at Raymond. It was crazy! To her, he might as well have not been there. Women! But he didn't mind. It was more comfortable that way than having to smile at her and acknowledge her, especially in front of Nora. It was Nora he was still worrying about after all. Anna could almost be taken for granted now . . . . .

Nora turned to him, and said, quite emotionally, 'Paris really is falling to bits Anna says. On the edge of total disruption. The students are still being beaten up. It's becoming real anarchy she thinks. She had to rehearse in a garage. She is staying until tomorrow.' She carried on talking to Anna.

He was bored now listening to their German and interrupted, saying he was going for a walk. They nodded approval, so he left them, to go exploring in the garden.

He found a tall cedar tree in a corner near the perimeter wall, and felt such a strong urge to climb it, and being hidden from the girls, he started to do so. Like all young boys it had been one of his favourite pastimes. He found a fork in the tree where he could sit and relax, surveying the scene in front of him. It was remarkably peaceful and tranquil - completely out of time. He couldn't see another house or farm building or any other human object except the walls of the garden. He felt safe and happy . . . . . although the feeling disturbed him. It had all been so sudden. It was all so bizarre. He kept telling himself he must not take it too seriously. The 'story' with Nora was fascinating enough, but the addition of Anna to it and to his bed, made the whole thing even more unlikely. He touched his head impulsively to make sure he hadn't been wounded as well.

Just at that moment something moved in the tree next to him and he almost fell off his perch with fright. Then he laughed. It was one of Nora's cats, curled up, as he was, in the fork of the next tree. It had noticed him and was looking at him suspiciously. It stretched and climbed up several branches until it was above him. There, it presumably felt secure again, promptly curled up in the warm sun and went to sleep. He sat in the tree for a long time wondering what was going to happen next with Nora and Anna . . . . . and what tree inside himself he had to climb, to be higher, to remain safe.

★

When he walked back towards the lake, the girls had disappeared. There was no sign of them in the house. He wandered about making a noise, and played the piano loudly. One of the cats appeared, but no-one else. He went to his room and tried to work, but Anna's perfume was still on the air . . . . . and now it disturbed him. And he'd not noticed she'd left her knickers on the bed. He was sure it was on purpose. He wanted not to, but he couldn't resist picking them up and sniffing them. He hid them in a drawer, knowing she wouldn't ask for them. He wondered if she was always as careless, or she was just marking out her territory.

He couldn't work, so he read a book instead. He had taken Nora's copy of Ernest Jones's biography of Freud, at her suggestion. 'You ought to know the history of psycho-analysis, one of history's great wounds inflicted on the spirit of mankind, as Freud called it!' Raymond was interested to read up on the subject, because it was Nora's raison d'être, after all, and she had insisted this book was the best place to begin. He read for an hour or so, but then felt drowsy and fell asleep. The wine at lunch had been stronger than he thought. Or so had Anna.

When he awoke, he was longing for Anna, but didn't know what to do about it. He was surprised to hear Nora working. As she talked he could hear the click of the tape-recorder switches.

He went downstairs to the drawing room, intending to play

the piano, and was surprised to find Anna there, practising her dancing, in a skin-coloured leotard. He was about to leave the room when she made a small sign, telling him to stay. He sat down awkwardly on the piano stool. In a way it was the first time he had ever been alone with her. Alone and fully conscious. It was time he took a good look at her, uninfluenced by the presence of Nora. Anna stopped the music and wound it back, obviously pleased to see him, smiling at him warmly, confidently, as if she'd known him for years, before continuing with her practise routine.....

His body was aching. He wanted so much to stop her and take her. She was dancing to him now, facing him as if he had been picked out of an audience, making sure none of her charms went unnoticed, unstretched, un-caressed. He was surprised at the length and beauty of her legs. He'd not noticed them before, under her skirt. Suddenly she turned directly towards him and smooched sensuously towards him step by step. He stood up apprehensively. She took him by the hand and led him towards the sofa. He still wasn't sure. Was she going to show him a tattoo or something? She made him sit down on it and stood staring at him, her legs apart. With one flick she undid two buttons on the leotard between her legs, and the costume sprung back. Moving from side to side she pulled the leotard over her head. But instead of falling down on him, as he expected, she knelt down in front of one of the armchairs and her head disappeared into the cushions. She caressed herself as he stood behind her, eagerly taking off his trousers. He went straight into her, and she winced..... he was so hard and determined..... so beside himself.

Afterwards, Raymond lying smashed out on the floor, she left him, kissing him lightly on the cheek, without even a German word, and presumably went to her room. He was an actor now, himself, mimicking a corpse. With difficulty he became alive again. Back in his room he wondered what might happen if she decided to sleep with him through the night, thinking, 'It's a good thing she's going tomorrow, or I'll have to stop climbing trees.' But that night she didn't come to him and he was asleep before he could get angry about it or wonder what she was up to. With Nora.

★

The following day, Anna left in the morning, while he was still sleeping. At lunch with Nora he sensed immediately she had no intention of talking about Anna, so he didn't mention her either, as if she'd ceased to exist the moment she left the house. Nora spoke to him exactly as she had done before Anna's arrival, as if they were still intimate accomplices, working together on a mystical quest. Tangible, physical reality was irrelevant.

She was eager to talk about her project. The text was now emerging as she had hoped. She was remembering whole sections almost word for word. 'It's all just flowing out now.' She seemed amazed at the extent and detail of her memory and marvelled at the miracle of consciousness. 'But when you think of it, the whole of psycho-analysis depends on this kind of memory! In some of my father's cases, people were able to remember whole scenes in extreme detail, pages and pages of dialogue, from events that had happened forty years before. At least, they said it was memory. I often question what is remembered and what is invented. But I've spent a year arranging my father's book. During that time I excluded everything else from my mind. It's not surprising it's so indelibly printed there. But what a relief! At this rate I'll have the bulk of the text on tape, probably in a couple of weeks or so. Once I have the essential structure, recorded and typed, I can remember the small details, and add them in. I am making verbal footnotes as I go along. At the moment I'm concentrating on the main thread of narrative, the linear flow of the whole story. Later I'll add the theatrical asides, the vertical bits.'

He said he'd started on his text too, even though it wasn't exactly true. It was eluding him really. He was still fiddling around, making notes. She was still eagerly talking about 'the mind' when he noticed she was moving her head stiffly. She was still in pain. He asked to look at the head wound . . . . . and she tried to put him off, saying it didn't matter, it wasn't hurting that much. 'Anyway, Anna brought me some really strong pain-killers! And by the way, some pills to help me work at night!'

Raymond was angry. 'But that is not the point Nora. The pain is not the point. That's the surface, the outside, the results. It is the infection we have to clear up, inside. Are you taking the antibiotics I gave you?'

She looked away. Instantly, he knew she wasn't. He demanded to see the wound. Reluctantly she allowed him to spread her hair and examine it. She had somehow managed to cover up the bald patch with an ingeniously arranged clutch of red, art-nouveau, egg-shaped combs .....

Raymond looked carefully at the wound and sat down slowly, looking sombre and serious, as if he was about to chair a meeting on 'Elastase in Connective Tissue Diseases'. She looked all coy and guilty as if she'd just been caught throwing a bomb into the Assemblé Nationale, in order to 'change its policies on Algeria'. In his most serious voice, and staring dispassionately at her, the way he looked at the mice in his laboratory, the one's infected with diseases he had given them the week before, he said, 'It is still infected! It has not healed at all. In fact the two sides of the wound have become even more separated. Now, it will have to be stitched, almost certainly. A hospital job. It hurts a lot doesn't it? But you know it's your own damn silly fault, don't you?'

She shook her head. 'Nope. Not really. I am oblivious to pain. I'm just too busy working so hard. I can't stop to worry about it. Anna's pills do the trick. The pain has gone now. I'm impervious to it.'

'What pills are they?' he asked her.

'I don't know.'

'Show me them!'

'Please don't ask me to do that ..... not now. Let's be mature about it. It's MY wound after all, my body, my problem - as you say, it's all my fault. I accept responsibility. Give me a few more days. I will take the antibiotics again. I just forgot really. Forgive me, please.'

He explained she would now have to take different antibiotics, having broken off before the first course was finished. The bacteria would have had time to develop defence against it. He was furious with her. Medicine was some kind of God to him after all. A belief in an order within nature that was predictable and with rational knowledge, could be understood and controlled. His future depended on his faith in this belief in form and order. But he could see she didn't care ..... there was a far away look in her eye. Her body was secondary, almost irrelevant She was now given ..... immersed in her mission.

He went to his room and found some new pills in the little black bag he carried with him everywhere, in case of emergencies. He would have been a great asset behind the barricades when the police charged..... or in an airport when a bomb went off. She took them with a glass of wine, insisting it was better than water. He shrugged. He knew she was mocking him, if only unconsciously. She knew as well as he did the effect of antibiotics was diminished with alcohol. 'If you don't want it to heal, it won't! Here you are with one of the best immunologists in the world..... and you are a total mess, with a gaping wound in your head!'

But she smiled. 'Here I am, the daughter of one of the greatest psycho-analysts the world ever saw..... and look what a total mess I am! With a gaping wound in my mind!' she said cynically, and for the first time he saw a shadow of bitterness cross her face that scared him. 'Who will cure me of those inner wounds..... Herr Docteur? The wounds inflicted on me by the love and care and attention my father devoted to me? He doted on me..... every moment of his life! Look at me now. Who is there now who can protect me from the wounds I received from such a perfect, generous love?'

She had regained her composure. She was enjoying feeling superior to him for a moment, talking about serious things. He was looking utterly confused, even upset, so she apologised for being so bitter. But her apology made him feel even worse. It was her intonation, not the words. She left him in no doubt it had taken an enormous effort to be so generous to apologise, even if it was a lie. She seemed to know she was turning the knife in the wound of his feelings, because the suffering she was talking about inside her, would make her even more unreachable. But that is what she wanted.

To his surprise, she suddenly grabbed a fly wisk next to her and went 'Spat' on the table and it made him jump. She burst out laughing. 'Damn it. Missed the little bugger!' She leapt up and went round the room swatting an invisible insect, which he knew wasn't there, until finally she yelled in triumph and pressed her finger on a black smudge on the wall, under a Piranese print of a prison. 'Voila! Et tu Brute..... Poor little mosquito, just happened to be passing, feeling thirsty, with a mild dose of malaria. Did you know we get malaria here, when its damp and hot, around this time of year?'

'No you don't!' he replied, knowingly.

She laughed. 'If you say so, Herr Docteur Immunologiste, we don't. But let me tell you..... if there was *one* mosquito in this lonely place with malaria, it would find *me*! Did you know I sleep under a net every night?'

'No, I didn't know!' he replied, coolly.

'Yes I do.....a huge net..... it is as big as the Milky Way..... as impenetrable as the barricades on Boulevard St. Michel..... as powerful as the magnetic force that binds the moon to the earth..... and yet, it too..... is invisible! There is an invisible wall around my bed......keeping everything out! I am as safe as sound..... I like that expression, don't you? Where did it come from, do you think..... why is sound so safe? When it is in the shape of words, it can kill, it can bring down kings and destroy empires! And seduce unwilling girls! Why is sound unsafe?'

'I don't know, tell me.' He guessed she was a little bit drunk. She was slightly unsteady on her feet. She was slurring the occasional syllable.

'I know why..... because it can slip into your ear..... like the Arch-Angel Gabriel..... without doing any damage ..... where it matters, between your legs!'

She sat down. She couldn't look at him. She was talking to herself really. She seemed quite drunk now. Maybe she was tired. Emotionally tired. Perhaps it was the result of her long, lonely hours talking to herself in her father's room. Words, words, words..... into the dull, lifeless microphone. Talking about her father's work, about her father's mind and spirit..... talking to her father.

He suddenly felt sorry for her, realizing the pressures she was under. Maybe his flirtation with Anna hurt more than she would admit. He'd tried not to notice or think about her real feelings concerning anything that had happened. Now he felt guilty for neglecting her, thinking only of seducing her! 'You are tired Nora..... You should take a nap. You mustn't over do it - push yourself too hard. Sleep for two hours before dinner, then you will be fresh to work afterwards. You mustn't go beyond your own limits.'

She held her head in her hands. She spoke very very quietly

and slowly. He could see her body shaking. He could hardly hear the words. 'But I don't have anyone to take me to bed, Herr Docteur, and tuck me into the bedclothes gently and tenderly and kiss me on the forehead and tell me to sleep softly and not to dream . . . . .' She was sobbing now.

He stood up and took her hand. She didn't look him in the face. She stood up, staring ahead, in a trance. He took her upstairs and along the corridor to her bedroom. He pushed open the door. The room was impeccably tidy. The curtains were drawn and a small night-light was still switched on next to the bed, as if she had been intending to come to bed. There was no sign of a net. He didn't know what to do about undressing her, but she flicked off her shoes and slipped off her skirt, as he stood next to her, holding her hand. She started to move towards the bed and he folded back the sheets and helped her to slip into them. He noticed the small wooden object she had been carrying the night he had found her, just peeping out from under the pillow. He pulled the sheets back and she curled up like a kitten, as she had done on that first night, the night of the barricades. He tucked her in, warmly. Her eyes were closed but she was smiling with pleasure. He kissed her lightly on the forehead. 'Goodnight Herr Docteur,' she murmured . . . . .

'Goodnight my little one! Be a good girl now. No dreaming!' he said, not knowing where the words came from. He slipped out of her room very quietly and went to his own room. After a few minutes, after not being able to work, he continued reading the Jones Biography of Freud . . . . . to try to avoid thinking about her.

★

After an hour or so reading, becoming fascinated by the revolutionary and competitive world of psycho-analysis, and trying to imagine Nora's father's role in it all, he decided he really must try to work on his own scientific paper. The notes he had made were on his table awaiting him. Everything was ready to start. But when he tried, he couldn't write the first words of the narrative. Every time he wrote something, he immediately thought of something better. But then that too receded . . . . . until sometimes he was left with a single word that was dissolving away continuously . . . . . losing every part of its obvious meaning. Somehow it was related to thinking too much about Nora. He wanted to know what *she* was working on at that moment, and more important, what she was thinking. Now she was telling him more about herself, opening up, admitting her vulnerability, it disturbed him because he was finding her more and more desirable, despite the fact that in his presence, she was cool . . . . . even cold . . . . . and she clearly didn't expect him to pounce on her.

On an impulse, he took one of the crisp new notebooks he had bought for his work, and decided to start writing a kind of diary. This was something he'd not done for years, not since his late teens, when after a disastrous love affair, he had decided to become a scientific journalist or historian, rather than a pure scientist, devoted to pure research. As he sat in front of the blank page, he remembered the earlier time and experience quite vividly. He had started the 'diary', knowing he had to start somewhere to 'teach himself to write'. The writing experiment had lasted a few months, before he decided he was not cut out to be any kind of writer after all, and decided to return to the austere world of scientific experimentation. After all, his reason for wanting to become a scientist in the first place had been profound. His sister had died of leukemia when she was five years of age, and he was nine, and he had vowed all his young life to 'revenge' her death, to work in the war against cancer. He had returned to the battle-front, determined never to stray from his cause again.

He was now certain he would stay in Nora's house for some time, until she seemed more calm, or perhaps until her book was on tape. Or until her wound was better. Or until Anna went off on her tour with her new dance project . . . . . or until . . . . . or until . . . . . . he felt he ought to stop trying to work and try to record his shifting ideas and emotions instead. Relax. He wasn't at all sure why, but he guessed that the pervading ambience of 'analysis' was catching . . . . . not unlike a sound-virus on the air-waves!

He started by recording the now fragile memory of his dream, but it seemed no longer like a dream, as Nora had said. It was too rational. He immediately went off on a tangent, and wrote several pages describing Nora, her house, the way he found her, and a short resumé of her, or her father's project..... adding a few random images from her description of the 'content of the case-history'. He sensed it might be a good story..... his interface with her, during her project's period of realization.

He wrote what he could, adding, 'Thursday. 'A'. The dance near the piano. The inside cover girl. Pleasant distraction!'

But he couldn't write more so he returned to the Freud biography. He was impressed reading about Freud's struggle with his self-analysis, which had resulted in a whole book, 'The Interpretation of Dreams'. The biography was open at the page he had reached before, and he noticed lines underlined by Nora in red ink. He flicked through the book and noticed she had underlined sentences and phrases through the whole text. It occured to him they were significant. Nora was always in so much control when she spoke, hiding everything, revealing nothing. By instinctively underlining certain lines, she was showing what she found at least provocative..... or especially meaningful.

He felt quite excited. He decided to copy out the lines she had marked into his diary-notebook, as if they were things Nora had actually said, starting with the page he had reached where Jones referred to Freud's first paper on the Seduction Theory......

'On 2 May 1896, Freud gave an address to the Society of Psychiatry and Neurology in Vienna entitled 'The Aetiology of Hysteria'..... According to Freud the paper met with an icy reception................

It is a valuable and comprehensive paper, and, although it adds little to the conclusions just mentioned, the arguments are so well marshalled, and the objections so skilfully forestalled, that it may well be called a literary tour-de-force.

'Referring to the proposition that at the bottom of every case of hysteria will be found one or more premature sexual experiences, belonging to the first years of childhood, experiences, which may be reproduced by analytic work though whole decades have intervened, he adds..... "I believe this to be a momentous revelation, the discovery of a Caput Nili of neuropathology."......

Krafft-Ebbing, who was in the chair of the meeting, contented himself with saying: "It sounds to me like a scientific fairy tale".....'

Raymond thought for a while about the curious image conjured up by the expression, 'Caput Nili', which he knew meant the 'head or source of the Nile'. Surely it had *not* been found at that time. It was only something to imagine. It was there but had not been discovered. Not seen. Not known. It seemed a curious choice of phrase.

He then noticed Nora had made a note in the margin.....'See page 379'. He turned to the page and saw she had underlined a chunk of the text there too.

'Up to spring of 1897 Freud still held firmly to his conviction of the reality of childhood traumas..... At that time doubts began to creep in although he made no mention of them in the records of his progress that he was regularly sending to his friend Fleiss. Then quite suddenly, he decided to confide to him ..... "the great secret of something that in the past few months has gradually dawned on me." It was the awful truth that most - not all - of the seductions in childhood which his patients had revealed, and about which he had built his whole theory of hysteria, had never occurred.'

Nora had added in the margin, 'Never occurred..... never occurred..... In other words, the women lie! What has been built, can always be taken down ..... but not vice versa. But men cannot build in the one place where they have taken women.' She'd crossed out the last two words.

Raymond flicked through the book, reading the lines Nora had picked out unconsciously. They were intriguing. She seemed particularly concerned with this turn-around by Freud. This volte-face. His retraction of the seduction theory. At first, Freud had said the seductions had happened, they were real, a physical, material fact. Seduction. But then he said they were not. They were merely imagined ..... a false memory. She had written this several times ..... 'A FALSE MEMORY' ..... in capitals. Once she had written, 'The best kind of memory to have when you are remembering the Warsaw Ghetto! Reference my father's text.'

Raymond started copying out the lines she'd marked. There were a lot. It was almost like a poem when he read them afterwards, each phrase out of context. A 'poème contrète'. Jane had read him some once. A friend of hers had translated some of them, from German, of a poet called Ernst Jandl. Jumbles of apparently meaningless sounds, fragments of words. But together, an explosive conjunction of associations, triggering memories, dreams . . . . . ghastly ideas.

★

Nora called him later for dinner. She seemed to be completely relaxed and herself again. She chatted superficially about the food . . . . . about the garden . . . . . her cats . . . . . some news she had heard from her friends about the riots in Paris. And once again she expressed concern about him, that he must be utterly bored, doing 'nothing all day'.

'Nothing? Not at all! In fact it's good news. I've started my scientific paper! I'll be very busy from now on, for a week at least, depending on how it goes. I've told you many times. Don't worry about me. I am very happy here. As you said, it is very peaceful. Idyllic. *Just* what I needed, a place away from the madding crowd, where I can work quietly on my paper.'

She seemed reassured. But as he ate, and drank the excellent wine she had brought up, yet again, from the cellar, he wondered why it was so important to her for him to be there, when before, she had been alone for so long . . . . . happy enough to be alone, working. Why did she seem to need him now? Or so it seemed. So he asked her. 'Were you really happy living alone here, after your father died? Not being a student any more. Didn't you have friends you missed suddenly? Or did they visit you here?'

She paused. 'You mean boyfriends, don't you?'

He was taken aback by the sharp tone of her voice. 'Well . . . . . er . . . . . yes I suppose so, amongst other things. Yes, I suppose so . . . . . boyfriends.'

She poured more wine for them both. 'I have always been happier alone. I am an only child. My father was sad in his last years. I told you once, he was glad to die. It's a terrible thing to say, I know. He was ill. Cancer. For a long time I was inwardly preparing myself. You know..... people always think every young woman needs to be, what can I say..... involved, needs to belong to people. With other young people. I was never like that. I have always been capable of making myself happy. I had a perfect childhood..... probably because I always felt loved, felt whole. Once in a while I get sentimental, don't we all! But I don't hanker for things..... anything..... I don't sit around longing for..... for desire itself. That's like a snake eating its own tail! Longing for a man? To be in love? Ugh. I watched other people and always felt sorry for them. One day of course, I will emerge from this extended period of latency, to use a psycho-analytical term. I'm sure. But I feel very happy meanwhile. If you want the truth..... the whole truth..... do you?'

'Of course!'

'I have *never*..... never had a boyfriend! Never! At school in England, we were all girls of course. Then I became a student in Paris. I never met anyone I could love, or even merely want. I saw what a mess so many of my friends were making, becoming so proud of their casual affairs, the more casual the better, so proud they could just fuck around and not get hooked, or care..... all the new freedom, which is as old as the hills really, people just *talk* more about it these days. Look at the Nineties, the Twenties, the Thirties. Berlin between the wars! Just read the novels and biographies of Paris in the late twenties..... Wow! Dynamite! And not all fantasy! Just read through the notes my father made in his case histories, ninety percent of which were women. Wow! It all went to pieces a hundred years ago. I often wonder why. Or maybe the myth of the marriage, the Christian family, was always a fraud, a useful fraud. But for whom. The state?'

She looked at him searchingly. 'Maybe!' was all he said.

She continued. 'I know that marriage ought to be the most precious thing in life, in the whole of our experience, if it works. I have never, ever, ever in my whole life met anyone who could say it worked. All the time and forever. Am I a freak? Don't I meet the right people? Am I living in the wrong place as well as the wrong time? I know that is terribly cynical. What do we mean by "worked"? That stayed virtually alive, renewing itself continuously. We read about it. There are some marvellous love stories in literature, in history. But it's so rare. I want to be one of those rare stories ..... Here, now, in 1968! Am I a fool? I want to be the ONE young woman of my generation who has a perfect marriage! You see how absurd it sounds. Am I not a total idiot, a false mutation? My friends thought so! I ought to be in a museum. Every single girl I have known from school onwards has launched themselves into the new freedom with a profound sense of mission. To prove what? To prove they are NOT going to be conned by men, at all, at any time? They will use men as they say women have always been used ..... and as for marriage! You must be joking. I see it as very sad. I see it as the ultimate split from nature ..... between the two essential halves of nature. Spirit and matter. So you see. Here I am. Already an old maid at twenty five ..... living with my cats, who disdain me really. And poor beautiful, lost, long suffering Anna. Biggest victim of all, because she does it all the time and experiences *nothing*! So she tells me. What a family I have. Oh yes ..... And there is the ghost of my father!'

He looked at her with confusion. He felt she was contradicting herself but he couldn't be sure.

She continued. 'You ought to say, "Ah! That's the point. The ghost of your father!" Something like that. If you were streetwise in the back-alleys, those anal city passageways of psychoanalysis. But the only difference between me and all my girlfriends is that I admit such things. About my father. And my father happens to be "really" dead. Because they have all killed off their fathers anyway, only symbolically! The father is dead. Daddy is dead. Nietzsche told us *that* ninety years ago, or whenever ..... We killed off God, first of all, and then slowly ..... only awfully slowly ..... realized we had killed off Daddy as well. We killed off the ability to love men for being men, for being "other"! All my girlfriends are out having a good time, as they call it, fucking around, screwing everyone in sight, having fun at last, free at last ..... But every time they are saying. "There! Look at me Daddy! I can fuck around just as well as *you* can!" What happened to the real Daddy they could love, who they wanted to love them? Needed to love to become whole? I'm sorry ..... but I am different. That was a failure aided and abetted by the mothers too, by the way! She encouraged the daughters to reject the father. But they must love him and fall out of love with him. Naturally. That is the essential pattern, the inner structure of nature. Only then are they free to relate to men for what they are ..... mere shadows of the Gods. To be loved for their weaknesses as well as their strengths. I am quite different and intend to stay that way. You know that don't you?'

'Er ..... Yes I do ..... I do now anyway!' He was feeling battered by the intensity of her logic, or irrationality ..... whatever it was. He'd not had time yet to decide if it made sense. He thought it might not ..... but he'd never seen her look so passionate.

'You knew it all along, surely? If only unconsciously - that I was not available? And that is where it matters. Unconsciously. You have known from the beginning I was not able to love you ..... not able to love anyone ..... not available to anyone on any level. Didn't you?'

He felt a lump in his throat threatening to choke him. She was right. He had known all along, really, but he didn't want to know that truth. He wanted to hope. He couldn't look at her. He didn't know what to say. He didn't want her to see how upset he was, that he was on the defensive. So he did what he usually did in such situations. Went into the attack. He looked her straight in the eye. 'I don't know what my unconscious knows Nora. Maybe its full of love. Maybe hate! I am waiting for it to let me know!'

She laughed. 'Good! You start to talk my language! It will tell you eventually, when you are least expecting it. You will be surprised, as we all are ..... by its passion. It's unexpectedness. But you see, you are already lost aren't you.'

'How do you mean lost?'

'Falling in love with Anna, the voluptuous, sexy Anna, the child of nature ..... if I may use such a corny phrase. You have made your choice! I don't blame you. She is lovely. You must get to know her better, if she lets you. You might have to learn Munich slang to penetrate the real Anna, but in the meantime, you seem to be doing fine. I shouldn't tell you this, but she thinks you are very sweet. She asked me to make sure you stayed here! I told her it was up to you. I have no power over you whatsoever, to keep you here, or make you go away. You are a man - quite free. She said I was to be nice to you, cook you nice meals, and make sure you don't go off into the town after the whores who sell themselves cheap - her phrase - around the station. Did you see them the other day, by the way? Some of them are quite spectacular for a small country town, with only a smattering of industry.'

Raymond was furious. He felt himself blushing. He had in fact noticed the whores, the evening he returned from Paris. There had been two or three standing near the taxis and they shouted to him. He always avoided whores, but on that occasion, probably because he was feeling confused in his feelings, he had almost gone off with one of them. She was dressed in a black leather suit and wearing black thongs around her legs. He'd never seen such an outfit on a street corner before, so easily available. But the truth was, he wanted Nora and her deliberate unavailability was eroding away his defences. He'd have probably fucked anyone, not to feel so inadequate. But then Anna had taken over and all was well.....

He couldn't avoid saying something. She was watching him keenly, perhaps enjoying his embarrassment. He felt he had no choice but to try to hurt her. 'Yes I saw them. One in particular looked very sexy. I almost bought her. But I didn't have enough cash on me at the time!'

He felt awful. How had she managed to twist his words so easily, and trap him? A minute or two before he wanted to say to her, 'I am like you. I too am dreaming of meeting someone to love totally..... the perfect marriage..... forever and forever'. And suddenly he was being cheap, trying to taunt her with his ability to buy a whore. He felt utterly miserable.

'Don't. I advise you not to, Herr Docteur. I happen to know there is a particularly virulent form of gonorrhea about at the present time, imported from Tunisia. It can disfigure you for life. They are keeping it quiet. It takes a long time to cure. It renders you infertile. I've seen some of the women. The victims! Except perhaps, *you* would know the right cure?'

He wasn't sure to believe her or not. 'How did you see the victims as you call them?'

'One of my father's closest friends was a doctor at the local hospital. I kept in touch. You can meet him if you like. He will show you..... if you are really interested.'

'No! NO! I am not Nora. You know I am not. You have

trapped me. Why? I don't want to talk about whores. It's not my style.'

She smiled fondly at him. 'I am sorry. It was too easy. That is why I despise my girlfriends. It is easy isn't it! Mocking love. Mocking sexuality for its own sake, in the name of love. I am sorry. It is an old habit. Even my girlfriends are behaving like whores, taking presents and holidays if not money, and then putting men down because they like whores! I'm sorry. I was being unfair. I happen to love the idea of whores, but the sacred idea, the primitive idea, the sacred prostitute in the temple. But *that*, Herr Docteur, is another question..... a past we can never never retrieve. The golden age of consciousness. Never retrievable. Like childhood, once it has gone, it has gone forever. You see, that is what marriage is, the opposite face of the same coin. The loss of childhood is forever. So what we long for is the gain of something else that is, that means, forever. That mystical illusion! Forever. That is the mistake. We do not seek a partner, a woman, to explore and grow old with. We yearn for forever-ness, because we have just lost it. We try to replace the lost fairy tale with another..... But alas, it rarely works. Only the person who stays a child forever, can achieve the perfect marriage. Like me! One day I will achieve it. I will find the perfect person. I will do it, because I have refused absolutely to grow up and be conned by the illusion of adulthood. I want NOW..... here and now, to be my 'forever'. I live in an eternal present. Why? How can I be so sure? Don't laugh! Because I am still a virgin!'

He wanted to mock her now..... it was his turn. But then he realized it was probably true. 'Impossible!'

'Yes I am. A virgin! I admit it. Are you surprised to meet one at last? We are almost extinct. But I have chosen to hang on to my sacred virginity..... *forever*. But it is not easy at times, I do admit. It was easier when my father was alive of course. He enabled me to do it, easily. Now that he is dead. I am more threatened of course. My barricade has been destroyed. I cannot hide behind HIM, which is why I have an invisible barricade around myself, to protect me..... protect me..... protect me from temptation..... from desire..... from desire for the wrong thing..... from desire for the sake of desire..... from desire coming only from loneliness, desire for a thing, an object.

I am preserving my love, as Lautreamont said, "For the creator of the Universe"! Amen. You must be bored to tears, Raymond, with all these words, chunks of mind, little word-pavés..... for the sake of a better word! One day I will tell you my dreams, and scare you away forever. When I want you to leave..... *if* I ever do! I will tell you my dreams. By the way. Would you like to see my etchings?'

Raymond let some of the wine slip down the wrong way and he started to choke. She came round behind him and hit him a few times. She hit him so hard he nearly smashed his face into the plate. But she stopped his choking.

She sat down, looking very happy with herself.

'Why yes..... er..... I'd love to..... Are they really etchings?' he spluttered.

'Yes and no! They look exactly like etchings. They fool everybody. But they are drawings I do with a knife and black oil-paint, a technique no-one knows about. I am doing a whole series for a story I once wrote, a kind of short novel. I want to do it with drawings. They all look very old, ancient, as if from the middle ages.' She paused, thinking hard. 'No! I've just decided I can't show you them, not yet! They are in my studio in the roof. But one of these day I will show you, I promise you. Later. I must not distract myself. I must keep to the real work of the moment, the here and NOW! The forever that is only today. My father's book. My work of building my invisible barricade around myself.....'

They said nothing for a while.

Eventually he said, 'Yes. You must go and work. And me too.'

She smiled fondly at him. 'Let's have a break in two hours. I will meet you at the piano and we can sing again.....' She didn't mention the dancing.

'It's a date!' he said.

But when she came and kissed him on the cheek, to clinch the deal, he almost burst into tears. He wanted her so much to know *him*..... to know what he was really like, to give him a chance. To see behind the role, behind the facade of having to be a predictable 'man'. But he knew she had no intention of getting close. She wanted him to keep his distance, to remain safe. Beyond the invisible wall..... where she would always find ways to keep him. One step wrong, like an alien organism, he would be rejected. Thrust away from her body. Banished. Forever.

It was not going to be easy. Thank God for Anna.....

★ ★ ★

Four

Later that evening, Raymond and Nora met up again and played the piano together. And then they danced. But much as he tried he couldn't avoid thinking about Anna, dancing more flamboyantly in the same room earlier..... images of her body swayed to music were flooding his mind..... so much so that he was almost tempted to abandon himself to the rush of the present and push Nora down on the sofa and perhaps she wouldn't resist him..... despite all her warnings. Mere words after all. What truth was hidden behind them? Nora's eyes were tight shut, so who was she thinking about? When he closed his eyes he could see nothing except forbidden images of Anna dancing, touching herself, stripping and revealing herself, kneeling and giving herself, arms spread-eagled on the chair, her bottom swinging gently from side to side to the throbbing music, legs apart..... knowing and wanting..... her vulva open and ready for him.

Nora was wearing the same perfume as Anna had been wearing..... or perhaps he was imagining it.....

But worse than the frustration was his annoyance with himself for feeling guilty towards Nora. Guilty for allowing the closeness of her body to provoke images of Anna, naked and abandoned. Betrayal was becoming a much more complicated notion than he'd ever imagined. Thought, words, images..... images igniting thought and provoking imagination..... such an involuted trinity, when suffused with desire..... especially frustrated desire. And yet..... did he really desire Nora? Physically? Did he merely think he ought to? That was probably the worst betrayal of all..... He was becoming so frustrated and confused, he moved awkwardly, deliberately, almost stepping on her toes, to break the perilous mood..... knowing he was drifting helplessly towards a vicious, spiralling whirlpool. Nora took the hint and they drew apart, their hands taking longer to separate..... reluctant to give up the small but so significant point of contact. She turned off the music, and looking slightly sad, smiled as if to say thankyou. But in the smile he thought he could see how aware she was..... how knowingly she was orchestrating their frustrated intimacy. He'd no idea how much it was arousing her..... she wanted him to be frustrated and confused..... clarity in such things, always petrified her. But this ambiguous terror seemed the only way she had left to try and reach him, to reach past her habitual lies, to be breached - to lose her veils. Those he knew nothing about, as yet, and would not have dared to imagine..... that would be revealed in the book maybe. Maybe.....

She led him to the kitchen like a child, where she sat him down at the table, obviously defeated. She almost thought of taking him, there and then, but the moment passed. But wasn't he perhaps the last chance she had..... to make sense of it all? To bring unity to her fragmented memories..... that collage of erotic sketches..... to bring unity simply because he was an accident at the right time? Was she not doomed only to desire such an anarchic confrontation with time? Otherwise she would remain forever entombed in the ghetto, which 'she'..... her subject..... was able to escape?

Nora said she didn't like to drink too much wine when she was working on the 'monologue', as she was now calling it, so she offered to make Oolong tea instead, to help clear her mind. They sat on opposite sides of the wooden table, neither of them willing to speak. Eventually Nora laughed. He was looking so deadly serious, almost on the point of tears, she had to breach the silence. 'We must look like an old married couple, to anyone watching us from outside!' She glanced suddenly at the kitchen curtains which she had drawn as they were sitting down. 'I hope there *isn't* someone looking at us from outside!'

He smiled and shrugged. 'None of my friends would believe it was me, such a defeated man, sitting all day like a ghost in his room, all alone and unable to work, dedicated to you, to helping you to work in your father's study, recording his book into a tape-recorder. I can't make sense of it any longer! Crazy. You must admit it's all a bit strange!'

She didn't want him to become more miserable, so she decided to ignore the self pity, not to rise to it and challenge it. But she was confused herself. 'Oh really? Now I see why you are staying here then, it's not for me at all. That is too much like hard work. It's for the sex! I am the madame. If I can't persuade Anna to come more often, must I find you someone else?' She looked up at the ceiling, as if trying to imagine who she could bring into their life together if Anna was naughty and stayed away too long. 'What we need is a maid. I'll go to the Agency. Last time they offered me a Vietnamese girl. People here are employing them at the moment. They are cheap, *and* you can feel you are helping them! The perfect hypocrisy. Would one of those do?'

He was utterly dismayed at her suggestion, for obvious reasons. Was she reading his mind now as well? Why had they suddenly got onto the subject of Anna? But wasn't it a compliment really, that she was so concerned by his sexual needs? People were so helpful these days! 'My assistant Jean-Pierre had already found me a Vietnamese nurse, the other day, when I was in Paris!' he said, hoping to appear matter-of-fact.

'Ah! So you *do* like Vietnamese girls. I might have guessed. I know why, of course - because they always look so young. Take their clothes off and you have a twelve year old girl! The small breasts, tight little bottoms, in fact almost no bottoms at all! They are all children, aren't they?' She looked fiercely at him, as if he had just committed the crime in front of her.

She had trapped him again before he had said a single word in defence. But he started laughing, so she had to laugh too. 'If I describe the pink velvet curtains on the window as 'sensual', which they are by the way, because they are a bit faded and a bit battered, a bit torn at the edges, but shaped like a woman's body, all curves, does that mean I'd like my girls wrapped up in an old curtain? Don't let's exaggerate too much. As it happens, I can't stand Vietnamese girls. Anna is much more my type, so voluptuous and willing!' As he said it, he regretted it.....

But she laughed again. She enjoyed such sexual arguments. Her father's work was almost entirely concerned with them, in a way..... the truth between the lines, in the spaces behind the words. 'We'd better not send you to fight in Vietnam, then, had we?' she said mockingly, but not too seriously. 'Although the soldier, poor chap, needs his recreation if he is to fight well at the front. Otherwise he gets up tight and starts raping civilians left right and centre. Doesn't he?'

He looked at her with such a look of being fed up with the line of conversation, she apologised, suddenly miserable knowing she'd been too aggressive. 'I'm sorry Raymond, I had this heavy telephone call earlier from an old girlfriend, all about her despair at the violence and political chaos. Her boyfriend is in jail. Also, Anna is always going on at me about Vietnam because of her play, the burning Buddhist monk and all that. I start to get it all muddled up. Especially when my girlfriend's sex lives are shuffled into their stories as well. I only wish they would leave me alone. Why don't they talk to me about fashion and pop songs and gossip columns, like most girls?'

'Yes indeed . . . . . why not?' he asked insinuatingly.

She looked down at her fingers. 'Yes. Touché. It's my fault I know. I'm far too serious. But one day I'll snap and all hell will be let loose, won't it?' She smiled but it was obviously fake. 'Then, it will be my wars too, sexual and otherwise. I know its my fault. Either that, or it's the monologue already taking it toll! Talking of which, I must go and work. And you? I worry about you all the time. Especially . . . . . when . . . . . I'm sorry Anna is not here to entertain you! It would be easier for us both, wouldn't it?'

He tried to smile affectionately, and even tried to laugh, but it sounded more like regurgitating a mouthful of frog spawn, after falling into a pond. She was looking really concerned. She had the same expression his mother always wore, when he preferred to work at home than go out, 'like other boys'.

After a moment's silence, he spoke, trying to appear as relaxed as possible. 'No problem. I will work too. I'm really getting into the swing of our night routine, now. By the way, I'm reading the Jones biography when I am bored with my own stuff. It's fascinating, as you said. It's not a history of a man as much as the whole movement. See you later?' he asked, not knowing precisely what he hoped for . . . . .

She came to him and kissed him lightly on the cheek, as she was already accustomed to doing, and he wished to hell she wouldn't, and didn't wear so much perfume. After she'd left, he stayed sitting at the table, playing Chopin's Funeral March on the edge of it. He had the curious impression it sounded better than on a piano. More mournful. Suddenly he started to panic. He wouldn't be able to stand it much longer. What if he tried to rape her? She would resist and he would become violent and not actually rape her..... She would have 'words' with which to defend herself. But it might clear the air. She would say something catty, and it would throw him enough to stop him, like, she knew he didn't want to be so violent really, so why was he acting as if he did? Or something like, 'But you know it's not *me* you really want to rape, is it, it's someone else? The question is, *who* is it really?' He would lose the moment and the momentum. He might even laugh. Probably he didn't want her at all. Unconsciously he just resented the ease with which she took him so much for granted and had palmed him off on her girlfriend.....

Was it only her unavailability that tormented him? He remembered some lines he must have learnt at school..... but couldn't say from where. 'Man is in love and loves what vanishes, what more is there to say?' Surely there were two kinds of desire, for what could be seen..... or what could only be imagined? Who was to say which was the deeper, the more important?

He had caught her looking at him strangely sometimes. He was sure she was sizing him up, physically, thinking something like, 'What does Anna really see in him? Why does she need to undress him and see him naked? Why is she so happy to lie back on the bed and let him penetrate her, fling himself about for ten minutes and then go..... aaggghhhh, or whatever sound you made at that moment?' She might then expect him to say something inane afterwards like, 'Are you alright?' Raymond was furious. Damn her! What *did* she think? But he hated being forced by her silence, her distance, to think her thoughts for her..... knowing he must be so far off the mark. But she gave him no choice.....

But it was the idea, the image, that she was a virgin, that was throwing him most of all, and he didn't know why. It was a kind of affront. There was an image lurking in the wings of his consciousness. What was it, on the material level, still there? He was a man, and men thought like that. They had no choice. They wanted to see it..... what was it like? He couldn't see it in his mind. He was used to imagining the spaces inside a woman..... what must be touched and filled..... rather than the mucous membranes, like the barricades, there to keep someone out.....

But suddenly he wondered again if she was fooling him. That

was so much more likely after all. It was absurd that she was still a virgin. In 1968? The truth was she simply didn't fancy him. She was being polite. He wasn't her type. She liked sailors or black men. Or homosexuals. There was no reason why he should be her type, after all. She probably had a very particular type, a quite certain image of the desirable. But her rejection of him still hurt.

He decided he must go to Paris the following day. Take a day off. Maybe go to a film. Get a waft of 'outside air'. He was becoming stifled inside the walls of her house now, even though he was fascinated by her, and still felt it was his duty to help her to be calm and complete the 'monologue'. But some time alone was needed. She was even starting to depress him, with all her complicated ideas and talking.

But the following day, he found he couldn't leave.

★

For two days he suffered. They repeated the 'rituals', the same routines and timing. It was important to her, she claimed, to be trapped in a very precise structure, while she was 'letting herself go' into the other woman's madness. Otherwise she would go mad herself. So he followed the time-table as she did, without complaint. In fact he was happy with it in a way, although he was becoming more edgy as time went by.

One evening at supper, she surprised him, saying, 'I am like a child who wants the same fairy story, exactly the same words every night, night after night. It takes time for them to be completely absorbed. The story must never change. Every night a rite, at the same time. Like sex in marriage isn't it? I am a creature of habit too, like my cats . . . . . I like habits. I need them. Does it annoy you?'

He lied, saying nothing she did annoyed him. He enjoyed her way of life. It was new for him, unpredictable. But afterwards he felt bitter again. He hated any situation in which he didn't know the truth . . . . . didn't have control.

★

Two days later, Anna arrived again, late at night, and slipped into his bed, and the next day he missed breakfast and lunch. On the bed in the morning, she showed him a folder of 'stills', of photographs of her production, and Raymond was utterly amazed by the masks of the Peaceful and Wrathful Deities..... and some of the flimsy costumes.

But in the afternoon, she and Nora spent the time in Nora's studio, with the photographs. Nora said she wanted to copy them.

After dinner Raymond found Anna alone in the drawing room and they danced for a while. Nora joined them and Anna chose some rather fast rock-and-roll music to dance to. To his surprise, Nora suddenly seemed to peel off her psychic straightjacket and started to dance with her, really wildly. He sat watching them both, amazed at the power of music to transform people - even bewitch them. They each moved so differently, even when they seemed to be copying each other very precisely. Then they found some slow music and they danced sensually, sinuously..... caressing each other..... until Nora suddenly became shy and came and sat by his side and Anna carried on dancing alone. Suddenly he noticed Anna was very drunk..... or so it seemed..... and she started to move even more slowly, out of sync with the music, twisting pain from her mis-timings. She was caressing herself provocatively.....

Raymond drank two glasses of wine quickly, while Nora went to the kitchen to get something, or do something. He knew he would have to be a bit drunk too. Anna was still dancing with herself, in a trance, turning herself on, her own audience, perhaps imagining herself dancing on the stage of the Paris Opéra as Elektra, or even Clytemnestra..... Either way, she was hell-bent on shocking everybody out of their wits and their seats.

Nora suddenly left him alone with her, after a couple more songs. Until then they had taken it for granted that Raymond wouldn't dance. It was his job to watch, to be the all-seeing eye. But at the door Nora turned and winked at him. 'She's far away at the edge of the universe. She's all yours. Can you get that far?' He nodded. He'd have a damn good try anyway.

Anna danced one more dance before she noticed Nora had left. Immediately she changed the music to a more roxy routine and proceeded to strip for him, and they made love on the floor and on the piano stool and on a chair and finally fell into the pink velvet curtains over the window, one of which fell down on them. Anna was indeed pretty drunk, but not too drunk to enjoy herself, and to keep escaping and getting him to 'take' her again. It was some kind of necessary rite with her. A continuous first time. Over and over again she said it, 'Take me - now!', then slipped away. It was the first moment of penetration she seemed to savour . . . . . but to his surprise, when she obviously wanted to stop playing this game and 'get on with it', she lay on her stomach and told him to 'Take me' . . . . . but she barred the way and indicated with a finger that he could vary the approach . . . . . so that's what he did. At the edge of the universe, everyone knows there are black holes . . . . . waiting to engulf unwary rockets passing by . . . . .

Afterwards she seemed happy, and smiling wickedly, speaking in an almost inaudible whisper, 'Nora like that!' She was learning English. He wasn't at all sure what she meant, but didn't really want to think about it, or know, especially at that moment. Or he was too drunk and exhausted to make her explain herself more fully, even in Munich slang.

He'd also been too busy with his passion to notice when it was that Nora finally slipped from behind one of the curtains near the door, to go, as she had said, 'To my father's study to work' . . . . . But Anna had known she was there. Watching everything. Every small detail. That is why she'd put on such an exotic, varied performance. She had a nose for Nora's strange ways, even though Nora always tried to lie to her too about everything. She too had her intuitions, her instincts, her ideas about Nora's perversities. That was why she had never brought a man back to the house. But this time it clearly didn't matter, as it was 'Nora's man' anyway . . . . . up to a point. It was a good opportunity at last, to break down Nora's defences. If Nora wanted theatre, she could have it. She didn't mind acting anything, if the audience was appreciative. She loved Nora . . . . . she didn't want to be *so* mean, and deny her the only real sexual pleasure she was capable of . . . . . or so it seemed . . . . . .of watching them . . . . . .

★

When Anna left the following afternoon, Raymond was exhausted, not so much physically - he had soon found his rhythm - but mentally, from trying to make sense of her English and his German. After a while they gave up trying, communicating well enough with silent tongues, and eloquent fingers . . . . .

By the time she left, he was happy to see her go. This time she had managed to prevent him from seeing Nora at all, who had hidden away in her various rooms, not even appearing for meals. Anna had heated some ready-made dishes for their dinner, which Nora had earlier taken out of the freezer. She seemed to be treating them like two naughty children . . . . . punishing them by ignoring them . . . . . but leaving them to get on with it.

The more he made to love to Anna, and enjoyed it, the more he dreaded seeing Nora afterwards, imagining she would need to treat him with greater aloofness, and detachment. He had no idea the opposite was true . . . . .

Lying in her bed alone afterwards, Nora was aroused exquisitely, watching the image of them in her mind, abandoned to their passion on the floor of her elegant drawing room. She knew that Anna was aware of her presence behind the curtain . . . . . a woman like Anna would notice such things. She saw at what point Anna started putting on a show, making sure the camera angles suited her. Nora had always suspected that Anna's real erotic trip, if not her *only* one, was to be the exhibitionist. No doubt she preferred to dance in front of men, but to dance in front of a woman . . . . . even if Nora was only acting the role of mother . . . . . would also produce in her the necessary shame . . . . . or whatever you'd want to call it . . . . . to make it really exciting.

Anna had often tried to make Nora talk about sex, without success, Nora always managing to avoid the question and turn it inside out, making Anna talk about her own lovers and their peculiarities instead. But from now on it would be different. Before Anna left, she and Nora had driven into town to buy some more frozen meals, and to Anna's surprise, Nora started to speak explicitly about the previously taboo subject. As she put it, 'Only for the sake of my monologue, for the sake of the book. I need to know some rather sordid details!' Anna was surprised by her sudden frankness, the naked curiosity. She had expected Nora to ignore the 'question' of Raymond, but actually watching them making love, had altered the situation. She had been there too..... part of it..... present.

Anna had always been sad they never talked about sex. After all it was one of her favourite pastimes. The silence on the subject was a void that often threatened their relationship. At least that was Anna's response. She liked to talk about sex, with girlfriends especially, almost as much as performing it. She had always wanted to know what went on in Nora's head - and body. Anna's theory was that Nora had been promiscuous at some time in her life and been very hurt by someone in particular, whom she'd be unwise enough to fall in love with. She'd then rejected the whole business as 'irrelevant', which was how she had summed it up once or twice, in superficial references to the subject. In vain Anna had said, 'You're quite right, maybe it *is* irrelevant, but it's fun being irrelevant. What is pleasure, if not enjoying irrelevance?'

That morning they spoke about sex and sensuality for the first time. Anna felt excited afterwards, knowing the ice had been broken. Now they might be really intimate, at last. As she left the house, she turned and looked back at it, not thinking about Raymond at all. He was now irrelevant! She had assumed the role of power with Nora. It was Nora now who had become *her* child..... asking 'mother' at last..... about the sexual mysteries that confused and worried her so much, despite the way she verbalised about it before, in a very superficial, masculine way. 'I presume you fucked him, didn't you? Oh good!' Just to know whether she'd fucked someone or not, had seemed enough. She had only ever seemed really concerned and upset when Anna had seduced Mathieu, the leader of their anarchist cell. He had been in love with Nora, but she had refused..... and refused. She told Anna she was convinced he was after more of her money and she'd given them as much as she could. But with other men they had both met, Nora didn't need to know any details. The details were taboo. Just to know, yes or no..... so she could imagine it.

Anna was already looking forward to coming back. She would put on an even better performance next time, with more variation, if only on the pretext of answering questions already asked, or not yet asked..... questions from Nora's project. 'Only for the sake of writing my father's book with more insight and understanding, of course!' Maybe she'd bring back some outrageous costumes..... maybe. Some really cinematic ones ..... the one's she'd collected, mostly from the thirties..... Berlin between the wars.

★

A short time after Anna was out of the house, Nora came down and played the piano, and Raymond guessed it was a signal for him to join her. He was surprised to see her heavily made-up, the colours exaggerated and extreme, almost as if she was going for an audition for a movie. Raymond's heart sank. She was looking utterly radiant. Ravishing. But in a trance. Nevertheless she was clearly excited to see him, eager to talk to him. She insisted they went to the kitchen, where he saw she had laid out all kinds of tasty little pots of food she had bought that morning in town..... He was amazed by the variety of delicious cheeses and pâtés, smoked hams and smoked fish, she had prepared for his pleasure.

As he drank the tea and nibbled at the food, he was thinking how different she was to any other woman he had ever known, or ever expected to meet. He prided himself on having known a few, and many of them had been complicated. But he'd never known a woman who only warmed up to him because he was making love to her girlfiend, and in her own house! He would have been even more shocked though, to know she had been behind the curtain, watching everything.....

He could see she was determined not to start the conversation, eyes focused elsewhere, so he asked her how the monologue was going.

'Oh..... the monologue..... why yes..... Marvellous! Now anyway! It was a bit sticky at the start, as I told you, but now I'm really happy about it. No looking back now. It's all coming back to me..... word for word almost, or so it seems. What amazes me is how well I knew it. Strange how some things get etched into your mind, and other things don't, as if there is an underlying structure that selects. Always above you. We are mere victims. You can forget a whole war. Six million people gassed, but never forget the first avocado pip you persuaded to grow in a plant pot, when you were a child. Or the little boy who pulled down your knickers. Why some images and not others? That is it the question. That is fate! That is the power of the gods over our little minds! Why some dreams and not others? It is only a terrible, anguished illusion that we are free. If we were free, we would not need to gas six million people here and kill other millions there. The lack of freedom is always within. And we are more and more trapped by images . . . . .'

He nodded. He was enjoying the food immensely. She was looking so gorgeous, he knew if he stopped eating, he'd scream at her and tell her to stop talking. He nodded again. She seemed almost beside herself with an irrational excitement. Her lips were quivering as she spoke, like butterfly's wings . . . . . She was tormenting him but the food would have to do instead . . . . .

She continued. 'But after all, my father and I had discussed his project many times. It was his great dream to have it published. He knew it would combine new psychological insights but also hint at many other things. Nothing would be explicit about the wider issues, but they were clearly so relevant. This case-history was the unravelling of a single knot . . . . . a very fascinating knot . . . . . more entangled than the knot of the Goddess Isis. I'll tell you about her sometime. My favourite! This story, this quest for a cure to madness, is happening now . . . . . to me. In my blood. I knew it was all there, just below the surface. How's the food?'

He gulped. 'Beautiful!' He knew she was high on something, but didn't dare to ask. He knew it would be the worst thing to stop her now . . . . .

She continued immediately. 'I had a beautiful dream last night. I was a little girl, watching an old man with a beard making a pot out of clay. I was laughing because he kept getting his beard in the way of the pot! But he was moulding it so perfectly with his hands, and his feet were running, running below the table, turning the wheel . . . . . suddenly I knew something mysterious was going to happen. He stood back from it and took a small, beautifully shaped stick of willow from his table and waved it in the air, like a wand, and then touched the pot. The pot was in the shape of a woman's body. Just a hint, no more. The waist, the buttocks, the breasts. Like some of those very early figurines of Mother Goddesses. Not voluptuous. But undeniably female. The little vaginal logo in the crotch like a

CND sign. But in the dream this was significant - this femininity of the pot. It had not gone unnoticed even to my young, innocent eyes. No such thing of course. Innocence is the greatest of all betrayals. Anyway..... Suddenly it was transformed, as if by a flash of light, to pure, shining gold. And then he gave it to me. I knew it was *so* precious, worth a fortune. Solid gold! Then I woke up. But you see, it is what I must do now, make gold out of his old clay pot. He called me his little willow tree at times, when I was just thirteen or fourteen, you know, when young girls become a bit too tall and a bit too thin and a bit gawky, but at times they look pretty with it. He said I was lithe and supple like his favourite willow tree. I used to sit under it whenever I was sad or particularly happy. It was my favourite tree in the garden..... I'd sit there, dreaming, my fingers playing with the water..... or throwing bread to the ducks. Most of all though I loved the black swans, such a contradiction, back to front in meaning, but I don't want to talk about them. Are they not against nature?'

'Yes I supppose so,' Raymond murmured, fascinated by her eyes and lips as she was soaring on the wings of the invisible source of excitement.....

Nora then suddenly changed the subject, to talk about Anna, and he nearly choked, the change was so abrupt. But she carefully avoided the fact of their love-making. Not one word suggested she was even thinking about that side of it. Everything about Anna was in relation to Anna herself, alone, apart from him, or to Nora herself, or to external events like the play that Anna was rehearsing. She told Raymond how they had met some months before her father had died, and had 'hit-it-off' immediately. She asked Raymond to explain where the curious English expression came from, to 'hit-it-off', but he had no idea at all. She said it was something of a contradiction. He asked her if there was a similar expression in German, but she couldn't think of one. He kept forgetting she was German, she spoke such elegant, poised English, and he complimented her on it again. 'Don't compliment *me*, my dear. Compliment one of your public ghettos for girls!'

It was the first time she'd called him 'my dear' and it seemed utterly inappropriate. But he could see by her eyes now, clearly, that she was high on something..... perhaps the pills. Mixing antibiotics with other things would make things much worse . . . . . She stopped to take several deep breaths as if she might be planning to choke quite soon, and asked him if he too was now managing to work well. He said he was, reasonably well, but he was also enjoying the biography of Freud, which was a revelation. She seemed delighted. He asked if she had a copy of 'The Interpretation of Dreams'. She said she'd find it for him.

After the meal, she suddenly blurted out . . . . . 'Come with me. I'll show you my studio. My work. My etchings!' She ran up the stairs ahead of him to the top floor, where Raymond had not yet ventured, and took him at last into the studio she had kept secret for so long. He was entering the inner sanctum of the temple. But he was not expecting the scene that confronted his eyes. What he saw disturbed him deeply. The walls of the room were covered with her work. There were so many images, it took him some time to focus on each one separately. They were black and white sketches that looked like etchings, as she had said. Quite a few of them had splashes of a single colour . . . . . a pale olive green usually . . . . . or burnt umber or a deeper brown. Occasionally red. The presence of the splash of colour made you read them as a painting rather than an etching.

But every picture seemed at first glance, to be the same, as if she had made a hundred sketches of one subject, never quite getting it right. When he looked more closely, they were all different really, but the variations were often quite subtle, almost unnoticeable. This was disturbing enough, the repetition of this single image, but then, even more disturbing was the eroticism in the pictures that took him by surprise and made him feel really uncomfortable. Yet he knew they weren't really erotic at all . . . . . not obviously . . . . . he had more or less projected this quality in his initial reaction. He couldn't be sure if this was her deliberate intention or not.

Every image contained only the same few elements. They were all related to the dream she had just told him about. He almost mentioned the association, but he suddenly felt he must not refer to it. He didn't know why. In each picture, there was a shape . . . . . which seemed to represent the earth, or a mound, or a pot, or part of a female torso, and going into each one, or coming out, or just touching each one, was part of a tree, often the small trunk of a very small tree, or a mere branch of a tree.

Sometimes the branch had leaves, but often it seemed made of the same textured material or substance as the pot or shape. The images were quite abstract. But he could 'read' one of the totally abstract ones because he had seen the others..... in which the pot or shape was more clear, or the branch of the tree was drawn so finely he could see the markings on the bark. On one small branch he saw the first signs of a bud..... a mere hint. On another, the bud had almost burst..... like the phallic tip of an amanita mushroom.....

'One thing you must admit,' she said, 'if you were to see one of my paintings in an exhibition, you would know it was mine, wouldn't you? Seen one, you've seen them all!' she said with a wry smile.

'Yes indeed, indeed.....' he answered, awkwardly.

Under her breath she muttered, 'As Anna reminds me often enough.' But then she spoke normally. 'I used to do lots of different images..... but then I found my theme. My myth let's say. We all have our own myth, and getting to know it is to become free. Free from fate. If only Oedipus had known his! Anyway..... this is really only the first exploration of the theme. I threw all my other stuff away. I burnt the lot in a huge bonfire in the garden, and spread the ashes on the rose garden. It started with the idea of growth, the tree growing out of the apparently inert ground. Then it developed. That, I suppose is what my work is all about. No? Growth. The seed becoming a tree. Look at these others!' She opened a huge black leather folder and showed him more drawings or sketches. All the pictures were the same again but this time the roots of the tree were exposed. He could almost see where the twisted fingers seemed to be trying to suck out the fluid and nourishment from the earth.....

'I'm planning my first exhibition for six months time. I'm an arrogant shit, aren't I? So they say. But I know where I am going now. I'll stay within this narrow range. All I need are my trees and my earthenware vessels. Surely, it's the most fascinating thing of all, putting that small seed into the ground, into the mud, and it grows?'

Then she dismissed him and he felt sure she was going to cry.

★

That evening she seemed more normal once more and they danced, but quite soon, Raymond was brought again to the point of screaming. He still didn't know where to begin with her. But still the time didn't seem right. Maybe never..... But he knew that some part of him wanted to tear her apart..... lay her down on the sofa and ravish her. This time he thought he could feel how tense she was, poised, poised like an animal ready for flight. One small guesture and she would bolt..... snap ..... escape. She lay her head on his neck, her cheek against his, but so lightly, it might have been a moth's wing. He knew he must not move..... not disturb her fragility. This light touch was all she could manage, yet. She was waiting for him to make the first move, so she could reject him, viciously. But how could she be so fragile and yet so brittle at the same time?

★

Later, in his room, he wondered if his attitude was totally wrong. But how could a mere man understand such a woman! Surely he ought to throw cares to the wind and grab her, as males of the species were expected to do. As her cats did after all..... But he knew she felt safe now, for the moment, and needed it that way. It would be grossly unfair to shatter that feeling of being safe with him. He must not abuse that. Even if he just made one small sign..... one passionate kiss, hard on the lips..... what would she say? 'How awful you are! How easy to betray isn't it? What about your poor girlfriend, Anna?'

In desperation he picked up the Freud Biography and it opened at a page where Nora had underlined the text again.

'The last letter from Ferenczi written in bed on 4 May, was a few lines for Freud's birthday. The mental disturbance had been making rapid progress in the last few months. He related how one of his American patients, to whom he used to devote four or five hours a day, had analysed HIM and so cured him of all his troubles. Messages came to him from her across the Atlantic - Ferenczi had always been a staunch believer in telepathy.....

..... followed by his sudden death on 24 May. That was the tragic end of a brilliant, lovable, and distinguished personality, someone who had for a quarter of a century been Freud's closest friend. The lurking demons within, against whom Ferenczi had for years struggled with great distress and much success, conquered him at the end.....'

She had made a note at the side.

'Ferenczi had the key to it all! To us all. If not to himself. Death and love. Love and death. I don't know how to keep him at a distance. To say no! If I say no..... he will penetrate my mind with his telepathy. Dead or alive he could have easily taken me.....'

Raymond assumed Nora had chosen this text because it related to the death of her father in some way. But he wasn't sure.

He flicked through the book again, reading more of her under-linings. It was no longer the Freud book he was reading, but her selection of it. He was reading her. The quotes she had underlined sometimes seemed to relate to her paintings. Most seemed to be about love and death. Some were about growth. They were fragments of a portrait of a woman unknown..... But one thing was certain. He knew she had underlined each line for a special reason. She didn't underline the quotes consciously. Raymond knew from his own experience that the guesture was intuitive and impulsive. A kind of slip..... not of the tongue. But of the mind.

He took his diary-notebook again. He'd not written anything more in it, having abandoned the project after the first day, as too indulgent. But he decided he must carry on and copy all the lines she had marked. There were not too many after all and they were already suggesting a pattern. If he had them all written down, in order, and read them straight through, would he not discover her secrets? It was worth a try. He started copying out the lines. He copied out several pages of quotes, but then felt an unexpected resistance. He stopped. He didn't see it as an act of repression. He was tired perhaps. But it was a crazy way to be talking to her about her secret self..... Damn her!

Almost in despair, he started again on his Immunology paper, and managed to work until he was tired enough to sleep. He could hear Nora talking to herself, or to her father, or to her wider audience, in her father's study. He tip-toed quietly and listened, angry he couldn't understand the German. He stood outside the door for some time, anguished at the irony of their relationship. Yet he respected her for her total dedication to the work. She was unrelenting. Nothing else really mattered to her. He had never seen this in a woman before, this sense of absolute certainty. He seemed to expect uncertainty. It was clear she knew exactly what she wanted and why. Just like a man. He knew that nothing could stop her. But her paintings related to another, different Nora. The one needing the image of growth. Could it be related to wanting a child? But whose? Or was he now being really sentimental?

He was tired. Depressed. Weak from thinking too much about her. Damn her! He was probably deluding himself. Her images were as much about death as growth. The trees, or plants, or broken off part of plants, were often stunted. Twisted. Gnarled like gristle. It was Nora who had said her pictures were about growth. The more he thought about it, he felt more and more sad. Her paintings were empty. Frigid. They were really about frustrated growth. A form of reversal of growth. Death of some kind. He felt miserable.

Wasn't he much better off thinking about Anna . . . . . and her lust for pleasure? And so, with her in mind, he decided to crash out and sleep. And maybe he'd go to Paris in the morning . . . . . and see how well it was collapsing.

Anna's breasts . . . . . to remember them or forget them . . . . . that was the burning question of the moment . . . . .

★ ★ ★

Five

For the next week, Raymond and Nora followed the same routine. They woke up around lunchtime, ate a light breakfast-lunch, went for a walk in the garden, worked for a bit, had tea, worked, had dinner, played the piano, and sometimes danced. Raymond felt unexpectedly peaceful, once he was managing to work well on his project, and time flew by. Nora taught him a number of German folk songs and a piano version of the section from the Brahms Requiem..... 'Denn alles fleisch - All flesh is as grass'..... which she said was very very important to her, but she couldn't explain why. It was something intimate between her father and her mother. When she sung the sombre German words, there was little suggestion of their origin in the bible. She made the music sound seductive and haunting, like Marlene Dietrich singing a song from 'The Blue Angel'. Many times she asked him to play the accompaniment and she would sing..... sometimes he thought she might cry she was putting so much emotion into it..... but always it was a sign that they must separate and go to their rooms to work. It was the 'finale'.

Quite soon Raymond accepted his fate, that he would never receive anything more from Nora than this sisterly affection. As he lay in bed at night he thought of Anna instead, even if it took quite a conscious effort, most nights, not to yearn for Nora.

At their lunchtime breakfast one day, he told her he must go to Paris - 'Maybe for two days, to find some scientific books I need, so I can stay here longer.' But she hardly seemed to notice what he was saying. She was always especially distant, just after waking up. It took her a long time to recover from the night's vigil with the tape recorder and her monologue..... and her trances. He had no idea that she was often so excited by the flow of images and words, she became careless..... and nearly overdosed.

★

In Paris, Raymond discussed the progress of his new paper with his director and asked for a further week off. 'Peace and quiet in the country looking after a relative' was proving an ideal situation in which to complete the long-overdue report. As Paris was still in such chaos, one way and another, with the student so-called revolution, the director thought it was sensible for him to stay in the country and work, and wished him luck. He wished he could do the same.

Raymond instructed Jean-Pierre to make some more routine experiments, having examined the results of some recently completed ones. Jean-Pierre said he'd not been too involved with the politics, as Beverly was proving harder to 'pin down' than he had expected. The Vietnamese nurse had sadly drifted out of his sphere of influence. 'She is probably making money servicing the policemen in their Black Marias in front of the barricades!' he grumbled cynically. Raymond guessed she was one of those who was lucky to get away.

But Raymond felt lonely already. He thought about Anna somewhere in the city, abandoned passionately to her rehearsals of her play and its timely message of Protest, and probably making passionate love to her director. But then he decided 'passionate' wasn't the right word really..... perhaps for the play, but not for her casual pleasures..... passion was what he felt for Nora! It was to do with frustration. He sensed that even if Nora and he became lovers, he would never reach her..... there would always be a void he could never penetrate..... but oh how passionately he would try, given the chance!

But he would have loved to visit Anna at her rehearsals, and he was annoyed not knowing where they were happening. He had asked Nora about Anna before he left, diplomatically and somewhat reluctantly - not wanting to hurt her, as he still imagined or hoped it might. She had turned away and shrugged. 'God knows where she is. This whole play business may be a front for one of her anarchist scams! It may not even exist. I am not her keeper at the best of times, and these are the worst. She is always secretive about her men and she is probably heavily involved still with the present events. She is particularly secretive at the moment!' she said, seeming resentful of her freedom.

★

At the station on the way back, waiting for a taxi, he noticed the same whore he'd seen before, wearing the same leather outfit. He was surprised at himself, having to think hard for a reason *not* to pick her up. After all, she was his 'type' in a way. She was probably pied-noir. The black leather resonated with, and emphasised her exotic colouring, especially in the half-light of the station forecourt, everything a grainy black and white. He had to wait some time for a taxi, eventually she smiled and waved to him, so he went to her. He was surprised she spoke quite elegant French. But she had a long scar on her arm. It could have been from anything, but he remembered Nora's warning, and cursed. Even if he bought her he would not be able to make love to her, recalling Nora's words. So she was repressing him even at this distance! But there was too much to risk and he didn't need her that much. He apologised. 'Excusez moi. Au revoir mad'moiselle'.

She replied rather coolly, 'Vive les Anglais!'

On the way back in the taxi, he realized she looked exactly like a whore in one of Godard's films. Or was it Chabrol or Truffaut? Or Pabst even? Maybe Bergman. Fritz Lang. Cassavetes.....
'Curse the cinema!' he said out loud, thinking of the girls he had gone to bed with because they merely reminded him of a scene in some damn film, girls who had always been so utterly boring and disappointing, not knowing the right lines, or the right slow-motion guestures. Films were dangerous!

Then he wondered about Nora in this context, trying to 'place' her in his mental files of cinematic images. He couldn't find the right file or she wasn't there. Perhaps *that* was why she fascinated him so much. She was too interior to be a subject for a film. The cinema cannot easily reveal absence..... Nora! Damn her! If only he could leave. Why did he allow himself to be so trapped? She didn't want him, he knew that now, but it was more than that. He couldn't relate her to anyone else he'd known - but only to something invisible inside himself - nor could he relate her to any girl in his vast mental collection of erotic scenes from films, which was clearly the key to understanding his attitude to the erotic. Because he couldn't file her, she was truly herself, unspoilt, unravished by any stolen image that would have sucked away her soul..... As she had told him, natives in the jungle knew, a photograph was always the theft of soul..... Nora was so far untainted with this threat of mute objectification. Or was she? Maybe he'd not yet found the right file.

★

When he got back, Anna was there. He thought she was looking tired and dishevelled, by which he meant very dishy. Later, she insisted they made love again in the drawing room. She had brought a costume back from the theatre and it was the most amazing thing Raymond had ever seen. She was eager to wear it for her performance. He didn't mind at all, it was so roxy, except some of the sequins came off and nearly choked him, and the feathers tickled his balls at one point, and they both started to giggle so much, he lost his erection. But they hunted for it through the numerous layers of kitsch material and eventually they found it again..... brought to life when he regained contact with the sleezy music in the background and he saw himself with his knees tight up against the back seat of an open-topped Cadillac Sedan at some all-night drive-in movie ..... After all, it wasn't stretching too much of a point, except on the desired physical level. She was an actress after all, even if she hadn't made it in the movies yet.

Afterwards, she insisted he played the piano and she sang, and Nora suddenly appeared from nowhere, just when he had buttoned up his trousers. They all had a wild time together, singing and dancing, drinking so much wine, Raymond thought he might lose his decorum..... but later, when they could barely stand, when Anna grabbed him again, he was pleased to see Nora slip discretely out of the room.

Anna sat astride his legs on the floor, and caressed him for a long time, kissing him gently before she made love to him very very slowly, moving her body as if she was still dancing, in long deep lunges over him, drawing him up with her as she pulled away. And when he ejaculated, to his surprise, she jerked back so he covered her bottom with the semen. But he was too drunk to care, happy enough if that is what she wanted.

Anna was surprised how much it excited her, knowing Nora was hidden behind the curtain..... she could have gone on forever.

★

The following day Anna left and Raymond and Nora slipped into their former routine. Nora didn't mention Anna at all this time, and it seemed better that way.

To Raymond's surprise though, she suddenly announced, 'I've got some good news! It's finished. The monologue! I've got the essential structure on tape. It is *there*. We can relax now. The basic text is there, and it's only a question of patiently fleshing it out..... which I can do in my own good time. You are off the hook, Herr Docteur. We can relax. I have some things to finish off tonight, some details. But I have an idea. A surprise. Why don't we go to a movie tomorrow, to celebrate, instead of working?'

He was surprised how relieved he felt as if he'd really solved a problem of his own. He said he was delighted and agreed a trip was a great idea. 'Near here or Paris?'

But she suddenly suggested, 'I have a better idea! I asked Anna where she was rehearsing. Why don't we surprise her and barge in on her? I think the play is close to the dress rehearsal. We know what her costumes might be like now, don't we!'

They agreed to leave the following morning for Paris.

★

That night, to his astonishment, Nora invited him to sleep with her. She said it so matter of fact, he nearly fainted. But she continued, 'Of course..... as brother and sister! I am not joking. I am not playing games, like so many women do. I'm not really hoping you *will* try to seduce me. If that is what you think, then *don't* do it. But I am lonely at night. It is so nice to hold hands in bed, surely, to feel someone close to you? I would like that..... but brother and sister. Promise?'

He didn't know what to say he felt so excited. So moved. Would he be able to handle it? He couldn't believe how relaxed she seemed to be, taking it completely for granted they could do it that easily. Hold hands in bed like brother and sister. She really was an enigma, to say the least. Rather sheepishly, he promised. 'Er yes..... I promise to be good. At least I will try!'

He changed into his pyjamas in his own room, wondering if she would make a move after all. Either it was rather a dumb ploy, which didn't seem likely of her, or she meant everything

she said about brother and sister. He'd soon find out.....
She was in bed when he joined her. He lay next to her obediently, holding her gently. She took his hand and laid it on her breast..... and that is where it was when he finally fell asleep, hardly daring to move. When he woke up in the morning, she was already in the kitchen preparing breakfast. She was very cheerful and talkative. But she made no mention at all of their sleeping together. Maybe she dreamt it.

*

They drove to Paris together as planned. She seemed very excited, as if they were going on holiday. She went shopping while Raymond called in at the laboratory. He was summoned to see the director immediately. There was a 'marvellous opportunity' to work on a three month project in America. It was all hush-hush, top secret, but very well funded and extremely well paid. If he wanted to go, he would be told the details of the work when he reached America. It was a special 'preparatory' course that might lead to some really interesting work there, if he wanted it. There had been some major discoveries recently in the field of the human immune system, which he ought to know about anyway. But he had to make a decision immediately and if he wanted to go, he would be expected to leave in two weeks time. The director had personally recommended him.

After this unexpected news, he went to a café and sat drinking a beer for some time, thinking hard. Hadn't Nora finished her work? She said she could carry on now with the further work necessary to complete a full text. He had given her all he could. He had nourished her while she needed it. But he had hoped that once the taping had been finished, he might entice her away from the house, invite her somewhere like St. Tropez for a few days. In the change of habitat she might be unsure of herself..... de-racinée..... and he might manage to seduce her.

But in his heart of hearts, he had by now accepted that she was 'off limits' to him forever. He would never succeed, however much he tried. Their night in bed together had convinced him of that. She hadn't shown the slightest sign of being attracted sexually to him. She was closed, as she had often said she was closed, protected by the invisible shell around her. He was fooling himself, telling himself he could change her. She had been so obviously happier with him once he was making love to Anna, he was a fool to delude himself she was available. Her invitation to sleep with her as brother and sister, confirmed she had no intention at all of making love with him. It was the cleverest kind of rejection. Apparently giving something, but really taking everything away. He might as well go to America and see what it was that was so secret, so much of an opportunity. It was probably the very best way of forgetting her.

★

He had time to spare and was browzing in a second-hand bookshop, when he found a copy of the Penguin edition of Freud's 'Interpretation of Dreams' and bought it eagerly. Afterwards he was annoyed with himself. Had he bought it to read, or to convince himself he was going to see more of Nora and not less?

Later, they met in a café. Nora was wearing some new clothes she had bought, in black velvet, with a long skirt. A small black battered pill-box hat, 'A *real* one from the Thirties!', had a red silk rose on it. 'I thought I ought to dress up for Anna's Dress Rehearsal! If she sees us, I don't want her to be ashamed of me!'

He told her about the proposed trip to America, and was utterly dismayed when she seemed really enthusiastic for him to go. 'But of course you must go! Heavens above why not? It is for your work. You are a scientist, and it sounds really intriguing. There is no reason to stay here, in lousy old France, which is falling apart at the seams anyway. What hope is there for you here, by the look of it? After all this chaos and structural unpheaval, money will be tight here for a long time. I am not an amateur, hypocritical Marxist for nothing, didn't I once tell you? You should go to America. Land of opportunity - and CASH! At least, see what they have to offer. I said you were free now. Please don't worry about me. You helped me with my problem . . . . . the most difficult one of all . . . . . getting started . . . . . and I will be eternally grateful. I will never forget your

sacrifice for me. I am pretty sure I can cope now by myself.'
It was at that moment he noticed blood trickling down the back of her neck. 'What on earth is that blood on your neck?' She looked down and then quickly away. 'Oh . . . . . It's only the old wound, not completely healed, and I caught it on the edge of a steel shelf in the clothes shop, while changing!'
He insisted on looking at it, and was dumbfounded to see it had hardly healed at all. 'But there has been almost no improvement! How on earth has it been like this, for so long? Why did you tell me it was perfectly alright? Perfectly cured?'
She looked guilty, and then almost angry. 'I didn't want to tell you . . . . . that . . . . . you had failed, did I?'
'Failed? I don't care! Failed or not failed. I just gave you the pills to take! Has it been sore?' He was too angry to absorb the fuller implication that it was *his* fault.
'Yes. Very. It has been really infected. But I went to the doctor in the village and he gave me some other antibiotics. Two days ago. There has been a lot of improvement since. In fact it is much better. I was silly to bang it, that is all.'
Raymond was furious. Not so much that she had said he'd failed. It had dawned on him by now what she'd said. He knew how easy it was to get the antibiotics wrong, without a sensitivity test. He was also annoyed he had taken her word for it that it was cured. He'd fooled himself. He had been sure it must have been healing, especially as she never referred to it. All the time it must have been causing her a lot of pain. Why had he not forced her to show him the wound?
'Don't be angry with me! I didn't really care, or even notice it much, really. I was *so* involved with the monologue, wasn't I? I didn't want to get involved with my stupid wound . . . . . my silly head . . . . . my boring body! We were so peaceful . . . . . it seemed unfair to bring it into the open. It is getting better now. So don't worry about it. You know I'm a masochist at heart!'
She stood up quickly and stormed off to buy a newspaper and left him still fuming with frustration and resentment. She really could be so boring! Most of all he was annoyed she could so easily and deliberately hide things from him. She was so secretive, so devious . . . . . it was this he hated most about her. It was the existence of her secrets that sometimes made him wish he could rape her, a poor revenge. But, now it was too late,

their time together was near its end. Had he failed her there? To rape her though..... maybe there was no other way of making her open up..... and escape her loneliness. He knew she was going to miss him whether she liked it or not and it would serve her right..... Damn her!

★

They drove to a suburb, and with difficulty managed to find an old church where Anna was now apparently rehearsing. Slipping quietly inside the building they found a couple of chairs to sit on, behind a colourful, shabby, motley group of spectators. They had decided not to tell Anna they were there, in case it made her too self-conscious. At least, that was Nora's excuse for preferring to gate-crash the rehearsal.

The director's assistant announced that Act One would start in about ten minutes and would last for about forty five minutes. There would be a half-hour interval, and then Act Two. It was the first of several expected previews before the full dress rehearsals, as they were having difficulties with synchronising the music and recorded speech tracks. It was a complicated kind of visual and sound polyphony.....

While waiting, Nora told Raymond about some other avant-garde events she had seen Anna act or dance in, and he noticed she didn't reveal the slightest hint of malice, jealousy or cattiness about Anna's obvious qualities. She celebrated Anna generously, even assuring him she found her very sexy too.

There were problems and the start was delayed a few more minutes. Nora suddenly mentioned 'the monologue' as she called it still. 'I must go immediately to Vienna, to my father's publishers there. They said they can help me to get my tapes copied and typed, when I rang them today. I didn't tell them what it was all about. Just vague outlines about the project. They were very friendly. They published all my father's papers and major articles. They were pleased to hear from me, saying they had something they wanted to talk to me about, anyway. I can stay there with some friends until the tapes are copied. I might go in a couple of days time, now that you are going to America. I didn't tell them what it was really about though..... not yet. And you? Have you made up your mind?'

He was surprised to feel his stomach slowly going taut. He didn't want her to be so cool about it all..... so detached, almost callous. He knew it was how most people treated each other in that day and age..... when what was desirable, had always to be new. He knew he was still rather old-fashioned, probably, compared to most, and he had no reason to criticise her. She had promised nothing. She had given him a very pleasant holiday in her home and generously provided him with Anna! It was her right to be so unreachable. He watched her carefully, objectively now, as she talked. Some part of him still wanted her desperately, even though he thought she would probably be utterly unresponsive to him, and probably to anyone else. It was surely *not* just him. She had decided not to be interested in sex, and she wasn't! It disgusted her for some obscure reason. The sooner he left her and went to America, the sooner he would escape the frustration and longing she still provoked in him, so mysteriously, despite his attempts to rationalise himself out of the predicament.

He asked her who she would stay with in Vienna. He saw her catch her breath as she said it. 'Some old student friends. Musicians actually. Not all my friends were anarchists! I met them in Paris. The girl was my friend. She played the cello. She is living with her lover. He plays the violin. It's funny seeing them playing together. A sexual duet! They always remind me of the copulatory advances of the Praying Mantis! The male is the violin! And she..... with such a gaping wound enticing him to his death!'

He laughed. 'While on the subject of wounds, you promise to get yours sorted out, I hope?'

'Of course I will! I'm no fool. I don't want to shave my hair forever. I'm not a Buddhist monk after all!' They laughed. She looked at him for some time, affectionately. 'You will go to America I think..... won't you?'

'Yes. It seems the best thing, from every point of view.'

She smiled at him fondly. 'I have a present for you. One of my pictures. A sexy one! I'll give it to you tomorrow. You *are* coming back tonight aren't you? Or will you prefer to stay with Anna?'

The question surprised him. He hadn't thought of staying with Anna. He assumed she would be staying with a boyfriend!

He hadn't thought about going home yet. He took it for granted he would take Nora back, and they would sleep that night, as before . . . . . brother and sister.

The director called for silence and the babble of the audience subsided. The make-shift curtains were drawn across the front of the bare stage area and the music started . . . . . the plangent beating of Tibetan drums accompanying the extraordinary 'Mahakala' singing of the monks, who could sing several notes at the same time. Nora told him about it in a whisper. 'They sing a whole chord . . . . . getting notes from different parts of their throats.'

Raymond thought it was a profoundly unnerving sound . . . . .

The curtains drew apart. Sitting on the stage in a lotus position was a monk dressed in saffron robes. Another dancer came forward with a can and simulated pouring petrol over his body. Then he poured a thin line of petrol from the sitting monk to some distance away, where he sat down. The other dancers crept onto the stage, humming. The sound was the sound of insects, mimicking the chordal music of the monks. Some of the dancers were dressed as monks. Others were dressed as Europeans, and onlookers. One was holding a movie camera, filming.

The man who had poured the petrol over the monk struck a match and mimed setting the petrol alight. The monk stiffened as the imaginary fire took hold and gradually smothered him. Raymond wanted to look away. Having seen the image on the television of the real monk burning himself to death, he could not detach his mind from this previous image, the real act he had seen, really seen, the image he knew of the real thing, even though it was film . . . . . now being recalled and seering into his mind and he was suffering as if he was really there, in Saigon, witnessing the monk's terrifying sacrifice. It was profoundly disturbing and he'd not expected it at all. It was as polyphonic as the monk's singing . . . . . as if reality could be perceived vertically on several levels at once. At best his response was all back to front. He felt sick.

The music got louder and louder and the dancers started to mime in a circle . . . . . a dance of death. The circle became smaller and smaller until the monk was hidden. When they stood back, the 'remains' of the monk's body was lying on a bier, hidden under saffron robes, his friends seated around him.

On the sound-track came a voice reciting the text of the Tibetan Book of the Dead, a meditation or explanation to the dead man of what he must expect after the moment of death. At first he will not feel really dead. It takes some time before he is sure he is dead. Then he will see a piercing blue light . . . . . and will start floating . . . . . in the realms of space and consciousness and time known as the Bardo . . . . . from which a spirit or soul can later be reborn into matter.

All the verbal images were mysteriously re-created on the stage by the lighting, the music and the dancers. Raymond found it very disturbing, intensely moving.

After the sequence with the blue light and the acceptance of being dead, the soul-spirit was then confronted by the Peaceful Deities, the Gods and Goddesses who represented pleasures and joys, but also the temptations . . . . . trying to persuade the soul to re-consider whether to choose Nirvana or to be born again . . . . .

Anna appeared playing the principle role in the Peaceful Deities and Raymond was pleased to see how beautifully she danced. He was proud of her and thought she managed to convey the needed sense of spirituality quite convincingly. He had been afraid she might appear vulgar and exaggerated, and he might be embarrassed, even ashamed of her. She was wearing an exotic headress of the Tibetan Deity and her face, with white make-up like a mask, looked unexpectedly young and pure . . . . .

★

Nora and Raymond slipped away during the interval and ate a quick dinner in a local café. The wine was good . . . . . and they talked about America and Vietnam, Paris and Vienna, Immunology and Marxism, the recent riots, Anna's poise and presence on the stage. Had they just met? It seemed to be the first time they had really talked for ages. Or at all! Raymond couldn't understand how he could have stayed in her house for a month and they had discussed so little about her role with her fellow anarchists . . . . . unless it was all a fiction. A romantic exaggeration. But as she was getting onto that particular subject, with some probing from Raymond, she changed her mind . . . . . and the subject, saying only, 'Anarchists? None of us are innocent in a democracy!'

Nora talked about her paintings instead ..... and about her ideas of the Tibetan Book of the Dead and its message of re-incarnation. Now she was already somewhat drunk, her eyes glazed. As she talked it was becoming something of a jumble and not particularly coherent ..... but passionate enough and Raymond loved to see her so animated, rising out of herself like a bird .....

She said she couldn't believe in re-incarnation in the popular sense. But she definitely believed in a kind of spiritual 'Telepathy' - which she saw as 'related in the same way the unconscious is related to the conscious. Like a tree to its roots. But the roots can only be seen obscurely! Imagined!' Even the idea of rebirth was probably a pagan or primitive belief derived from the observation that children resembled their parents. 'Don't forget, in the beginning of human history, they didn't know that the sexual act created a child. Sex was for pleasure alone! Like it is again in these pagan times! Re-incarnation occurred only on the telepathic plane. Call that spiritual if you like. But then matter responds, as it does to all such resonating forces. But think of it ..... Four of your children out of five looked different, then suddenly a child would be exactly like a parent, or as often happens, exactly like a grand-parent. Or like the man next door! This was all a great mystery. They saw it as re-incarnation into the flesh. *But* of course they experienced telepathy all the time. It was a natural feature of those cultures which depended so much on drugs to assist visionary experience. Telepathy was a fact and taken for granted. Their ancestors spoke to them, directly and indirectly. Mostly in dreams. Especially when they were in drugged trances. Then they heard voices! Yes indeed! As we can if we try and a few of us do! Just as recent military experiments in America and Russia with certain psychedelic or similar drugs have proved the mind is opened to all kinds of other messages .....'

'Not my territory at all!' Raymond said, sheepishly ..... He'd always preferred to stay lucid ..... as he called it. Nora wanted to say, 'or blind as a bat', but she resisted the temptation.

She continued, explaining it was all down to semantics probably. The inadequacy of words to describe such things. At its heart was the notion of faith. And the observation of cases of possession . . . . . by other beings. Telepathy was a fact, in the sense of re-incarnation.

Raymond nodded, 'Yes, I see what you mean . . . . . '

She then said she was trying to imagine a scientist's theory on the subject. 'I am of two minds. Such things are clearly possible, but we have not interpreted it right. Obviously, it is more mysterious than they say. Ferenczi believed fiercely in telepathy. It is like a dream. The truth is encoded within the text. But I don't want to talk about it. It is hard to imagine a soul floating in space, seeking rebirth and finally doing so . . . . . as the Tibetan's believed and said they had proved time and time again . . . . . entering the woman's body, 49 days later, to be reborn, entering the woman's body because of desire . . . . . an incestuous desire to be reborn. I don't entirely agree with that side of the story. It is possibly a kind of frequency influencing the egg immediately after conception. On the level of molecules. DNA and so on. It is hard enough surely, to believe that children desire their parents, as Freud said, without having to believe the act of re-entering a woman's body in re-incarnation is an expression of physical desire. Anna and I had a big argument about this other night. Of course she believes everything is Eros! Everything physical in the universe is suffused with an energy to join up, to unite with everything else, which she calls the erotic. Wishful thinking if you ask me - or a neat way of justifying her behaviour. Daughter of Eros. Daughter of our pagan times! Not like me. Still tied . . . . . a victim. Victim of the past. Haunted by ghosts! How lucky she is to have inherited only a void in which to float . . . . . '

Nora had given Raymond her copy of the 'Tibetan Book of the Dead' the night before, suggesting he glance at it so that the images and ideas would not be entirely alien. He had found it incomprehensible, but weird and strangely fascinating.

★

Act Two of the play started with clangs on a huge gong and the frightening appearance of the Wrathful Deities, as if reverberating in on the plangent ringing air, and the stage was suffused with menace and horror. The 'spirit' of the dead man had become 'formed' in the first part of the play, acted by an actor dressed entirely in black..... so that most of the time, thanks to the lighting, he was totally invisible. He only 'appeared' when he was seen against another person. A silhouette, suggesting a shadow.

As Act Two developed, his fate was to be 'devoured' each time by the Wrathful Deities. They seemed to have wings. Their bizarre costumes, copied from the images found in temples and on the wall-hangings called tankas, were voluminous and flowing and each time they easily engulfed the dancing-floating spirit. Raymond couldn't help recalling some of the electron micrographs he'd seen of the white corpuscles or lymphocytes in the act of engulfing marauding cells in the blood stream, but he didn't mention it, thinking it was rather out of place in the mystical ambience of the play.....

The narrated text developed from the meaning of the Wrathful Deities to the next phase, the growing desire for rebirth..... and here, Anna came into her own. She was the Scarlet Woman, as Nora described her in a whisper, the embodiment of sensuality and desire. She was hidden behind a disguised Deity and emerged at the end of the scene - not unlike a Praying Mantis emerging from a chrysalis, as she stalked her victim, doing everything she could to seduce him, to persuade him to give up his spirituality, and choose, through her, to be reborn again in the flesh. Now she was in her element..... the temptress, the erotic promise of renewal..... the power in nature that our ancestors worshipped, that allowed the grass to grow again after it had died..... the same God or Goddess or power surfacing in every mythological system..... as when the waters of the Nile, stemming from the body of the God Osiris, the Source of the Nile, fecundate Isis, the Goddess, who in the barren season is the dry earth waiting for the nourishing water, which then transforms the inert wasteland into life-giving pasture..... as the semen in the womb makes a child grow.....

The text had been ingeniously modernised..... the choice between Nirvana and Rebirth being brought into a new context. The monk, through the unprecedented and unimagined act of killing himself, seemed to have lost the privilege of choice ..... unknown except to the Deities, he was doomed to extinction. Neither a return to matter or going beyond to nirvana. An incomprehensible full stop. In essence, he had shown by killing himself, that he did not wish to return into matter in any new incarnation. He had destroyed even the hope embodied in the concept of spirit . . . . .

The dance became more and more orgiastic . . . . . and Anna peeled off layers of her costume, until she was almost naked. Now, love and death had become inseparable, indistinguishable, the desire for the one, the desire for the other . . . . . she had been transformed into death itself, into the desire for annihilation . . . . . le gout de néant, de l'infini . . . . . but she danced around her victim so seductively, as far as Raymond was concerned, she made even annihilation, if that is what she symbolised, a fair bargain, she was so tangibly desirable. But maybe that was because his perceptions were polluted with material memories.

Raymond turned to whisper to Nora and noticed she was in one of her trances. She was sitting on the edge of her chair, as if preparing to leap off into infinite space. Suddenly she gripped his arm so hard it hurt, and he knew she was really unaware of his presence. He was just something to hold on to. She needed to grab something solid. Then she started to mouth words, but no sound came. Raymond wanted so much to hear those words, he almost screamed out to her. But then the words slowly became audible, of their own volition. Words were like ghosts, their one desire was to be known, to register their meaning into human consciousness. 'She must . . . . . she must . . . . . must kill him . . . . . I want to see her kill him!' Raymond had ceased to exist. She was now sitting bolt upright, like a statue, totally identified with the dance . . . . . and Raymond was torn between watching her, rigid at his side, and Anna on the stage, dancing the sensual, tempting dance of death . . . . . devouring her victim by sucking him whole, so it seemed, into her body. He had not imagined, from his superficial reading of the text the night before, that the sacred mystical treatise of Mahayana Buddhism, the Bardoh Thodol or Tibetan Book of the Dead, could be so tantalisingly and painfully erotic . . . . .

Nora was weeping, tears gushing down her cheeks, as she gripped him even harder. He sat spell-bound beside her, fascinated by her expression of total abandon to the images in front of her. She looked so utterly beautiful. Suddenly the music reached a climax and the dancer annihilated her helpless reluctant lover . . . . . sucked him into oblivion.

On the stage, there was a sudden, total silence. Everyone in the audience was silent too, shattered by a battering of words and music and images. Then slowly the music from the beginning began again, and the action was re-cycled..... another monk was coming forth to be reborn, reborn into the scenario. He was coming to the centre stage to sit in the lotus position, to communicate momentarily with the Deities, and wait..... to be covered in petrol..... await the striking of the match. The fire.

Nora was watching the stage so intently, gazing into the folded scenery and props above it, Raymond wondered if she might be seeing something that wasn't there. But she suddenly remembered Raymond, turned to him and whispered, 'Wasn't it the sexiest thing you ever saw, like you and Anna in the drawing room!' and she looked back at the stage, unaware of what she had said, or having said it so casually, as if he knew. The words didn't have time to register on Raymond.

At that instant, to Raymond's amazement, Anna came back on the stage to enact another scene. While the monk was slowly covered with petrol to repeat the first scene, Anna came to the front of the stage in front of him. She had become a movie star! A vamp, dressed to the nines in all the glamour and the gear. The music was unmistakable..... Hollywood. The narrator's voice was now confused, jumbled, intercut. A tower of Babel. The mysterious, sublime text of the Tibetan Book of the Dead was intercut with awful American jargon recorded from movies and newsreels. It took a while for Raymond to realize the message, that it was America raping Vietnam, raping the Buddhist culture of the country..... offering cheap, obvious, vulgar sex in its place..... raping the minds of the gentle, agrarian people with its awful brand of cultural pornography, considered to be the norm. The most desirable, sickening norm.....

Anna, Movie Queen Anna, had taken one of the dancers from the back of the stage, a pure looking youth, a novice monk, and was seducing him. The youth couldn't resist of course, she was so tempting and gorgeous. Raymond felt awkward watching Anna making love to the boy, even when the act of sex was simulated, although it was the closest thing he had seen on a stage to the actual thing. In a Soho strip club it would have been closed by the police. In Paris you could get away with such things.

Raymond wanted to close his eyes. He didn't want to see what was coming next. He wanted to shut off the ouside world, to say to himself it wasn't happening, just as some of the images of the war itself in television newsreels had forced him to close his eyes . . . . . not wanting to see, or be forced to believe it was really happening.

Anna's orgiastic frenzy was mounting, enraged by the refusal of the dead monk to be reborn again through her body. The narration suggested America's naive, Christian, racist resentment of the Buddhist ideas of the Vietnamese religion and culture, the essence of the nation . . . . . She was determined to revenge herself by devouring the young novice monk with her sex. Raymond was in a state of such utter confusion, he didn't know what to feel . . . . . or think, or even if he was capable of keeping his eyes open. He wanted to shout out. 'No more!' He looked at Nora. She was still spell-bound . . . . . in a trance, moving strangely.

A painful thought came seering into his mind. The play's mixture of sex and violence, just like war itself, was really turning her on. The way she was moving, he felt sure she was masturbating. Her thighs were twitching. She was pressing a book she had in her hand, against herself. It was too dark to see precisely. Perhaps he was being unfair, imagining it. But everything about her suggested ecstasy. Or was it that he wanted to see the image in his mind . . . . . her pressing it against her own sex? Damn her! Even now he wanted to know what he could never know . . . . . what, in her woman's body, was she feeling . . . . . as waves of excitement spread from that imagined point in the centre of her being? Women were so different! Always so unknowable, if the truth was admitted . . . . . and was it not obvious, here and now, it was Anna that she loved? Why had he not thought of it . . . . . and yet if so, why had she offered her to him on a plate? Suddenly, he felt so much resentment - as a flood of ideas and images came to mind, suggesting he had been cheated, lied to, deceived so blatantly - that he wanted to hit her. But then he saw the tears in her eyes . . . . . and he felt guilty. He'd been wrong again! Surely he had been wrong. He felt waves of something spreading out in his own body . . . . . a kind of profound sorrow..... spreading out from a centre within himself, an invisible centre in a huge widening chasm of emptiness..... and he had no choice but to forgive her, even as she was at that moment betraying him so absolutely, unconcerned that he was present at her side. He was a fool! Even now, he was falling in love with her a little more..... because she was so unreachable, so unfathomable..... even though his mind was saying it was irrational, dangerous and destructive to do so. Perhaps she was really evil..... cruel and evil. A witch! Hate was rising..... but he managed to push it away. It was too easy to hate..... to hate women just because they were different..... a different race almost!

He looked again to the stage as Anna was making love to the young man..... the American movie queen molesting the young Vietnamese novice monk..... as the sound track built up its message of hate..... He was feeling so split inside himself, he was seeing himself with Anna, on the drawing room floor, on the piano stool, on the sofa..... and suddenly he heard what Nora had said, as if the words were coming from a previous dream. He'd not noticed them at first. Why had they washed over him so easily? 'Almost as sexy as you and Anna on the drawing room floor.....' Had she accidentally seen him? Slowly he realized, image by image, that Anna had choreographed their love-making so that Nora could see everything! He felt such a fool. And there she was on the stage..... fucking the young man. But he still couldn't be angry. His instinct was to laugh. 'Hey you guys..... how's this for a funny story!'..... or were they words in the play? Perhaps it wasn't true but if it was, what did it mean? He knew that Nora was utterly confused. Perhaps Anna too. Everything was confused. That was what he was witnessing, that the play was so brilliantly revealing..... documenting..... he just knew he was witnessing so much confusion, so much pain, fear, terror..... outside his life and inside it. All structure falling apart. Cultural anarchy. Cultural pornography. Culture become pornography. An entire generation seduced by instant fucking..... and killing. Killing to feel real. Killing to create images that can be seen..... to prove you are powerful, because when you cannot embody the power to love and be loved, everything becomes unhinged, all hell let loose..... collective despair and madness disguised as passionate freedom to be as anarchic as possible. Everyone was acting as if they were so knowing, so much in control, but under it all, they were so lonely, so fucked up..... so unfree! Trapped by pornographic images, above all else. In every film, every magazine, every advertisement. That was the new fascism. Advertising! Selling objects by selling sex..... and mostly sexual greed and frustration. Masturbation disguised as mass production. He was almost crying himself. The wine had been very strong. And Nora's words. What had they really meant?

The sound track was giving it all..... the hell of Vietnam and why its images were tearing a generation apart..... and he didn't know if the words were his own, or floating on the air.....

He closed his eyes and listened, not wanting to see more. The images had become too real. Seering and enflamed. Apocalyptic and murderous. He heard the sound only..... he remembered Nora asking about the deeper meaning of the expression 'as safe as sound'..... So he was partially safe. He heard the play end with the orgiastic cry of pleasure from Anna, as she killed him or had her orgasm - he would never know which - drowned by the sounds of the Vietnam War, and in the background, fading out over it all, the voices of the monks chanting..... and he put his arms round Nora and put his head on her shoulder. She put her hand on his cheek, and then kissed him gently, still not detached enough from the play, like him..... not yet realizing she made the terrible mistake, that she had told him the truth..... a kind of truth he probably ought not to know..... wasn't capable of witnessing. That she had given him to Anna so she could watch them fucking.....

Afterwards, he couldn't speak. She calmed herself, wiped away her tears. 'My God! It was exactly like one of my dreams!' she said and pulled a face at him, trying perhaps to make him laugh. She stood up and took his arm and pulled him out of the church. 'I want to be alone. Completely alone. Let's not see Anna! Let's go home..... but drive carefully..... I always get so emotional at all of Anna's plays, especially one like that. Please forgive me.....' She was crying again, but wanting to cry and letting herself cry. 'War frightens me so much. Only men makes wars. Does patriarchy depend on them? Can it be *so* wrong? Sons killing fathers and fathers castrating sons. Images of war and sex, and sex and war - the primal scene - unforgettable when they are in the family blood, as mine. They haunt you with their telepathic power. This war now in Vietnam was the trigger for our protest and rage. It radicalised us above everything else. Its images. If they could kill there, we must kill here. How long will if be, after it is over, before we forget it? A year? A week? A day? Where is the next war to film and see on television news? They'll make sure one is available. It sells televisions! And commercials. Imagine..... an advertisement for nappies immediately after the news! How long before Hollywood gives us films about its heroism in Vietnam? I am raw at the moment. Raped by images! It is a war, the same war I've just lived through again in the monologue, inside the Warsaw Ghetto. Filmed in every small detail by the Nazi soldiers. Edited. A neat, eloquent montage. THAT was her worst problem! They filmed her pain. Her crime! Was it really not so long ago, or so long ago? What is long ago? Long ago is something we are merely already forgetting..... a year, a week, a minute ago..... between commercials. Because they are instantly forgettable. Our biggest threat is that images must become instantly forgettable, or we will all go mad! We are becoming conditioned to be blind. Instant forgetters. Junkies of absent time - la vrai vie est absente - addicted to the present. So we will forget Vietnam in weeks..... and allow another Vietnam to become real and alive and filmable. Who am I? I am a book of images. An exhibition of paintings. A nightmare. There are images I cannot show you that I can never forget! That when you read my father's book..... his book and mine now..... you will understand! And then you will forgive me for being such a cold, wooden bitch!'

She slept all the way back in the car, and Raymond was pleased. He didn't want to talk about anything. He needed time to think.....

★

Arriving at the house, Raymond had to carry her inside. He was worried. She seemed far too 'out of it', merely from the effects of the wine, and he wondered if she was really ill. Perhaps the infection from her head wound was creeping round her body.

He decided he might leave her asleep on the sofa in the drawing room - virtually in a coma - and take a look round her various rooms. No doubt she was taking loads of pills, presumably supplied by Anna. With the antibiotics and the wine, no wonder she was so crashed out. But once inside the drawing room she started to wake up, almost in a panic. She groaned and then smiled, happy to be home. 'In the car ..... my God ..... I had the most awful dreams. Were we chased by the police at one point?'

'Of course not. I drove very slowly.'

'Oh good. I was sure they were after us ..... which would be the last straw wouldn't it, now that I've got the book almost finished? Mind you ..... it's so erotic in parts, it will probably be burnt on a pyre somewhere. All the time I was dreaming we were on the road to Rouen!'

Raymond, presuming she meant 'The Road to Ruin', said he hadn't seen it. 'Was it with Dorothy Lamour like the others?'

'No silly, Joan of Arc!' she said, giggling. She hugged him affectionately. By now she was bright as a button, and becoming childish, which was her favourite method of dealing with Raymond. She suggested some cheese and more wine.

They sat at the table in the kitchen, but went immediately silent ..... still not free from the mood of the play. Still numbed by its savage imagery and its emotional nakedness.

Raymond remained silent, to provoke her to speak first. He hoped she might refer to her faux-pas about witnessing his 'spectacle' with Anna in the drawing room. But she didn't mention it at all, and later Raymond wondered if he'd not jumped to the wrong conclusion. Maybe it was all in *his* imagination. She was not referring to what she had seen, but what she had imagined, what she had assumed was happening ..... She was upstairs in her bedroom imagining it. Or in the kitchen listening. Who would not? Of course she would have images of it in her mind. He wondered why he had presumed so quickly that she meant it literally ..... and the more he thought about it, he presumed he was mistaken. She was merely showing off that, despite appearances, she knew jolly well what it was all about ..... if ..... IF ..... she really was so naive and innocent on the subject, which he was still doubting .....

After some time she broke the silence. She said she was

sad they were having to separate, but hoped it would not be for too long. However, it was a good thing really. Her next step was to go to Vienna and sort out her father's book. She was ecstatically happy to have got so far with it, and successfully cheated the woman who had stolen the manuscripts. 'The amazing thing is, I feel it is almost word for word as my father wrote it. I could remember things so clearly. I was a good student at last! I felt he was reciting it to me. Telepathy. He would be proud of me. He would have hated knowing I was an..... an..... I was involved so to speak. Not that I was really! Why do I always get things back to front?' She was not quite herself.....

Raymond asked her why she had never told him more about her studies and political activities. After a pause, trying to smile but not really succeeding - she was looking slightly scared - she told him, 'I don't know why I didn't tell you. The truth is, I didn't study anything! In England I took my advanced levels..... philosophy, psychology and politics..... I even did biology at 'O' Level. I got a place at University there, but instead, I came to France to be with my father..... I sensed he was dying. My project was to take the exams again in France, to enable me to get to University here, but it was too complicated. The work here was far more advanced than in England. They are way behind there. That is how I got in a mess. I had a friend who was broke. She looked a bit like me, especially on photographs. She wanted to live and work in America. She needed money..... because she had some friends - drug pushers I think - the French connection and all that - who could get her a fake passport, a forged one. So I paid cash for all her papers, which included a French passport of course. Think of it. What fun. A new name, and *her* place already waiting at University. It's fun being someone else! I arrived at the Sorbonne to study Political History and I knew nothing about it really. Not from the French point of view. I tried very hard to *become* this friend of mine..... but..... I won out in the end. I failed. I failed myself. I am my father's daughter. It was too hard for me to escape my destiny! But I am still her legally, on her papers.'

'What was her name?' Raymond asked, already puzzled.

'I shouldn't really tell you. I can tell you the first name but

you will never never never believe it. Not in a month of Sundays! I cannot tell you the surname in case the police capture you and interrogate you.'
'Why on earth should they do that?'
She smiled her all-knowing smile again..... 'You never know!'
'Go on. What was the name?'
'What's in a name!' She laughed. 'Can't you guess?'
'You said I would never guess in a month of Sundays and now you expect me to. It's Thursday! Time has suddenly shrunk hasn't it?'
'It always does,' she said, softly, almost sadly, 'when you are just about to separate.'
'I can't guess.'
'Anna!' she exclaimed, laughing.....
'You're joking?'
'No! My student friends know me as Anna. To them I AM Anna. In fact I don't see myself as Nora, any longer. It was only by a mistake, a careless mistake, I wrote that name when you had found me. Very strange in fact, that lapse. It still puzzles me. I never never could understand why I wrote Nora, when I had become so accustomed to writing Anna, instinctively. My cheque book is Anna now. But I was still dazed of course from the wound..... from the blow. Also I was touched by you saving me. I was more conscious than you thought I was..... but still I couldn't be totally conscious. We were sharing a dream..... You were the brave knight, saving me from the fiery dragon, my initiation by fire! Taking me off on the back of a handsome, prancing white Deux Chevaux! A fairy story..... and it made me feel like a very young girl again. Which is why I lapsed, and wrote Nora on my note to you. It's been a strange experience for me all this time, you calling me Nora..... and Anna having to do so too! Whenever you call me Nora I feel I'm twelve again! And never been touched!'

The more she talked, the more he felt uncomfortable, not sure she was telling the whole truth. He couldn't think why she should lie, but her voice was different. Brittle and sharp. She was exuding an aggressive confidence. There was spite and bitterness in her voice, which gave him the impression she was acting..... lying. He decided to test her.

'Show me your cheque book!'

She reached for her hand-bag and showed him, carefully putting her thumb over her surname. It said Anna Ursula M.....

'Really it is better you do not know my fictions. My other, unreal life, in case of trouble. It was a silly thing to do really..... but I had this profound desire at the time to go underground. To be an anarchist. Ironic in the light of recent events! The desire at the time NOT to carry my father's name was quite irrational. I went through a phase of rejecting him..... like all girls do. My poor long suffering, ever loving Daddy. I didn't want his name. It was like being married to him. Especially since my mother died. I wanted to be myself, someone absolutely different. This girl was desperate for money, so I got the money from my father, telling him it was for something else. An abortion for her. And some blackmail money. She was from a very good family. He understood. He gave me the money and I gave it to her. I became free! I bought my freedom with money and crime - not by analysis! She became an American girl and left for New York, forever, on the false passport provided by our friends..... she was now called Maria Schwarzkopf. Suitably middle European, to go with her looks. She thought she was Hedy Lamarr, really! Ecstasy! I took over her abandoned identity. It suited me fine. But it was hard, very hard, keeping it from my father. When I met Anna it was perfect. I told her the whole story. That is one of the reasons I moved her in with me! When people called up for Anna..... he thought it was for her! Brilliant! Then I got my own phone. He didn't want to be disturbed, so the problem ceased. Of course I still have all my real papers. I am two people you see..... very convenient at times..... troubling at other times. But I really do embody the myth of the age, don't I? What a privilege. The age of the schizoid self and collective schizophrenia. The split soul. Schizo-phrenia comes from schizo-phrenous, split soul.' She smiled at him, coldly.

'Yes I know,' he said, equally coldly. The more he seemed to discover about her, the more puzzled and confused he became. And frustrated. In the past, the more he knew about a woman, the less he desired her. Except Jane, who had managed, by her other-worldiness (as she called it) to remain intangible, so he always felt he could love her, though in truth, they had drifted apart. He wished it was simpler. He was sure it wasn't entirely his fault . . . . .

But now, he and Nora were parting . . . . . so would it matter if she rejected him? If he messed it up? Once. If only once . . . . .

He was watching the corner of her lips quivering as she spoke. She spoke English with an accent that at times seemed a mere hesitation, a loss of breath between syllables, a kind of lisp, as if she was saying one thing but meaning another. She never said what she meant . . . . . but now he was watching every nuance of movement at the edge of her lips . . . . . to see a sign . . . . . wanting desperately to kiss them, rather than to listen to more lies . . . . . surely she sensed what he was thinking?

'You will forget me as soon as you are in America, you know that. You'll tell your new sexy American girlfriend - won't take you long over there - you'll tell her you met two crazy girls in Paris that you are glad to be rid of. You went to a riot, to be present at history - or by chance - and much of history is chance - or to be a student again, to participate in it all and you picked up a poor helpless creature, bleeding to death, who turned out to a spoilt little rich girl with a huge house that got burgled, who then pimped for you and supplied you with a sexy German girl, child of her times, with no notion of the meaning of the word inhibition . . . . . with whom you learnt little German, but became adept at sexual mime. From me you had lessons in psychoanalysis, which you found all poppy-cock. That is what you will say about us, and it will be true!'

He shook his head from side to side slowly, but he knew she would reject any other version of the story - her story - the one she had choreographed, mistress of ceremonies . . . . . so he said nothing.

She poured out more wine for them both. As she was drinking, she suddenly whistled loudly . . . . . as if trying to stop the Trans-European Express at a level crossing . . . . . and he jumped. She looked towards the door and after a minute or two, one of the cats came in. 'You know what I call them don't you? Their names!'

'Anna and Anna?'

She laughed, spontaneously. 'Very good. Excellent Herr Docteur. One love to you on that one - your point! But not quite.

Well their names are German of course, but I will give them to you in English. I call them "Reality" and "Fantasy". Pretty don't you think, even in English?'

She stroked her cat and picked it up. Reluctantly it stayed a moment or two on her lap but preferring to be on the floor, jumped down and starting walking round and round her legs. Once again Raymond noticed what perfect legs she had, swathed in black net stockings. Damn her!

'Which one is this one then?'

She looked carefully. 'I don't know. I never know. I don't even know when they are here together. I never knew. They are twins. I don't want to know. But I do have a great fear..... a real worry.'

'Which is?'

'What will happen if one dies? The one remaining will have to be both. She will become so confused, so threatened by monotheism! Aren't we all? One day I will call her "Fantasy", the next day, "Reality". What an agonising identity crisis. Watch me!'

She spoke the first name sharply in German, but the cat ignored it. She then gave the other name, and the cat looked up at her, questioning. 'Ah good,' she said, 'at least *she* knows who she is!'

Nora looked at Raymond with her eyes narrowed. She was enjoying her game. 'One day you will visit me, in the future, and I will be Anna for you. In every sense. OK? When you come back from America..... I will show you that I too can dance, and in my dance, bring together the two opposing Deities, as Anna did, but mine will be Freud's of course. Am I not my father's daughter? My Deities will be Eros and Thanatos, what else! By the time you come back, my father's book will be finished. I will have proved to the world and to myself, how you can tell the difference between reality and fantasy in a little girl's memory! And, in the process, I hope..... I will have taken down, brick by brick, word by word, dream by dream..... the invisible wall around myself.'

Raymond was sure he saw tears in her eyes, but she averted her gaze. She stood up and came to him and kissed him lightly on the cheek. He already sensed what she was going to tell him, and he braced himself for it. 'Goodnight..... I'll see you tomorrow morning. I am feeling too tense and upset this evening, with one thing another, to take the risk..... of betraying myself. Please forgive me!' She left, to sleep alone.

He sat in the kitchen for some time..... drinking the excellent wine and eating more cheese. He was angry with himself..... or with her..... telling him she would see him after he came back. As Anna! THAT would mean he would be thinking about her all the time, which was NOT what he had planned to do. As Anna! He had planned to forget her. But perhaps he was being stupid. He would soon forget her. If he wanted to see her, he could. Maybe he'd stay in America and never come back. If so, it had been a pleasant interlude, a quiet idyll in the midst of an otherwise chaotic month. And anyway, he must not forget Jane..... and his promises to her.

However, recalling the Anna of the evening, he was becoming aroused sexually. The images of her on the stage were flickering in his mind, like static under the surface of grey storm clouds. He wanted to bring her now, here and now, into the drawing room and fuck her on the carpet, until it singed her thighs, or straightened out her coccyx. He wondered why he was feeling so aroused suddenly..... and aggressive with it. He couldn't fathom out how Nora always turned him on sexually, yet apparently not towards herself. To others. Then he almost wept, saying out loud to himself, 'What a fool I am. It is Nora I want and I ought to have the guts to take her, if necessary with violence. It's our last night. She said she was a masochist..... does she enjoy actual physical pain, or enjoy the pain of denying herself pleasure? That is the question..... but what have I now to lose?'

But the telephone rang. The ringing stopped as Nora picked up the receiver in her room. A minute later, she came back into the kitchen. 'You're in luck! It's Anna. She is at the station. Blind drunk from celebrating her play. She is so drunk I could hardly understand a word. She kept trying to speak English. Maybe she thought I was you! Please go and collect her in the car. She daren't take a taxi, in case she ends up in a brothel in Tangiers!'

★

Anna was indeed very drunk. When he arrived she was propping up a lamp-post, talking to the whores, and didn't notice him parking the car a few yards away. When he reached her she beamed. She seemed very excited. 'From Munich, from Munich!' she kept saying about the girl she was hugging, as if neither of them were able to stand up without the other. The girl asked him in French if he could handle her, or if he needed any help. It was not the girl in black leather. He looked round for her but she wasn't there. Pity.....

Raymond took Anna's hand gently, as if to take her away, but there was no immediate response. She stood her ground. He guessed he ought to yank up her skirt, push his hand between her legs and hoist her on his shoulder, like marines are taught to carry bodies, but if the police saw him they might think he was carrying off one of the whores, for a free bash, and arrest him. 'I am Hedy!' the girl said. Anna babbled some German to her. She turned to Raymond and said, 'She doesn't want to go back to the house. She wants the three of us to go back to my place. She wants to enjoy herself. She says she will pay!'

Raymond was rather drunk himself. The whore was not exactly pretty, but she was young-looking and her mouth, her teeth and smile were clean and bright. She was wearing a 'little-girl' dress, presumably to appeal to men who liked schoolgirls. Close to the lights, the number was a failure. But at twenty metres, she could have passed for sweet 16. She knew he was sizing her up, so she stuck out her breasts to improve the image. Sweet 36B. Out of place on the girly image, but..... Raymond was tingling. She'd made her point.

The three of them soon arrived at Hedy's flat, which Raymond was disappointed to see was spotlessly clean and utterly bourgeois. A whore's habitat ought to be Kubla Khan or the Hanging Gardens of Babylon. He had never been 'into' whores, so didn't know their only passionate desire was to become bourgeois. Hedy explained she usually entertained her clients in a hotel, but Anna, being German, was already a friend.....

Raymond wasn't sure what to do, so decided to wait. It was their scene, that much was certain. He was a mere pawn..... willing to be lost for a night..... He sat in an armchair and Hedy gave him a very stiff whisky. The girls went into the bedroom and he heard all kinds of giggles and merriment. He decided he was really going to enjoy himself, whatever happened. If only to spite Nora.....

He drank the whisky eagerly. Then he decided the room lighting was too sharp. Everything was far too clear. Real. He wanted everything dim. He switched on a small light on a side-table and switched off the main light. The girls were making so much noise it sounded like a dressing room at Les Folies Bergère..... at least, that was how he was seeing it and no-one was going to contradict the image inside the private confines of his own mind. Not even Nora.

He poured himself another whisky, and was soon feeling ready for anything and everything. When Hedy back came into the room, the school-girl look had gone. She had let her hair down and it was surprisingly long and clean looking. She was wearing a very roxy negligée, and the obligatory pink frilly stole around her neck, black net stockings and very high heel shoes. She said they were ready for him now, and promptly dragged him into the bedroom, laughing.

Through the fog now enveloping his mind, her bedroom resembled something out of Kubla Khan or the Hanging Gardens of Babylon, and he couldn't see Anna for lace hangings on the ornate four poster bed. But what he thought was a polar bear carpet used as a bedspread turned out to be Anna..... and then the fun began.

Hedy started to undress him while Anna peeped from behind the white fur. Raymond was hesitant at first. This was a play he'd never acted in before. He did - and he didn't - want to show them how erect he was. How complicated such things can be at the best of times! Hedy politely stood back when Raymond insisted he wanted to take his own trousers off. She went to a cupboard and produced a silk bath robe which he was delighted to slip over his nakedness. She was a professional. Perfect timing. She knew exactly how long to be discrete.

Anna spoke to Hedy and she translated. 'Anna wants to be the director tonight, for once in her life. She says she wants you to make love to me now and get it over with. Then we can have a drink, and can start all over again and you will perform better! The first one is the dress rehearsal!'

For a moment he thought he ought to frame some kind of

objection, as it smacked of a feminist put-down, but then he thought to himself, 'My God. She's quite right. What a damn good idea!'

But then he had another, worrying thought. Anna's remark! 'A dress rehearsal!' Had she seen him and Nora watching her on stage, and that is why she was so keen to come back? But he didn't have time to think about it further. Anna had emerged from under the polar bear-skin and dressed in one of Hedy's more daring outfits, red and black lace and all kinds of leather things, Raymond was too given to the dream. She dragged him to the bed and started to kiss him and fondle him. Hedy lay down next to them and opened her legs and crotchless knickers. Anna pushed him into her and hugged him and kissed him and encouraged him . . . . . though it wasn't necessary. It would have needed his mother to hold him back. He let go, until even the whisky couldn't numb him any longer.

Anna was a good director. He felt more relaxed having ejaculated, knowing there was more to come. They relaxed and drank on the bed, in silence. Then Anna started to caress Hedy, and Raymond watched . . . . . until he had to join them. And he was going to take his time, this time . . . . .

At a moment of semi-repose, a most unworthy, unwholesome idea surfaced uneasily into the murky swamp that had recently been his mind, to which he imagined he was barely attached by a kind of long thin umbilical membrane, enclosing a precious part of his body . . . . . proof that the phallus is what holds men to their egos . . . . . the thought being, 'Christ, Anna can't afford all this!' Then the idea mutatated into something more malicious. 'But I bet she finds a way of charging it on Nora's account . . . . .'

By the time he was finally spent, the two girls were out cold too, or were acting as if they were - perhaps to expedite getting rid of him. But he couldn't imagine going anywhere, so he took the white fur rug and lay down with it on the long sofa in the sitting room and crashed out, a polar bear that had been overlong breaking some ice.

★

In the morning he was woken by Hedy. As he poked his head out from under the fur, she smiled quite fondly at him and stroking the fur, as if it was part of him, said, 'Time to come out, little bear. It's spring. You look as if you've been hibernating all winter!'

He and Anna drove back to the house late in the morning, after visiting the shops in town to buy some things for the house. He couldn't understand why she still couldn't speak any French. He asked her in German. Why no French? She smiled. 'I am a dancer!'

There had been no mention of money on leaving Hedy's flat and he hadn't pushed the point. He wondered if he would get a bill later.

Nora greeted them warmly, as if it was quite normal for them to spend the night elsewhere. They drank black coffee in the kitchen until Raymond excused himself. He was feeling too awkard in their presence. The story would come out in the end, but it was best it was from Anna. It was time to pack . . . . . and he packed the Freud Biography without asking Nora if he could.

★

The three of them drove back to Paris in the afternoon, and the girls were babbling and giggling like schoolgirls most of the time. He hoped Anna wasn't now telling her about the night before. If so . . . . . he had not performed quite so well as he'd imagined. But he was happy not to need to talk. His mind was like jelly and his body like lead. Somewhere between, he was a fishing line, floating . . . . . feeling he might have lost the bait.

The two girls were sitting in the back and from time to time he looked at them in the mirror. Now, he had become a mere chauffeur! Who was it? Oh yes of course . . . . . Eric von Stroheim. Ah well. They weren't aware of his presence at all. But he wasn't bitter. Why not, he thought, maybe he'd been used, but so what, he'd had a great time. Maybe that was only an old fashioned way of looking at things but it was the point of view his education and background had instilled in him and there was no shaking it off. Even the cinema hadn't changed it. It had merely made him more romantic . . . . . But who was to say it should ever be anything more? Much had been shared and given and taken. He was still growing up. But the sooner he got to America the better! Time to move forward.

His strange, tangential lapse from reality ..... his peripheral merry month of May 1968 ..... was over. He'd picked up a mere slip of a girl behind the barricades ..... it had all been like a film ..... but his innocence was still largely intact. And so was hers, apparently .....

It was strange that film could only reveal what was there ..... it was hard to film something that wasn't there. Hard to capture invisible truth, whatever that might mean ..... perhaps it could only be achieved in the cuts, in the spaces, in the violence inflicted on the narrative flow. Something like that.

The girls were still giggling like two teenagers in the back. He loved them both really. He was going to miss them .....

★ ★ ★

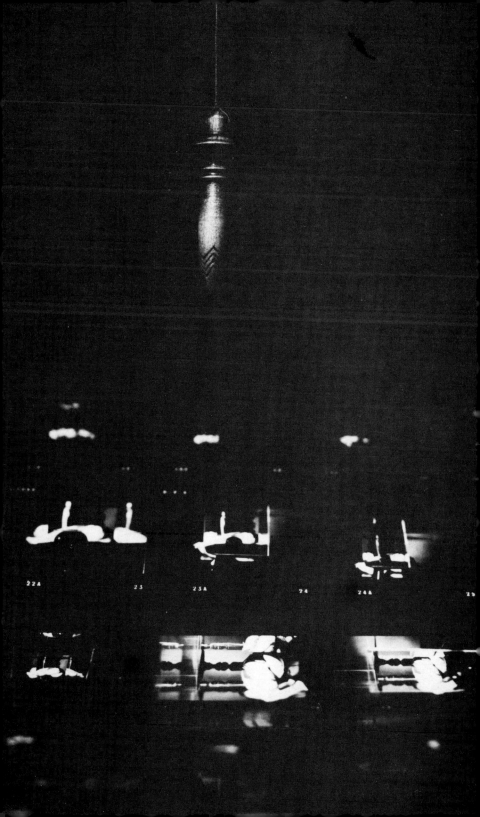

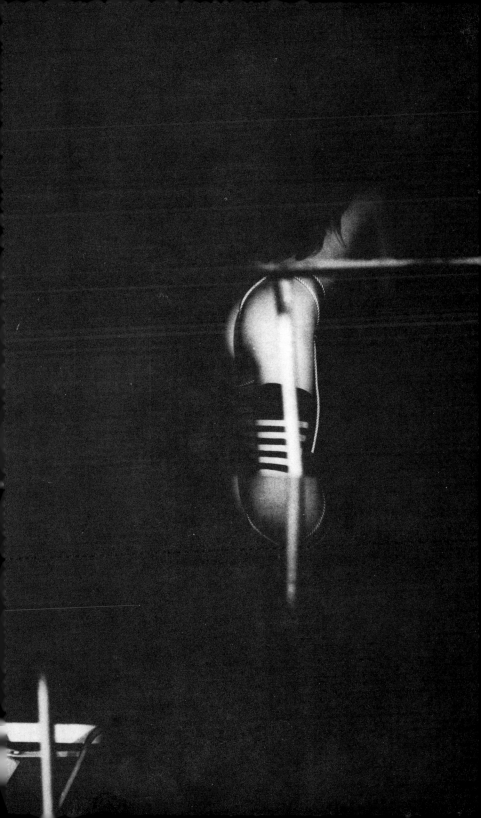

Part Two

Six

Nora took a plane to Vienna a few days later and went immediately to her father's publishers. She had told them no details about the way her father's project had evolved, except that she needed their help to transcribe a number of tapes, and afterwards, their advice in editing and publishing the final manuscript. They had indicated they would be pleased to help and advise, and were intrigued to know more.

The director of the publishing company, Doctor Andrija Kaczmarovska, a Polish aristocrat, had himself trained as a psycho-analyst, at the same time as Nora's father. But being too impatient - he had once told Nora and her father - to listen to patients complaining about their parent's inadequacies rather than their own, he'd gone into publishing instead. Amongst general books, school text books and fiction, his Company published various scientific books and papers, mostly to do with psycho-analysis.

Nora met him alone in his office the morning after she arrived, handing over the tapes with instructions to treat them in the strictest confidence. She said nothing about the theft of her father's manuscript, but explained she had worked with it, but with some difficulty because it was 'very fragmented'. She had used various other fragments of text, also handwritten and difficult to read, and excerpts from a very private diary. She had done the work on tape because she had a 'block' about writing and couldn't type. After the text had been transcribed, she would take it back to Paris and complete the work of structuring and editing.

Doctor K. as he was known, assured her he had been a close friend of her father, owed him the deepest respect and would do everything to comply with her wishes. He was eager to see the final text, which he felt sure he would want to publish. Everyone in the small world of psycho-analysis had been saddened by her father's untimely death, and there'd been much talk about an unpublished major work . . . . .

Doctor K. had an eye for pretty girls, and Nora knew she could twist him round her little finger if necessary. With gushing smiles, he'd said she had grown up to become a 'lovely' young woman, and he was sorry she was the daughter of his colleague, and 'part of the family so to speak'. Nora knew that if she fluttered her eyelashes and bleated something like, 'Good heavens, do such things matter nowadays in these swinging times?' he would have dragged her onto the couch in a flash. Like striking a match to a thin stream of petrol accidentally or deliberately spilt on a pavement.....

★

She stayed with her two friends in a small village in the countryside, near Vienna. She was sad to discover they were quarrelling bitterly. She had the sneaking feeling it was since they decided not to play Schuman and Bach, but Schoenberg and Bartok. She did her best to keep out of their way, and went for walks alone in the nearby forests. She loved drifting like a shadow amongst unfamiliar trees..... alone..... talking to them like strangers met in a dream..... but then she spent hours sitting under a favourite tree she remembered from her previous visit, where she would relax and read. She felt really peaceful, at last, knowing the tapes were being transcribed. Freedom was close at hand.

A few days later, Doctor K. called to say the first batch of type-script was available for her collection. She went immediately to his office, and was surprised to be introduced by him to an attractive young woman, Agneta, whom he claimed was his niece. Nora felt immediately it must be his mistress. Apparently Agneta was doing the typing.

She and Agneta went to a pavement-café to talk, while Doctor K. was busy. Agneta explained she was half Swedish, half Viennese, and worked part time for the publishing company. Most of all she wanted to talk about the text that was emerging from the tapes. She'd found it fascinating. It was beautifully 'written', and she told Nora she had a perfect sense of timing and phrasing. Nora told her she had studied Literature at the Sorbonne, and had always wanted to write, especially fiction, but found it very difficult to write with 'her hands'. The breakthrough had come when she decided to use a tape-recorder. Agneta clearly knew quite a lot about psychoanalytical language and theory, and they talked over a few points. Nora confirmed it was her father's most 'seminal' case history that she was re-constituting from various fragments, the main manuscript having been partially destroyed. Agneta looked a little puzzled and said, 'That explains things. There might be a slight problem. From time to time you feel it's a woman speaking, not a man at all. Especially in the most intimate sequences!'

Nora was worried for the moment. Had she put too much of herself into it? 'No problem. Please mark those passages - underline them with red ink. I'll go back to the original notes and re-phrase it. Thankyou for pointing it out.'

Agneta was gazing at her attentively, scrutinizing her face as if she was looking for someone else who wasn't there..... and murmured, 'It's a very harrowing story. If it comes out as a book, it will shock people, terribly. Most people dare not confront such truths about other people, never mind themselves. It might offend some people too. Have you thought of a title?'

Nora nodded..... 'I had thought of "The Blindman".'

Agneta smiled. 'Yes..... I've reached that far. The game the woman, when she was a little girl, used to want to play all the time with her father. Very touching. Blind Man's Bluff!'

Nora didn't want to elaborate further. Agneta was not yet half way through the tapes. She would see the deeper, sadder signifance of the title later. It was during one such innocent game of blind man's bluff, that the father took advantage of the game, and of being behind the blindfold..... as if he had mistaken her lithe young body for someone else's..... and had first fondled her intimately. Their game of blind man's buff had led to many things, and would be re-enacted by the woman..... as an adult..... not being able to make love to a man, satisfactorily, without being blind-folded herself. Often being bound by ropes. Whether or not the events had been real or merely fantasised by the young woman, who later saw a film, or photographs, of a young girl being seduced in such a predicament, had been one of the problems confronting Nora's father during the analysis. Later the woman 'fused' the images together in her mind..... into a kind of multi-layered polyphony..... fusing, confusing, fusing them with the parallel images - and facts - of the young girl, filmed by the Nazi soldiers in the Warsaw Ghetto.

Nora found Agneta attractive, and wanted to know if she was really Doctor K.'s mistress. She couldn't ask her directly, knowing that if the idea offended her, she might reject Nora in some way, or even subtly revenge herself by corrupting the text, or at least, deliberately taking a long time over it. The veracity of the text was in her hands at the moment.

Eventually she invented a story. A complete lie. Sometimes you need lies to uncover the truth. 'It's funny you are half Swedish. I knew another girl in Vienna two years ago, who was half Swedish. Her name was Gul-Britt. I forget the surname. She was lovely - the mistress of another colleague of my father's - a very brilliant man. I ought not to mention his name. I am *never* that indiscrete.'

Agneta blushed and turned away. Nora was pleased with herself. She'd been right! To her surprise, Agneta said. 'Yes, I think I heard about her. It must be the same one. Is she still in Vienna do you think? I would like to meet her. There aren't many of us half-castes about these days. Was she dark like me, or blonde?'

Nora replied, 'Blonde..... very typically Swedish looking. You know the type. Pretty without being gushingly sexy!'

Agneta was looking at her intently. She couldn't tell if Nora knew she was bluffing. In fact, she desperately wanted to talk to her about herself and Doctor K. Suddenly she relaxed and decided to take the plunge. 'You said all that because you wondered about Andrija and myself didn't you?' She smiled kindly at Nora.

'I did wonder!'

'Is it that obvious?'

Nora paused for a moment or two. 'Probably not. But I always pick up on such secret relationships. I resonate! I have a nose, a Jewish nose for such things. I am my father's daughter after all! I see forbidden scenes..... illicit sex hiding under every cobble-stone..... often when I don't want to! You can't expose yourself to psycho-analysis and remain blind. Except to yourself of course.'

Agneta laughed. The ice was broken. 'How long are you

staying in Vienna?' she asked Nora.

'Until you finish the typing. Then I'll take it back to Paris, work on it a week or so, and come back here. Or maybe the final revision will take me six months. I don't know.'

'It won't take you that long. It reads very well, already, very smoothly. In fact it has probably gained by being absorbed and given out as a monologue in one go. Analytical people write very awkwardly most of the time, turgid and circular and with all kinds of convolutions. I have difficulty typing it, let alone understanding it. Your arrangement of the text flows beautifully. It has a poetic quality about it. Your father was a very sensitive and gifted man!'

Nora looked down and turned her head away. Her hair fell over her face but she left it there. For some time she followed the movements of the pigeons fluttering about the tables. She wondered how many of the couples there were lovers . . . . . and if it mattered. Surely such things didn't matter? Life went on just the same . . . . . how right was she to assume that our worst behaviour often came from mis-directed sexual energy? And some of the best too . . . . . like art. Painting. Music. Religion. People didn't like such ideas. Truth based on analogy rather than rationality. They had ridiculed Freud for saying such things for the first time. He had been a courageous man. As was her father. It was true. Her book might be hated by a lot of people . . . . . but she didn't care. A lot of people she knew were hateful.

Agneta was looking at Nora fondly and she felt comfortable. She liked Agneta. She liked to think of her and Doctor K. in bed together . . . . . as little girls liked the idea of grandma and the wolf. And themselves too . . . . . better that than being like Anna, wearing red shoes that would never never never stop dancing . . . . . always waiting for a man who was wise and clever and sensitive enough to take them off. So Anna had once let slip. Drunk. Or like herself, to see the ghost and persuade him to fall in love with someone else - your best girlfriend - and go away and leave you free . . . . .

★

Two or three days later, Doctor K. invited Nora to dinner at his apartment, with Agneta. Nora guessed Agneta had told him she knew about their liaison. She felt quite uncomfortable about the the invitation, but couldn't refuse it, although she felt confident she could handle it. He was sure to take the dumb approach and try to get them both drunk..... just like Mathieu had done a couple of times with very little success. Mathieu! All that seemed a long way off.....

But whatever plans Doctor K. might have had were dashed even before dinner started.

'I have something for you Nora. You remember I told you there was something here of interest for you. You forgot to remind me. We came across a brief-case of your father's papers. It has two combination locks and we have never opened it. I remember he said it was copies of all the papers we published here. Anyway, it is your property now of course.'

He handed her a leather briefcase. There was a similar one at the house. She knew the numbers. On one side it was her father's birthday and on the other, it was her own. She pressed 281, for 28th January and then 253 for 25th March. It sprung open.

Wrapped in purple tissue paper, was a copy of the manuscript that been stolen.

She nearly fainted. She had no idea it existed. Her father had never mentioned it. She flicked through the pages. It was identical to the one she had started working on such a long time before.....

'I see it is something important!' Doctor K. said, noticing she had gone quite white.

'Er..... er..... perhaps. I don't think so. It seems to be a copy of a manuscript. A book by a friend of his, by the look of it. Ferenczi I think. I think it is 'Thalassa'. Thank you anyway. Perhaps my father made notes in it which might be valuable. Or it is an original manuscript. It might be worth a lot of money, especially if it *is* Ferenczi's 'Thalassa'.....'

She closed the case and jumbled the numbers. Her heart was beating fast. She was dismayed, scared but also excited, intensely alert. Her whole body was tingling as if she'd been making love for hours without an orgasm. She watched the other two for the slightest move. But inwardly, she was trying to confront the 'meaning' to her - the new fact of the re-discovered text. It could be the worst thing to have happened. She had a deep sense of foreboding. It was like being at a funeral and seeing the coffin lid opening..... or meeting Adolf Hitler alive and well in an Argentina suburb..... selling paintings, perhaps his own, or a new encyclopaedia of the occult.....

She sat numb at the table, barely able to eat the dinner, giving the impression of not noticing any of the sexual innuendos that started to flow from Doctor K. She would have played with them earlier, and teased them, as if she was available, and then politely removed herself after coffee. But she was feeling so dé-racinée..... she made no effort to please..... only to be polite.

After a short while Doctor K. got the message, and changed the subject from the latest society gossip and the risqué plays he had seen and erotic books he had read, and they talked instead about the student revolution. 'Weren't you there Nora, when the fun started?' Nora decided to explain a little about her part in it, only to annoy him. She resented his tone of 'put down' as if it was just a student prank. So she admitted she was a member of a small but deadly serious Maoist revolutionary cadre that had probably helped to get it started in Paris. 'After the naive, adolescent police action at Nanterre University, we knew we had the chance to escalate it into Paris. My friends were real anarchists though. I was rather naive and tagged along with them. I would have probably gone the whole way mind you..... and blown people up..... but then I got wounded!' She smiled sweetly, as if throwing bombs was second nature to her. Maybe it was. She bent her head and parted her hair and showed them the wound, covered with a plaster.

The Doctor feigned deep concern. 'Oh la la..... quelle horreur!' He knew she was mocking him. Still..... she was her father's daughter and he had been an activist - albeit on the plane of ideas - all his life. Especially in the last ten years when he became contemptuous of the whole process of psycho-analysis, claiming it was a hoax, with very limited use in extreme cases, a perverse method of maintaining power over people..... 'psycho-analysis exists to re-assert the patriarchal delusions necessary to man-kind' he had once written in an unpublishable paper. He was pretty sure the so-called 'text' that Nora was working on would be totally unpublishable. Far too radical. Riddled with sado-masochism too, her father's obsession and undoing.

But Agneta was genuinely worried. 'But there is blood still seeping through the plaster, isn't there? Is it still bleeding, now? Why is it still that bad?'

'Er . . . . . yes . . . . . it's very boring. It won't heal. I am on the third series of antibiotics. There is some poison in it I think. Or a foreign body. But it will heal eventually. I just tell myself it is not there. It didn't happen. I forget it. I'm immune to it now. I have some very strong pain-killing pills!'

Doctor K. left the room for a moment and Nora spoke quietly to Agneta, making light of her participation in the riots. 'I'm glad I got out when I could. The police were after my friends, knowing they were anarchists. They had been watching us for some time. I had to be very careful. The others have disappeared. Gone underground from necessity. I warned them. I told them there is never peace, it is always war. You have to persuade the people first and then the government and that's too slow these days. Anarchy seemed to speed things up but people don't bother to understand the underlying motives. I don't know if they are in jail, hospital, or plotting something really bad. I had concussion for a while and lost touch. They will reach me again soon though, when things are quieter.' She didn't say . . . . . 'For money, if nothing else'. She'd never admit now that she'd been the main financer of Mathieu's group.

Doctor K. returned while Agneta was telling her about the student riots in Germany. She said it was all inevitable after Rudi Dutschke had been shot . . . . . Doctor K. errrred and ummmmmed and ahhhhhed, as if he was either listening, or had suddenly regressed to a babe in arms . . . . . he was really fed up he wasn't going to get both girls in bed together. But he enjoyed watching them and he was relishing the idea of punishing Agneta afterwards. He could easily find a suitable pretext, like her enthusiasm for Nora's anarchist ideas. That would deserve a special beating . . . . . threatening the very structure of the State! Tie her up and really hurt her, although he'd kiss away her tears afterwards, of course. Her father had been a diplomat in Vienna, but had disappeared during the war, trying to help the Jews escape to America.

Immediately after dinner, Nora politely excused herself and left, telling Agneta secretly that she was sorry but would explain later.

★

That night, alone in her room, Nora took out her father's manuscript and fingered it carefully. The paper, copy paper, was very very thin, almost like human skin. She poked her finger through the title page, half by accident, half from impatience. The sudden rebirth of the original text had thrown her completely.

She didn't know what to do. She thought of destroying it, but then she started to read it. After a few pages, she lay down on the bed and wept. She had lied to Raymond. It had been some months before when the manuscript had been stolen. The theft of the television and other things, was an isolated, second incident. A real burglary. After the theft of the text, she had deteriorated, not knowing what to do. It now seemed like years ago. She had no idea why she had asked Raymond to come back with her. It was a kind of joke really..... but..... the most amazing thing of all..... his calm presence, his Englishness, perhaps reminding her of school, had triggered her into action. She had been blocked for so long, but his mere presence there, so polite, so undemanding, especially sexually, had aroused her, mysteriously, indirectly. He had been the necessary catalyst. Also the wound. That was significant. Quite weird. And the way he had 'saved her'..... 'liberated her from the police'. It had been a moment of synchronicity..... one of those mysterious moments of fusion, confusion, co-incidence, of polyphony as she called it..... and suddenly, the flood of words had come from her..... the text that Agneta was now in the middle of typing. It had been an unexpected month, of so many internal rifts and fractures..... an earthquake breaking the surface and an underground river bursting forth where it was least expected. Truly it had been 'Dessous les pavés, la plage..... '

She recovered herself and started to read the manuscript again, to confirm her suspicions. After a few pages she skipped to the centre, and skipped again to the end. What was she to do now? The text she had spoken into the tapes was indeed based on her father's text..... indirectly. But..... but..... she had always suspected her father's text was not quite true. Even a total lie. And her version of it, she knew..... was the truth! Her version..... on the tapes..... that was so utterly different. It hardly resembled her father's version of Frau S.'s story at all.

What she had written had become a work of fiction..... a novel..... based on the central image of her father's text, the little girl playing blindman with her father. Blind man's bluff..... blindfolding him with a scarf and leading him through the woods, chanting, 'I am your eyes Daddy..... you are blind Daddy. You cannot see the world any more Daddy. Take care, you don't fall..,.. don't worry Daddy..... I will guide you..... I will lead you. I am your eyes Daddy..... through ME you can see!'. She knew it was the story of Antigone, the daughter, leading her blinded father, Oedipus, after his loss of power, and abandonment of the city. His desolate, despair-ridden years in the wasteland. Paris here and now today. She knew her novelisation was closer to Antigone than to her father's text..... and YET..... on another level, the unconscious one, it wasn't. The central images were right. Were true. Authentic. The essence..... The essential truth, had not been violated by her sensual reformulation of the text. She knew she had fused-confused other images. Oedipus with Freud and Freud with her father, and Tiresias with Oedipus ..... the two blind men, fighting over forgotten images of the past. Long buried..... to be unearthed by a young girl, poking in the barren earth, the scorched earth of the ghetto, with a small broken stick. She knew she needed to think of her own father as blind too..... so as NOT to see her growing up, the two of them alone in the big house, alone, he growing old, she growing up..... sprouting like a plant in all directions.

Her text was a novel. Yes. And yet it was the truth. Her father's text was a literal case-history..... a triumphant vindication of a new kind of analytical theory and method, yet was a cover-up. Perhaps some would say, a lie! The woman in fact had been cured..... patched up for the road. She had lived, survived, even got married..... avoided killing herself, which she had seemed hell-bent on doing. But her life had become a lie. A play, in which she felt she was a mere marionette. The past pulling the strings. Tying the chords around her body. The thongs. Maybe it would have been better to have killed herself, because that would have been the truth. But she had survived the Warsaw Ghetto..... so how could she *then* kill herself? Afterwards? How could she tell Nora's father he had cured her, yes..... but the world was still too sick to be lived in, unless she compromised herself, sexually, in order to be satisfied?

Nora was confused..... excited..... miserable..... lonely ..... her head was aching badly. She had forgotten to bring more pills with her, the ones Anna got for her, that were Morphine derivatives produced by some hippie friends of hers and mixed with alcohol, were almost as good as heroin for numbing the pain..... numbing her feelings.....

She could hear her friends quarrelling. She lay back on the bed..... drinking wine..... listening to them. She knew they would fight until they ran out of words. Then they would make love, passionately..... desperately..... violently..... and she wondered if they needed the threat of separation all the time, of loss, of death to their love, so acutely contrived, so viciously persecuted, in order to arouse desire in each other. She wondered why desire always seemed to wane so quickly. What was needed to keep it alive? Was it possible to define love as a mysterious quality that kept desire alive? That didn't seem quite right. There could be love, she knew, with no desire at all. Or so it seemed. She was glad she was avoiding the problem..... and she thought of her father..... how his desire had waned so quickly..... so her mother had once told her in a moment of weakness. She knew she had been right, choosing to be safe. Which meant alone and lonely. Maybe that was better than being rejected. No longer desired. As had happened.....

She took out her sketch pad, and made some drawings. Drawing was her only relaxion when thinking was so painful. She did a funny cartoon of a violin making love to a cello. The one playing Bartok, the other playing Schoenberg, but at the same time. It was how she felt at that moment. She was the cello, her father the violin. But then she returned to her theme..... a small twig growing out of a barren landscape, or a small twig in the hand of a girl, searching..... for something..... buried and lost. Eventually she went to sleep, drunk from the wine ..... desperately lonely, thinking of Agneta and Doctor K. making love on a piano stool..... and of a little girl with her father, the blindman, leading him..... into an impasse from which he could never escape. She had once found a reference in his diary..... 'Now I too am trapped in a ghetto! But it is surely not entirely my own fault..... the anima, that dark goddess, also knows how to kill, for her own pleasure!'

★

The following day Nora felt she had to return to Paris, being so upset, and left instructions for Agneta to send the remaining transcribed pages to her by post. As Anna was away in Aix presenting her dance-play at the festival, she would have a quiet week to herself, to work on the two texts. Her own and her father's.....

There was a letter from Raymond, from a boat in mid Atlantic. He hated flying and had decided to travel to America by luxury liner, during which time, he told her, he could catch up on new Immunology papers..... but more important, further discover the truth about her, for which he now had the key.....

'I'm sorry to say this, but my memory of you is already quite blurred. You always made sure I couldn't know you. You have your reasons for not revealing yourself, and I respect them. We all have things we prefer to keep hidden. You have been so exposed all your life to people who "revealed all". Friends and patients of your fathers. You were right probably, to become war of spoken words..... of talking too much!'

He had presumably meant to write 'wary' but had written 'war' by mistake. Or 'aware'?

'I took the Freud Biography you gave me to read. Hope you don't mind. I didn't dare ask you for it, in case you refused. I know it is a pretty bland book, but it is easy to read and as you said, it is an ideal introduction to the ideas of psycho-annalysis. The world you were brought up in! I am becoming fascinated by the subject. I hate to say I sometimes spend more time reading about P/A than Immunology.

But the copy of the book you gave me is also a biography of you! A secret revelation of YOUR inner self. All your slips, you mere slip of a girl! Freud tells us we reveal so much by slips of the tongue. (As by kisses!) Well. They are slips of your pen, guided by impulse, intuition, the spur of the moment. All the sentences YOU underlined . . . . . in red ink always.

Forgive me if I play a game - I'm learning from you! I started copying those "chosen lines" while I was in your house, but there were too many distractions! (Love to Anna!) Now I am going to annalyse you, by compiling a text that YOU wrote, using the words of the Freud Biography. I will let you know all about yourself soon, what you are really like, behind that cool facade of yours.

I walk on the deck and gaze at the ocean and think of you, looking at the lifebelts, seeing "H.M.S.TITANIC" on them, but I may be mistaken. Maybe I see things that are not there. I am getting my cats wrong! But the pull of the sea on my spirit, threatening to suck me down into its depths, is real enough.

A couple of quotes to wet your appetite!

> Page 640. 'More serious was the dreadful day when Anna Freud was arrested by the Gestapo and detained for the whole day. It was certainly the blackest day in Freud's life. The thought that the most precious being in the whole world, and also the one on whom he depended, might be in danger of being tortured and deported to a concentration camp, as so commonly happened, was hardly to be borne.'

You wrote in red ink. "Antigone! And the poor wife . . . . . now so irrelevant. No-one writes about Freud's wife!" Further down you underlined,

> "There had grown up in these years a quite peculiarly intimate relationship between father and daughter. Both were very averse to anything resembling sentimentality and were equally undemonstrative in matters of affection."

You underlined it and wrote, "What is never seen is the passion! Passion is for what must be hidden. Even if is turned back on the self. Especially with women, e.g. Frau S."

On page 615; the footnote. "In America some former pupils of Ferenczi have sustained a myth of Freud's ill-treatment of Ferenczi."

You wrote, "Freud could not accept F's belief in love rather than power. That in the process of analysis, the patient seeks the mother not the father. Ferenczi was a feminine man and gave them feminity which was much more effective. And he seduced some of his patients. Tant pis. I would always allow myself to be seduced by such a man in power..... to see behind the words..... to see if he had a soul."

Missing you..... with much love..... Raymond.'

★

Nora was angry. She felt threatened. She resented Raymond's theft of the book with her marks on it. But after a walk and talking to her ducks, she started to forgive him. It was a harmless exercise really, and not without its charm! Then she managed to laugh at the idea. She saw him assiduously copying out all 'her' quotes, putting them in order, cutting them up, re-editing them, like a documentary film, a collage of sentences and phrases. Penetrating her mind despite herself. It was quite a clever idea. Good for him. He was improving!

She thought of her father's text suddenly. Thinking of documentary film reminded her of the documentary film Frau S., the woman of her father's case history, had been working on when she first came to him to be analysed. The film that had precipitated her breakdown. She had been asked by her Film Production Company to do research in the Nazi Film Archives for an intended film about the Nazi invasion of Poland, including the Warsaw Ghetto. It was to comprise Nazi newsreels from the outside, and footage shot inside. Both in parallel, to show the lies and hypocrisy. She had told no-one in her life up to that time, that she herself had survived the Ghetto, after so many devastating experiences. It was too traumatic a subject. At first she had tried to resist the film project, but then she felt it a challenge. Perhaps it was right she should 'go back there'..... see it from the other viewpoint, through the eyes of the Nazi soldiers who had filmed it all so neatly and coldly. So objectively. It might enable her to stand back from it too, become objective about her own private suffering and memories and achieve a catharis, a release.

But the experience had been too complex, too harrowing, and she had collapsed, threatening suicide, ending up with Nora's father, who was just starting as an analyst. That is how it had all begun.

Nora wasn't sure at first why she made the connection, thinking of Raymond on the boat editing the book, looking for clues about her, but then she saw an association. He was like the cameramen in Frau S.'s story, observing her against her wishes. He was making a 'photographic montage in words' of her inner thoughts, her unconscious guestures. A voyeur in a sense. He might be able to uncover things about her she would have preferred to hide, or would always have hidden from him. She was being analysed by Raymond! He had pulled a fast one on her, but she didn't really mind. It was not as if he was reading a diary or something really *too* close. After all, the text she had marked, the bland, totally 'corrupt', white-washed biography of Freud by Jones, was hardly the source for any truly devastasting insights on human nature, she told herself, rather smugly, forgetting it was not so much the words themselves, but the selection, the juxtaposition of one phrase next to the other. It was the 'joins' that mattered..... the 'and's..... the 'eroticism' implied in all connections, even words.....

Yes. That was it. Raymond was now the voyeur! She thought more about it. But is not every voyeur, like herself, not so much interested in the two people making love, but watching the part that joined them..... even if momentariliy, tenuously? The 'and' around which the dance, the wheel of life and death and birth, seemed to turn..... the penis that momentarily, vicariously fuses-confuses-joins, and by analogy, the universal principles of male and female, the Yin and Yang of the Tibetans..... anal-orgy, as she had once written, by mistake.....

She would have been much more worried if Raymond had

taken her copy of Ferenczi's 'Thalassa', which she really loved, which had always meant so much to her in mysterious, intangible ways. Thalassa..... the sea. The book she called her 'sexual bible'. Later, she must look at it, and see just what she had underlined in *that* book!

On an impulse, she went upstairs to her studio, to her bookshelf of favourite books, and selected some books at random..... flicking through the pages until she found the first underlining......always with her red pen. Some of them alarmed her.....

In Freud's 'Totem and Taboo' she found;

'The avoidance of the name of the deceased is as a rule kept up with extraordinary severity.'

And a few pages later.....

'But the other, the incest prohibition, had, besides, a strong practical foundation. Sexual need does not unite men; it separates them.'

In Hesse's 'Steppenwolf' the book opened on a page where she had underlined;

'He held a glass up to me and again I saw the unity of my personality broken up into many selves whose number seemed even to have increased..... the separation of the unity of the personality into these numerous pieces passes for madness. Science has invented the name schizophrenia for it.'

In Rilke's 'Notebooks of Malte Laurids Brigge' she found;

'Twelve years old, or at most thirteen, I must have been at the time.'

On another page;

'But what he did not wish to forget was his childhood. To this he clung.'

In Macdonald's 'Lilith' she found;

'Every time I slept, I dreamed of finding a wounded angel, who, unable to fly, remained with me until at last she loved me and would not leave me; but every time I woke, it was to see, instead of an angel-visage with lustrous eyes, the white, motionless, wasted face upon the couch.'

In the 'Upanishads' she found;

'Life is father, mother, sister, brother, tutor and guide. If a man speak cruel words to a father..... people say 'Shame upon you for such cruelty', but if, life once gone, somebody shoves them back on the funeral pyre with a poker, where is the cruelty?'

In Djuna Barnes 'Spillway';

'Do not repeat anything after me. Why should children repeat what people say?..... Katya will go with you. She will instruct you, she will tell you there are no swans, no flowers, no beasts, no boys - NOTHING, nothing at all, just as you like it. No mind, no thought, nothing whatsoever else. No bells will ring, no people will talk, no birds will fly, no boys will move, there'll be no birth and no death; no sorrow, no laughing, no kissing, no crying, no terror, no joy; no eating, no drinking, no games, no dancing; no father, no mother, no sisters, no brothers - only you, only you!'

In red ink she had written - 'Like heroin. Sometimes the only way to forget the images that won't go away.'
In Breton's 'Nadja';

'What was so extraordinary about what was happening in those eyes? What was it they reflected - some obscure distress and at the same time some luminous pride?'

Quickly, urgently, she flicked to another page..... it was becoming painful.

'Who goes there? Is it you, Nadja? Is it true that the beyond, that everything beyond is here in this life? I can't hear you. Who goes there? Is it only me? Is it myself?'

She took down Freud's 'Dora' Case History but put it back, not daring to open it. It was the same with Wilkie Collins' 'The Moonstone'..... one of her most cherished books. In it, is not the truth hidden and found in an opium dream? She took de Quincey's 'Confessions of an English Opium Eater.' Did she dare open it? There was poor Ann..... the child prostitute ..... whom he could never never forget. The images could never be eradicated, even with more and more opium.

There were many underlinings. The first one .....

'But I found, on taking possession of my new quarters, that the house already contained one single inmate, a poor, friendless child, apparently ten years old..... amidst the real fleshly ills of cold, and I fear, hunger, the forsaken child had found leisure to suffer still more from the self-created one of ghosts; I promised her protection against all ghosts whatsoever!'

She'd written in red ink - 'Ghosts! Alas, they are often real. Mere memories of the night. See page 139.'
Quickly, her heart beating fast, she turned there.

'The case of poor Ann the Outcast formed not only the most memorable and the most suggestive pathetic incident, but also that which, more than any other, coloured - or (more truly I should say) shaped, moulded and remoulded, composed and decomposed - the great body of opium dreams.'

She'd written ..... 'cf. Frau S. case history. Child prostitution was rife in earlier days, like those of de Quincey. It still is of course, elsewhere..... but hidden now. That's the only difference. Hypocrisy. For the anal fucking monotheists, incest must always be made a crime so they can enjoy it.'

She snapped the book shut and went back down to the kitchen, where she nervously poured out more wine . . . . .

Damn Raymond! Damn his meddling mind! But these were distractions! She must work. Her first work must be to re-read her father's text, the only way of escaping herself. She must compare it to her own, to see how well she had taken the main ideas in writing her version of the story, transforming it into a new, deeper truth. She was a woman after all! How could any man truly dare to say he understood a woman and her sexuality! The arrogance and hypocrisy of it . . . . . Especially someone as beautiful, as complex, as wounded as Frau S. God help those men who fell in love with beauty . . . . . the essence of intangiblity.

Frau S! She had the memories of her meeting this woman to take more into consideration, with whom she had once been on good terms, even intimate terms. She had discussed with her, once, some time ago, many of the themes her father elaborated in his text . . . . . These memories too ought to be drawn on. She must flesh the story out now, even more . . . . . and she must stop using that expression to herself! All little girls dream of having their father's baby . . . . . even when they think there is only one door to open. A pure gold baby. Very valuable.

She whistled and after what seemed like years and years, waiting waiting for doors to open, the two small trap doors at the bottom of the main kitchen door, both her cats came in. Why had she made two doors and not one? They never came in at the same time! She asked each one their name, to make sure they remembered. She offered them food but they rejected it. There were too many juicy baby ducklings to catch and eat at the moment to need human subsidies . . . . . from tins.

One day she would make love to Raymond and Anna together . . . . . and shock them both with her precocity!

Then she unpacked. She took the copy of her father's book to the safe. She didn't want it stolen again! She glanced at its title-page . . . . . which had not been on the copy she possessed, torn off ages before, before she became interested in it.

'The Invisible Wall' 'A case History - A Cure.'

★

Later that evening, slightly apprehensive at being alone, she started working on the parallel texts. She wondered why she missed Raymond so much. She had not loved him in any way really, but she had needed him 'there', out of sight, while she entered the labyrinth of her father's imaginary, deliberately forgotten text. But now, she had her father's real text again in front of her. The situtaion was different. Couldn't she do without Raymond? Forget him, as he deserved to be forgotten? She had found him gentle, passive, but ultimately un-inspiring. But she had tried to be kind.

All night she worked, amazed at the differences between the texts. She had thought she had been reasonably close to the original man-uscript. But now, reading the first part that Agneta had typed, it seemed written by someone else. The more she read, the more amazed she became. She was frustrated she didn't have all of her tapes transcribed yet. But already it was like reading someone else's work completely. But when she read her father's text, however, she felt it was her own, even though in principle, she disagreed with much of it. Yet her father's text now seemed to be closer to the truth after all, and her own text seemed to be more definitely a kind of novel. A fantasy. Almost as if she had experienced her father's text as a trauma in itself, and she preferred only to remember a fantasy version of it . . . . .

Now she felt possessed again, as she had been when recording with the tape recorder . . . . . very high on one thing and another . . . . . possessed by his ghost . . . . . communicating with her by telepathy. And yet. Had it all been an illusion? Was not her text, so different to his, proof that it was all illusion? Like their love had been . . . . . or was that being too unfair to him? He had loved her desperately to his dying day. And love can bewitch.

At four oclock, tired, tense and lonely now in the hour of the wolf, she played the piano . . . . . singing her version of 'Denn alles Fleisch es ist wie Gras'. Most of all she was missing Anna. She wondered if she should try and find Hedy, the whore. Anna had told her all about it. Anna couldn't keep a secret from anyone. She was always an open book, which is why Nora loved her. Maybe Hedy might be good for some research, some unusual insights into the theatre of cruelty, of sexual nightmares . . . . .

Nora had gone to the station the day after Raymond had left

and watched Hedy from the window of the station café. She looked too nice, she thought, to be a whore, even though a provincial one. They were usually more ordinary. More accessible. Ordinary women who had decided not to be enslaved. But when she saw her being picked up by a derelict, seedy looking man..... she shuddered with physical nausea. Seeing the 'waiting' had been quite fun. Seeing her being bought, being chosen, being taken, was disgusting. When it became flesh, even the spirit could lose all its charm, as she well knew. Oh Daddy! But she would have liked to have talked to Hedy nevertheless, and discovered why she had become what she was. Was the decision entirely one of money? Doesn't the stranger offer the permanently new? Wasn't Anna's biggest trip, always the unknown? The present-tense rite of total non-self? Isn't what is truly, profoundly desired, the instant escape from the brooding self? To become the force of desire itself, devoid of all personality? And yet in Pabst's 'Lulu', did she not finally meet the most new-renewable of all? Eros and Thanatos as one? Fused and confused? Death at the knife..... Jack the Ripper? The film's subtitle at that moment was 'Christ is risen'. She'd never understood that one, nor did her father.

She went to bed eventually, wracked with fatigue - she'd almost overdone it - wishing she had chosen two cats who were domestic, silly, soppy cats, who would sleep on her bed, close to her body all night. Why had she chosen the only kind of cats who were untameable, only just decent enough to remain vaguely attached to the house and make the occasional guesture of recognition? When it came to cats she was clearly a masochist.

She had forgotten again to take the antibiotics. Her head was becoming really infected again. It was such a terrible bore. And now the pills Anna had given her for the pain, seemed to be losing their effectiveness against it. She wondered if she might be forced to go back on heroin again. 'No! Not until the book is finished! For the trance, yes. Not for the final touches,' she said out loud. She took some sleeping pills and managed to crash out.

★

The following day she received an unexpected telephone call from a friend of Anna's. She too was a dancer, she said, but she was out of work. She needed somewhere to stay for two weeks while she sorted out some emotional problems.

Nora usually refused to have anyone around except Anna, but she knew she was quite fragile at that moment. Maybe it would be good to have someone around, even if she didn't like her. Being a stranger was useful too. She was Danish she told Nora, and had also made money modelling. But she was broke. Anna had told her that Nora was a painter, so she wondered if she could model for her, in exchange for the food. Nora had never drawn from life, and the idea amused her. She met the girl at the station and was pleased to see she was dressed quite soberly and was quite pretty in a cold kind of way. 'I am Dorothea' she said, in English, 'but you can call me 'Dot' like everyone else if you like.'

Over supper Nora told her she worked at night at her writing, but in the afternoon she often painted. She asked Dot what she intended to do in the future, when she was 'herself' again, hoping she might reveal why she was feeling a bit 'broken'. Nora could see from the opacity of her skin, that she had been through some kind of trouble.

She obviously didn't see too far into the future. 'Don't worry about me. I will read..... walk in the garden..... practice dancing. Wait for Anna to come back. She has always been a very good friend. I'll be fine.'

Suddenly Nora guessed what was wrong. She was psychic with girls. She looked her straight in the eyes, 'I knew a girl a year ago who was ill, with the same colour as you have now. You were pregnant I presume?' she said quietly, coldly, ruthlessly.

The girl looked surprised and hurt. 'Oh..... Did Anna tell you then? I asked her not to.'

'No. Anna never mentioned you. She didn't tell me you were going to call.'

The girl played nervously with her hands, tears in her eyes. 'Yes. You are right. I made a mess. At first I wanted to keep it. Then it was almost too late. I couldn't afford to pay a good doctor. It went wrong, but I am alright now. Anna told me you would let me stay a couple of weeks until I became strong again. I had nowhere else to go.'

Nora smiled kindly now, now that she knew the truth she wanted to know, that she had been prepared to hurt to uncover.

'Of course! You can stay as long as you like, until you are better.'

She thought of Anna. Now she was like one of her cats, bringing back 'presents', young birds that were broken, but not quite dead, chance and fate having tormented them and broken their wings. Nora had always tried to save her own garden's poor little creatures, her own family, but she had always failed. They had always been wounded just enough to guarantee their subsequent death. That was the morality of cats. She looked fondly at the lonely girl in front of her with the broken inner wings. 'Do you mind? I hate the name Dot. Can I call you Dorothea?'

She seemed astonished. 'Oh yes, please, please do. I hate the name Dot, but everyone calls me that. I go along with it. I've longed to be called Dorothea again! Please please do!'

Nora watched her, cowering in front of her, and felt suddenly protective towards her. She just hoped she wouldn't be like one of the ducklings . . . . . that seemed to get better for a few days, but then keeled over one night and died.

★

For the next few days, the two girls preoccupied themselves with their respective problems. Dorothea, happy to be for a moment outside of life and time, allowing her body to recover from her abortion. Nora, confronting her two contradictory texts.

They went for a short walk in the garden together each afternoon. Afterwards, Nora took her to her studio, where Dorothea stripped naked and sat awkwardly in various positions, while Nora tried to draw her. She found it almost impossible to draw what she could see in front of her. Dorothea's body was sumptuously beautiful, lithe and flowing and quite voluptuous. She knew it was the kind of body a man would have desired instantly . . . . . even worshipped . . . . . but all the time she was looking at her, she was thinking of what was no longer inside that body, what had been forcibly removed, what had been loved and wanted for a brief moment, a temporary lapse of reason, then feared, and eventually killed. Nora saw the body in front of her as an empty husk. She couldn't help it. The more she sketched, hoping to capture the voluptuousness, the more she ended up drawing her usual kind of drawing..... There was an earth there of sorts, but it was the same wasteland, and the tree-body-limbs trying to grow in it, were dead. But she made one or two drawings as realistic as possible..... for Dorothea's sake, although she had promised to show her nothing until she had finished a project, a 'series' of images that together would capture the whole.

Nora felt sure there was still milk in her breasts, and in one fleeting, irrational moment, she nearly went up to her, wanting to squeeze her breasts or even suck them, to find out..... but she checked herself, expecting Dorothea's reaction to be negative. Maybe if she had decided to keep the baby, she might have surrendered to Nora's desire and wallowed in the narcissistic voluptuousness of it..... maybe.....

Dorothea fell in love with the cats immediately, which Nora knew was inevitable, and spent a lot of time trying to find out where they were hiding, as cats do in the day, waiting for the darkness when they could hunt again. Each day they chose a different place, as if to deliberately confuse her, but she crept around the garden, as silently as possible, stalking them, not leaving a branch unturned until she found them. They were nearly always sleeping up a tree. But her greatest pleasure was finding them still asleep, all curled up in a bed of moss or grass..... in the soft womb of the earth. Not having heard her stealthily seeking them out. Nora was happy for her to have found these small pleasures.....

★

But Nora had a serious problem now with her project. She felt she was losing control. The simplicity had gone. She now possessed her father's original text again and the first half of her own monologue. What was still missing was all the work she had done transforming it, before the theft. What had gone, was becoming more important than what was still present. Also, she was having to fight the sensation that her father's text was nearer to the truth than she had been prepared to admit, and her text was a novel. Or at least a novella. But as Agneta had said, it had a certain beauty of style, a consistent unity. The more she thought about it, the more she felt she ought to publish her own text as a novel. The sense of 'fiction' was unnerving. Each time she read through it, it was as though it had been written by someone else.

In the act of sitting up all night talking spontaneously into the tape recorder, in a trance, like one of her father's patients - he had given them LSD sometimes - it was almost as if she had tapped the voice of another woman completely..... telling the story from another, new, completely different point of view. The text was splitting into too many simultaneous levels..... Were there so many selves in each of us? Ancestors?

But she kept asking herself, what did it matter what she published? What mattered was only the expectations of the person reading it, what they expected it to be. She played with the idea of trying to publish all three texts. First her novel, then her version of her father's text, if she could re-do it now that she had the original text again, and then her father's text in all its nakedness. But then she laughed. There should be a fourth viewpoint to complete the quaternio! A fourth gospel! God's ideal viewpoint, like nineteenth century novelists! Ideally, Frau S. would then publish *her* version, the truth as *she* remembered it. For Nora, the most important question was becoming whether she should be honest with Doctor K. and Agneta, or deliberately lie? Even more? What a labyrinth of lies it was all becoming. In that sense it was still vital and alive..... Not tell them what the final text was at all.....

It was all getting so complicated, so many layers of meaning and truth derived from the one set of initial events, her mind was becoming dangerously blurred. Might she not go mad? Before, she had felt it was all in her head, in control, formed - but now she needed the texts, the actual words on the paper, to remind herself all the time of what was *that* particular version. She sensed suddenly, that if she kept on with her attempt to synthesise the versions, in one way or another, she would lose control of the whole project..... and it would start to disintegrate ..... she too. In the same way she had started to fall apart when she had come back from her school in England, to be with her father again..... when she knew he was dying..... and at that time, the only way she had bought time..... avoided a total breakdown..... was to go onto drugs..... an artificial kind of wholeness, a false unity, but one she temporarily believed in enough to hold herself together, to stop the fragments falling irreparably apart..... as if they were all inside her body, gnawing at her and at themselves..... losing their coherence. Their meaning.

At the time of her first crisis, she had told herself it was all really quite funny..... and had started to keep a diary. By chance she had recently found the diary and read what she had written on the first page......

'Am I my father's daughter, or am I not? Here I am, the daughter of one of the most revolutionary pyscho-analytical thinkers alive today, and I am having a nervous breakdown! Yet here is the TRUE irony. It is the ONE thing I cannot admit to HIM!

I can't reveal anything to him. I am the one person in the world he cannot cure, he must not try to cure. I have only one choice it seems. A few days ago, a girl-friend gave me some heroin. I felt good. I felt relaxed. I felt whole. I felt calm. I felt I could cope. She told me about a famous doctor in England who had carried on being a doctor all his life, just taking a small dose each day, always in control. Not injecting it, but taking it with wine, like the great Romantics used to do. Then it was called Laudanum. Opium mixed in wine. She had a friend studying English Literature who had managed to find a source of the right kind of heroin/opium and mixed with wine, it was a God-send.

It numbed me. It was a barricade against my own fears, attached as they were on objects and images of the outside world. I became immune to the world that was threatening to attack me and fragment me into a million pieces.

I have arranged for her to supply me regularly and I have decided to keep this diary. Like Jean Cocteau did!'

Nora was upset how naive it seemed. How much older and more mature she seemed now. Yet at that time, she had been so sure of herself! She was reading her old diary when Dorothea knocked on her door and asked to come inside. She seemed very upset. She apologised, but said she had decided to leave, immediately.

It would be the best thing to do for everyone. She thanked Nora very much. She was ready to leave . . . . . now. She had phoned about a train and a taxi.

Nora was worried. She could see she was very disturbed. She told her she ought to stay, but she refused. Nora went upstairs and took one of the drawings she had made of her . . . . . and gave it to her as a present. It was the first of the drawings she had been allowed to see. She looked at it, a little surprised, even hurt. She didn't know what to say. 'It is not very realistic is it . . . . . I hope?'

Nora promised that if she wanted a more realistic one, she would do one later, from a photograph. She said she'd done a few that were as realistic as possible, but none were flattering. 'But you should keep this, because this is my real style. I told you I don't draw realistically. It is better you have this, because it will be like the ones in my exhibition. It will be more valuable in the future, more characteristic of my true work!'

Dorothea thanked her. She would have preferred a drawing that looked like her. She might have sent it to her mother. But it didn't matter really. Time was running out, anyway. Could Nora lend her some money for the taxi and train?

Later, Anna told Nora that Dorothea had deliberately done nothing about the infection in her womb, until it was too late. She not only killed the baby but also herself.

★

The following morning when Nora came down for breakfast, one of her cats was mewing outside the kitchen door. It had something for her, which was too big to pull through either of the two trap doors . . . . . the body of the other cat. She had dug it up where it had been buried. Later she also brought the kitchen knife that had been buried with it.

After crying, Nora tried to cuddle the cat that was still alive, but it kept its distance, sitting watching her but allowing no contact. Each time she stretched her arms out to hold it, it backed away. She whispered its name gently, and then the other name, but it reacted to neither. She had always known it was the other cat who reacted to both names, but even then, only when she felt like it.

Nora called up her friend who bred the cats and asked for another one. She was promised a kitten when one became available. They were difficult to breed in captivity. In a few months time perhaps.

She sat in the kitchen drinking tea, trying to control the surging feelings of bitterness towards Dorothea. No wonder every time she had tried to do a portrait of her as soft and gentle and feminine, the image had come out hard and cold looking. Arid. Sterile. But after some time and much effort, by thinking hard about other images, peaceful and tranquil, she managed to diffuse her feelings . . . . . telling herself, 'It was better the cat, than herself, here in my garden.'

Feeling distraught, she went to Anna's room. She had not been in there for months. She respected territories, as she wanted others to respect hers. But it was so untidy she lost her breath. Her first thought was a strange one. 'It looks as if a cyclone has hit the gardens of Babylon!' She glanced at Anna's diary which she normally locked in her desk. She flicked through a few pages. It was her diary-project. Anna was still trying to write her strange book, her memoirs, called, 'Daughter of Kubla Khan'. A kind of sustained Opium reverie. A modern version, so she said, of the kind of dream that Coleridge was supposed to have had when he wrote the famous poem. Anna's 'book' - a kind of auto-biography disguised as a portrait of Coleridge's poem - was written as if by a teenager with a mental age of twelve or maybe thirteen, but did have a kind of mad logic. She was the Abyssinian damsel with the dulcimer . . . . . and it was all seen from her eyes. Slave of the harem. She showed it to Nora from time to time. It was probably insane, but Nora couldn't be sure. Parts were truly visionary, or seemed so when you were as high as a kite yourself . . . . . un serf-volant, high on sacred mushrooms . . . . .

Anna gave the impression to everyone she was nothing but a dumb blonde, albeit dyed, interested in acting and dancing, mysticism, drugs and sex. A child of her time. Nora knew this was actually the real Anna. But some boyfriend had sown this crazy idea in her that she ought to be an intellectual as well. It was ludicrous. She couldn't even spell. She'd learnt the word Opium in English but always wrote it as 'Hopium'. Her work was really a kind of comic strip cartoon. But she meant well. She just wanted to write the ultimate 'trip' about the Sixties! She said it was the beginning of the end. Why not? She might be the one to do it when all the historians had drowned in a sludge of facts.

Nora suddenly had an idea. The next book she would write would be a portrait of Anna! Yes. Perfect. As Salomé. She had once started a poem about Anna, as the dancing daughter of Herodias..... its opening could be adapted for the start of her novel-biography about Anna......

> 'Anna was always Salomé - daughter of her time - the temple dancing girl, in love with death. In the night-clubs, her temples, she could be found each night, giving head to mindless hedonists.....'

No! She was being unfair. Why? In fact Anna was quite bright. Hadn't she been studying sociology in Munich until she opted out for 'life'? At times they had enjoyed some quite intelligent confrontations. That is why she had joined Nora in Mathieu's group, promptly seducing Mathieu of course..... but she had been pleased to give him Anna. She'd been a birthday present.

Nora sat in the room for some time, stupified, surveying the extraordinary untidiness. She had once believed that people who were untidy in their minds, usually kept their private places very tidy. It balanced outside and inside. On this theory, Anna was really quite organised inside that pulsing body of hers. In fact Nora knew she probably was. Often she was much more organised than she was. The truth, and it made Nora very sad, was that she knew Anna hardly at all, despite their year or so of contact on one level and another.

Or none. There had always been an invisible wall between them, from the beginning. Nora knew that Anna loved her, but was wary of her. Anna depended on her now, too much. For money, for the house, for protection. And there was the unspoken bond..... that they never really talked about afterwards ..... their bouts from time to time with heroin, and the times they helped each other to get off it..... as if they had merely caught a lousy flu. Those were the only times they had come really close. Nora jealous of Anna's abandon, and Anna jealous of Nora's calm and her money. But there was love there too, above all else, pushing these jealousies away, down beneath imagined cobblestones.

Nora started searching. She knew what she was looking for. It was a small chinese red and black lacquered box. But she couldn't find it. She sat again in the chair and looked round the room, wondering where Anna would hide it. In the most obvious place probably. Nora would have taken up the floorboards to hide it. Anna, she knew, would have hidden it somewhere silly.....

She went to the desk and was surprised to find it open. Normally it was locked. Anna was becoming loose. Obviously she'd lost the key. She might even be in love. Inside the desk was her copy of the Tibetan Book of the Dead, and Nora flicked through the pages, remembering Anna's dance, recalling her sexual excitement when she had watched it, which had taken her so much by surprise.

On one of the shelves was a round box and Nora *had* to open it. She knew exactly what it was. It was the box in which Anna kept a 'dutch cap'. She wanted to know if Anna was wearing it! Pills made her go fat. She shook the box and it unexpectedly went 'clang'. She opened it eagerly. Inside was the little red and black box. But it was empty. She was annoyed and frustrated. But then it occured to her there was far too much of the white talcum powder in the box that normally kept the plastic cap dry. She wet the end of her finger and tasted it. It was what she was looking for. She took out the chinese box and left it in Anna's desk and took the other box down to the kitchen. She mixed a small dose into the wine and drank a glass, telling herself a small dose would not hurt her. After all, she was under a lot of strain.

Without it, she would not have been able to bury her cat. Whose name might even be 'Reality'.....

Nora found a spot under her favourite tree, and dug into the soil with her bare hands, wanting to feel the dampness of the soil and its rough texture. She wanted to see her hands all brown and messy and smelling of dead leaves and humus..... the earth's excrement. After she had laid her lovely cat's ravaged body into the hole, she sprayed the ground with a whole bottle of Anna's scent..... L'Air du Temps..... to kill the smell of the cat's body. She didn't want it brought to her as a present again the following morning. Or be found and eaten by a fox.

In the afternoon she tried to paint in her studio, her strange little 'drawings' made with black oil paint on prepared white paper, like old etchings, like a 'still' from an old black and white movie..... searching, searching..... the true meaning of her images, still seeming to be unknown to her. Beyond her touch.

In the evening she drank another glass of wine with a mild dose of the white powder, before going to her other room to do her other work. She took her copy of Ferenczi's 'Thalassa - A Theory of Genitality' and started copying out the sentences and phrases she had unconsciously underlined in red ink when she was reading it. She had read it many times.

'It was reserved for psycho-analysis to rescue the problems of sexuality from the poison cabinet in which they had been locked away for centuries.....

..... in the matter of sexual enlightenement of children even the most liberal approach boggles at the riddle of how the child comes to be in the mother's body......

..... it has to be assumed that there is such a thing as specific anal technique in impotence of the male. In all these matters we must confess our deep ignorance.....

Children are fond of fusing pleasurable activities of the most various kinds into a single act..... the well known activities of perverts customarily strive for such a summation of erotisms, most conspicuously in those voyeurs who obtain.....'

These were the underlinings from the first chapter. Nora looked at them, now juxtaposed, trying to recall why she had underlined these particular sentences, trying to see if they expressed a unity of trend. She was convinced they didn't..... and felt suddenly, acutely bored. Cold.

She flicked through to the last page. She had underlined the very last lines of the book.....

'In the light of the considerations here briefly resumed, the male member and its function appears as the organic symbol of the restoration - albeit only partial - of the foetal- infantile state of union with the mother and at the same time with the geological prototype thereof..... existence in the sea.'

Nora took a pencil and wrote next to it;

After May' 68 the new meaning - 'Dessous les pavés, la plage' - the collective attempt by a generation of psychically abused children to expose the repression and implied sexual anality of those in power! To liberate their authentic feelings.....'

But she was now already drifting, finding it too hard to read. She wanted to sit back and watch the images unfolding as if from nowhere, surfacing into her mind. She put a tape in her machine, made by a friend. It was a whole tape, an hour long, of the sensual, caressing sounds of waves of the sea, pulsing, seeking, leaving, beating upon the body of the beach..... the mother's blood inside the womb..... and she put it on repeat, and drank some more red wine, with a larger 'touch' of the white powder, and lay on her bed..... becoming quiet, stilled..... away from the need for ideas of the erotic..... the most repressive of all..... the invisible wall dissolving away as she became more and more inseparable from the images conjured magically in the imagination, tapping deeper memory, by the systole and diastole of the sounds. Rising and amplifying as the moon pulls, as the mother is caressed and penetrated and loved and her whole body shudders in orgasm..... and is the child listening or asleep? She was murmuring fragments of words ..... as if they too were dissolving back into her own inner sea. 'La mer..... la mère..... Lamour..... Lemarr..... Dorothea Lamour. Hedy Lemarr. L'amer..... l'amertume..... les gouffres amers..... les amoureux, les amoureux.....'

Until she finally let herself fall..... falling asleep, saying thankyou to the Goddess of nature for creating the sea..... and her cats..... and willow trees..... plants that lived under the sea and moved and swam and devoured each other..... and poppy plants..... and willow trees..... the existence of which, and the thoughts inside her which they provoked, images, memories of subtle, erotic things truly touched by the hand of a child, helped her to avoid enfolding on herself, as an endless layering and interleaving of dissolving tissues..... without roots. Without needing to seek out hard roots. A thousand leaves. Soft buds blossoming. Sea frothing like milk. The milky way. Wandering, wandering..... lost in a sea of quiet ecstasy, dreaming of eternity, beautiful with emptiness, not needing to become anything..... all life spent..... not before but after.....

★ ★ ★

Seven

A few days later, a parcel arrived with more pages of Nora's monologue, dutifully typed by Agneta. In the parcel was a letter from her saying she would come to Paris in a few days, bring the remaining pages, and it would be nice to meet and talk about something 'important'.

Nora read the new pages eagerly, not knowing what was coming next in the strange novella she had created in those days 'off' with Raymond. She had been right not to tell Raymond about drinking a little of Anna's 'potion' every night before talking into the tape-recorder. He would not have coped with the mental rejection that it implied, in addition to her continuous, but apparently necessary physical rejection of him. For the meantime, anyway . . . . .

But she was unprepared for the new part of the monologue. It was even more weird than the first half, straying into all kinds of unexpected areas. She was embarrassed by how erotic it was. Had she gone too far into her own misery?

She went upstairs and lay down on her bed, close to tears. She wondered if being so emotional was due to the laudanum. Was she getting close to the limit again? She didn't want to pass the point where it could be controlled, but in her present mood, she might soon become really addicted again, although it was the only switch she had to switch off the world, and switch on the ghost dance. Maybe there were other ways, but that was hers, for the time being. It helped her through the more difficult periods . . . . . and seemed to provoke her into creative activity . . . . . but it had to be small doses. She had always stopped before becoming enslaved by desire for it.

It seemed to be more the problem with the texts that was upsetting her. Layer upon layer . . . . . as translucent as membranes of skin. If only she had someone to touch, to bring comfort . . . . . to touch her gently and warm her deadened body. The more upset she became, the more she longed for Anna, although now it was always Raymond and Anna . . . . . or Hedy and Anna and Raymond, acting in a play she'd written long ago.

The images were often torture. More than anything in the world, she resented being aroused sexually, merely by her own confusion. Her own inner emptiness. But there seemed to be no escape again, and it was always best to try to make it interesting.....

She unlocked a secret drawer in the back of a black lacquered Chinese cabinet, and took out the antique wooden object of carved and polished willow, which had supposedly been a replica made in the nineteenth century of an Ancient Egyptian spinning top. That is what her father had told her it was. It had belonged to her mother. Nora had found out one day, while casually looking at a book about Ancient Egypt, that it was probably a weight..... a perfectly balanced weight..... that was suspended on the end of a piece of string..... in order to ascertain the exact direction of the vertical. Her mother had collected beautiful wooden objects, but this was the only one her father had not sold. It was the one she most cherished, he had once told Nora.

Her father though, had underestimated the memory of the child. Nora had remembered her mother's love of this small, sacred wooden objet-trouvé, only too well. She also knew that it was not a replica. It was an original object, found in the tomb of a dead King..... or a dead Queen. Now it was sadly bereft of its original, sacred function, to ascertain the exact direction of the vertical. In the next world, which was around us all the time if we had eyes to see it, except we lived in too few dimensions to do so..... her mother had once told her, when she was too young to fully understand..... there was no gravity and everything was vertical..... and if something descended from there, into matter, it was by choice.

She held it in her hands, rubbing it gently, as if preparing it to make fire.....

She was feeling close to the edge. She had to do something dramatic, otherwise she might end up in a worse state. She went to Anna's room and searched through her wardrobe, petulantly looking for something new to wear. It had to be new. Something she'd not used before. She found a rather vulgar dress, made of cheap red lace and decorated with stupid black leather thongs. She slipped into it, although with some difficulty, and being impatient with it, she caused the thongs to cut into the skin on her thigh. She sat at Anna's dressing table and taking her old, used tubes of theatre make-up like tubes of oil paint, squeezing them viciously to extract the last gobs of paste, she painted her face with thick layers of it, as extravagantly as possible..... daubing bright crimson lipstick on her lips and rouge on her cheeks and more lipstick on her nipples. Then she piled on as many trinkets and baubles and cheap jewelry she could find, covering her breasts. Some wildly coloured gossamer thin veils, from another of Anna's previous ballets, she wrapped round her neck. She was almost a wooden doll, a marionette, waiting to be animated by invisible strings, to be plucked by ghosts to make her dance. She picked up a small bottle of body oil.

When she was satisfied with her appearance, and it would have pleased even King Solomon, used to being tricked by beautiful women, talking birds and flying thrones, she paused for a moment, breathless. Then she went down slowly, as if to a dirge, a cheap, painted doll descending a winding mahogany staircase, to be viewed by as many pairs of lustful eyes as possible from different viewpoints, an erotic collage singing a song without words, wafting into the drawing room where she made a flamboyant entrance, bowing to the piano or something, anything..... the applauding audience of ghosts..... closed the curtains roughly, disappointed there was no-one hidden behind them, put on a tape she had made of herself and Anna singing 'Denn Alles Fleisch es ist wie Gras', and danced with the image of herself in the long, bruised mirror that she had put up over the worst patch of faded silk on the wall that had torn and fallen, the shape of a gaping vagina. She gazed entranced with the corrupted image of herself or the someone else in the mirror, its silvered surface was so pock-marked and scratched, it made her look as if the film had been made at the turn of the century, or an image etched on a cheap tin tray.

When the moment was right, she took the wooden spinning top and dipped it in the body oil, before caressing herself with it, very very gently, trying not to think of Anna being fucked..... but thinking of a weeping willow tree hanging over a still pool of water, the leaves on the end of the thin branches that fell down like plaits of hair, flicking over the surface as if they were guiding the movements of irridescent beetles scurrying over the surface and sea horses bobbing along underneath, as if the round pond was a circus for the entertainment of birds in the trees..... and cats..... but she couldn't hold the 'stills', the arrested frames..... they were not the truth she needed at that moment. She returned to Anna..... and danced wildly, a whore, seeing the leaves around her cunt, opening and closing as Raymond's prick went in and out..... digging her out.....

Afterwards, she lay on the sofa and dozed, peacefully, abandoned on some distant shore..... next to a silent lake, the colour of lapiz lazuli, its surface now reflecting hovering dragon flies and kingfishers......

★

When she woke up, she went to the kitchen to make herself Darjeeling tea. She whistled a few times out of the window, and after a few minutes her cat came in, looking as sleepy and dozy as she was.

'I hope you haven't been up to the same tricks as your mother!' she said to her mischievously. 'Listen my little one, I am going away for a few days. Maybe ten days, and Auntie Anna is away too. You are going to have hunt for yourself again. You have been a bit lazy lately, haven't you? Spoilt? You are not to be lonely!'

The cat looked up at her..... and Nora knew she understood.

★

Paris was still in chaos. She tried to locate her anarchist friends, but they had all gone underground. She phoned another girl-friend who like herself had been a reluctant member of the group. 'They had to leave. Damn it, they couldn't cope with all the success they were having, but *not* having. Imagine! A bunch of fanatical anarchists..... watching the whole city grind to a halt. They were really upset. A few lousy students had achieved more than they could have imagined. All their methods were redundant. It was the last thing they could cope with..... a city already on it knees. If they'd blown up the Bastille, the credit would have gone to the Sorbonne students, now sitting and arguing in committees with the Unions, pseudo politicians already enjoying the misuse of power! They have gone underground to wait for life to return to normal, when they can become useful anarchists again, embarrassing the communists and the extreme Right at the same time!' Nora laughed. She hadn't thought of it like that. She guessed there was some truth in it.

'Tell me really, where are they?'

'In Germany..... trying to bring that Self consuming industrial Monolith to its knees. Going for some big company directors. Do you want to contact them?'

No. Later. She wanted to stay in Paris for a while.

She took a room in her favourite hotel in Rue Gît-le-Coeur. It was small, very seedy and very cheap, full of resident homosexuals and a few whores who considered themselves high class because they had permanent rooms there, with their own back entrance. They had become known as the 'back-entrance girls', and had developed the speciality to go with the name..... why should the 'back-entrance boys' at the front, have all the fun?

She felt quite comfortable there, she didn't know why. She knew one of the homosexuals, a painter, quite well and often had coffee and croissants with him in the morning in Place St. Michel.

The morning after she arrived they met in the lobby, and he was soon telling her all the news. His version. The city had been in sublime chaos, sublime, and he waved his hand towards the crossroads where Boulevard St. Michel severed Boulevard St. Germain. 'We were told the city was giving birth to a revolution. You see that intersection over there? I've re-named it, 'Le Carrefour Mons Veneris'. It was where the city finally opened up its legs to give birth to the something promised..... that great ugly beast slouching from where was it, to be born?..... just there, and what happened! The old hag was pushing so hard, out came a bunch of fascist police from her arse flinging turds at everyone, and the baby crept back inside. But it is still there, abiding its time! One day it will come out. Maybe!'

Nora was surprised by the intensity and vulgarity of his imagery. Obviously he was still upset by it all, and hadn't got it under control. Normally he was delicate, effete, talking about nubile blonde-haired Greek sailors in Marseilles, whom he spent all his time drawing for a project about Socrates..... 'My favourite intellectual sodomite!'

She remarked on his coarseness. 'The revolution has not made a poet out of you - unless it is some kind of American Beat Poet.'

'Poet..... my arse!' was all he said on the subject, knowing she was probably sending him up..... and not like the Greek sailors..... although he quite liked phallic bitchy women ..... which is how he saw Nora, although she would not have seen it as a compliment. To him it was.

★

She spent the day in the Louvre, where she often went when she wanted to find herself. She was buried in there somewhere, she had once told Anna, who said something like, 'I didn't know the Mona Lisa was actually *buried* in there!' She said that whenever Nora was telling lies or talking about sex, the smile on her face had always reminded her of the Mona Lisa.....

In the evening she saw Godard's film 'Alphaville', and afterwards she felt sad. She wished she looked like Anna Karina..... so cool and spiritual, and yet voluptuous as well. So irresistibly desirable. She drank beer in a café, thinking about her problem with her texts, when an idea came to her. Maybe she should take her text and her father's text and shuffle them together like a pack of cards..... close her eyes and cut out whole chunks, shuffle them up again and see what happened. The idea appealed to her. She murmured to herself, 'Funny if it came out exactly like a novel by Colette..... or Francoise Sagan!' And she doodled on the napkin..... 'Bonjour Triste Frau S.'

She tried to put her finger on the problem why she was really feeling so close to the edge again. Close to the open space. Was it seeing Anna actually making love to Raymond? She had watched Anna making love to almost every man she had ever talked about..... but in her mind's eye. She enjoyed imagining beautiful girls being ravished by strange, faceless men. Or was it because she had felt she might not be able to talk to Anna now? The opposite seemed to have occurred. She could talk more freely. Or was it the trauma of the texts, the rediscovery of a copy of her father's original manuscript, and fearing she couldn't cope with the reality of it now..... could not edit it . . . . . could not impose form on so many loosened fragments? She had been given too many opportunities. Too many choices. Like being available to all the men in the world, no longer a virgin. Who to choose? That seemed to be the problem, more than anything. Choice. Too much choice. Anarchy.

The image of Raymond and Anna was haunting her more and more. Was it because, for the first time, her erotic fantasy was not based on some photograph or painting or dream? Now it was an 'actual' image. Memory. That sharp-edged sword. The source of so much self-inflicted torture. The unforgettable. Raymond really screwing Anna . . . . . fucking her hard on the floor. In, out. Anna arching her back up to take the thrusts as deeply as possile. She had always feared she might be disgusted, witnessing the real thing. In her dreams, the man was a mere shadow. It was the girl she always concentrated on watching. She was always soft and gentle, like a jelly fish. Now it was different. She could see Raymond, a living sculpture . . . . . and he had a nice body. In particular she liked his bottom. It was tight and small. Michelangelo would have masturbated seeing it. He was trim and clean and not hairy. She mused for a while on the image of him, trying to compare it with other images she had clung to over the years . . . . . and was surprised how unclearly she had remembered images in films or photographs, of men. Pretty girls she had always been able to recall, precisely. Whether she liked it or not, she had to admit, the real thing was more enticing, more numinous . . . . . more painful in its absurd abandon, choreographed by an octopus. There's ink in your eye . . . . .

It had seemed a stray impulse that made her slip behind the curtain. She had not planned it. After all, it was the first time she had allowed Anna to make love to someone at the house. It was her suggestion of course. 'Raymond said you reminded him of Shelly Winters!' She was off like a flash. It was bizarre that it was Raymond. She had liked him from the start, but for the wrong reasons. Her private, interior ones. But he was nice looking though not handsome. Very English looking. He didn't seem at all overtly erotic. Rather bland. But he had saved her. He had bathed her wound . . . . . She put her fingers on her head. She could feel it was still a little damp under the plaster and very sore. It was determined not to heal.

Later she wandered up the street to where Raymond had found her. There were all the signs of the recent chaos still littering the street. Most of the cobble-stones had gone. The trees seemed naked without them, sticking up from bare soil, naked without their sculptured skirts. She remembered the night clearly and she remembered why she had gone there, really..... not for any of the reasons she had told Raymond, or anyone might have assumed. To see what it was really like to stand in front of a row of uniformed soldiers, faceless black helmeted police, armed, and menacing. The promise of brutality. Fascism. But she had admitted these reasons to Anna before she left, and Anna had seemed quite shocked. It was at that moment Nora realized that Anna loved her, in a protective kind of way..... and it had comforted her. Given her added strength to go out and face all the faceless Daddies.....

She had needed to experience the scene, feel what it was really like..... tangibly, objectively, outside of herself, in the so-called dimensions of the real world..... because after all, it was the central image in her father's book. The primal image of its meaning. Frau S.'s image. Her incandescent memory, so desperately alone, facing the Nazi soldiers.

She had been shocked to discover how urgently she felt drawn towards the uniformed police..... wanting to surrender to them..... wanting to give herself..... a sacrificial victim. Certainly, she wanted to be hurt, she knew it..... and it had aroused her, not her mind but her body, so much that she had almost experienced an orgasm without touching herself. It had frightened her enormously..... and she had run towards the police eagerly, wanting more. God knows what she would have done had she reached them..... but the cobble-stone had hit her from behind, thrown by one of her friends. Just in time. Some of fate's blows can be kind! Ironically, she had fallen at the hand of her own people, as if they were the ones to draw the line. Repress her. An incestuous betrayal. She had been dragged back and abandoned by her family, until Raymond had found her.

She had still been semi-conscious..... she could have become conscious with an effort, but she didn't want to. She wanted to appear unconscious to maintain the erotic tension..... as Raymond had carried her so galantly down the street and away, until the car had stopped for them. All the time she had been aroused to such a pitch of sexual excitement she didn't know what to do with herself. In the taxi she had slumped over Raymond..... and moaning as if in pain, she had touched herself, secretly, finding an extra tension in his presence..... a total stranger. Strange he didn't have a knife. Her orgasm caused her to shudder so hard, Raymond seemed to react as if she'd just died next to him..... and he'd shaken her to make sure she was still alive. How little men know of women, at the best of times.....

The whole experience had terrified her. She had never imagined she could be so intensely excited. Especially in such an oblique situation. So, it had been by accident she had brought Raymond into the shadowy curtains at the side of the stage of her most intimate being..... where he had then become an essential part of its new transformation. And he was still there, figuring in it, with Anna now. To erase him from the script now, would be like putting on a play, Oedipus, without the King. He was now inextricable from her drama..... She had even thought of seducing him, of finally surrendering her virginity, soon after their next meeting, but then Anna had arrived, and she had found the perfect solution. It also postponed the problem of their desire for each other that had been mysteriously mounting.....

She walked slowly, a little sad, remembering how intense that night had been..... shuffling along on the bare patches of road, on the sandy soil which had been under the cobble-stones..... and she was chanting silently to herself, 'Thalassa, Thalassa, Thalassa'..... She loved the word, it sounded so right to her - onomatopoeic - the simple word that said so much, the first, most primary symbol that Sandor Ferenczi had chosen so aptly for the title of his radical, revolutionary book..... revealing that the act of love was an enactment of regression by the whole self, not just the penis, the whole imagined self back into the womb..... into the womb of sleep and dream..... back back back to touching a physical, elemental memory of the sea..... the sea in the blood..... the brine in which the baby grew inside its mother's womb. The source of all being.

She realized suddenly, so sharply it made her stop in her tracks, it was just that, the sea, that was lacking in her drawings!

She should have the sea beneath the layers of sand and soil..... beneath the mud. Why had she left it out always? The most obvious thing? Was that perhaps what the young girl in the ghetto had been digging for in the mud? All along Frau S. had said to her father, 'The little girl was digging for food..... for food..... just for a small morsel of food! I know..... I know..... I know..... because it was me!'

Nora had often thought Frau S. might be lying. But she'd always insisted she *was* the little girl in the Warsaw Ghetto film, seen, seen time and time again, forever, digging in the mud for food with a small stick, the most harrowing image in the whole film, that summed up its horror, its unimaginable inhumanity. One of many images the world would sooner forget.

It had been central to Frau S.'s delusions, her madness, if that is what it was - her claim that it was *herself*..... this starving young girl with a stick in her hand, filmed so elegantly by the German soldiers..... so perfectly in focus, so neatly framed ..... the soldier's hands not even trembling with the heavy hand-held camera. She had pointed this out many times. 'His hands were not even trembling! There he was, watching a starving child digging in the mud looking for food, trapped inside the walls of the ghetto..... just waiting to die..... and he stood there, filming..... making a record......capturing it, forever. For..... ever. For whom? And his hands were steady. If they had been twitching, could he not have been forgiven?'

Nora was excited, her thoughts carrying her away. 'Perhaps the girl was not digging for food. Why should she think there was food in the mud? Perhaps we should imagine she was dreaming of being on a beach..... a serene, beautiful beach ..... a long way from the sea..... perhaps she was remembering a holiday when she had once dug into the dry sand with a small wooden spade, and to her surprise, into the dry hole had seeped the sea, bubbling merrily, gurgling, JugJugJugJug with excitement. She didn't know it was so close, just under the surface of the earth's skin. Was it not the sea she wanted to touch again..... to drown in..... even more than food? The sea in which she could dissolve away in the embrace of eternity? Free at last from earth's hell, earth's soldiers dressed in honour of the sky god, in the glow of the rising sun, forever?'

Nora stopped in the first café nearby and asked the waiter for a beer and ten paper serviettes. She turned them over and scribbled. The new idea excited her. It was nothing to do with her father's text and it was nothing to do with what Frau S. had claimed was the truth ..... both before and after the analysis. But it was a profound, numinous image that appealed to her, that touched something deep inside. An instinctive knowledge. She would incorporate it into her version, anyway. More and more she was coming to an inescapable conclusion. To hell with truth! She would give *her* naked monologue to Doctor K. and tell him it was her father's text. And the new key, the answer to the riddle ..... was a mere image. The same image but back to front. Reversed. The young girl in the film, who Frau S. claimed was herself, was not digging in the mud for food ..... but for the sea ..... for the source inside herself of her own sensuality. No longer looking for something real. Reality was intolerable. Dead. But for a symbol. The source of all symbols. And inextricably confused with that need for a new way of seeing, the symbolic way, Nora sensed, she had tapped her own budding eroticism and enjoyed being watched by the soldiers ..... in her torn dress. Everything else that Frau S. had claimed had happened ..... her being actually seduced - given by her father - was a falsification of the truth. Call it fantasy. Maybe she had found a way of smelling the sea and feeling it in her hands .....

★

Back in the hotel she wrote feverishly for an hour or so. Then she decided to write to Raymond .....

> 'Dear Docteur, you have a very sexy bottom. I liked you best when Anna was on top of you, going down on you ..... your prick vertical ..... '

But she screwed it up and started again.

'Dear Raymond, Anna misses you. She rang me and told me. But I miss you too! Yes. I do. Sweetly and gently. The house has been sombre without you. I felt so secure with you there in my house, invisible, but inside the walls. When are you coming back? How is America? How is my Freudian Annalysis coming on? You wrote Anna-lysis! Did you not see the slip? Did you ever bugger her? How could I know? What have you uncovered about me in the words of Mr. Jones? Read no further. It is very simple. I will tell you everything there is to know about myself. When I close my eyes, when you take away the veils, when you peal off the outer layers of skin, when your finger pushes through the meagre defences we women are cursed with..... you will find only one thing. The sea..... Thalassa! La mer..... la mère. Fused together in an eternal embrace, before men emerged and decided to wander..... seeking wombs and tombs. Can you swim? But in such oceanic depths? So deep that all is paradox? Beyond rationality? All is ANAL-ogy! Are you good at under-water diving? If so..... I will be waiting for you when you return! With love..... Nora. (Le Déluge! La Source!)'

She read it through, and laughed. 'Why should I tell him? Let him discover for himself! Then if he drowns, it will not be my fault!'

She tore it up and threw it away.

She tried to listen to music.....

She wished her name was Leila. 'Le' plus 'I' plus 'La'. It was a girl's name in Arabic, suggesting 'Of the night'.....

Eric Clapton got it wrong, writing Layla.

That night she slept soundly, unexpectedly peaceful again.

★

She stayed in Paris for a few days, happy to be away from her house and the feeling that she ought to be working on the text. From time to time she made notes, which was enough to keep the project alive inside her.

She went to movies, and suffered. If only men and women were all as beautiful as that..... She went to the Louvre several times and meditated. If only men and women were all as beautiful as that! But she felt more at peace there. It was a forbidden pleasure, feeling peaceful, when the city was still in such turmoil. She didn't read the newspapers. The headlines were provocative and distracting enough. She didn't want to be drawn back into any kind of involvement, or confrontation, with her old self. Her curiosity about fascism had been momentarily assuaged. Something had been born inside her, due to the so-called revolution and its momentary passion. A promise of optimism. She was happy, brooding..... her project, its final form now gestating inside her.

Anna telephoned her from the house to say there was a telegram from Agneta, who had been trying to reach her by phone. She was at L'Hotel with the final part of her 'monologue'. Nora asked Anna how the cats were. She said they were fine. Except the second one didn't come until the following day..... or during the night.

Nora met Agneta the following day in a café. Agneta was looking very emotional and hardly gave Nora a chance to speak, producing the typescript and placing it nervously on the table between them, as if it was dangerous. Nora didn't pick it up, waiting for Agneta to speak. 'It is very very moving Nora. You have done a marvellous job. Amazing. The extraordinary thing is how it 'flows', as if you have taken all the little blocks of text written by your father..... I compared your text with some of his former papers, and I checked references to the present case-history..... you have taken the blocks and eroded the edges, as if you dissolved it into yourself and it has come out more fluid..... softer. I'll be frank with you! Perhaps too frank. But it is almost as if your editing has created a whole new work. It is now androgynous. The text has become a marriage of ideas between a man and a woman. AND of course it is so much more moving because it is between a father and a daughter. It gives the impression..... I hope it is not false..... that your father, in dealing with Frau S. shows a kind of sympathy and generosity of spirit in dealing with her, that is very very rare in psycho-analysis. In men I might add! This book is unique. There is very little work to be done on it. You'll see. Am I boring you?' she asked, disarmingly.

'Well of course not! Are you crazy? I am flattered, and delighted!'

'Good. Then what I am going to tell you now will show you why I came here to see you. I had other things to do in Paris, of course, but most of all I wanted to speak to you directly. I don't think you realized the true nature of my relationship with

Doctor K. We have been lovers for a year or so, yes..... but I came into his publishing company originally as an editor. I didn't do the typing. I lied to you. I gave it to an Agency. I have a position of great authority in Doctor K.'s company. He is a weak man, a womaniser. He made a lot of money publishing rubbish. He has clung to the psycho-analytical stuff because I have been pushing him to do so. Secretly he is bored with it. He wants to cut the list from his company, and sell it. Frankly it doesn't make much money. If any! I have been getting closer and closer to the centre of the wheel, and now, most of the events in the company revolve around me! He calls me Circe!'

Nora said, 'I guessed from your earlier comments in Vienna, you were not merely a typist!'

'Good. Now listen. The text as it stands is unique! I don't know what your father actually wrote, but your "structuring" of it has given it a poetic quality that will make it very publishable. Handled right, it could make a lot of money. However. It could die a death if it just came out in the boring Psycho-analytical list. Or it could come out in that list, but be published simultaneously in a paperback, with the intention of reaching a wider audience, immediately. I would promote it carefully, with great respect, and use the "outside" story..... that is you, the daughter who found your father's notes and put them together, resulting in this moving work, produced by you both. THAT is a very good story after all. It will touch people. And the fact that the story..... I use the word story..... IS a story, not merely a case-history, is very important. It is different from Freud's "Wolf Man" or "Dora". It is more like a novel. And it is a collaboration. Your idea of taking the story of the little girl who played Blind Man's Bluff as a child with her father, who abused her, and linking her to Antigone..... making the Warsaw Ghetto, the fallen, plague-ridden modern City equivalent of Thebes..... is brilliant. And Freud as Oedipus! Marvellous. We should tell the truth, no? The truth outside the book, as well as inside it, to promote it? What do you think?'

Nora felt too emotional to speak. Delight and terror, all mixed up. She nodded. It was beyond her wildest dreams. Eventually she asked Agneta, 'Does Doctor K. agree with your plan?'

Agneta turned and called the waiter. She turned to Nora. 'Have a brandy or a cognac or something fierce, to celebrate?'

Nora didn't usually drink brandy before lunch but she agreed to have one. She told the waiter it must be in a large round glass. She could look into it and swill the golden liquid around, catching the sun, as if she was looking into a magic ball, imagining a rosy future.....

Agneta continued. 'The situation is more complicated I'm afraid. I have NOT spoken to Doctor K. about it, for a very important reason. What I am going to say now is strictly secret. No further than you and I!'

The brandy arrived.

Agneta's eyes narrowed, and Nora thought she looked quite beautiful, she was thinking so hard. It was nice to see a woman who used her mind to calculate and plot.....

'For the last six months I have been unhappy with Andrija, let's give him his name at least! He is generous and fun at times. But he is so narrow. He has no finesse, no style. At first I thought he was sensitive. He is actually, but to all the wrong things! He is not really interested in women. Like most men, he doesn't dare to know them. I am sure I don't have to elaborate. Six months ago I met someone else, and started to betray him.' She paused and drank her brandy.

'A younger man?' Nora asked.

'Er..... No..... not exactly. Two years younger than me, yes..... but not a man. A woman.'

Nora was annoyed with herself for not having said it first. The notion had flickered through her mind as Agneta was speaking, at the speed of light. 'Good for you. Teach him a lesson. I thought he was too obvious!'

'Exactly! Well. Her name is Marie-France and she works in Paris and is French of course. We met at a conference, and she is also an editor for a publishing company. To edit a long story short, oops, she has a lover, who doesn't know about us of course..... who is very rich. Very rich indeed. He owns companies all over the place. Marie-France and I started a project two months ago which is now coming to fruition. Her friend is going to buy the Psycho-analytical Series Andrija publishes in Austria and Germany through a company of his own in Munich. Much of this series has not been released in France. We can do it. But..... much more important..... he is backing Marie-France and I, in a modest publishing venture.

As we are so much outside mainstream publishing, as yet, we are calling ourselves "La Marge", hoping not to stay in "The Margin" forever of course. I will carry on editing the German Series. BUT, we have his backing to look for any new kinds of books we want to publish. He knows we will encourage "Women's" books. Books by women for women about women. He doesn't mind. As long as a lot of women buy the books! He has given us a certain sum of capital. If the project succeeds, we expand. If not, it folds up. Fair enough. Marie-France and I have found a small office near here in the roof of a Fashion House, which is great fun, and we are starting to collect some titles. I have stolen a young novelist from Andrija, who was fed up with him! Marie-France has taken a couple of her authors. We have a small nucleus. Exciting?'

'Very!'

'Marie-France was in Vienna last week where she read your book. I made a copy of it for myself! She agrees entirely with me, that with careful editing - it doesn't need much - we should publish it. We want to, if you agree, and it will be one of our books at our initial launch. It will have a better chance of succeeding.'

Nora's brandy was eddying around her glass. She had found a position in which it caught the sun's rays. It looked as if her glass was full of fire..... water on fire. She didn't know that 'Fire in the Water' was the hieroglyph for war. She gulped some of it down and it made her splutter. Agneta patted her on the back, gently rubbing the back of her neck until she regained her composure. Nora still had tears in her eyes, from what had gone down the wrong way..... and thinking of her father's text, now to see the light of day!

'What do you think?' asked Agneta.

'I don't have to think. It is all yours. I am thrilled. It could not be more exciting. And it will happen here in Paris. I am flattered too!'

Agneta embraced her and kissed her on both cheeks, before suggesting they made a kind of agreement on the spot. 'But..... We have very little money. We can't pay much advance. But if the paperback takes off, which it will..... we'll have much more to pay you. We will give you a very good percentage.'

'Good heavens! Don't worry about that! I don't need money. When my father died I inherited a lot of money, even though it was all my mother's. He was hopeless really, never made much from his work. Too much of a dreamer. So I don't even need an advance. My mother's family are very rich. For me the pleasure is to see my father's work in print, to hold the book with his name on it. How will you do it?'
'As you want? Have you settled on a title?'
'Yes I think so. I was going to call it "The Blind Man", because of the game she played all the time with her father, but I think that is wrong. It's not what it is really about. Sexual repression and the abuses it leads to. I think it should be "The Invisible Wall", because it was his own title, and this emphasises the Warsaw Ghetto image. I think it should be written by my father, edited and transcribed by me. Something like that. Then you can refer to his other papers and things. Also it will allow it to enter into the world of psycho-analysis, as it should, as his final statement, his final synthesis.'
Agneta agreed that it all sounded okay. She told Nora the break with Doctor K. was imminent, hopefully, in a few days. He had no idea that she was leaving him. She smiled cynically, and looking away, murmured quietly. 'I don't feel sorry for him, AT ALL, but his other mistress . . . . . that little whore, will be badly beaten for a few weeks, and I don't envy her at all!'
Agneta held up her glass and invited Nora to a toast. 'To "The Invisible Wall".'
But Nora said, 'To "La Marge"!'
Agneta called the waiter for the bill. She was eager to move on, to tell the good news to Marie-France. 'I will have contracts ready in a couple of days. We must meet and decide how to do the final editing and knock it into shape.'

★

That evening Nora was lonely. Excitement always made her lonely. She was so excited about her book, she didn't know what do. She wondered if she should try and find some of Anna's friends. She knew the cafés where they could usually be found. But then she decided it might be wiser to knock herself out. But the phone rang and it was Anna. Nora said, 'Very strange, I was just thinking about you. I was just about to take a walk and look for you!'

'Very strange, my chinese box took a walk, too!' Anna said, mischievously.

Nora apologised, saying she had used some of the 'Vie en Rose' powder because she really needed it. She'd used hers up on writing the monologue. Anna asked her if she was alright. Nora wanted to cry, but Anna was the last person in the world she could cry with. She asked Anna what she was doing. Anna could hear the anxiety in her voice, and was worried. She knew how irrational and destructive Nora could be at times. 'I'll come to Paris, now, on the train. I want to see you. I'm lonely and bored. We could go to a late night movie..... or to the theatre..... or even a night-club and dance!'

Nora whispered, 'I would love that Anna! Come to my hotel. See you later.' Anna told her she was sure one of the cats had gone off hunting beyond the garden. She was worried what might have happened to it in a territory it was not entirely familiar with.....

★

They went to a late-night movie, and afterwards ate a simple dinner in a small restaurant. Anna had a lot to tell about the chaos her play had caused at sedate old Aix-en-Provence. Afterwards Nora asked her if she wanted to stay with her in the hotel. 'It's pointless going off to your friends so late!'

In bed together for the first time, much to Anna's surprise, Nora started to caress her hair, and then her neck. She kissed her shoulders and then her breasts, very gently. Nora was surprised how totally passive Anna was. She hardly moved. Anna wasn't so sure how to handle it, knowing how complicated Nora was. At times she had even believed she was still a virgin as she'd often said, although she wasn't entirely sure of that. She often wanted to find out, as virgins were a curiosity these days.

But now, their bodies were touching. Anna had known it must happen one day, but she still felt unprepared. It would have to be Nora who chose the pace..... who would delineate the extent of the territory of her body to be conquered, on this first occasion. She was always the boss.

Nora was content to kiss her breasts and stroke her bottom. She lightly touched her pubic hair but didn't press further. Anna moved her hand to show she wanted to fondle Nora but Nora took it and placed it back at her side. Anna got the message. Nora wanted her to be entirely passive . . . . .

Even at school, Nora had never made love with another girl. She had been in love several times, but had never been able to transform it into physical tenderness. As she caressed Anna, she worried that she was arousing her and she would be frustrated, and not able to be satisfied without a man. She decided there was only one thing to do. She slithered down and to Anna's surprise she parted her legs and opened her vagina with her fingers and caressed her. When she thought Anna was moving her position so that she could do the same to Nora, she slipped further down the bed and kissed Anna's thighs and then she turned her over and kissed her bottom . . . . . until she knew Anna was being drawn more and more out to sea by waves of sensation. She was surprised how wet Anna was. She was sure she had never been that wet herself. Then Nora licked her bottom and then her vagina and pressed hard and firmly . . . . . and kissed her until she hoped Anna was satisfied. By her movements, Anna knew Nora still didn't want to be touched in return. It had been a tentative beginning.

They fell asleep without saying anything. Anna had wanted to say something like, 'Why did you always make it so difficult?', and Nora wanted to say something like, 'Why did I always find it is so difficult?', and they both wanted to ask, 'Why did it only happen now?' But silence prevailed. They were happy falling asleep in each other's arms . . . . .

★

When Nora woke in the morning, Anna was dressed. Nora still didn't know what to say to her. Eventually she knew it was up to her to speak. 'I wanted to know what Raymond felt. I'll tell you something . . . . . Now I know he had a great time!' And Anna laughed with her. Then she told Nora she had to run, and they embraced gently before she left.

Left alone, Nora wondered what Marie-France was like . . . . .

After breakfast, Nora wrote in her notebook.

'The Invisible Wall is going to be published. But in what form, I've still not decided. I'm still not sure. I don't share their certainty. Yet. To reveal all or hide? I take, but I still cannot be taken. But at last I may have thrown a cobblestone. Je detruis, donc je suis.'

★

Nora spent the day wandering around. Drifting. She couldn't settle. She bought some clothes she knew she didn't want, deciding later to give them to Anna. They would suit her better anyway. They weren't black. It had been the first time she'd bought clothes that weren't black.

But something inside her was threatening to undermine her new confidence. Was it merely excitement? Was it so powerful? It was as if a hitherto unknown, precious, winged part of herself was threatening to escape the increasing tension, by propelling itself away like an arrow.....

She walked head down, counting the squares on the pavement, not daring to look up, convinced that a stranger, a thief of some kind, was waiting for her and would jump from a high building nearby..... so she decided not to go to Nôtre Dame..... he would jump off the highest pinnacle, and screaming, arms outstretched, fall and crush her into the grey concrete under her feet. If she looked up she would see the body hurtling towards her and she'd stop, terrified, and in stopping, she would be killed. Her only escape was not to look up. She had to keep on walking, walking..... if she was to avoid the collision.....

Then things got worse. She could only describe it as suffering a heightening of her power of recognition. She was recognising more and more faces in the street, until everyone was known and familiar, had been met somewhere before, until there were no more strangers. She wanted to stop everyone and ask each one where she had met them before. She was losing the ability to distinguish people, one from the other. All the young men were resembling the Rimbaud she had seen on newly printed posters, the young women were becoming Anna Karina, the old men Jean-Paul Sartre, the older women Simone de Beauvoir. People were fusing into the single image of one person. Was this confusion, merely caused by an over-flowing of unattached desire?

Perhaps these sensual aberrations were withdrawal symptoms from her several days of 'La vie en rose', but it had never happened before. Maybe it was Anna's pills. But she felt so excited, so close to victory. Could it be that? But didn't it also mean she was now dangerously closer to being found out? Uncovered. Unmasked. Unveiled. Perhaps invalidated. The truth she had so long repressed was unavoidably surfacing. If she was to tell the whole of her own truth, the book would have to come out as a novel, with no reference to her father or his text at all! A novel, a pure fiction, all the characters with different names. No reference to any kind of objective psychological truths. Was it not an illusion anyway? Would it really be betrayal of her father? Perhaps that was preferable . . . . . than the truth.

Or was this being so unsettled, because she had finally kissed Anna's breasts and fondled her and felt her so wet and so excited, pressing as deep as she could into her flesh, hoping to discover the source of so much sap rising from deep within her? She thought of her favourite weeping willow tree, its fingers in the lake, but reversed in function, pulling water up and back through to its roots . . . . . she would like to be like that. Inside out. Upside down. Like the cabbalist's tree . . . . . as her father always said of her . . . . .

She rested in a café, exhausted by the complexity of it all, tired from clinging to the part of herself that wanted to shoot off like an arrow, from her taut, bowed body. She couldn't escape the question looming up. Why was she never as wet as Anna? Even when she had watched Anna and Raymond, even when she had been stoned out of her mind and dancing for herself, with herself, in the mirror, in Anna's clothes, she had never been *that* wet. She was wet inside, but not like Anna had seemed . . . . . overflowing. Was she imagining it? However much she tried, she couldn't get this image out of her mind. But worse, she hated being so distraught by such a childish question about herself and her sexuality. If only she and her mother had been given time to share such secrets, how different it would have been . . . . . Nora missed her terribly at times. Though she didn't lack of experience, she wasn't naive at all! She knew enough about psycho-analysis, hysteria, neurosis, psychosis, madness, nymphomania, sexual perversions, amanaphysis or what the hell Ferenczi called it..... She knew as much about sex as anyone she knew, especially what was really going on behind the act itself, which was even more important. How the mind was dealing with the illusion of being put into second place for a while. How dreams gave a man an erection in his sleep. How women..... also had such sexy dreams. Were they not erect too, in their modest way? Oh God! All those necessary mental acts that preceded the physical, she knew all about. The spirit..... had she not decided to call it..... and its lonely wanderings searching for the oases of matter. No! Damn it, she'd go it all wrong. The lies must end. But she'd get there. Soon!

Why though, should she be so distressed by the difference between Anna and herself? After all, she had barely started. Perhaps it was selfish resentment she felt that Anna was so lucky, free of the labyrinth of questions and meanings that stood between her and her surrender to the oceanic. For Anna it was so easy. The beach was a very narrow strip of sand, barely visible. A few skips and a jump and she could dive straight in. Why was her own beach so interminably long and treacherous, full of quicksands, with the sea almost always out of sight? A straight black or sun-shining line on which she had no words she dared write, whereas at the end of the day, as night opened its mouth and sucked away the day, it might become a blood red line, underlining clouds, delineating the horizon, the horizontal.

But now she was thinking about Raymond again. Why had she let him go so casually? She could have easily persuaded him to stay. One word, one physical guesture, one passionate kiss, and he would have waited..... she could easily have convinced him that America was a hell-hole of menacing panting women and bomb-throwing Vietnam war protestors. Both would scare him to death and make a complete fascist out of him overnight.

Why had she deliberately pushed him away? At first it had seemed so right. He was chosen by recognition - resonance with her past - was this not nature's pure expression? Why was she still afraid of confrontation with her past? Those tortuous images? She'd lost her nerve. After all, she'd made the decision at the very beginning to give herself to him. Everything about the situation had been right. So many things before had seemed like one long premonition. The external situation of the riots was trite in comparison to her inner feelings. The chance facts were preposterous. But the symbols had been right. She had felt it immediately when he picked her up and hobbled down the street with her, after parting her hair and saying 'Oh hell!' when he saw the wound in her head. He'd been so gentle, so romantic. But also so punctual, arriving exactly at the right moment in the symbolic logic of it all . . . . . And he was so unlike all her other friends, with his cool mind and delicate sensibility. Perhaps he was none of these things, she hardly knew him. But if he was none of these things, it didn't matter either. Raymond was the man to do it. To lie next to her while she caressed him, because he would be awkward at being chosen to signify a fusion of all the others she had rejected. He would have to be passive. She would take the initiative, lying on top of him, just as she enjoyed lying on her sacred wooden object, on a small silk pillow. Or would the real thing always be disappointing - nothing could be the same again? It had been the same with Frau S., in a way.

She took the little wooden weight from her pocket and placed it on the table next to her glass of beer. She wondered if it really was a plumb line or had been a toy or game . . . . . a spinning top. She stroked it like a mouse. 'You and I have been through some sordid adventures together, haven't we!' she murmured, affectionately.

Now she would have to wait for Raymond to come back, in his own time. Perhaps it would be right if he returned at the moment her book was published. It would be more appropriate to surrender herself to him then, whether he liked it or not. Perhaps she would become soppy and sentimental and soft, hoping he would love her as well, although she was confident he already loved her quite a lot, despite or because of her resistance, her 'absence' . . . . . She knew he would have some affairs in America, but he would return, perhaps loving her even more. But love was no longer relevant to the equation, anyway. Best not to think about it.

It was strange, Anna had never really talked about him. He had seemed never to exist to her, at all. But after all, it had been her suggestion to Anna that had started it all. Anna had spent an hour or so the following day looking for a picture of Shelley

Winters in one of her piles of film magazines..... Nora didn't dare tell her she'd invented the whole thing. It was like all incest. Betrayal engendering future betrayal.

But now, Nora needed to talk to Anna about her book, and its potential betrayal of her father. How could she discuss such things with anyone else? But in speaking to Anna, rather than to a tape recorder, she might discover the true way out of her own fantasies, the one's that still imprisoned her, and had structured the book. If she got drunk enough, she might be able to go the whole way, taking her the way she had to, to make it worth while. Let her do the same. It might shock her, but after that, everything could more easily come into the open, into the light.

★

That evening Anna called her, asking casually what she was planning for the evening. Nora wondered if she ought to be vulgar like a man and tell her, 'Let's go for dinner and then screw all evening!' She hoped it would never come to that. Anna suggested, 'Why don't we go the ballet..... to Béjart..... you always said you admired him, and it was the only ballet in the world you found entirely erotic? Why don't we go there? Or the Crazy Horse?'

The Ballet wasn't on, and the Crazy Horse was full. 'Probably full of American journalists,' said Anna, 'writing about the May revolution.' So they went to Montmartre, to a seedy club where some girls were stripping. Nora got bored quite quickly. It was too real. 'I have better than that at home!' she told Anna and they went back to St. Germain and found a quiet café for dinner.

Anna was still feeling quite nervous towards Nora. They had been friends for so long, and there had always been many undercurrents of implied sensuality between them, but Anna had never been able to talk about them and Nora had deliberately acted like a school-teacher with her. Even now, Anna wanted to hold back..... She had so much to lose with Nora. A kind of security she couldn't find anywhere else. But if Nora forced the issue, she'd go along with it.

Nora couldn't resist asking her if she had ever made love with girls. Alone. She knew she had indulged in quite a few romps with several people at once. 'Before I slept with a boy for the first time? Yes. Very innocent things. But since then, you are the first. You are the first ever..... in a real sense!'

Nora wasn't sure if it was true, so changed the subject and spoke about politics and anarchy and the theatre..... and dance and movies and the Mona Lisa. And then, the strange sensation of meeting a hundred Rimbauds in St. Germain. Anna said it was certainly withdrawal from 'la vie en rose'..... nothing worse. She wasn't to worry. Just to stop it again for a while.

After the first bottle of wine, Nora ordered another, this time an expensive Rosé. 'La vie en rosé. A Rosé is a Rosé is a Rosé. She wanted things to go smoothly. She had decided what to do with Anna in bed, earlier in the day. She presumed Anna wouldn't mind. These days, wasn't everything old hat? It was her misfortune to have passed it by. She guessed Anna must be game for anything, which was why she had been to a sex shop and bought what she needed. Whether she'd dare to use it though was another question.

However, Nora also wanted to discuss the new complexities created by the promise of publication of her book. But she felt great reluctance to start talking about it. She couldn't make the first move. Then she laughed at herself..... although it wasn't really funny. That is why she had always been so lonely, not being able to make the first move about anything.

She wanted to talk about betrayal - and the pages still left out of the manuscript - the truth she was determined to put in somehow. 'I see you are worried about something,' Anna said.

So finally she was able to say it. 'Yes..... There are some things I want to talk about that are very important about my book. Sexual details. I must get them right. Very intimate, perhaps perverse, if there is such a thing. But I can't talk about them yet..... not now, not here, not until we're back to my hotel. Afterwards. Do you understand?'

Anna blushed. Nora had never seen her blush. Nora laughed and Anna looked even more embarrassed. Nora asked her why she was feeling shy, or whatever it was. She looked quite sad. 'No-one has ever said they want to make love to me because THEN they can have an intellectual conversation with me afterwards!' They both laughed.

★

By the time they were back in the hotel they were both drunk. But Nora had bought more wine during the day, together with a small tape recorder to play music while they made love. The German Requiem of course but some other music too, including Clapton's 'Layla'..... She had also bought some black trousers and a black silk shirt for herself.

She ordered another room for Anna. 'For the whole night Madame?' the Concierge asked, accustomed to renting rooms per half hour. 'For an hour!' Anna answered abruptly.

Nora wanted to prepare herself for Anna, alone, and Anna was happy to do the same in a room of her own. She changed into the clothes Nora gave her, 'for tonight, but also a present.' When she came to Nora, she was pleased that Nora had draped a red scarf over the small bedside light, to make the room more mysterious. It was almost so dim they might not see each other. Nora knew how she wanted to handle the rite she had planned. In some respects, she was no novice, even if so much might still be imagination.....

They drank wine in silence, flecked with a mere touch of 'vie-en-rose', until Nora finally laid Anna back on the bed and undressed her, savouring the effect as if she was pealing a luscious fruit. A ripe mango perhaps. She stroked her and covered her with the perfumed oil she had bought, wanting to see her naked and glistening in the dim light, imagining her as the girl on the cover of Nerval's 'Voyage en Orient' she has seen earlier in the day. 'Le rêve est une seconde vie.....'

Anna was surprised when Nora's oiled fingers explored her bottom. When Nora turned her over onto her stomach, she decided not to think about anything, why, or what it meant. She listened to the music, relaxing as much as she could, knowing she must if it wasn't to hurt too much. She hoped Nora didn't want only to hurt her. But Nora was very considerate and gentle as she eased the well oiled rubber dildo into Anna's anus ..... licking her clitoris as she pushed it in and out.....

When Nora seemed to be satisfied with Anna's squirmings and moanings, and had relaxed, Anna slipped away and tried to make love to Nora in return. Nora allowed Anna to caress her, but when she tried to be more forceful, Nora pushed her back gently saying, 'Not yet..... one day I will say yes, you know it, but not now!' But she allowed Anna to kiss her body and the flickering gentle touches aroused her so much she allowed Anna to go down and down until she kissed her vagina . . . . . until she was almost prepared to give way . . . . . but she managed to divert her from danger. Anna was astonished to discover that Nora was still a virgin after all.

But afterwards, lying close on the bed, limbs still entwined, Nora was eager to talk about her book. Anna was surprised how quickly she managed to snap out of the intimacy . . . . .

First Nora explained how the book was going to be published, all the details, and the situation with Agneta and Marie-France, mentioning they were lovers 'too'. Anna was disturbed by the sudden flow of words, especially when she would have preferred to crash out. But this was typically Nora. Full of paradoxes as usual. Anna said it was all exciting news. 'Go on!'

Nora propped herself on the pillow before continuing. 'Exactly. From every point of view it looks promising. I should be happy. But I'm not. The text I narrated into the tape-recorder and gave to Agneta is a complete fiction. They say it is a perfect fusion between two minds. But I know they have not *really* read it at all. If they had, they would have seen through it. They should have been smarter than that. But they may be right, on another level, because they know nothing of the truth, as I know it. All they know is my text and for them it works. For me it is betrayal, but what should I do? For the sake of whose truth? My dead father's? Should I mess it all up now, say it is all wrong, go back to square one and try to write the whole thing again, with my father's sacred and immortal words merely linked together with my verbs and my little observations and innuendoes and so on? What can I do?'

Anna didn't know what to say. It had sounded simple and ideal. Now it sounded utterly complicated. But being an actress, she knew what it was like to have to follow a text, to learn lines, so she suggested, 'why not get a blank piece of paper and write down what it is you are saying with your novel and what it is you believe in, deep down. Are they the same? If so, the actual text is totally unimportant. You can fool everyone if you want, just as I do as an actress. When I play Elektra, I am Elektra. For two hours we all enter the shared fantasy. Not unlike making love! It is no different with your book. You have achieved a distance from one side of its truth. So what? I think you should publish it as it is. But what was your father's text *really* about?'

Nora hesitated. She had almost forgotten. She was still quite drunk..... 'Er..... my father's work *was* very important, that's what is awful. His ideas were revolutionary in his time, saying such things like, sex for men and women was totally different and so, certain conflicts were inevitable. The essence of love was compromise, accepting that passion was destructive. Men and women seek opposing meanings and needs from the sexual act itself. I don't need to elaborate. We know all that!'

'Right!' Anna said, but not entirely convinced. She started to say, 'But it's also fun, and.....' but Nora wasn't listening.

'He was scared by the mounting social problems caused by patriarchal repression, the way it split men and women and tore society apart. Every individual reflected this internally, because men and women are both being forced to live as "men" in the patriarchy, cut off from their femininity, both acting as men, in the narrow sense too, to survive in a society structured by male values. He saw peace as a natural harmony, a balance between these two energies. Now there was a permanent imbalance and there would be permanent war. All war is territorial, fighting for portion's of the mother's body, the earth and her resources! It was not the conflict of Eros and Thanatos. That is how the patriarchy wanted to see it. By inventing Thanatos they were trying to get themselves off the hook. It was the patriarchy who invented Thanatos - the death wish! It was their way of operating. The basic split was between masculine and feminine ..... objective in the culture and subjective with every self, male and female. We are all androgynous at the deeper, significant levels. But patriarchal values drive a wedge inside us, split us from head to toe, encouraging the male with promises of power and suppressing the female, saying it's too subjective and indulgent. All emotion! Useless. Not productive.....'

'I see.....' Anna said, finding it hard not to ask her to tell her about it tomorrow. She would have preferred to sleep.

But Nora was in one of her trances, caused by one excitement and another..... 'The ghastly failure of pyscho-analysis according to the Gospel of Freud was because it was based on a deliberate lie. A monstrous cover-up. If little girls *were* seduced, psycho-analysis was defunct. If they imagined they were, psycho-analysis could be magic and exorcise some of the ghosts. Best to say it was always imagined ..... but he *knew* that sexual hysteria was derived from actual seductions, but he "abandoned the theory" and said all hysteria was based on fantasy. The girls, always girls you notice, needed to delude themselves with fantasies, and were experts at it. Men wouldn't do such a thing! Women were prone to hysteria, hardly ever men. But this was a terrible, fascist deception ..... to hide the fact of mass abuse of women by the patriarchy! Invariably starting with children. Abuse is physical and real, or subtle, on the level of words and images. In a child it is always both, simultaneously ..... different and yet the same. It is pain either way to be abused physically or abused as psychologically worthless and a nuisance, children merely tolerated, most of them the result of nature's accidents. So let's all abandon truth, if Daddy Freud did! Let's say the Warsaw Ghetto was a fiction film made by a bunch of Nazi soldiers! My father was so angry with Freud, he was scared of being called anti-semitic!'

Anna poured herself a drink. It was the Nora she knew. Nothing would change her. Nora offered her glass for more wine and nearly fell off the edge of the bed. They both laughed and Anna thought it might stop the flow of words, but ......

'My father respected women's power ..... the awesome power of women's sexuality. He was Tiresias, he who denounced Oedipus! Oedipus re-incarnated in Freud. All-seeing Tiresias! He who had experienced sex as a woman and as a man. When asked about sex, Tiresias said ..... 'If pleasure in love be divided into ten, nine parts go to woman and one to men!' My father quoted Jung. "Man cannot stand a meaningless life." He changed it to, "Man cannot stand meaningless sex." Sex for a woman could be meaningful, purposeful, in a profound sense. Never for men. They can't grasp that meaning, which is why their frustrations became so desperate. In all their sex is the discovery of absence, the re-discovery of loss. Emptiness. A void. They strive to go beyond the body of the woman, transcend it into a space that opens up and engulfs them. L'amour fou. An intangibilty that is always a psychic betrayal. It parallels the loss of unity with the Mother's body. In the sexual act the man cannot become as the sea and re-enter the womb ..... he is always a rock on the shore ..... every time he makes love he affirms his separation, his primal loss. He knows it and reasons himself into hell. Only through becoming a father does sex become profoundly fulfilling and meaningful. How often does that happen these days? A woman can have a baby and become a mother, and there's a point in it all, a fulfilment . . . . . a telos . . . . . an end result. This is always known unconsciously by a woman, whenever she makes love, which is why sex is so often crucial and important - so much more important than for men who can enjoy it for being casual - except some women who act out the men's fantasies, who enjoy being trapped into enjoying the same superficiality. But strip women from this meaning and they become worse killers than men. Nothing is more dangerous than women acting as if they were frustrated men. They *know* something has been taken. Stolen. Not the penis but the child. No wonder men end up playing their sexual power games with objects . . . . . with territory . . . . . with guns and other symbols of male power.'

Anna was floating . . . . . not exactly asleep. Her bottom was too sore to let her fall asleep easily. It reminded her she had a duty to listen to poor, lost Nora. But it was getting harder and harder to make sense of it all. But she was still trying . . . . . Poor Nora! She missed the reference to women being casual about sex, merely mimicking men . . . . . she loved being casual. Free of responsibility.

Nora continued, 'With a woman, with nature, men experience the empty spaces . . . . . the void. O world intangible we touch thee! The conquest of nature, and then of space! How often men worship space! Is nature so threatening? Perhaps. We must start to feel sorry for men and forgive them. Even his sperm gets stolen by the woman, so his unconscious tells him! Men, my father said, and there was much of the feminine in my father, were made very lonely by their sexuality. They wanted to grasp and touch and hold and possess, but it is always an empty space into which they fall. A woman wants to grasp an object. She does so. And then the fruit of the act. Her child. She grasps the child. Both men and women suffer that primordial alienation from the Mother, but woman stretches out and can touch herself, wait, be patient, and is mother within herself, and takes and makes an object. She feels it inside her. It becomes a child. Men never achieve the goal of sex, which they seek unconsciously, of re-entering the womb, swimming again in that silent sea! La mère.

Only the sperm does that. It is his whole body and being that desires this union, as Ferenczi would have us believe. Thalassa! Man is always betrayed. His essence is stolen. I felt so sorry for my father. I wanted to be everything for him. Tangible. No wonder man rejects his failing in love in favour of power!'

Nora noticed Anna was asleep. She ignored the tape of the German Requiem in the machine and switched to 'record'. She had to carry on, thinking, thinking aloud ..... had to get rid of the words ..... had to believe there was someone listening, somewhere, to whom she could finally confess. And it had to be a woman ..... even if she was asleep.

'.......... So! The seduction theory. Some psychoses in women were due to actual sexual traumas. They *are* seduced either by the father or another man. But we forget ..... alas we forget. If only we could have a film of the event! A document of the crime ..... 'Look, here I am. Nazi solder number 67568. Proof is in the film. Here I am raping a whole people ..... here, look, a pretty young girl, a mere child digging in the sand! Aren't I clever. I built a wall around a whole people and starved them to death. Why? Why Anna, why? Why did they need to do it? What drove them to it? What passion was so frustrated, it transformed into that? It displaced into that? I am a woman too Anna ..... What we need to know is the truth. How can we ever know it? Did he really do it or did we imagine it? The mind is right to forget. Leave it in peace. Leave it closed. Shut. Do not prise it open with the psychic scalpels of psycho-anality ..... ANALity ..... THAT is the story of my father's book. Or should I say of Frau S's book! Did her father fuck her or not? And why did she think it was one of the soldiers? Was she really the little girl filmed in the Ghetto, or just want to imagine she was? Can we never forget - must we ever forget - what can we do with the ghetto inside all of us now?'

She was sobbing now but Anna was deeply asleep, snoring. Nora clung desperately to her body, caressing her buttocks gently, not wanting to wake her. It was enough to cry into her hair ..... and to hope to fall asleep, despite trying to imagine what it must be like to be a man ..... to desire her woman's body ..... a man, a lonely cut off man, who nevertheless for a moment ..... a passing moment ..... even the irony of that ..... had something real to push into her and make her object too ..... for only a passing moment until he loses even contact with his own body, that went into her as hard and gnarled as the branch of a tree, a golden bough from the tree of sacred knowledge, that thrust inside as an alien, and left part of its memory in the primordial sea ..... which would return, as a child ..... unless of course he made a deliberate mistake. The ultimate betrayal. Filthy lucre ..... shit ..... she knew all about it. Proof too. Images in her mind. Memories, otherwise transformed by the needs of the soul into image-ination ..... there was no longer any difference in this modern, soulless, filmed world .....

But she was falling now ..... and fell asleep at last. Was the recorder still listening?

★

The following day, after breakfast, they separated, both having things to do. But in the evening they met up to drive together to the country. They had not yet talked about the previous evening. It was raining heavily, and visibility was bad, so Nora drove slowly. It was hot and humid in the car and the sound of the rain added to the hypnotic ambience. They listened to music on the radio for some time until Anna asked if she could switch it off.

After a few miles in silence, Anna spoke. 'I'm sorry I fell asleep last night when you were talking. Tell me again about your book, if you want to. You know I am interested.'

Nora tried to make light of it ..... 'I was drunk and babbling on ..... mostly rubbish. Just trying to get things into perspective.'

After a pause, Anna asked her, 'Why did your father fail with writing his book? And why is it a betrayal if you make something out of it, even if it is your own?'

Nora answered immediately. 'It is not only him I betray. You're right. He's dead. It doesn't matter that much. It is Frau S. I am betraying, isnt it? It is her life, her secrets.'

'Does it matter, if you use different names?' Anna asked.

'Probably not. But she is a woman and one of us.'

Anna laughed. 'And she was very beautiful wasn't she? Tell me about her.'

'Yes..... alas. That was the problem. My father was always in love with her. How could he not be? But she was his patient and according to the code, the strict laws of psycho-analysis, you do *not* seduce your patients. But he loved her. That was the problem.'

'Tell me about her..... go on. Was it that bad?'

Nora took her recorder and started the tape of the Requiem. She had pressed the pause switch and not the record switch the night before and had recorded nothing! Tant pis! Mere words. She put the volume switch low, so the music was peaceful in the background.

'The irony is, Frau S. gave my father all his insights. It was her ideas that dominated him..... woman, the Mother, Mother earth..... mut..... mud..... Man always a wanderer..... an outcast, like Oedipus, left to fight for the invisible..... the unseen, that can no longer be seen because he is blind. It was she who as a child had played the game of blind-man with her father, and then she played it with mine! She blinded him with her beauty - and her tragedy. War as the inevitable sublimation of psychic loss. Loss of the mother.'

Anna interrupted. 'She was a powerful woman!'

'Yes. My father didn't stand a chance. His saving *her*, messed up his whole life! Ironic really.....'

They listened to the music for a while, as soon as the 'Denn alles Fleisch' sequence came on.....

Then Nora continued. 'She was in the Ghetto, trapped inside the wall, being starved to death by the German soldiers. But she survived. Her father bartered her for freedom. She was seduced by one of the soldiers and he helped them to escape. She was about fourteen at the time. Probably.'

'Poor thing,' Anna murmured.

'A valuable virginity! Her mother had been murdered by the Nazis. Frau S. was the only child. Years later, being a very modern woman, she was working - in the Cinema. She was obsessed by films and photographs. One day she was asked to compile old newsreels for a series about the war, including the Warsaw Ghetto. When she saw the footage secretly filmed by the German soldiers, she collapsed, saying she had seen herself. She even said she *then* remembered being filmed. My father discovered it couldn't be true, the cameraman was hidden from view in a truck. She took a few frames from the film and blew them up. She had a still made. It was a young girl, in rags, digging in the mud. On the soundtrack were the words of a later narration, saying the young girl was digging in the mud looking for food. Her fragile balance of mind and body was broken by seeing the film. It had forced her to remember. The repressed material had surfaced. She came to my father..... with one obsession. Never to make love again. She said she had been seduced by many of the soldiers..... That's enough now!'

'Go on!' Anna said, 'I always wanted to know the whole story! You only ever gave small, tantalising, conflicting fragments!'

'Okay..... My father was just starting his practice in Switzerland, when she came to him, and he says in the Introduction of his proposed, but unrealizable book, "I was just embarking on my chosen profession. I had recently married and my life seemed ordered and secure." His experience with Frau S. so unnerved him that he was preoccupied with *her* story for the whole of his life. He once said to me. "She is free now! I cured her. But me? I carry all her guilt, all the guilt for this ugly world created by men. I am now stuck forever inside the Ghetto, worrying about the truth of what really happened to her!".....

..... Of course, this merely meant he was in love with her! How could he not be? She was beautiful, socially privileged. Very rich. All the family money had been safe in Switzerland. They lived there in great style, with the hidden secret that her father had sold her, exchanged her body to buy their freedom, and regain their fortune..... From the orthodox point of view she was incurable. How could you efface such a *fact*? She could be taught to forgive perhaps, but never to forget. But the discovery of the film had made it impossible for her to forget. It etched the images anew on her mind..... resonance, form provoking form, mirrors face to face with mirrors, the most dangerous of all nature's experiments, the unfathomable polyphonic way she evolves..... evolution, the cycles of endless revolution.....

..... So the problem was now much worse after discovering the film. The fact of the creation of the Ghetto was bad enough. The systematic murder of a whole race of people was inconceivable in human terms. But..... how could they film it? What Frau S. couldn't deal with was the idea that a soldier could stand there and film it. To cold-bloodedly record the act of detached genocide. It heralded a new kind of human consciousness. Total, absolute objectivity. Separation from all feeling. What kind of insanity was that? But more important. What caused it? Something did. It must have. Such things don't just happen. My father said it was rationality..... so-called science-based rationality..... which evolved naturally from Jewish monotheism! Ironically he was forced to hate the Jews too, intellectually. At the end of the war, with their presumed victory, were the Nazis going to gloat over the film as if it was pornography? The primal scene, the primal crime, endlessly repeating?..... But as he said. If you intellectually hate the Jews for their monotheism, that means you are rejecting the Christians too and the Muslims. But that is so. They were all responsible for the holocaust. Anyone who waved the flag of rationality. Reason implies the genocide of the feminine..... and nature and human nature, in its roots, is feminine, part of the androgynous unconscious..... the house of reason, la maison de la raison..... is built on sand. As Noah and the other Babylonians and Sumerians knew, the ark of the human spirit must be a floating vessel.....

..... Frau S. became obsessed with..... "What was going on in the mind of the photographer?" Her soul had been stolen and trapped in his mind! She had to "become" the cameraman, her imaginary or possible seducer. Thief of her soul. My father said that is why she became obsessed with having her photograph taken. Might she see her soul there, after all? She had been a fashion model, but later she often posed for erotic pictures of one kind or another. Later in her analysis, she said it had started in the ghetto. One soldier in particular had taken many photographs. It's like the sick world we live in Anna. All images and photographs. Billions of stolen souls. Adverts and visual shit! Everyone hoping to see themselves on film, imagining it might reveal their stolen souls!'

They drove in silence for a while.

'I will always love you Nora..... I will always stay with you if you want me!' Anna said suddenly. Nora was too disturbed to reply..... It was as if she hadn't heard.

Nora continued, 'My father took a bold step. Let us assume Woman is totally different to man. In his notes he often wrote

"Womb-man" to remind himself. The average man would say of Frau S..... poor, sad, helplessly deceived and misused woman, whom no decent man would ever take on afterwards! To have been sold, raped, taken, used, and what a trauma for her poor father! Let us assume woman is different. What else did she know at that age? He took the recurring images and dreams of the woman and realized she was thinking the way *men* do. She was obsessed with the image of the little girl, pushing the stick in the mud. She too was punishing herself with the man's point of view. The truth had been different. She was enjoying every minute of it. At that age, maybe she was a terrible flirt. Maybe she found the soldiers very desirable? No woman would like to hear that would she? Do you cringe at the thought? But children are often very perverse. It is quite natural. The problem in her life became, that no man ever afterwards could satisfy her sexually. Not without certain acts of the theatre of cruelty.....'

They finally arrived at the house. Anna took Nora's keys and opened the two locks on the big gates. Nora was feeling more relaxed now. She had started to really talk and soon it would be over. And then maybe she could forget the facts and return to writing her novel. The facts would lose their power to repress her.

Over supper, Anna insisted she told her the rest of the story. She knew it was bubbling inside like a volcano. Better for Nora it should all flow out, otherwise she might go mad. Ideas can be like alien organisms in the blood.....

'You must read the book!' Nora said, laughing. But then she became serious. Sad.

'Forever afterwards she needed her soldiers..... her men in uniforms with the power to abuse her. My father knew she had been too young to be moral and ethical. Merely sensual. BUT. And this is where the story becomes almost impossible to credit, and where my father had the biggest problem of dealing with her. He never knew whether it was true or not, but Frau S. claimed that when she and her father escaped, with the help of one soldier she says she really loved, she was so sexually developed, so frustrated, so cut off from everything that had become real..... so cut off from everything we would call normal..... from despair and spite, she seduced her father.

Clearly she didn't have a chance!'

Anna seemed very distressed. 'How can such a book be published? What women will ever read it? It will be a terrible flop!'

'No, the story as I have written it must succeed, for both their sakes! The hard edges are moulded now. I did a Freud on it and abandoned the seduction theory. I said the whole sequence with the father was *imagined*. A fantasy. Not true. My father could never publish the Case-History because he wanted to tell the truth! And yet, he had no proof. People might have ridiculed him. In the end he *did* believe it was true. You see why I am worried? What to say and what not to say?'

They ate in silence. Anna asked where the other cat was. Nora said she would return when she wanted to.

'My father believed her in the end when a dream revealed that her greatest sorrow was that she could never have her father's child! So, you can appreciate why she never wanted to have the book published! It is too harrowing..... too naked..... too bizarre..... too unbelievable..... too subversive..... too anarchic. People would *have* to refuse to believe it. It is not what they want to believe. They would prefer the lie. That she had been irrevocably broken by her experiences. That she was the victim. *That* is why Frau S. stole the manuscript. She knew I was going to publish it. But! Here's the ultimate irony. The real reason is that her father is still alive. She didn't want it published for reasons you might not assume. It could be veiled in secrecy, all the names changed and so on. As I have done in fact. However, her father would know it was her, and did not want the "story" to be released. But she wouldn't have minded really. She believes in the truth, however harrowing. She has much integrity. After all, the Warsaw Ghetto was a fact. The truth. She too asked, why did men need to do it? To assuage what fears? What tygers stalking them in their dreams? But here is the truth. Maybe the only one in this galaxy of subversive cover-ups! Her father has threatened to cut her off financially if it was ever published - if *she* allowed it to be published. It all boils down to money! She is the only person who can stop it. While my father was alive, she persuaded him not to do it. When he died, I became the threat. She has stolen it not to protect her story..... her modesty..... or anything like that. But to protect her inheritance. Simply to conserve the money that is due to her, which will enable her to carry on living..... freely! How can I forgive her that?'

Anna didn't know quite what to say. 'Amazing..... I wouldn't have thought of that. It was all due to money in the end?'

Nora continued. 'What I have done is to transform the book, make the truth symbolic but not factual. I have written the story from inside the Ghetto but showing how her entire sexuality had become fixated in a particular rite. You see, after my father had "cured" the woman, she became happy to go off looking for soldiers and anyone she fancied who would enact her theatre with her. He freed her for that. It was her only sexual trip now. So take it! My father did cure her. He made her fulfil herself, live out her myth. To bring back the two faces of Janus..... reality and fantasy..... and make it one face. He told her her script was not to become the prevailing socially acceptable one, a dutiful wife with lots of children, as the Freudians and their patriarchy would deem to be "cured". She became a woman of the world, of the "real" world..... the only world she could perceive..... broken and raped and misused and Godless..... undeniable in its absurdity. No wonder she would never become a good mother. She became a femme fatale, with her money and her pretty young soldiers..... or the men she dressed up as soldiers. But here is the deepest irony of all. She became a brilliant psycho-analyst! An expert on curing German soldiers who in the war had done a few things they would forever feel guilty about. Which father could they allow to forgive them? None in a patriarchy! She became so clever, so tender, so understanding. She taught them to forget and forgive too. To forgive themselves. She showed that charity was the only way out, the only solution. She became a great nurse. She nursed the enemy. It was hard for my father, who loved her so much. He cured her only to lose her.....'

'And we dare to think we have problems!' Anna said, eating some cheese. 'We kids of the Swinging Sixties - wow - it makes me feel ashamed.....'

'What hurt terribly, was, that she was better at analysis than my father. Men always feel guilty about anality..... of seeking anality. She was convinced from her studies, that most women seem to secretly enjoy it. She made some wonderful observations in her work. Great insights into the true nature of sado-masochism. But she has refused ever to publish it as ascientific fact. She writes novels instead and 'papers' for her friends. 'How could I betray my analysands? I would be the same as the photographer inside the ghetto, recording the sorrow and misery and madness of my victims.' She wrote poems as well. She has many pseudonyms, behind which she has remained hidden.....'

'In the book you should call her Salomé, hidden behind so many veils!' Anna suddenly blurted out. Nora looked at her in astonishment, but decided to continue with getting the story off her chest.

'I want to publish my father's case history of her cure, but I don't want to hurt her. What can I do? Don't you see?'

'We will sort it out,' Anna said, noticing that Nora was almost crying. Suddenly Nora blurted out, 'And then there was Raymond..... fucking Raymond!'

Anna said nothing. She couldn't see the connection. Nora was in one of her trances now..... talking mostly to herself.

'Fucking Raymond! He made it all worse, turned the knife in the wound. It was his suggestion, the tape recorder, that has made it all so complicated, when my father's story dissolved into my own. I just closed my eyes and imagined I was a patient of my father, talking to him. What came out was strange even to me. It is full of half-truths..... some would call lies..... but where are the absolutes? Show me! I know it works. As Agneta said. The work of a truly androgynous mind! My father's and mine. Our child!'

'Hunger is an absolute,' Anna said, in a daze. She stood up and went to the loo.

When she came back she said, 'Nora..... if I was a man, and if you were not so complicated, I would ask you to marry me!' And they both laughed. 'But promise not to talk in bed before we make love. But publish the book anyway. Publish and be damned. After all, as you said many times, there is no truth in the written word, or the painted picture, except the fantasy it provokes. Make it the perfect fantasy, but sell it as the truth. If you sell it as fantasy, a novel, it will sell 200 copies. If you sell it as the whole ugly, ghastly truth, it will sell thousands of copies. But you and I, will know it is everything and nothing and neither! Tant pis!'

'Isn't that being immoral?' Nora asked.

'Immoral! I have been immoral all my life and enjoyed every minute of it! It depends what you mean by morals. Sex is another absolute my darling! If you want to enjoy sex in our broken world, it has to be immoral! As long as I know my partner is enjoying himself, knowing I am desired, that I give pleasure in taking my own pleasure, that is enough for me. Do the same with your book. Give it away generously for what it is. Be a woman! Don't hesitate like you do. The time has come to surrender your so-called morals - and not the least, your virginity! Throw yourself into it like a lamb to the slaughter. You'll discover what passion is. I can tell you! Sheer relief!'

Nora laughed. 'I was intending to lose my virginity, but I sent the right man away!'

'There is no such thing as the right man, except the one who is there - unzipping and getting ready to do it. I suggest you just put on a fur coat over your nakedness . . . . . you are too skinny by the way, you must eat more . . . . . go out and pick up the first man you think looks the right shape, ask him if he wants a virgin and charge him 2000 francs. When he pays up, lie on the bed and tell yourself a moment's pain is worth 2000 francs. After that it will be pleasure all the way . . . . .'

Nora thought about it for a while, seriously. God! Maybe Anna was right. 'No Anna. It was Raymond who was there at the moment the revolution's blood started to flow. It must be him. I'll wait for him to return, to complete the crime. He doesn't know how lucky he is. *He* is the stranger you speak about . . . . . the perfect stranger . . . . . because he almost took my virginity that night. He didn't know it. But it was the first time I rubbed up against a man and had an orgasm from sheer excitement. He had no idea. He thought I was dying in his arms. Le petit mort. Isn't it strange how little they know about us women and yet they have written ten thousand books about our sexuality, as if it was all created by and for men? The libido is masculine Freud assumed most of the time. Mine isn't, anyway. Mine is female. If not both or neither. Pagan I'd say!'

★

The following day Anna left. They had slept together but not made love.

Nora woke up deciding she must work at her paintings. She was determined to surprise Agneta, who'd not seen them yet. That was her plan now, to finish her series of paintings and arrange an exhibition at the same time the book came out. The paintings would be her own..... entirely her own..... from nowhere except her own inner being..... telling another kind of truth, hopefully, a purely sensual truth. Her carapace was cracking. She had indeed, at last, cast the first stone.....

As for her father's book..... it was strange how she still deluded herself about it, protected herself from the truth about it. Poor Daddy! He had become so confused, more confused with every revision he made, confusing Frau S. and her past, with his own fantasies..... but worse still, he had utterly confused Frau S. with Nora herself. Nora was the true, reluctant subject of the book, although her father had never allowed himself to become conscious of this. Many so-called facts were mis-placed, put into the wrong context, or wrongly interpreted. So much for those life-rafts called facts..... any piece of drift-wood would do when the storms were really blowing.....

Perhaps it was a compliment really. After all, her father was trying to elevate the narrative above a personal case-history, trying to reveal that every woman was a daughter in a patriarchy, a victim, because the patriarchy depended so absolutely on repression of everything feminine.....

Poor Daddy! She couldn't help forgiving him and loving him..... although she dreamt of him often, his hands bleeding, desperately building a concrete bridge over a river, magnificent and ingenious, but going nowhere to nowhere, not knowing the way to go was along the river.....

★ ★ ★

Eight

Nora worked on her painting for several days. She couldn't face the writing. She still wasn't sure how to cut the new pages into it, that were essential to make it truly her own book. Her own work. No longer a betrayal of her father or Frau S. Perhaps a betrayal of herself, but for that she was prepared to be responsible. It must be her viewpoint, her side of the story made clear in its context of the three of them. It must be about herself and how she found her way to survive too.

But she was feeling very lonely. She missed Anna more and more. And every time her cat came in, she couldn't forget the other one, who could never return. The pleasure she ought to feel at the one who remained was spoilt by the memories the unknowing creature always brought in with her of the one who was dead. Trailing memories..... She was now permanently in the company of a ghost, which was her other self. How Nora had always seen herself.

She called Agneta, who was eager to hear more about the new, unexpected final solution to the problem of the book. She didn't admit she was worried. What had Nora been up to, with the 'drastic pruning' she talked about? Throwing the baby out with the bath water? But she didn't know Nora well enough yet to realize that if she spoke about pruning, editing, cutting, she was really more worried about putting something in..... or vice versa. Agneta suggested she'd come for a weekend with Marie-France, during which time they could finalise everything. Time was running out.

The following day Anna returned, so Nora postponed Agneta and her girlfriend until the following weekend.

Nora asked Anna if she would pose naked for her in her studio. She didn't want to do any portraits of her, but simply wanted to try and capture the slopes and curves of her body where it reminded her of sand dunes..... But Nora was hoping that the fact of being naked in front of her, might tempt Anna to talk about her various men, in more detail.

Anna stripped willingly, after the usual excellent wine from the cellar, and struck a pose. Nora said it looked too like 'Victory' so she relaxed and tried again until Nora shouted 'Stop!' and Anna froze . . . . . now looking like a mermaid trying to hide the tail. If that is what Nora wanted! But the ruse to make Anna talk, didn't work. Anna claimed she remembered nothing about her lovers. Once gone, forgotten. She gave her body every time - any time - but nothing of her mind. The body was easy to take back. But Nora insisted - at least Anna could tell her what her sexual fantasies were. She said she had none. But Nora argued she must have some, if her father and the psychoanalysts were to be believed, and they had listened to the harrowing fantasies of thousands of people . . . . . crippled people whose minds, being so wounded, could be read like an open book.

'None!' Anna insisted.

'You *must* have fantasies. Without them we can't survive!' Nora insisted.

After many pained expressions, Anna answered, 'Maybe I have only one fantasy, to meet the man who can show me what my real fantasy is! But I don't need fantasy. That's the point. I go along with it *all*. All sex is a fantasy! Just doing it requires going over the edge of the cliff everytime. For me, all sex is theatre . . . . . *that* is why I am an actress and a dancer don't forget! The act of theatre is the central meaning of my life. Not sex. Theatre is first. It is primary. Sex happens to be part of it, though so few people admit it. I'm like Genet. You can only dare to deal with the horrors of reality when you know it is pure theatre. Pirandello knew it too. It was Pirandello who turned me on to the theatre. I saw "Naked". It tore me apart. Ever since I've been "One character in search of a fix"!' She laughed. 'It is the search for so-called truth - the one that is predictable, that is illusory and doesn't exist - that is fascism. As you said, reason is the big con - the trap - the religion for which wars are fought. For me there is no separation, as there is with you, between so-called reality and so-called fantasy. Mere words. It's the words that separate. I can't use words like you. I mistrust them. I know what my body wants. Music. Feelings. Instinct. Intuition. Food. Air. It seems so easy, so obvious. I've thought about what you said, that thinking like we do came very late in evolution and on the evidence, must be a terrible mistake. I do everything I can to descend to my feelings . . . . . even the bad ones. With those, we came through the first ten million years. With reason, we are struggling after two thousand years, joyously breaking the most sacred, fundamental laws of nature. You're right. It depresses me. But there seems to be no escape from the totalitarian vice. I heard someone say the other day they were "born a catholic". I laughed. We are all born pagan and I certainly was - and have remained so ever since.'

Nora said she agreed but it was all too abstract - she wanted to hear about her sexual fantasies! She knew she must have some. She must dream! Why were people so ashamed of their fantasies? Were they a kind of running away from the truth? Anna looked miserable. 'I am on show today. Don't try to penetrate my mind. Just stop at the surface and enjoy my body!'

But Nora felt uneasy. If she could get into Anna's mind and her fantasies, she might dare to seduce her again. Also she would enjoy it then, otherwise it would be meaningless. Empty. If she knew Anna's fantasies, she could manipulate them. She didn't know why she needed to, exactly. Perhaps because she had recently revealed her own. All this talk of rationality! Maybe that was her fantasy, that she could be rational! In the name of rationality, one hundred million people had been legally murdered in the twentieth century alone. Perhaps Anna was right. Better to keep one's fantasies for one's own stimulation . . . . . better keep them secret.

Nora asked, 'Don't you dream of someone who might make it different? Who might tap things you'd not imagined? Who might undermine your certainty? Someone waiting in the wings, some tall dark stranger who in some golden age of the future will waft in and transform everything? Someone who will know you, your innermost secrets, the utter truth, without you having to tell him? Instant recognition?'

'But that implies a future. There isn't one!' She laughed as if mocking herself a little. 'I am a child of the times. Addict of the eternal present. Every day is my last. *So* exciting. Like being in a permanent war. Why hold back, why keep the orgasm down, why postpone for the aftermath? Sex is only fun in the present, the psychotic present. That is where I leave it! When he's there, he's there. Otherwise? I forget it. I desire what is in my hands.

Not what isn't!' She was pouting as if not to be entirely believed.....

'It can't be that easy,' Nora insisted.

'I don't worry about it, as you do. Why make it so complicated? For me it is not complicated, because I don't analyse it all the time. You get further and further away from it, the more you seek a reason for it. I never think about it except when it is there, in front of me, in my arms. I can go for weeks without sex, but suddenly I feel an itch, as if I am about to start a pearl and I start looking around. But that's the point. There is obviously a way I look, because I just look at someone and I think, he's the one, and they never fail to see the sign. I never miss. It is impossible to hide desire, however much you try, for those with eyes to see! He becomes the one, subject to a few qualifications. Must be under ten foot six! The stranger becomes familiar - family - for a moment. That's enough.'

'I don't believe it is ever that easy!' Nora said, convinced Anna's whole detachment and coolness was a pose, hiding something.....

'If you mean, is it always ecstasy? Then no. It's never First Communion ever again after the first time. If you spend your entire time wanting it like that, then it will always fail you. It is different each time. You meet some quite interesting men amongst all the hacks! You get to really talk to people. I like that. The point is, if your expectations are too high, it will fail you. If, like me, you know damn well it is fickle and frail, like most human activities, it's okay. When you go hunting, you don't always catch something. Only some days you bring back a full bag. You must accept it is a very delicate game really, and you win and lose..... and often, there are no winners or losers. Then you will enjoy it, simply, for what it is. And often it will be more than your expectations. Those moments are the ones you never forget and cherish forever. Some of the times I enjoyed, barely scraped the surface. No mutual probing at all. The greatest time might be a man you spent one night with. In your whole life, maybe an hour. Maybe you made love in the back of a Chevrolet, and had a pain in your neck for a week. You enjoy the pain because it reminds you of it. Maybe it was someone you lived with for six months. I forget the ones who hung around, more easily. Because there was time, all the questions were asked and answered. Time to assimilate and forget. Duration is unimportant. The time I remember most of all, lasted only a few hours, and I wouldn't have missed it for anything. And we hardly got going at all, physically.'

Nora attacked. 'So you *do* remember one time as better than all the others. So tell me why. It touched a fantasy perhaps?'

'No. I don't want to. That is the one time I cannot talk about, because it was unique, simple, the best. Pure, pure present. If I talk about it I will spoil it. It must remain secret, because it was perfect. Unexpectedly and by chance, everything was right. Let me keep it secret. And therefore sacred.'

Nora looked wistful, and gazed towards the window. 'You are right. I was like that once. Why did I change and spoil it all?' Anna wasn't sure what she meant, but decided not to push her to explain. She didn't like talking about such things anyway. Not in this analytical way. Joking as girls do, yes. So this was why she was asked to pose naked for Nora's painting - supposedly - to be trapped, unable to escape an interrogation? But she forgave Nora. She knew how fucked up she was about everything, especially sex.

Nora became silent, concentrating on her brush strokes.

Anna was feeling angry suddenly. That was it. An interrogation..... an in-terror-gation. Not an act of caressing with the eyes, not an act of love at all! Some thoughts occured to her and she couldn't stop speaking. 'You delude yourself Nora. You are not really interested in sexual fantasy, or any kind of fantasy. You are interested in knowing..... analysing..... being able to predict and control. Your search is for clarity and structure. Order. Form. What you lack! The very things that sex is *not* about, and should never be about. You are looking for a way out, by thinking. But from what? You are forced into believing there must be fantasy and you betray yourself. Stop looking for rules and hidden explanations. Stop being a fascist! Why else did you go to Paris wanting to be in front of them? When you can forget such thinking, and just fall into the sea and swim..... because you have to..... you will have arrived. When you are swimming, are you thinking about why and how you swim, or why and how we evolved from fish and then lizards and then birds? Why we left the sea in the first place? Why we like to leave the womb to be born? It happens. Just go along with happenings..... nature has its own wisdom.'

Nora was deeply hurt. She almost panicked. She couldn't speak for some time, but she guessed it was the truth. Eventually she managed to say, 'Alas ..... most of the time ..... I even hate swimming too!' And they both laughed ..... much to Anna's relief. She thought she might have gone too far. People who dispensed so much 'truth' as Nora did all the time, about those shifting inward currents of consciousness, those below the surface, hated hearing it about themselves.

Nora was looking puzzled at the drawing she was making. 'The sand-dunes are voluptuous enough!' she said. 'But the sea is out of sight. A mere straight line on the horizon! Must I walk out to it? Or be patient and wait for the tide?'

★

The following day, Agneta rang, full of excitement because she'd met a young woman who was opening a small gallery in St. Germain to be devoted entirely to women artists, to be called 'The Opening'. They were planning some possible projects together. She was keen to see Nora's paintings. 'For us poor Women, at last, it is all happening!' If she liked them, she would be every happy to arrange an exhibition to coincide with the publication of the book. Was there any way perhaps of linking the two ..... in subject-matter, for the advertising, the promotion?

Nora thought about it for the rest of the day. It was exactly what she had dreamed, as if she'd created it by wanting it so much. There was definitely a link between frustrated desire and premonition - no wonder the oracles of ancient Greece had always been women - though not forgetting some poisonous creeping-vine leaves fermented with mushrooms and honey! How could she link the book and her paintings? She mulled over the title ..... 'The Invisible Wall'. Although there were quite a number of images that referred directly to images in the book, she had been developing in new directions since Dorothea had posed for her, and Anna too ..... and since she had 'thrown the first stone' as she hoped. The sea was creeping in for a start ..... moisture to the roots.

She didn't want to make the parallels too close ..... if she could avoid it..... but suddenly she had an idea. She rang Agneta back. 'I have a title for the exhibition, if it happens of course..... 'THALASSA'..... the sea! La mer..... la mère!' Agneta said she would talk about it when they visited her. It all sounded wonderful and exciting..... Gosh! It was going to be such fun!!

Afterwards Nora wrote in her notebook, 'What I will probably end up hiding in the book, might I be able to reveal in the paintings? Perhaps I can be like Anna and enjoy being an exhibition-iste?'

★

Anna was away during the following day, but promised to return for supper. In the afternoon, Nora drove to the town and bought some smoked salmon and filet steak and various small bits and pieces she knew Anna liked. She also bought ten rolls of black and white film..... but only after visiting a commercial studio, where a craftsman made signs..... shop signs mostly, painted on wood or cut out of plastic. She had visited him a week before, asking him to make her a special kind of transparent perspex box..... without a back side, a side on the back. He had rung to say it was ready.

At supper, after letting Nora speak about her book and the pains of cutting, editing, rejecting, losing, maiming, spoiling, transforming, fragmenting - you name it - Anna talked mostly about a new play she was thinking of doing in Munich..... yet another re-make of 'La Ronde', but this time, for the *first* time, written and directed by a woman. She'd not seen the revised play-script but knew it was set in Berlin between the wars and hopefully would be a devastating exposé of the underlying fears of men towards women and how their world was constructed as an attempt to deal with those unconscious fears..... to give the impression they didn't exist. Something like that. Anna would play two different parts..... one was the the prostitute of course.

They talked a lot about such fears..... sol versus luna..... but Nora tried to make Anna admit she was afraid of men too sometimes and afraid of the power of her own sexual feelings ..... Anna thought about it for some time before replying. 'Sex would be terribly boring without fear! If we can't open ourselves to the unknown we are as good as dead. I had an affair with a mountain climber once - and nothing could be more unknown than that, to me! I asked him why he did it - not the sex - the climbing! He told me he was terrified of heights and got so much satisfaction from overcoming his fears!'

Nora laughed. Anna added..... 'Fucked like a Capricorn too. Took his time. Inch by inch to the top! The old goat!' Nora laughed again and was pleased. Anna was more than tipsy and seemed jolly enough for her next project with her.....

After the crème-brulée, and more wine, Nora asked Anna if she would pose again for her, but not for her painting. She wanted to take some photographs..... not ordinary ones..... but through a strange box that had been made for her. With invisible walls.....

Nora was astonished when Anna seemed really confused, embarrassed. 'Sexy ones?' she asked nervously.....

'Well..... perhaps. Yes! But not vulgar. Beautiful sensual images. Naked of course, yes..... but sensuous. A celebration of your body not an exposé.' It wasn't perhaps true, but.....

Anna didn't say yes, and Nora was terrified she was going to say no, but after a further, agonisingly long pause, she murmured to Nora, without looking at her, 'On one condition. A promise. You never see my face! My body yes. But never my face!' Nora was so relieved she went round the table and put her arms round her and gently kissed her on her cheek from behind.

'Of course. Anything you ask. I want the images to be very abstract anyway. I want the box to cut you up..... to fragment the image. I think it will work. I've done some experiments looking through the camera with objects. It is just an idea..... an experiment. I want you to be aware of the point of view, the two eyes that watch, that's all.'

In dreams though she often saw the voyeur as a cyclops..... but watching two people of course..... or the same in reverse.....

Nora took Anna to her bedroom and gave her a black leotard and a black chinese silk dressing gown that had belonged to her mother. She told Anna to go to her room and make herself up - as heavily as possible - almost a mask, with lots of white powder. 'Almost a clown. To make you an object! In case we catch your profile. Call me when you're ready and I'll come for you.'

Nora changed too, into one of her tight black cat suits and made herself up in the same way. There was a tall mirror in the black room in the roof where she would do the photographs and maybe she would take some pictures in the mirror of both of them..... She took a bundle of black underwear from the bottom of a cupboard. Maybe she would use them, as props..... and two black leather whips. Cats of nine tails..... only as props.....

She climbed the stairs to the floor 'in the roof' and unlocked the door of the black room. She had made sure it was very warm.

The walls and ceiling were painted with matt-black paint and the carpet was also jet black. The only window was covered with floor-length black velvet curtains. There was a tall black stool and a black comfortable chair. But also a painted white stool. In the centre of the room, directly under the two spotlights, was an old child's cot, made out of metal, also painted white. In front of the camera on its tripod, on a black table, was the perspex box. If the light was in the wrong direction, it disappeared. According to where the spotlights with narrow beams were pointed, parts of it came into view. At a certain angle the perspex sides cut the image into fragments and distorted some fragments against multiple images of each other. Whatever was seen through the box was reflected in four directions, inside..... the empty back side was always open.....

When she brought Anna into the room, Anna gasped. 'My God! How long has this been here? You can't see anything at all..... except the stool and the bed! It's the weirdest room I ever saw in my life!'

Nora laughed. 'It is my photographic studio. I don't want backgrounds so I painted everything black! You'll soon get used to it. It is very peaceful. Soothing. I meditate here sometimes.' She started some music..... very very quiet in the background. It seemed miles and miles away..... a flute Raga..... the night sky was devoid of moon, was infinite, and yet inside the room..... penetrating everything..... the inside open to an infinite distance.

Nora took many pictures of Anna..... draped over stools, over the chair..... and lying on the floor..... in the black leotard, in the underwear, naked. Sometimes with the whips, suggestively lying across her flesh. Sometimes with her wrists tied. Finally she did some of Anna naked in the white bed wearing only striped stockings..... She finally took some images with herself in the mirror, behind a wooden screen, like metal railings or bars, painted black..... images suggestive of some of those described in her father's book. In her book now..... Frau S.'s images that had haunted her for so long. Once published they would die..... lose their power to repress.

'They will give me ideas for my paintings! Maybe I will use one for the cover of my father's book. Maybe I will get some made into lithographs, hard edged black and white or some printed grey, and then I can use them to paint over..... cut up into collages. I don't know yet. It's an idea that's all..... just an idea. Let's see how they come out. If we don't like them we can always throw them away!'

Afterwards they smoked a little, drank more wine and meditated. But as much as she tried, Nora couldn't reach outer space, getting no further than the nebula of her own body outline, so she suggested they made love instead..... and they made love on the black chair..... Anna still dressed in the striped stockings and a torn black flimsy slip.....

But afterwards, Nora felt awkward and sad. Profoundly frustrated. She knew she'd made a mess of it. There had been no resonance. If only she had the courage to let go, tie Anna to the bed and whip her..... Hadn't they both read all the books? Why then was she so inhibited? Surely Anna might enjoy it if she knew it was an image, a dream that often occurred to Nora, upsetting with its confused edges, its ambiguity? But she didn't really want to *do* it, that was the trouble. Always the same problem. Watch it maybe. She loved imagining-looking at pictures of pretty girls in all kinds of available poses, but hated the responsibility of poking things into them. But hadn't she only suggested it because she thought Anna expected it? Anna had often joked about some of the photo sessions she'd been roped into..... as she put it. Often literally.

★

The following morning Anna left early for Munich to en-role for her new project and Nora worked steadily on her paintings.

From time to time she tried to write the book but it was drifting away from her. All she wanted to do was cut it. Cut whole chunks out. She had decided she would never write another book - of her own, but especially in symbiosis with a text of her father's! It had taken too much out of her. She had been drained by the whole thing. She was going to become a painter. She was starting to really enjoy it. Paintings mixed with photographs perhaps. She'd find some way of combining the two. Dissolving edges, overlapping meanings.

While walking in the garden and talking to her trees, she thought of a way of structuring her exhibition, to give it focus - a clear meaning. She would do a drawing for every single quotation from 'Thalassa' that she had underlined several years before, when she had first read the book. That would teach Raymond a lesson!

But reading the book again, she was disturbed to feel she disagreed with many of Ferenczi's ideas. They still seemed too orthodox at times. But she liked his concern with images, physical images. He related ideas about consciousness and feeling to the nature of the physical world, to the physical body. The psycho-analytical ideas became irrelevant as her 'stolen' text, the quotations, became the focus. She found she could create images that were obliquely different to the words. She found she could make an ironic statement about the phrases, by making an image apparently different to the quote. A symbolic interpretation. She found she could 'say' more, the more distance there was between - separating - the image and the words.

She became more and more excited by this new project, as images and phrases resonated and set up all kind of provocative meanings. She worked every spare minute of the day, obsessed with her images . . . . . and her ironic, tangential interpretations of the Ferenczi text. She copied out the phrases on large pieces of paper and put them on her wall, trying to interpret even some of the most un-visual ones. It was a challenge. She saw the words as masculine, trying to penetrate the feminine images . . . . . and sometimes she wrote words on the drawings, often in red letters.

She took . . . . .

> 'Then occurs the final and decisive battle between the desire to give away and the desire to keep the genital secretion itself.....'

and made an image in which the semen was the spume, hovering on the grey steel knife edge of the pounding waves..... curving into the shape of rocks, like women's breasts and buttocks.....
She started to have fun with the quotations, cutting them up into smaller and smaller fragments until she was only left with single words. But the smaller the phrases the wider their meanings until a single word was effectively meaningless. It was the context that gave it life.
She would start off each day's work, reciting new texts, written in huge black and red letters on white paper pinned on her studio wall, until one would jump out and she'd work on it, trying to find an image that would give it life..... But there were many texts that died before she found a use for them. Too abstract and analytical, but most she could mould to her own uses.....

> 'Excitement engendered by erotic looking, hearing and smelling.....'

This became her image of the voyeur, all eyes and hidden hands..... probing fingers..... opening pages, leaves.

> '..... displacement downwards takes place not only during the sex act but throughout life.....'

A face in which the mouth had become an anus..... with grey hair like sloughed off skins of snakes.....

> 'In the auto-erotic stage of this evolution the sexuality of each separate organ of the body or instinct-component exists in a state of *anarchy*..... which is lacking in all regard for the weal or woe of the rest of the organism.....'

A barricade over which a naked woman's boby is draped, her sex wide open..... soldiers wearing masks.....

> '..... there is no part of the organism that is not represented in the genital.....'

A huge phallus with a face on it..... the mouth, a rose.....

> '..... to regard the phallus as a miniature of the total ego, as the embodiment of a pleasure-ego.'

A naked body, curled up like an embryo, sucking its own erect prick, entitled, 'The fascist.'

> '..... the entire genital warfare rages about the issue of giving up or not giving up a secretory product.....'

A mouth, a knife, a wound out of which semen is oozing, not blood..... an open hand in which is a small pearl or drop of liquid..... in the background, a wall suggesting the ghetto.

'..... the purpose of the sex act, can be none other than an attempt on the part of the ego - to return to the Mother's womb.....'

A street of barricades behind which is a huge vulva and in it, as far as the horizon, a tranquil sea..... as if in a black and white photograph..... framed by the lips.....

> '..... the whole organism achieves this goal by purely hallucinatory means.....'

A girl's vulva in the shape of an opium poppy..... her two fingers touching in a Buddhist guesture..... her toes in the sea.

> '..... gratifies by means of the ejaculation, egoistic tendencies making for the release of tension, but, in the form of hallucinatory and symbolic (partial) return to the womb so unwillingly left at birth.....'

A woman giving birth to the sea and a huge distended phallus..... its mushroom-shaped head forcing itself out into the world, with a small eye in it, like a cyclops.....

> '......the human-being is dominated from the moment of birth onwards by a continuous regressive trend toward the re-establishment of the intra-uterine situation, and holds fast to this unswervingly, by as it were, magical - hallucinations.....'

She couldn't find an image for this one..... A portrait of Anna maybe, as a dead mermaid. Her hands crucified by nail-words.

But this one seemed easy.....

> '..... every symbolic association is preceded by a stage in which two things are treated as one and so can represent each other.'

A prick in a vagina in a prick in a vagina..... leaves..... petals..... mille feuilles. But it was really a drawing of a rose. Its stem and thorns. Three roses as one rose. Falling apart and yet still whole perhaps..... its roots in the sea.

> 'Aggressive impulses are manifested in the sex act in the violence of possession of the sexual object and in penetration itself.....'

A faithful drawing of a photograph from the Warsaw Ghetto of a soldier, seen from behind..... under his feet, drawn in pencil, a beautiful naked girl..... very young. In her hand, a broken twig..... across the bottom, on separate cobblestones, the title, 'Daddy'.....

> '..... the leading zone of genitality, in which in the male is definitely in the urethral, regresses again in the female chiefly to the anal.....

She couldn't find an image for this one either. She wanted to draw a picture of a girl's arm into which a needle was injecting heroin..... but she had never done this to herself. She couldn't lie about something so important. She had always drunk it with wine, to bring momentary escape from reality, not masochistic pleasure. But if she'd had a photograph of Frau S. she would have found a way of mutilating it with words, and using it as a collage..... but her father had destroyed all her photographs.

*

Nora cancelled the visit of Agneta again, saying she needed more time to edit the book. There was the new passage that was proving difficult..... but it had to be there.

Over the next week, working like mad, her paintings became more explicit, even what she might later call 'pornographic', as she fused/confused her layers of meaning..... the beach and the sea, the mother and her child, the penis and the vagina, anus and breast. She could only retain her original obliqueness and subtlety when she was dealing with the child with her stick poking in the mud..... the Ghetto as an anal fantasy of possession..... each image, each phrase becoming interchangeable as she stripped away the cobblestones in search of the sea..... as the little girl, Nora was now convinced, was digging in the hard earth, looking for the sea, her Mother..... rather than being dug into to find the shit. It was her Mother she had been looking for..... as we all were, adrift on a sea of concrete.

*

When Agneta and Marie-France finally arrived, impatient 'to tie things up', Nora took them immediately to the drawing room, where hundreds of images were pinned up, all looking like stills from a black and white movie, hand coloured afterwards with splashes of colour.....

Marie-France was a serious looking young woman, with large spectacles, too large, pale skin, and a sharp efficient face. But she had a pretty smile, a trim figure, and shapely legs.

They both seemed embarrassed at first but then struck a pose of mature detachment. Agneta said they were shocking and Marie-France said they were harrowing - but both agreed they were impressive and powerful and worthy of an exhibition. But it was Marie-France who said, 'Don't use the titles on the pictures. Use them to inspire you, but then throw them way. The images are enough to exist entirely on their own, without any further references, even though the references are provocative. It's going too far. But keep the words inside the pictures, when they are for a reason.'

She said she especially liked the image of the girl, a numbered prisoner in a torn dress being led through a garden by a man's hand. Just part of his uniform was visible. It was entitled 'en parole', the words in red letters on the image, around the hem of her school dress. Agneta suggested, maybe, maybe they could publish a book afterwards, where the quoted Ferenczi lines under each picture could make a very thought-provoking linear narrative . . . . . a meta-text, though she agreed that in the exhibition, the words should be absent. 'It will be much more erotic that way too. There is nothing erotic or romantic about words after all. Not any more . . . . . until women learn to write about their deepest feelings and experiences! Like you, Anna!'

Then they talked business. Because they were eager to start their publishing venture in a few month's time, they wanted to get Nora's book ready for the launch, so it meant instant decisions. Marie-France suggested to come down in the week and help Nora to edit it. Nora was apprehensive, not so much about the book - it had seemed already to have started it's own life - but about Marie-France. She had that predatory air about her. So she said she would go to Paris and stay in her little hotel, promising the book was nearly finished and it would be ready on time.

That night, lying in bed, thinking of Agneta and Marie-France, presumably making love, she thought of Anna. She was glad Anna had been so cutting about her thinking, thinking, thinking, analysing. But her being a 'fascist' as Anna had put it, was still disturbing her. She had never imagined a woman could be a fascist. In truth Frau S. had worshipped at the shrine of fascism . . . . . Maybe the women of Germany were as much to blame for some of the things that had happened. But that was another story . . . . . at least she was starting to lose some of her feelings of aggression, that had such difficulty in finding an object to focus on . . . . . perhaps painting her images was starting to heal something in her. As for the book, the more she seemed to be turning the knife in the wound . . . . .

★

The next day she received a disturbing letter from Raymond. He was desperately hurt and unhappy. He wanted to tell her the whole story, knowing she would understand, but he couldn't. But he had met a young assistant at the laboratory and started an affair with her, even becoming 'serious' about her. Nora's fingers twitched as she read the letter. But, Raymond explained, something terrible had happened.

She had gone to a laboratory in Texas for a month's special study, to observe some new work there in connection with a viral disease that had apparently killed some people in a place called Lassa in Africa. Not blacks but white missionaries and nuns. The blacks seemed to be immune. They had some blood samples from the victims. Some Green Monkeys also from Africa were used in an attempt to cultivate the virus in their blood. Something totally unexpected had happened, that he ought not talk about, as it was being kept highly classified. Later the world would be allowed to know the facts. But he had to tell someone. He knew she could keep a secret. But *not* to tell Anna, who couldn't!

The monkeys apparently, were also carrying some hitherto unknown disease..... a new virus, which was so dangerous to humans it had instantly infected a number of people in the lab. Either that or the viruses had inter-acted in some unknown, unforeseeable way in the monkey's blood producing a new virus. All the people in the lab who had contracted the virus had died - except one - even though every normal precaution had been taken to prevent infection. Whatever it was, it was devastatingly lethal. It had all happened very quickly. The victim had 'flu' for a few days and then the temperature shot up and they were dead. His new girlfriend had been one of them. He was devastated, and the whole community dealing with Immunology had become tense. 'There is more to the subject than we suspected. But work must go on. Alas, from such dangerous experiments, we learn valuable new things.'

Nora felt very miserable that night. Really awful. She was sad for Raymond, but also for herself, because she had betrayed herself. Some part of her had felt glad the girl had died. Raymond might have married her! She hated feeling such aggressive feelings towards another girl, simply because she 'belonged' to a man she felt was close to her. Not belonging, but

close. She knew that love ought not to be possession, but.....
She couldn't hold back those primordial waves of hate. As she
fell asleep, she was thinking again about something she had
wondered about but never actually clarified. Every one of us is
capable of murder. All it needed was an anarchic situation and
all hell let loose.....

Maybe some part of her was preparing herself to try to really
love Raymond..... after all there was no-one else..... but it
frightened her. It was so irrational.

★

For the next week or so, Nora spent all her time in her studio, painting and drawing, quite happy being alone. She received the photographs of Anna and was surprised how weird they were, and didn't know how she could use them. They seemed so different to her other work, almost as if created by another person. She might not be able to use them. They were too naked..... too suggestive of cruelty. The desire to hurt and revenge.

When Anna came back, Nora eagerly showed her the new paintings, and was happy when Anna said she was now 'really getting somewhere', although they would still shock a lot of people. She must be prepared for hostility. Men could make images like that, but not women! Nora said the lab in Paris had messed up the prints of the photographs. She'd get them later.....

That night they slept together, but Nora merely put her arms round Anna and fell asleep. Anna decided Nora was not really interested in making love to her. She had needed to do it, to get it out of the way, maybe just feeling she 'ought' to do it. But Nora did tell her she had decided quite definitely to seduce Raymond ..... 'If you don't mind. After all, he was only on loan!'

She wrote a couple of sweet, encouraging letters to Raymond, saying she was starting to remember the details of the night he had found her, as if it had been a dream that had been temporarily repressed, but she was gaining access to it again. She told him she remembered his face when he first bent down to pick her up, the fire from the burning barricade reflecting on his cheeks, as if he was a salamander that had slipped out of the fire and burrowed under her defences. Her letters surprised him. He couldn't remember any burning barricade, but was flattered the way she was suddenly talking to him.....

She didn't tell him her wound was not healing still, and even getting worse. She was worried about his reacton to it on his return. She hoped it wouldn't put him off..... but it wouldn't heal. The slightest thing opened it up.

She was taking the vie-en-rose again because it seemed to help her to work. To relax. After even a mild dose, a mere touch, all she needed then was a new quote from Ferenczi, and she was away.....

Her images pleased her, at last becoming more fluid, and she knew she was starting to achieve what she wanted. The suggestion that every part of her image was inter-acting with another part, that every shape was male or female, but often both, and all of them part of a whole, and the whole was a kind of voluptuousness. It was not an illusion. On the surface of the images, the parts were really copulating. She knew she had once been capable of that voluptuousness and she would be capable of it again. What Freud - poor guy, he wasn't all wrong, she told herself one day - had called polymorphous perversity. Without being it, you couldn't know it. That is why children were so different from adults. Being without yet needing to know. Open to anything. As she had once been.....

She read more about Ferenczi. She hovered between liking him and rejecting him, many of his ideas deriving from Freud and no longer tenable, but he had come to some brave conclusions about the nature of the archetype of the feminine, which Jung called the 'anima'. But she sensed he was a warm man, a loving man, soft and sensuous and capable of mistakes, who loved women for being different, for being women. He had broken the rules of psycho-analysis and been rejected for it, and in the end, treated by Freud as a pariah. He had kissed his patients..... held them close, and shown affection. He believed in tenderness, and knew that it was this tenderness that his patients had missed as children. That was another kind of abuse, to deny them tenderness. To treat children as objects, often talking about them as if they weren't there, could do irreparable damage. He also wrote that the analyst should be prepared to exchange his position with his patient, and show that he too is

fragile, incomplete, fragmented, and seeking wholeness.....
tenderness..... and he allowed some patients to become the
analyst for a few sessions. Such ideas were anathema to the
orthodox for whom the intellectual fascism was the chosen
ambience. Nora wrote in her notebook that no wonder many of
the patients 'transferred' to the analyst when he behaved as a
cold detached impersonal robot. It reminded them of their
fathers......the analyst merely repeating the mistakes was not
enough. It was taking 'still' photographs. It was not putting
them all together into a flowing line and making the story
whole.....

Why though was she so obsessed with Ferenczi? It seemed
irrational now. Why couldn't she give him up? Afterwards, she
would have to find out why. But she felt close to him. The idea of
him made her feel warm. It was quite irrational.

But she liked his celebration of the feminine, and rejection of
ANALysis. He said that men could never successfully cure
women, because in the very nature of the act of the patient
returning in time to the earliest memories, to the earliest traces
of trauma and experience etched on their minds, if he was
successful, he took the patient back to the time when relating
was impossible. At that stage, only identification occurred.
When the patient has reached these crossroads, the patient
needs a mother and not a father. Thus, the very nature of
psycho-analysis was flawed, because the more successful the
regression in time, the more the patient became a child..... and
sometimes even an infant..... and needed to identify with a
loving, tender mother, *not* a cool, detached, rational father-
analyst. It was probably what she needed too, most of all.

The analytical circle around Freud rejected Ferenczi and he
died a broken, unhappy man. Freud had even supported a
rumour that Ferenczi was totally insane at the end. Through
identification, he had become as mad as his patients, absorbing
their madness. In other words the analyst's code, the detachment, was to protect the analyst! But he was merely broken,
after years of devotion being rejected from the inner circle as if
he was some alien body in their stream of consciousness..... and
the vision they had of imposing it on the whole world. That kind
of madness is invariably frustration, knowing you are right and
the world is wrong.....

In his final days, freed from a lunatic asylum, the great German poet Hölderlin had written, looking back on his life, that his madness has been one simple thing. Frustration. Being unable to communicate the whole truth. Not being able to select a small part of it and be comfortable with it. Nora pondered for a while her own frustration and that of her generation looking back on images of the past, the ghettos and concentation camps, that had been inherited in their blood like falsely mutated genes - image-genes, with their own species of poison. If it was impossible to do anything about them - erase them or understand them - tell the whole truth - what could one do with the frustration? Become inert and immune? Fight the body politic, but with what? Anarchy, because they were was no organised revolt? Find worse images? There was no such thing. Or go quietly mad? Find ways to turn off the world with drugs..... which was an act of aggression in itself, hating oneself? Certainly it was unwise to ponder the images too carefully ..... certainly *not* to identify with them. But it was her childhood..... her inheritance. Her ancestors in the blood. The archetypes. For a while, Frau S. had been mad in that kind of way.

But Nora was now understanding how her father, in arranging for Frau S. to be trained with one of Ferenczi's pupils, had forced her to reject him and his wavering ideology. Only in his later years did he realize she was right and try to revise himself, trying to re-edit all the images into a new montage. That was the story of the book, really. His own self-analysis. Not that of Frau S. at all. But he still loved her and by then it was too late. No-one feels comfortable with an old man who abandons so many early ideas when he is old, because he is lonely and unsuccessful in love. It must have been harrowing for them both. Nevertheless, everything good in her father, Nora knew, had come from Frau S. in one way or another. So had she been right to steal the manuscript? Nora was starting to think so..... and she had been right with her father's book, to cut out everything she felt was false..... and untender. Analytical, rational, unpoetic. Not androgynous, treating the male and female principles and powers as equal in the story of developing consciousness. She had done to the book what Frau S. would have done probably. Maybe she would even accept it now. Maybe. Not that it mattered. She didn't care what she felt. Phallic bitch! She would reveal the deeper truths about herself with her exhibition anyway.....

One morning she made the final decision. Just like that! Or so it seemed..... The book would be a pure novel, and so, being fiction, she could put what she liked into it! Fiction. Fantasy. The imagination, whatever anyone said. Nothing more and nothing less. She'd pare it down to the bone. It was she herself now. Free. Free from Frau S. and her father. It would be pure fiction, not disguised as anything else. Except life maybe..... and she'd found a way of inserting the difficult passages. But it might be fun still, having done that..... to suggest it was a true case-history and confuse everybody - as Freud had done with his abandonment of the seduction theory! Only this time it was back-to-front.....

As to her paintings, she arrived at the same conclusion as Agneta and Marie-France, that it was wrong to have the titles on the images. If the image needed the title, it had failed. She was hoping they were serious about the book of images they talked about..... she could see it already in her mind's eye..... a collage/montage story, a type of photo-roman..... like an illustrated film script, images and words. It was something to consider for the future. And it was the very existence of future - a future tense - no longer clinging to a past - that she needed to believe in. As Frau S. had once written to her father. Her experience inside the ghetto had been entirely that. What else could it be? An eternal present, because time had been stripped of its future tense. And the past had been stolen forever.

Nora felt optimistic..... the future was becoming exciting, almost as if it was growing inside her like a child. She was even making plans. Firstly, give up the vie-en-rose forever! Secondly, she would be content with a modest exhibition. A foretaste of more to come. The book, she hoped, would truly free her from the past. But, most of all, after all the excitement..... she'd allow Raymond to take her virginity..... because it was his really to take. Would he know what an honour it was? Not that such things were valuable nowadays. No shutting up young girls in tribal huts so that the sun wouldn't touch their skin..... no being seduced by mere light! Light, the all seeing father's gaze..... his sexual power embodied in light, with all its threats, and later to be embodied in the light of reason..... the most threatening of all..... because to see and be seen at all was to rip open and desecrate at that sacred, sacrificial time. Once her virginity would have been valuable. Once it was. And she had liked it. It meant *she* was wholly valuable. A valuable expression of being.....

But the times were a'changing..... blowin' in the wind. Either way, if Raymond was impressed or not, it didn't matter. It was now becoming a bore!

Once that was gone, the seventh and final veil, she would be ready to fly on gossamer wings.....

★ ★ ★

Nine

When Raymond finally returned to Paris many months later, Nora's book had just been published. She presented him with one of the limited edition, signed copies. He also just missed the private view of her exhibition, her Opening, but she took him to the gallery, apprehensive of his reaction, although she had held back most of the very erotic images. She was not ready yet for a full frontal attack.

He was very moved..... most of the images were still black and white, with gashes of colour..... limited in texture and style but that was what made the impression of them all together, so compelling..... but the range of her ideas had expanded enormously. Most of all he liked the mysterious blue and green seascapes..... with the ominous black and grey rocks on the beach..... that were like parts of human bodies..... turned to stone. Petrified with fear. At being watched perhaps. But most of the images were sensuous and evocative.

In the months of waiting, Nora had planned an elaborate seduction. She had spent the previous week arranging her house..... the right wine, food, decor, clothes. She even bought him a strange suit that looked like a uniform, with a couple of badges on it. Really it was a hunting outfit made in Austria, in green serge material..... in case she needed, at the last minute, to dress him up in it..... rather than going the whole way and making him into a soldier.

She didn't tell him about the prepared theatre at her house. She took him first to dinner where she had taken Anna. Throughout dinner, she was aware of the wooden spinning top in her pocket. Unconsciously, before the sweet, she took it out and laid it on the table. He said he remembered seeing it the night he had picked her up. 'Picked me up?' she said, 'Be careful what you say! I was never a pick-up for anyone!' He laughed.

He asked her what it was, exactly. Or what she thought it was. He was smiling. He had remembered it clearly, and by chance, now knew exactly what it was .....

She said, 'It is Ancient Egyptian of course. Probably a plumb line. The real thing or maybe an early copy. Roman perhaps. They copied many of the wood and stone objects found in Ancient Egypt. It was not a sacred object, but practical - used for building. I read about it in a book by Flinders Petrie about Amarna. They were used to measure the exact vertical. So a wall could be built exactly straight. As they are now. Either that, or they were spinning tops ..... a kind of toy or game.'

Raymond laughed. 'Not at all! I met a guy in America. A real freak. But he was very clever. He had one almost exactly the same as that. He bought it in Paris, he told me. They are sold in a little shop that sells all kind of esoteric and occult stuff near the Louvre. A modern copy.'

'That's probably right,' Anna said, but insisted hers was a very old one - the real thing. It had belonged to her mother. And her mother was very particular in such things.

He fingered it gently. It was a beautiful object he said, serene in its simplicity. He said it felt and looked genuinely antique, the real thing. Authentic. He noticed a fleck of blood on it, but chose to ignore it. Then he smiled knowingly, pleased to be 'one up on her' for once. 'My friend was into lots of occult things. Dowsing and so on. Tarot. Crystals. But especially pendulums. You see. Look, yours too. It is on a string. It was his theory that it was a pendulum. The Ancient Egyptians knew all the tricks. Magic. Divination. Telepathy especially. Extra-terrestrial communication. My friend said it was definitely a pendulum. He used his for finding oils and minerals under the earth. And water divining. He used to earn all his money in Arabia, where they paid him a fortune for finding water with it. He could just walk across the desert with it, in likely places of course, and whenever it was deflected from the vertical, in a certain way, he knew there was minerals or oil or water under the sand, depending on the degree of deflection.'

Nora was shocked. It was something she had never thought of. But it was obviously right! She had a friend who used a pendulum. She had used it for finding things underground, too. Sometimes she just used maps. She was very good at it. She had taken it up when her mother had been killed in a car crash. Nora had always been convinced she was trying to find the body of her mother, restored to the earth. But she never told her, knowing if she did so, and made her conscious of what she was really looking for, she would lose her powers of divining.....

Nora held it in her hand and stroked it. When she thought about it, it looked like a pendulum. She had once read about Egyptian Magic, a book by Florence Farr, an actress and a member of the Golden Dawn. She had given up her career and gone to live with her lover in India who became a Buddhist monk. The Egyptians had clearly used hypnotism to regress people to former lives. Ferenczi had been fascinated by hypnotism and so was Frau S. Frau S. had written a controversial but convincing case history about a person being 'possessed' by a former identity..... but she never allowed its publication. She had also been fascinated by Steiner's theory that the youth of today were possessed, literally, by the souls of people killed in the last war. Possession, thought Frau S. was often a better explanation of memories of former so-called 'repressed events' ..... they could be from past lives..... past traumas..... past seductions, of children or otherwise. In some cases a child might remember being seduced by her father and it was in a former life. Such things had been revealed under hypnosis. Often they had used pendulums to induce trance..... Nora knew the Ancients were experts at using pendulums. She laughed at herself, wondering why she had got it so wrong. She had missed the most obvious point! It wasn't used when erecting a wall, for finding the vertical..... it was for finding the moment when it was deflected from the vertical..... by water under the ground! Under the cobblestones.....

She was feeling very disturbed. Dissociated. She had not wanted to think about possession. Frau S.'s obsession. It had always scared her. But now, this whole story about the pendulum had disorientated her so much, she decided to abandon the project of taking Raymond back that night. But then she started to panic. She knew she was wanting to run away. She decided she must not do it again..... Her possession must cease to be possession by a ghost..... it must become real. At last. A man possessing her body.....

Coolly, she took Raymond back to her hotel, and booked two rooms, as she had done the previous time. She had one of Anna's red and black outfits with her. She had slept in it at home, whenever she was alone. She drank two double whiskies secretly in her room, while Raymond was in the other room, having been ordered to prepare himself. He was not entirely sure what for, exactly. But with her, he was prepared for anything.....

As soon as she felt her head falling to one side, away from the vertical, she went to Raymond's room and dragged him back to her room, in which she had dimmed the light. She lay immediately on the bed. She lifted her clothes and opened her legs, having bathed herself with oil. She wanted to get it over and done with. He was so excited, he was not going to be held back by anything, real or imaginary......

Nora was amazed how easy it was. It was only the blood everywhere that convinced Raymond afterwards that Nora had indeed been a virgin. Or so she said. She was pleased with herself. She had managed to do the whole thing without showing Raymond that her head wound was still infected and weeping slightly.....

In the morning they made love again..... cautiously at first, but then it was fine. Then Nora insisted he take her in her bottom, because, she said, cheekily, the torn membrane was sore and might become infected. He was amazed at her precociousness, but was too overcome with desire to question anything. Nora decided she had wasted an awful lot of time, for no good reason at all. Maybe. Now at last, she might stop opening up her wound at night, in her sleep, with her fingers..... or with the spinning top. No! The little pendulum......

*

At breakfast in the little café in the square, she made him talk about his work. He said it was top secret. He couldn't tell her too much. He was hoping to carry on with the research in Europe, but wasn't sure where. The work was being funded by the Military. She tried to force him to tell her more, but he said he could only hint at the truth. The government had evidence, so they said, that the Russians were developing certain chemical and bacterial weapons. The Americans had come up with an idea to develop a kind of vaccine or artificially produced virus. It might take five years to develop, and many years to test, safely. The main purpose of the product, was to break down the human defence system. It might be an ingenious way of wiping out a whole enemy.

Nora said it was a frightening idea, and morally wrong. Raymond assured her there were thousands of side effects of the research that would be beneficial. It was all part of finding out how the immune system worked. It was merely a way of getting extra finance, really, and already there was evidence that certain viruses might have come intact, and in huge swarms, from outer space. Probably the remnants of old comets. These alien viruses might one day be lethal. Like those ducks in her pond! The unwelcome visitors that he was expected to shoot..... It was imperative to know everything possible about the way to deal with such things..... such invisible enemies that lurked in the blood and fluids of the planet, which in one blow, could wipe us out.

He said he was expecting to go back again in a week or so, for a few months. He didn't say Jane was meeting him there.

Nora didn't mind he was leaving. She knew she needed some time, maybe even a few years, to get herself organised, by herself, on her own, before she took things too seriously. She was grateful for the way he had taken her, tenderly, and without too many questions. He wasn't at all sure if she hadn't been cheating about her virginity, but it really had been difficult at the beginning. He wondered how she had done it, if she was cheating.

He didn't know that she was very sore indeed and had faked nothing at all, perhaps for the one and only time in her life.....

★

Later in the day, alone, she went to her Exhibition to listen to people's comments, but no-one was there. She looked at the comments in the visitor's book. She was surprised that no-one had mentioned anything about sex, or sensuality or the erotic. The images might well have been real rocks, a beach and the sea..... a stick in a child's hand poking in sand or mud..... the hint of a torn skirt or underclothes in the corner..... trees, branches, seeds, roots..... visible stone walls..... real cobblestones and barricades, and not obstacles between people. It occured to her, maybe not one of her images was the least bit erotic. No other person could know, after all, what such things symbolised for her..... or at least..... had done so for so long..... Images of the past from which she hoped she might never be free.....

★

In the evening, Nora wanted to be alone. She stayed in the hotel, thinking. The phone in her room rang several times and she knew it was Raymond. She had told him she would call him, but had not said when. He had assumed she would need to see him, after their shared 'rite'..... and he couldn't face being alone, not having really talked about it. He was desperate to see her after she had gone to so much trouble to convince him, true or not, that she had chosen him to be the first one to take the momentous step. He was afraid he had failed her in some way, because she didn't call him, wanting to see him. Or, much more likely..... as she probably always had done in the past..... she had indeed cheated him. Maybe being a virgin was some kind of fantasy that turned her on..... and she acted it out every time. That seemed much more likely knowing how secretive and devious she was. But if that was what turned her on and gave her the most access to pleasure...... what right had he to grumble? He'd given up trying to understand women and their peculiar attitude to their own sexuality anyway. As long as they took him to bed, for whatever reasons they kept to themselves, that was enough. The body did the rest.

But he was missing her desperately. Damn her! She'd done it again. And he'd forgotten to ask her for Anna's telephone number.

★

The following morning, without contacting Raymond, Nora set out early to drive back to her house in the country, listening to her tape of spaced-out excerpts from the 'German Requiem', singing a different song altogether in opposition to it but hardly noticing the dissonance and wondering why she would never see Raymond again, or at least wondering why she was wondering. It was obvious really. That particular movie was over.

She turned the volume of the tape down. She still couldn't turn it off completely but it became so faint, the folk-song she was singing sounded less off key. At last she could look forward to being silly and childish and careless. She hoped Anna might be there . . . . . and if she was, she'd insist they got drunk and had a wild party, just the two of them, to get each other softened up for what was to come. Then they would invite all their friends from Paris for the weekend - her theatre friends and the poor lost souls of the anarchist group they had belonged to, if they were not all working for I.B.M. She'd throw open the doors of her house - no longer her asylum from life - and everyone could bring along a stranger and they'd all get stoned out of their minds and if it didn't become an orgy, then the Swinging Sixties had died, nine months short of the decade's end . . . . . She'd fork out for an up-and-coming - forgive the expression - pop group . . . . . as loud and crude as they could find . . . . . all raunch and not the slightest finesse . . . . . riff raff . . . . . and if Mathieu came, she'd show him a thing or two in bed . . . . . Why had she been so dumb and wasted so much time? Not that the sex was much to write home about, let's face it, although it had its moments and as Anna had often said, you meet a lot of interesting people that way.

She stopped to get petrol in a small town, drank two cocacolas from the ice-box in quick succession - she'd never felt so thirsty - and she had to start - gettin' to like coca-cola - yanked out the Brahms tape and bought a tape in a small music shop near the garage of The Rolling Stones instead, 'Between the Buttons' . . . . . nearly invited the young guy in the shop back home, but decided not to. Not yet. Not there yet.

Drove on.

Humming along with the music, she was thinking fast. It was time she became more sociable and got involved with what was really happening. Maybe there *was* a revolution still occurring. Such things didn't happen on the streets really. That was when they accidentally boiled over, or were provoked to do so by a curious juxtaposition of accidents. When the spiral of events cracked under the strain, at a cusp as it was called, and all hell was let loose. Pandora's box spilling over as it must from time to time. The May events had merely resulted in increased and more organised repression by the police and the State. The revolution's aims had failed totally to change things on the outside. Now it was worse and it would get ever worse as time went by. Change must be wrought in a more subtle way. Through the spirit. She wasn't an anarchist any longer, if she ever had been one really. She was now regretting the money she had dished out, month after month to Mathieu and his hangers on - petty crooks, pick-pockets, drug pushers, so-called bank robbers like Mathieu himself - 'Nationalise the banks - or we'll rob them!' - frustrated bourgeois girls and other assorted romantic dreamers - in those heady days - before it had culminated in the May events. Mathieu! What a joke! But he had worshipped her and maybe it was her fault. When had it been? March..... two months before the events..... when he was already planning the bomb for the TWA offices near Place Opéra..... at last she had decided he deserved the reward he really wanted and had gone to bed with him. Oh the hours of preparation, trying out all of Anna's gear! What a night that had been! Thank God she'd resisted him to the last, poor sod. Hardly a leader of men. It took him all his time to keep sixteen pill heads to a once-a-week, hush its secret, anarchist shout-out. Still he meant well..... risked his neck a few times..... got caught for speeding twice..... he just wanted to make a better world by blowing up the old one first. But the build up had seemed fun, she couldn't deny it. She'd been as dumb as the rest. Dumber. It was her money they sucked. But come early May, the first few days shooting had been messy. Everyone getting their lines wrong. She'd been right to get out. When it happened, the movie was being directed by the wrong directors.....

She stopped at a phone box and tried to ring Anna, lovely crazy mad delicious sexy Anna - at a number she 'might' be at, but no-one answered. She was never anywhere at any number. That was her charm. No numbers or any thing could ever pin her down. Except for the duration of a moment's fleeting passion, when any number was available. That was the essence of her desirability. Addicted to the present. You need never feel responsible for her. She was truly free. Why couldn't the whole world be that way? Fleeting but joyous with it. If it was, would it all grind to a halt as they said? Oh Anna! Was it only her unpredictabilty that embodied her seductiveness? That, yes, and her Carol Baker baby-doll mouth and Shelly Winters breasts and strawberry jelly wobbly bottom and golly-wog head of black, manic pubic hair. What man or phallic woman could resist her? But even Anna.....goddamit.....under her own roof.....she'd failed to enjoy! Too busy with her wretched book and boring psycho-analytical ideas. What an idiot she'd been.....

She drove on. Maybe she'd miss her village and drive on to the end of dying earth and fall over the highest cliff, joyously, into the sea.....la.....m.....a.....m.....e....r....e....mama .....ma.....mary glands.....

.....but her mind was racing on ahead, free-wheeling now, almost.....she was getting there.....going home but not home, going places.....

......The revolution was always going on in our blood, which we leach from the mother like her milk, even in the womb .....wasn't it happening in the blood, all the time? The desire for freedom. For freedom to desire..... She'd get in touch with Raymond and ask him to look for the desire-corpuscles..... they must be there. No-one thought of looking for them. Maybe the more you fucked, the more you created them. Was it all merely hormones? Ah well, if that was so, here's praise to the little chemical buggers! But somewhere they had to convince somebody! She'd write to Raymond and tell him he was barking up the wrong tree, or sniffing it like a dog. There was a sexy black goddess living inside the heart, in her secret chamber, with a sieve made out of bone from a whale's nose, filtering the blood, just as the ancients had always known. She was in touch with the angels.....who dream us.....and Anna knew all about dreams. She said they were caused by a psychedelic drug called 'hypnotamine' that seeped into the blood as you masturbated in your sleep, to tune you into the floating minds of the not-really-dead who were desperate to talk to you.....and advise you, if you were smart enough to listen. Darling Anna.....Salomé, kissing the head on the silver plate, the head of the depraved Prince of Future sons of Christ Rationalists.....all set to start the Cosmic Light Company selling heaven and hell.....the only two options once you ate the bread and drank the wine. Baptism my arse! Who were they trying to fool? One day she'd find someone to do a ballet with Anna.....and Anna would play a voluptuous tree spirit, the one inside the tree that was cut down and made into the cross. She'd be singing to Him, oh why the capital 'H'? - still trapped inside the axed wood, trying to tell him he'd got it all wrong. She was the fruit of the sacred tree. To understand the holocaust you had to understand the demand made on the human spirit by reason..... and it was the Jews and the Christians with their monotheistic, self-castrating Oedipussy rationalism, who were responsible for pushing human hope too far..... so that it all went snap. Cracked open like an addled Ostrich egg in the desert sun. All hell let loose. They gave us hell on earth and transformed the world into its image..... and filmed it to prove that if you think about hell and sin and guilt and repression and hell and hell for long enough, it happens..... and yet we must learn to forgive ..... they were only victims of a whole complex of ideas they'd been sold, taught to barter with at the market, filthy lucre ..... ideas and images castrated from their source..... and women could be castrated too, as they were in Africa..... and what was Aphrodite but a penis cut off from the baby-munching father and thrown into the sea..... as the ancients knew with their all-seeing eyes..... now we see through the photographic lens, darkly..... Anna, gorgeous voluptuous sexy Anna Aphrodite..... you who contain it and generate it, the sperm and spume, that devilish potion that sunk into the depths of the miraculous seas where the sirens swam..... a potion that persuaded the fish to grow arms and legs and lizards to grow wings and the algal slime to mould itself the shape of dreams and out walked man on all fours..... opening the doors of perception until his blood told him to imitate giraffes and strive for the highest branches and the highest fruits and he stood up on his back claws and it wore down the sharp talons but the sharpness went up and up into his brain and he invented sin and guilt, those imaginary heavy metal wings that are designed only to make us fall, without which we could not become victims of the crooked priests and state..... but as an afterthought, someone invented forgiveness..... but by that time it was too late..... the human spirit had been born, briefly like a butterfly on its one day's flight from eternity..... and now it was dying again..... in the flames.....

Anna had given her some pills to stay awake. She'd taken

four. STAY AWAKE! My God Anna, what do you take to get carried away?

..... Anna where are you? Scarlet woman, Whore of Babylon? But she was crying now. She had to slow down because of her tears. She switched on the windscreen wipers but they didn't take away the smears, the brine and acid tears. Wasn't the car her body after all? So the adverts were wrong. Anna had once done a filmed commercial for a Volkswagen Beetle ..... she was told to drape across the bonnet as if she wanted to make love to it, as usual wearing next to nothing next to nothing ..... and she got so horny she said, fancying the cameraman, if the wretched animal had suddenly sprouted a metal prick she would have sucked it off ..... Eros and Thanatos ..... the truth would have been the same couple after the crash. The tangled metal and flesh, fused together at the speed of light and sound ..... image and soundtrack united again at last, the here and now, but the sea was still running away with the sun outside of frame .....

But she was crying so much she had to slow down almost to a stop, but then she was off again ..... faster now .....

..... Why wouldn't it rain and she would know she still had power over nature's bio-rhythms? Imagine the sun, it heated up the sea and sucked it into the sky and it rained on people's faces, and they drank it and it became tears ..... and blood ..... her head was still bleeding! Why didn't she think of such things still, as she did when she was a child? Awe and wonder were the true parents. The man and woman acting as if they were, were mere outcasts from the sacred garden. An apple a day keeps the the doctors away and their sacred message, that an apple a day keeps the bowels functioning. Doctor Faulkner ..... You were sweet really. You still had a childish sense of wonder, despite your dedication to a life of desire for the less and less, the smaller and smaller, the more and more victimised. One day you'll look into a microscope having found the ultimate aggressed, threatened particle, that can withstand the entire immune system, that fucks it all up. The secret it of it all. Now we can work back from that and see how it works! The answer to the burning question, how, rather than why? You'll turn up the microscope's magnification and see a small part of its reflecting mirror broken off. In its scarred sacred surface, your own scared face. Yourself! Something you could have known all the time by loving yourself.....

..... Wonder was knowing that in the spume of the sea, were all kinds of simple beautiful creatures dying to be born..... dying in a trance.....

She turned up the music. What fun it was all going to be ..... not needing to care any longer. Just to be herself. To say okay - carry on with your world. I'm not going to be part of it! She would go somewhere beautiful. With her money, if she ever got it, she would take Anna round the world, three times ..... gathering herbs and mushrooms all the way..... and learning how to make love to her properly and be loved in return. And sharing lovers along the way..... and at night she would curl up against Anna's breasts and murmer, mummy, mummy..... instead of clinging to the silk sheets as she had done for so long and murmured, daddy, daddy..... gone were the days..... gone..... gone..... if she could just hold it all together. The next week might be the danger period. Struggling down the vaginal passage a second time..... she must practise not waving her arms about when she was excited.....

..... This time round she would embrace the whole world - not the narrow en-ghettoed world of her father's worst fears ..... the whole world of mummy and daddy seen as one..... yin and yang in permanent copulation to make the whole..... not in murderous competition. She could love her own body, her own feminity now..... and celebrate it. And share it, even with men occasionally who would go on being mystified, and lost, which was their apparent myth and they were clinging to it, but in their mystification there was passion..... and that had to be respected......they all reached shore occasionally on the stinking, corpse-laded empty boat, guilty about the slain white bird, but ready to tell some tall stories..... Oh les beaux de l'aire..... the poet souls in the bodies of the albatross.....

..... It would be her mission now - if that wasn't too strong a word - to be an artist of sorts and create work that was not about herself and her own personal problems, but about the angst, still about and growing like cancer, that was infecting everyone open to life..... The zeit-geist - the ghost of time - everyone was suffering in exactly the same way as she was, deep down, beneath the surface details. They were all the same victims of the same forces. Now it was going to be fun. She'd almost had a break-down, trying to persuade herself that Raymond hadn't been chosen by the Gods! Had he not rescued her, like Frau S. had been rescued? But the blow too! No. It was all different but she had tried hard to put the pieces together, glued by the false significance of coincidence. In the end he was as good as any other passing stranger. She'd been broken by someone else, long ago. Now she'd broken out. All in front of her was open space..... vibrant with the need for her to express her new-found passion. Passion no longer focused into a single act! What cruel confidence trick that had been. Those wily old patriarchs of old! We can't have our daughters, let others pay! And thus rationality was born from their swollen prick heads, and guilt from their atrophied balls. Passion to change people and take down more walls, the walls they were putting up every day..... if you let them.....

..... Oh Anna? Can I do it? Do I have it in me? I think I can see the way ahead? Or will I retreat again into my lair? Is there anyone now who can stop me? Anyone? Anyone? Anyone but HER? That woman! The other woman, without whom there can never be the delicious forbidden taste of betrayal..... Will she try? Or will she leave me alone..... leave me free at last? Oh if only she too would die! If only I could dare..... to kill her too.....

She was going too fast now. She nearly hit a truck on a corner. But the speed was exciting. Was it cocaine maybe, slipped cheekily into some other capsules? No! That was different. Anna had said they were calling it 'Sunshine'.....

..... it was something new. New! Ecstasy, something new? As new as the Shamans of Mexico, and they'd been talking to the Gods for five thousand years. It was as new as that. Merely five thousand years old, this new way of thinking and seeing ahead. Seeing for seeing and not merely for looking at. Voir pour voir, et pas pour regarder. Luc Dietrich had said that after taking a whole film of identical photographs of a close-up of a wall. The shop-keeper said, Sorry they didn't come out! But they did! he said. He wanted to see if the wall had a soul. Everything was coming round full circle. Reason had failed. Any fool could see that, surely? But the new way of thinking was going to take people by surprise. There would be a lot of pressure against it. Even bigger black marias, and tanks and guns. All of that, again, against a few people who said there would be green rays you couldn't see..... but who meant really, that they believed in feelings rather than ideas, of going down down rather than up up. Down towards the feminine soul, the daugher soul, in its rivers and valleys, and not towards absence..... above the summits..... where double-headed eagles soared on metal wings, on illusory mental thermals the hot head fascists had called spirit.....

She had tried to give her father access to her soul..... because he didn't believe he had one. In the clefts, the cusps of the dark valleys where streams flowed.....

And then she saw the huge truck coming at her..... it was on the wrong side of the road..... surely? It was on the wrong side! Oh had she spun round and was going backwards? Backwards?

So..... she was going to be cheated. She knew it! Yes. She had been reborn only to die.

Why was it taking so long? Would it be better if she closed her eyes?..

Would she see her whole life flash past like a billion single frames of film going through the projector at the speed of light, or would it be the speed of sound - as safe as sound - bloody fast anyway? But there was silence. No-one would tell her the truth.

She closed her eyes and slammed on the brakes, surrendering ..... to something. Someone, some one maybe. The power of one to infinity. Was it one, or infinity? Or both? A paradox? Mummy and daddy fucking.....

If only she had been close to the sea and could have flown over a cliff into it. She heard the brakes screaming. All screaming was a kind of braking. And the car slurred to a stand-still. Jug Jug Jug Jug silence.

Still. A single frame.....

As still as defeated time, known as death or absence..... being yonder.

She felt something lifting out of her body and away..... leaving the broken wings behind for a new body..... next time she would be a bird and truly fly. Wise enough to avoid cats. She was fed up being stone.

It was pouring with rain. Why hadn't she noticed? She could hardly see through the windscreen.

But there was no truck. Had it passed by on the other side?

She turned round quickly. It was one of those long roads, dead straight, dead straight for miles with two neatly planted rows of Plane trees, proving man's geometric ingenuity, planted on either side for motorists to crash into, at the smallest lapse.

She was scared now. She was going over the top ..... she had been warned. The lorry was probably her beret slipped over her left eye. Fancy dying, just for that? Was happiness even more dangerous than angst? Until you got used to it .....

Yes .... still a victim after all .....

She drove the car very very slowly now and was relieved when she realised where she was, a mere kilometer from her neighbouring town. She limped into the town-centre and parked the car in the market square. She went to a shop and bought some things she needed. She was feeling very nervous and shocked. She was even more shocked some days later when Anna told her the pills weren't 'Sunshine' after all but some tranquillizers to relax you and help you sleep. She'd got the two boxes mixed up. They did make some people utterly miserable. Most people just crashed out, glad to be able to switch off the world.

Maybe she'd slept all the way ..... with her dead father .....

She took a taxi back home, not daring to risk the final few kilometers.

★ ★ ★

Ten

When she arrived at her house, Nora was alarmed to see a large car parked outside the gates, although she recognised it immediately. A black and silver 1932 open-topped Mercedes Limousine - now almost priceless, and probably the one used by Himmler. She told the taxi driver to drive in front of it, got out and shouted, 'On my account!' She opened the two locks on the huge gates, surprised to find she'd only locked one of them, and although it was still raining lightly, she walked through, head high, her lovely black hair glistening and blowing in the wind. She was about to close the gates in front of the other car, but realizing she was being too bitchy, she waved it to drive in. Once inside it stopped for her, but she walked ahead, up the long drive in the centre of the road so the car had to follow behind, slowly.

The limousine parked in front of the house and the uniformed chauffeur opened the door for Frau S., who emerged elegantly. She was looking immaculate, wearing a three-quarter length black coat with a voluptuous fur skin collar, leopard or jaguar, shining and new, obviously recently killed and imported illegally. Nora thought to herself..... 'Now the big cats have been hunted almost to extinction, trust her to collect their skins.....'

As always, Nora caught her breath when she saw how beautiful she was, how well preserved. The ravages of time had passed her by. Having so much money must have helped, Nora reminded herself begrudgingly. Her cheek-bones were too smooth and perfect still, for her age. Nora knew the skin must have been stretched over the delicate bones underneath, pulled tight, cut and then stitched, by the most expensive hands that money could buy. Nora was flushed by a montage of images ..... metal and skin, the metal blades that could kill and skin leopards but also make women beautiful again.

Frau S., also cold as steel, was looking her straight in the eye and Nora shuddered. This woman still had the power to make her shake in her boots, with her haughty look of Marlene

Dietrich. But to the chauffeur, Nora couldn't resist whispering cheekily in a broad American accent, 'Thaaannnnks Eric!' She didn't know his name, but his pseudo-military uniform reminded her of many things, not least the film that Frau S. had written a lengthy, highly acclaimed psycho-analytical critique of.....
'Sunset Boulevard'. Quite formally Nora shook her gloved hand and said politely, her German accent now suddenly strong, 'I am pleased to see you again, after so long. Von't you step inside?' Nora spoke better English than Frau S. so had always spoken to her in English.

Nora showed her into the drawing room and asked if she would like tea. 'Yes darling, Darjeeling preferably!' she drawled without emotion, smiling patronisingly. But her eyes betrayed her. Nora was sure she could detect a certain reluctant warmth. She seemed unexpectedly relaxed. Not as cold and tense as she had been on their previous meetings.

Nora went to the kitchen to make the tea. She'd picked up a letter pushed through the door by her gardener, and she sat down at the table and opened it.

'Darling Nora - unbelievable news. You are going to be even more rich - and even more famous! We have been approached by a film producer, working with Paramount. He has read your book and wants to buy the Feature Film Rights immediately! He says it will be a very serious film but it could also be very commercial. He seems a nice chap. Quite young. He's American but makes films in Europe. He might try and get Truffaut to direct it he says. Wow! Or Bunuel!?

Why did you change your phone number? Was it because of Raymond, as you said you might? Naughty girl. But serve him right, leaving you when he did. Please call immediately. Come to Paris and we'll find a good agent to represent us both. The producer guy is quite handsome. No names mentioned yet! Better be careful! We don't want to lose you to the movies already. Better get writing your book about Anna immediately. Maybe "The Prodigal Daughter" might be a good movie title after all. A Sixties Salomé. Weren't we all? Just make it sexy! Not so many heavy ideas this time. The producer said he might have to cut most of them out and leave

only the story. If the money is right? He wants it to be in English and not American. Enlightened guy! He thinks Paul Schofield for Helmut. An unknown German girl for Nora. As for Frau S. Jean Moreau in her prime of course, but who in England has that kind of mature charm? We'll go to Munich together shall we and Vienna to "cast the daughter".....It will be fun looking! This is the BIG TIME!
  With love, Agneta and MF.'

★

Nora folded up the letter and put it into a chinese tea pot. Not the one she was intending to use for the tea.....

She heard Frau. S. playing the piano. She could never resist touching something precious and rare, like an immaculately preserved Bechstein Grand. Nora thought she must be in a good mood. Normally she played heavy German music, like Schoenberg or Bartok. This time she was playing Strauss Waltzes instead. Maybe she was trying to put Nora falsely at ease.....

Nora slipped quietly up to her room, powdered her nose and checked her make-up, adding some lustre to her lipstick and blue shadow to her eyes. She fondled her breasts and pulled down her sweater, surprised her body still looked the same, showed no outward signs after her rite of initiation, of dismemberment so to speak, the previous night.

She took the tea into the drawing room and Frau S. stopped playing the piano and sat down on the sofa opposite her. They sipped tea in silence. Nora was going to force her to throw the first stone.....

'So here I am again, after so long! But this time I come to praise the daughter of Caesar! Congratulations on the book Anna. It was fascinating and moving. It will be a great success. It will bring you and your father, much respect, I am sure of that. And you managed to do something that I didn't think you were capable of, at your tender age, and bruised as I know you are. You wrote about very delicate subjects in a most respectful way. Without bitterness. Congratulations!'

She spoke so gently, Nora felt sure she must be telling the truth. Could she be so cruel as to start like this, if she was intending to turn it all round and attack? But with her, anything was possible. Nora'a knees were shaking. She was surprised how relieved she felt, thinking it was all going to be smooth, but it would have been unfair, she knew, if Frau S. had reacted negatively. 'I did my best to respect everyone concerned!' she said somewhat coolly. 'Which is why I called it fiction of course.'

'You did more than show respect. You created poetry. You took human suffering of the most perilous, intangible kind, and made it touchable . . . . . and touching. I was very surprised, I do confess. Very surprised. As you know, I was expecting something very different. I had always expected the worst, with that material, in anyone's hands. But I was wrong. You produced the best. Thankyou!'

Nora could see Frau S. was on the edge of becoming emotional, which was most unlike her. She too was becoming more tense though, after the initial optimism, and her head wound started to throb and the pain was suddenly quite penetrating and sharp. It was a sign of impending troubles. She had been dreading any new kind of emotional confrontation after the extremes of the previous weeks. The publication of her book, her exhibition and Raymond deflowering her. God she hated that expression, but it was the one she always used, involuntarily.

'Did you visit my exhibition?' she asked Frau S.

'Yes. I was coming to that next. Of course I did. And it moved me to tears! It is hard to tell you how surprised I have been. I feel slightly shocked that I underestimated you. Of course . . . . . I knew you would have to change your father's book. As it was, it was useless. Too rational and naked. Wooden. Hopelessly indulgent, and completely untrue most of it. Pure fantasy. But I thought you might make it worse, out of reverence to him. I had no idea you would have the courage to change it, transform it so radically. Of course, and don't be offended, it no longer reflects many of your father's ideas . . . . . of his case-history as he called it. But that doesn't matter. You were right to say it was a kind of novel, an autobiographical novel based on your father's texts. The fact that it will be accepted for some time as your father's text and ideas as well, don't let it worry you. You have plenty of time. You need not discredit him. You need *never* discredit him if you show so much care as you have done so far. In the meantime you must carry on painting. You have the promise of great talent. One day you will write more novels and I await your development with much interest. You are a very talented young woman and grow more lovely every time I see you. Why on earth are you still living here alone, in this heavy, dreary house? Merely to keep legal possession of it?'

Nora was overwhelmed by Frau. S.'s congratulations. All this on top of her trip in the car! She held back her tears. 'No, not really. I feel the presence of my father's spirit here. But anyway, I prefer being alone. I can only work when I am alone. Except the book. After the manuscript was taken, I needed help. I used someone. Yes alas, I used him, that is the word. He came here while I wrote my book. He suggested I narrate it into a tape-recorder. One long stream of consciousness monologue! I was afraid it was awful at first. A kind of verbal diarrhoea! But it turned out to be fine as you see. We have hardly changed a word. It's a novel, a long way from the truth, pure fantasy perhaps. But it was not me writing it really. It was another person talking through me. I was possessed. So maybe it is the truth after all, which I never knew. How was I to know who possessed me? I wonder who it was?'

Frau S. smiled, knowingly. This was her territory and she was glad Nora had phrased it that way. 'You have put your finger on the true mystery of human consciousness. We all hear voices all the time. Our stupid culture tells us it is all us, me, the ego. Very few people want to believe we are mere lenses through whom others may speak as well as we ourselves. If we allow ourselves to be receptive, passive, like mothers receiving the sperm inside their wombs..... we can be moulded by those voices, those forces of love and a direct message from nature's own mind too sometimes.....'

'And *your* novels mother, did you write them in the same way?'

Nora had made a slip. She had called her mother..... She pinched herself on the wrist, she was so annoyed with herself. If the Egyptian plumb-line, the pendulum, the fetish had been in her hands, she might have dug it into her wound from annoyance and frustration.

Frau S. looked down at her hands. She fiddled with her rings. One ring, a gold one with lapis lazuli stones, was also from

Ancient Egypt, recently smuggled out from a new, secretly opened tomb. 'Er..... my novels. Er..... yes. I suppose so. Everything seems to be created by tapping into some profound inner source of being..... in that sense, yes, always.' But..... she couldn't control herself. Nora's slip of the tongue had unnerved her, thrown her off balance. Nora was usually so cool. So bitter. So absolutely in control, dishing out hate as if it was something precious, artful, hard to have honed out of the bedrock of human instinct. She knew her hardness was probably Nora's only means of self defence and she had become immune to it. But now, this slip of Nora's tongue..... it was too unexpected.

She turned away so Nora might not see her. But she couldn't stop herself and started to weep......staying correct and upright and still on the edge of the sofa, but looking towards the marble fireplace with its carved caryatid figures, away from Nora, tears falling down her cheeks. Suddenly Nora noticed that her cheekbones, in profile, which had been so smooth before, appeared to be wrinkled now..... as her mascara ran down them in dark rivulets. But Nora herself was trembling ..... her hands were clenched. She had made a mistake to call her mother.

Nora went to her and broke down immediately, she too drowned by floods of tears. She knelt down in front of her..... but for a fraction of a second she remembered how Raymond had done the same, kneeling down on the floor in front of Anna..... then she thought, why do such images insist on surfacing at the very worst times, as if they are determined to hurt us? How can you escape, when your own unconscious becomes your worst enemy? Even as she was crying, she was trying to think herself out of it. But she lay her head in Frau S.'s lap. Her hands clutched Nora's head and it hurt the wound, but Nora burrowed into her lap and her mother pressed her hard against her body..... and they both sobbed..... and the tears they both shed came in wave upon wave..... together..... as they tried to erase the scarred memories of the years of silence and separation..... since Frau S., her mother..... had left the house and Nora and her father..... ten years or so before.

Nora could only say, 'Mother..... mother'..... and her mother could only say..... 'My child, my child'......feeling so upset, she fell back on the sofa. Nora snuggled up close to her, half on top of her . . . . . and they lay next to each other, like that, for some time, like two lovers who had just made love. While Nora lay there, her mother's heart beating so hard she could hear it resonating in the bones of her skull, a thousand images seemed to pass through her mind . . . . . a collage of recent memories, all of them messed up and confused, from her various versions of the book and many of them recalling the images in her exhibition . . . . . all of them unexpectedly erotic. Was she now discovering her eroticism had belonged all along to her mother? She knew, if she had been a man, she would have seduced the woman lying next her, passionately, as Anna had said . . . . . from relief. But she was grateful not to be a man, after all. Even though such distinctions had ceased recently to seem so important.

After what seemed an age, their emotions came under control and they pulled gently apart and looked intently into each other's face, managing to smile and finally, to laugh. 'We look like a couple of witches after a Sabbat!' her mother said.

'We are a couple of witches,' Nora murmured and her mother agreed it was probably true.

Nora said she needed another cup of tea and went to the kitchen to make it. Her mother joined her there, and sat down at the kitchen table, wiping her eyes with a Dior handkerchief.

It was now difficult for them to talk. There were too many things to say, it was impossible to know where to begin. They also had to learn a new language and as Nora thought about it, listening to the kettle boiling, she wondered if she should do as Ferenczi had suggested to his patients . . . . . persuading them to act as a child . . . . . she should go and sit on her mother's knee, and talk baby sounds . . . . . the first beginnings of a new language. Instead of doing it, she told her mother what she had just thought instead, and her mother smiled. 'You are a clever girl. Quite right. You make the right connections. You can do it if you want. But maybe you don't need to, now you admitted the desire for it. In so many ways I am very proud of you!'

Nora couldn't stop herself saying it, it had become so instinctive to do so, although the words had escaped her before she realized she ought to have held it back, perhaps, this time, 'Am I not my father's daughter?'

Her mother didn't seem to mind. She smiled. 'Yes ..... your father was a brilliant man. Too brilliant. But also too wounded, and like all men dominated by the myth of the Puer, the eternal child, he had a broken wing. He was too kind, too passive. Finally he needed you, it seems ..... to bring one small seed of his work, but the best part, to fruition. To mend his wing, even after his death .....'

Nora sat down at the table and poured their new tea. Her mother was still finding it hard to look her in the eyes. Suddenly she blurted out, emotionally, 'But am I not my mother's daughter too, at last!'

Her mother almost started to cry again, and it took some time before she managed to regain her composure again ..... 'Yes indeed Anna. Perhaps I can call you that now! The name we gave you. I hope so. I haven't done too badly myself, have I? Even though there were a few ups and downs!'

Nora knew she had done a thousand things more than her father had ever dreamt of. He had been weak really. A failure. It was she who had excelled in everything she set her heart to do. She continued, 'There are so many things we have to talk about, I don't know where to begin. You will forgive me for becoming Nora and not Anna will you?'

'Yes of course, I am not a psycho-analyst for nothing. It was necessary. You needed to become someone else. Someone, anyone who was *not* the creation, the product of your father and mother. We failed you miserably. The name we gave you was ours, showing you belonged to us. You chose Nora to be yourself ..... and even better with a new surname ..... as if you had married yourself, I might add.'

Nora looked wistful. 'I was the only one left, who knowing the truth, might marry me!' she said.

But her mother laughed it off. 'Rubbish! Don't do that masochism number with me Anna ..... let us put that behind us. You have suffered yes. As we all did in our various ways. But suffering is normality. Do you want to me merely normal? Or better than normal, above normal, more than normal? If so ..... then rise above it. Forget it. Your suffering is past. You have a real friend now. Your mother ..... the best friend a girl can have! You know that ..... ' and she looked at Nora intently. 'I always knew this would happen, especially when your father died. But I had no idea it would be the book that would bring us together. The very book I feared would separate us forever! It has joined us! I thought you would use it to prise us more apart..... an act of indecent exposure, to publish it with all its nakedness. But you clothed it, transformed it, made it a poem. It showed me immediately that you still loved me. No..... I won't say that..... that you were still wounded and needed to rediscover a mother's love. Your book was a message to me. But probably not known to you consciously. But not just to me personally. To all mothers. That is why I cried when I saw your exhibition. I could see immediately, knowing as I do, as did Tiresias, the language of birds, of symbolic images, it was the universal Mother you were searching for. As we all want..... and need now at this terrible motherless time..... she may be our first experience of loss, but later we grow up into reason and discover it is the entire earth we have lost. But I said to myself, I am a poor mother. One of the worst. But I am still a mother..... and I am your particular mother..... so why couldn't you start with me, with all my imperfections..... start to re-discover me in your search for the universal Mother, who is so much more important than your personal one? There will only be one mother you will know deeply enough to feel satisfied with though..... which will feel truly authentic. Yourself! When you become a mother. Meanwhile, start with me. Mother me! It is what I need now too. I was pretty useless, I know, and there are no excuses. Too late for that. Well, perhaps there were a few, as you said so generously, so forgivingly, in the book. You wrote, we can never forget the crimes we are victim of, but we can forgive. So here I am, to be forgiven!'

'It is you who must forgive me mother! I was a very violent, determined child.....'

'Yes, you were always grown up, always a woman. But I didn't help. I was your mother and allowed you to feel I had rejected you, and then stupidly sacrificed you to your father. With our betrayals at the hand of our parents, we reflect the crimes of nations. How can it be otherwise? Nature is a hall of mirrors. How else does it evolve except reflecting upon itself? We must not seek revenge, which is what we want, which we instinctively desire. We must find the difficult way to reconciliation - forgiveness as you said - which we often instinctively mistrust. It seems weak. Feminine. Can you forgive me? Are those tears in your eyes, or pearls?'

Nora wiped her eyes. 'Both! You were never far away mother. I knew all along I would not have wanted to do my father's book, if it hadn't been about you, even though I sensed it was in essence, wrong. Full of the need for revenge. He tried to expose your secret truths for revenge. I knew it was true, so many of the details - the incest and so on - but that kind of truth became untruth when it was exposed for the sake of revenge at having lost you. The book *was* a letter to you, it's true. I realized it after I had done it. Only when I read it, I knew. When the two girls who published it wanted to do it so much, I knew. I said to myself. They too feel cut off from the mother..... their particular mother, but also the hope of motherhood as an experience. Cut off from the Mother archetype and her mysteries. Oh the double bind, the double loss, never to be initiated into her mysteries! All that has been lost in the secular ghettos that are modern cities, the places where we are expected to grow and live. I knew I was so like the two girls that published my book, like them, and like so many women of my generation..... and men too..... in which the shared myth was to be cut off from the archetype of the nourishing mother..... oh the men too, they have it almost worse, cut off just as brutally. All they are looking for is tenderness, affirmation they could be truly loved by woman, not merely desired! And all that would lead them to the lost ability to respect the world of nature, rather than feeling the need to rape it with their technology. To conquer it.'

'Well..... what a relief. It's going to be fun, Anna!'

Nora agreed. Because she had spent so much time, albeit unconsciously, searching for her mother, now that she was 'there' in front of her, it felt so natural, so obvious, she already felt relaxed about it. She had a weird perception, contraction of time, as if it had only been a few days before, not ten years or more when she had attacked her mother in this same kitchen with a wooden salad knife..... and she had been rushed to hospital with a savage wound across her head. And her decision afterwards, never to come back home. The home in which she felt no longer wanted, needed, loved by Nora or her father.

Ten years or so before..... several days later, from the

hospital, she had telephoned Nora, whom she knew was just becoming a young 'woman', and had said something devastatingly cruel with its terrible unconscious logic..... which she knew had been psychologically inept, but she was emotionally crushed by that time by her husband..... but what she said was motivated as Nora knew, by the *desire* for revenge..... revenge for years of aridity. A woman scorned. 'You can have your father..... he is all yours. I hope he does better with you than he did with me!'

Now, all that seemed like just a few days before, as Nora gazed with wonder at her mother..... with awe at her strength..... and yet humble too before her weaknesses..... able to forgive, because now she was a woman too and knew some of the problems. 'Oh mother!' She whose various face-lifts helped to create the sensation of defeated time.

Nora told her she had the impression it was just a few days before when she had gone away. 'Gone away?..... You mean when I was evicted, thrown out, booted out, by a screaming she-cat of a girl, when I was carried off to hospital in an ambulance with a six inch wound in my head! The next knife cut from you my darling and it would have been my throat!' She seemed almost annoyed, but they both laughed. Nora wanted to tell her about the wound she had received too, at the barricades, and had kept open and 'alive'..... not exactly deliberately, but not entirely unconsciously. Maybe to show her that she too was now equal. Then she decided it was too symbolic, too obvious. There was no subtlety about it, so she kept quiet and didn't mention it. In fact she never mentioned it to anyone, and it healed very quickly afterwards, without any need of antibiotics. So much for doctors.

'The house is looking very clean and tidy!' her mother said. Nora looked away. She was dreading there might now be a confrontation about money, a serious set-back.

Nora looked away. 'Anna!' her mother said, loudly, almost harshly, and Nora looked up quickly, fearing the worst. 'I have some very good news for you. I have decided to give it to you. When I read your book, written by a young lady called 'Nora Flood', I said to myself, even if Anna doesn't want to see me or speak to me..... even if I have read the 'message in it' wrongly..... I will give her the house. So it is all yours now, your rightful inheritance. In fact everything you want is yours. I will give you the house and all the money your father left, but didn't leave, held as it was in my trust. We will not share it. It is all yours. I don't need it. I want it all to be yours.'

Nora replied quickly, 'You don't have to do that mother. I know all the money, everything we ever had was yours. I know my father never made a penny, and spent a fortune. You don't have to do it.'

Her mother smiled and put her long-fingered, elegant hands, with the crimson laquered nail varnish, towards her across the table. 'Let's not play games any more. The house is yours. I can afford it, you know that. I will make a new trust for you, as I did for your father. You will have as much money as he did. I will pay off your debts. I know about them. What you don't know is I guaranteed them at the bank. You thought it was credit against your father's will. It wasn't. He left nothing, only debts. I guaranteed it secretly at the bank. I was happy to do it. I always knew it was only a question of time. And here I am, now, after the flood, a dove, carrying a small branch of peace.'

Nora stood up and went to the window. She looked down at the willow trees and the lake, and she felt whole, complete, at last. She had thought, after Raymond's assault, she would feel she had lost something. Empty. It was curiously the opposite. It had all been part of the gnarled, root-ridden path she had taken back through the sacred wood to find her mother, still as ever the High Priestess in its central, shadowy glade..... the tall trees bending over, a bower, a temple with a roof of leaves. But now they were more equals. Nothing had been lost. Everything had been found. She could become a real woman at last..... and show Anna a thing or two. But she'd keep the name Nora..... and the fake passport. They might be useful if there was a real revolution, another war. Meanwhile she'd have a good time, anticipating it. When every day might be your last, there was no excuse for not having a good time..... Anna had told her often enough.

*

Nora suggested a walk in the garden, the garden her mother had planted even before she was born.....

In silence they walked under the tall, beautiful trees, in full leaf, the new ones planted amongst the old as if seeds had been blown there by the wind. Nature's garden, as once it had been, everywhere, the primeval forest. Without geometry, but expressing perfect harmony. The only trees revealing the touch of human hands were the four symmetrically placed willow trees.

After walking without speaking for some time, holding hands, they sat down next to the lake. Nora whistled suddenly, startling her mother, and after some time her cat came to spy on them, but wouldn't approach too closely. Nora guessed it was probably the coat with the fur skin collar which her mother insisted on wearing, even though it was quite warm in the garden. Nora mentioned it. 'My fur? Maybe? Your cat is very wise, recognising we are exterminators. The Jews, the big cats, the jungles. I wondered at the time who would be the next Jews they needed to wipe out. No wonder I identify with them in my usual, ambiguous way, being in love with irony and not forgetting paradox! I learnt early that human hope didn't grow on trees, but under the permanent threat of worse suffering.'

Nora threw a stone into the water and some ducks browsing nearby, not out of curiosity but looking for bugs in that particular spot, bobbed jerkily away as quickly as their little legs could paddle them.

'About the book . . . . . why did you put those extraordinary photographs into the middle of it? So unexpected? Not entirely relevant, except to suggest the mood?'

Nora laughed. 'It started as a joke but the two girls liked it. They wanted to sell the book! My reason was quite clear. People pick up novels and see all words. So much time needed to plough through all those paragraphs. People nowadays are addicted to images so I thought I'd bung in a few erotic images. People would buy the book thinking it was sexy! Also though, they were proving my point. That we are all capable of being seduced, and of failing ourselves, betraying ourselves for a few sexy images!'

'But . . . . . forgive me for saying it . . . . . there was also one part in the book I didn't fully understand Anna. I have an unfair advantage I know, of knowing the truth, as well as knowing your father's version of it. But I couldn't understand why you brought in the strange emphasis in the section about the justifiably invented "story" of the seduction by the father, that it was the woman, a mere girl, who made all the running, which you elaborated on with some detail, blaming it all - unexpectedly - on the girl. Then living sexually as a wife with the father ..... hardly likely! And then it all turns out to be a fantasy, conjured up for revenge. This made for some confusion. Why?'

Nora gazed into the water. Of course her mother had put her finger on the flaw in the book. It was never clear whether the seduction had taken place. And the aftermath, living together in relative harmony, was utterly romantic and even sentimental ..... the alien chapter.....

She tried to laugh it off, 'Am I not my mother's daughter?' She looked guiltily at her mother, who was gazing searchingly into Nora's eyes. There was no escaping this stare, and Nora knew she was determined to talk about it. Nora didn't really want to, but then she knew she also wanted to. It was weak of her to want to abuse her mother with truth she didn't want to hear. But her mother must have guessed the truth. She was too clever not to have done. It was better they spoke about it.....

'Can't you guess?' she asked blandly.

'I have imagined a reason..... the obvious one..... constructed an involute of images as de Quincey called it..... but I may be wrong. Often the most obvious, to an oppressed unconscious, to a spirit dominated by external or internal fascism, can mean the exact opposite. Surely I don't have to joke and ask was it reality or fantasy, referring to the 'phallacy' - spelt with ph - of the seduction theory and its unlawful, wilful abandonment. The question will always occur to the reader, did the seduction take place or not? That was the point, I presume? Only I would know you invented the whole thing.'

Nora looked into the water. Her mother was choosing her words carefully. Fascism! Internal or external. It was the same either way, real or imaginary.

'Mother, you are the only person in the world who can know what parts are you and what are me. What a privilege. What a responsibility. When I came back from school, I was very lonely here. He did what he thought was the right thing to send me away. But it meant I needed him more, missed him more. The pain became physical and awful. It was masturbation and fantasies, or that. It was inevitable under the cirumstances, surely?'

Her mother looked into the lake. 'Yes I suppose so. Sad but inevitable..... as earthquakes are inevitable, and death is inevitable.' But she still didn't know whether to believe Nora. From what she knew of her father, it was utterly unlikely. Why had Nora needed to invent such a thing, then leave it so ambiguous?

Nora felt awkward. 'Perhaps I will write another book about it! The whole truth. What it has made me, never knowing. Inert. A stone!'

Her mother put her hand on Nora's knee, but she edged away.....

Nora continued. 'I want to tell you the whole truth mother, to get rid of it all, once and for all, but do I know it? Do you know why I hated you so much, why I set about tormenting you, until I drove you out of the house?'

'I didn't know at the time, but from reading the book, reading between the lines, I presume I know. Buy maybe not. You did say it was a novelisation of a case-history. And then only fragments, "seeing synthesis"..... Tell me.'

Nora took out the wooden pendulum and placed it on the grass between them.

Her mother winced. 'So it was you who stole it? I thought it was merely lost.'

'Yes. I stole it when you were in hospital. Father sent you all your things, afterwards, but that was missing. I took it.'

Her mother nodded and looked away. 'I gathered from the book you had known that your father and I were.....' but she couldn't finish.

'Yes mother. I knew. I was very precocious and knew too much for my age. But look at my parents! I seemed to know when I was ten. Maybe earlier. Do not underestimate a child's knowledge of sexuality, to quote you! The unconscious knows all, ALL the time. I had it all worked out. I saw you one day, masturbating, alone in your room..... using this wooden toy. You always made a mistake. It was always when my father was asleep, and you put on the music to drown out the sound, but consequently, you couldn't hear me either! So when I heard the music, I knew what was happening. Most often, it was here in the drawing room! I watched from behind the curtains.'

Her mother shuddered and looked away. How could she have been so naive, so careless? Why do parents need to think their children are not sexually aware? Is it not because it means they become sexually aware of them? When adults say children are not sexually aware - before Freud that is - it means, 'I am acutely aware of my children sexually!' There was no escape. That is why some tribal peoples allowed their children to see the parents making love. At first they tried to separate them, thinking they were fighting, but then joined in, caressing and stroking. 'You are right Anna. How clever you always were. I always played the German Requiem. I even danced to it sometimes, didn't I? I always preferred to dance. It seems more of a rite, that way..... not just misery.'

'Yes..... "Denn alles Fleisch" in particular was your favourite track. But you and Daddy had your own bedrooms, and I thought, presumably you met from time to time to make love, because I knew about these things, in my fantastic, romantic way. But then I saw you masturbating. That seemed to define everything. The lack of love. The lack of passion. I had been masturbating for some time too. I must have said something like, 'My mother is like me. It is fantasy..... not real. But I also said, she is failing my father..... my poor father..... instead of going to him and making love, she satisfies herself and thus betrays him. I became more and more sorry for my father, and I assume, unconsciously I was determined to get rid of you..... to take your place..... and fulfil his needs..... and mine!'

'Yes. That is how it works. A classic story.'

'I resisted going the whole way, of course, and he did too, however hard I tried. He was impeccable. He was so correct, so loving, so tender..... he became a mother to me as well as a father. Can you imagine that, can you?' she snapped suddenly.

'Yes. Indeed. Only too well. Your father was always very feminine as well as masculine. That is why I loved him, and admired him so much. It is so hard for a man to be both. It is such a risk for them to take. Very few men in my world were like him. It is easy to be brutal.' But she was looking hard at Nora. She was sure she was lying..... why did she need to and why was she continuing with the pretence?

'Well, it was his femininity with me that was his undoing. If he had made an overt move to "take" me I would have been too afraid, I know, and escaped and it would never have happened. But he became more and more loving, tender, kind, motherly, as I said. So I was able to draw him closer and closer to me, passively, sensually, until erotically..... until he loved me too much to be able to defend himself. I made all the moves mother, every single one. It was me all along the way. I was responsible. He was entirely passive..... but being an analyst, no doubt he was fascinated too..... How could he not be? He was betrayed by his own mind and its inevitable curiosity. I became part of his scientific research, another psychic amoeba under the mental microscope. He simply could *not* resist going along with it, once I had decided it was going to happen. I intended to be his ultimate case-history! I was the fulfilment of his theories, and sublimation of his deepest fears. It was nothing to do with fantasy this time, it was me, his own daughter, perfecting my technique, drawing him closer and closer to me. I broke down the invisible wall around him and took him..... and he had no choice to go along with it. I made him feel guiltless..... freed him from guilt, because I made the running and because..... well especially as we found a way of..... doing it, without, without risk..... not going the whole way..... of.....'

Her mother could see Nora was becoming very emotional, but she said nothing. Nora had to take her time, if she was determined to reveal everything, kill all the ghosts, and it was essential to purge oneself of the worst memories..... they were the ones doing the damage. But she couldn't stop herself probing more, 'How do you mean Nora?'

Nora was lying with her face in the grass and she sobbed a few times..... 'Please don't ask me to describe it! Please please ..... just accept we were lovers for several years, until he decided I ought to be weaned from him, and find another man to discover what it was all "really" about..... or whatever.'

'How do you mean..... lovers..... and why did you need another man to discover what it was "really" about? Why don't you say it? What you did? The word? Say the word, it is very important. Don't beat about the bush! You are running away..... you're holding something back!' She presumed Nora must be lying. It must be all prefabrication. She needed to invent the story to hurt her..... the only way to deeply hurt her.

Revenge herself..... on her going away. When the mother was absent, you seduced the father, hoping to find the mother in yourself. That was the way the patriarchy worked. It killed off the lunar power of the mother..... with its solar mystification. Thus enslaving *all* the daughters unconsciously..... forever. But Helmut had tried to be different, she knew..... even though it had made him impotent in the process, he too a victim of the patriarchy's expectation of him as a man - to be like the others. Fucking rather than making love.....

Nora sat up and straightened her back. She looked at her mother directly, faking arrogance. She'd had lots of practice. 'My father was a gentleman! I know this may sound nonsense. But it was what I wanted.'

'What was?' her mother asked, but Nora was retreating, starting to hate her again and refused to speak for some time.

She seemed to be fighting a demon. Her face was white, her hands clenched, her eyes closed. It was just a word. It had no means of penetrating anyone else's consciousness with the numinous power it had for her, so why worry? For others the word would refer to some ideas or images in a book, or a film - second hand - once removed - like war was to her anarchist friends..... so why bother to try and share? For her it had a thousand and one different meanings now..... so why give it out as if it had one? As she couldn't believe in one God and was still determined to cling to the hope for a perverse polymorphism again..... If she could, if she only could..... How could anyone describe with "documentary" words, the breadth of such an intimacy? It would need poems, music, actors and actresses and the illusion wrought by identification..... and then catharsis..... Why was she, her mother, still unaware she was instigating such tangible, physical terror, by forcing her to describe with words..... bring her dark secrets into the light of day? She would only be free when she could tell her mother what she thought of *her*, still now, that she was a fascist! That it was women like her who allowed fascism to thrive! No! She did not want it de-sanctified. Why couldn't she be left alone..... left alone..... left alone..... as she had always been..... to work things out for herself? She had withdrawn once before and found protection inside a self-made cell of four walls, building it inside her heart..... she'd huddled there and tried to save the two of them from a disease she saw creeping up on them..... that later she found words for, in her so-called "studies" - angst - ennui - impotence - that arid lifeless silence as if ghosts didn't have the power to see each other..... But eventually she had been forced to revolt against the void now creeping up on her too, a wall of indifference, and take sides..... now it was too late..... she had only to save herself.....

'Go on. SAY IT! Say it Nora. Tell me what happened between you and him. If you can't say it, that is why you MUST say it, don't you see? You are still the victim. Say it, to kill it. You will be its victim until you share the pain. Share the guilt..... so why not with me? You know I know already! I read between the lines, the areas of silence, in your book.'

'Yes mother......the gaps, the spaces, the silences..... but silence is golden so they say..... but isn't gold the light of the sun, the solar all-seeing eye transformed into matter, brought down to earth, the mystical sexual power of the father become flesh? What about that ultimate, technological, excremental mystical vision of the Nazis, the master race who would become Gods..... and in order to do so, they had to wipe out the other, the other chosen race? Is not gold, for which we are bought and sold, not the sexual power of the father transformed into filthy lucre? So the earliest poets, the first mythologists, told us a long time ago..... at the time when the prison-house of reason was closing its gates..... the myths! The only truth worth knowing is of the unconscious, which knows all..... which desires all.....' she said weakly..... she was seeing images in her mind that had long been hidden behind mere words..... thinking, thinking, as now, thinking that words were walls too..... could be piled, word on word like brick on brick so that texts of words became walls of psychic ghettos..... how many bricks were needed to build the ghetto of the ego? No wonder people built them for real.....

In the ensuing silence Nora noticed the clouds were becoming menacing..... little birds were skittering about frantically, looking for places to hide. Perhaps. That was how she was seeing it. Maybe they were chasing each other for fun..... seeking relief, as Anna called it..... looking for open branches on which to get sopping wet. A delicious, free bath.

Nora wanted it to rain and rain and rain..... and she could sit there and not move, and enjoy watching her mother get soaked..... 'No mother..... I prefer to avoid saying it!' But then she laughed. 'May I quote? "But love has pitched *his* mansion in the place of excrement!" "HIS" mansion, you see. So even love is masculine! Oh mother. I seem to know too much, but probably know nothing. I seem to see it all..... I see the sordid roots of so much so-called knowledge, so much evil ..... knowledge exploited as power..... but can't you see? I can never know if my vision is pure and right? Do I not merely see what I am conditioned never to forget?'

She was battling to regain her stance..... to sit up and look her mother straight in the face..... but it was still so hard. Perhaps her mother knew the truth about her father after all. Perhaps he had always been the same.....

'Nora! Just say what happened and you might become free. Why not try it? It was one of the laws of psycho-analysis after all, and it often works! Even these devious suggestions admit nothing. You have always played too much with words. Sometimes they are all we have to share, all we have to go on..... do not destroy them because they sometimes fail you.' Nora sighed and threw a stone in the water and sighed again, hoping it might hurt to give the impression she had heard it all before.

'............Yes, mother, I know the rules......
You don't need to tell ME, my father was one of the great psycho-analysts! And.....
I..... he.....
At least there was no mystification, no hypocrisy between

US..... it seemed natural..... and I was happy to know where I stood!'

There was some urge, some desire inside her to get the words out but something was still blocking her.....

'I..... I.....
I allowed..... all.....
all our love making was.....

an..... and..... he..... he.....
Damn you!
You know I can't.....
and I.....
No! No! I don't WANT to!.....
.....
Ask that of me and you will lose me, again.....
Forever this time. Forever!
So why should I say it, describe it if I don't want to?

It..... it..... wasn't filmed, and in that I escaped a worse fate, and there is no proof except my word. I won't give it. No. I know you want to hear it. Tant pis! Maybe it is not true. Maybe I imagined it. Let us leave it at that. An impasse. If I am to be free..... and for years, for years I have been struggling to be free, have I not? Haven't we all been struggling with black, black images from the past? Trying to say they were evil instead of trying to understand why, why, why, if possible, and forgive? I would have killed to become free! If I am free, now, it is free NOT to say it! I don't want to say, in words..... to you or anyone..... what happened..... the words are ugly..... a pornographic text..... my memories aren't ugly..... and so, if I MUST keep it to myself and can never be free, I will never be free. I know I'm confused, maybe contradicting myself, but I am happy to accept the limits to my freedom. Freedom must never be limitless. Freedom is a contradiction. It is accepting to be free only so far and no further, otherwise it is anarchy. I prefer not to be made 'whole' if it means exposing the secrets..... what was sacred, even though it was dangerous and destructive. The sacred is always the sacrificed. Sacro facere ..... to be made sacred..... I was old enough to know and accept responsibility. Good God! In Ancient Egypt I would have had two children by that age!'

Her mother said nothing, feeling sure there was more to come, and wanting it all to come out, love and hate all jumbled up, the one parading for the other. It didn't matter. Such was the truth we must cling to, if we are to avoid being mere cogs in the desiring machines of Metropolis.....

Nora continued, spitting out the words this time, 'All passion is destructive if it is not let loose within limits. It needs an object to limit and frame it. Left on its own, floating on air, it becomes insanity, a mania for power. Passion forces us to see and need symbols, and all symbols are as destructive as passion itself, destroying our comfortable view of reality. All symbols are the lie to reason, yet are the deepest truth, for consciousness has its roots in the sea of symbols. I made a drawing of the ego as a shark, swimming on the surface of that impenetrable ocean. Maybe it was not a good image, but, you remember that painful, luminous sequence in "Chants de Maldoror" when poor, mad, helpless wanderer, Maldoror, shoots the sailors in the sea after the shipwreck and sharks devour the broken and struggling bodies? Then he swims out in the blood-red sea to the fiercest of the sharks, a female, and mates with her? I still have your priceless illustrated leather bound copy of that book, which I stole, mother! Maldoror is mad of course. A perfect example of insanity the psycho-analysts and others would say. But what a perfect symbol for the ego and the unconscious, their savage devouring of each other, the predicament of the human race! No more insane than Belsen and Dachau and Auschwitz, those creations on earth of that most destructive Christian and Jewish symbol . . . . . Hell! The underbelly, the flipside of the coin of guilt. Judas needed thirteen pieces of silver, but you can go to hell for one. Photographs are cheap! Hell is the mirror image of guilt and is the true betrayer of the human race. Hell is reason, pure and simple. What we have killed and lost with our reasoning, is the ocean, the mother of emotion, feeling, love. I too was betrayed, when you went away. I was left with only pavements.'

'Not by choice Nora, you know that!' But Nora wasn't listening. Her eyes were closed. The words were still coming . . . . .

'I . . . . . I took my revenge, my frustration and rage - rage because I had no-one to talk to . . . . . I took my revenge out on the police at the barricades . . . . . at least, I tried . . . . . .if I had been given the gun I paid Mathieu to get for me, the organiser of our cell . . . . . but he was a coward when it came to actual confrontation . . . . . I would have used it! I'd have killed the buggers! At least one. The random shot. The stranger. And yet . . . . . maybe I would have killed the wrong man. Half a man. Can only a man bring me back to that ocean and teach me to swim? Then it is only a man I can blame. I could never blame you, you the one I wanted to return..... in whose eyes I could discover myself. A man I would have killed. One I only hated rather than loved and hated. Tant pis. Such is life. People living out half of themselves. But it was as much the mother's fault..... The Nazis tried to kill the wrong people. Everyone but themselves. They were right with their cock-eyed mysticism to attack monotheism, but wrong to attack the victims of it as much as they were. Brothers in shame and fear. They should have looked inward and killed something wrong in themselves. Their fear of the feminine. Oh fuck it! Words words words ...... wasn't that Hamlet? But I say, if a word is a word is a word it becomes a symbol! It is symbols, myths, that Oedipus can never render translucent. We are all the children of Oedipus! Oedipus castrates himself with reason and then takes it out on everyone else, which means women and children, and then builds machines that embody reason to further negate the feminine..... to make sure..... and yet his own blood still knows the truth. He hates himself for what he does and kills others to avoid the truth. The fall of the sphinx was the fall of mankind..... she killed herself from despair at the stupid rational answer Oedipus coughed up!'

'Yes Nora..... yes. But these are things we couldn't hide from you! We too, mere parents, must live on the knife edge between reason and the unconscious. That ghastly thin fragile membrane! Occasionally it snaps. What could we do? Show you the real world or hide you from it with a blindfold, and then let you discover it for yourself, too late, when you ripped it off?'

Nora laughed but the laugh was hideous somehow. She sneered and snarled and her words were contorted, the snarl of a jaguar in the night who has found another creature of the night at its favourite water-hole. 'The blind-fold? I had one until recently! The vagina is blind-folded well enough, mother, until someone rips it off! But I offered Tiresias the way into hell! It was not your fault..... I saw well enough how dangerous the world could be..... and how important to learn to be immune to the worst terrors. But I still don't know the answer. Certain images refuse to be forgotten. They must belong to the gods! You see I WANTED to be my father's daughter, whatever he was. Frail and weak but loving. Prey to his desire to understand the feminine, so much it crushed him, took away his strength. It scared him! I can forgive him. I, Antigone, have done so, when he was alive, a thousand times, and since, a thousand times. And now, once again. But no man could have done otherwise, who was a man. But don't say it is myself I cannot forgive, or I will hate you again, mother!'

Her mother was playing with her hands. 'He was a gentle sensitive man. He was whole in that sense yes. He was in the wrong world, that is all. No-one appreciated him for it. He would have gone to Jung but Jung had praised the Nazis!'

Nora continued, 'Maybe I was not always proud of him, sometimes ashamed, but I loved him, as he was, a man with a broken wing. But we flew at times together. I loved him, without question or doubt. And to have been alive and really loved is to have flowered. That is the ONLY word I give you mother. Love. He loved me. And imagine how privileged I was, I had a god who would go on his knees for me! If we cannot love in such a way - with forgiveness - those so close to us, so in need of our love and affirmation, so weakened by passion, there is no hope for love, or us as people. All love must be loving someone who can embody the ghosts we can never kill! Those who have no bodies and are doomed to cry in the crack in the pavement. If love becomes displaced downwards by mere pleasure, we will become ever more arid again and create a worse hell this time on the bosom of mother earth. As we did, he and I. Oh world intangible we touch thee! Oh world incomprehensible we clutch thee! But *that* was not part of it. Our hell was simply missing YOU..... he and I acting as if I might replace you! In hell, it is sexual passion that stokes the fires. It was probably my fault. "I shared, as much as in love-making something abstract is ever shared, the guilt and responsibility." Weren't they your words in his book, mother, his book that is now my book? Our book? A family snap-shot album. I am Nora now..... not Anna any longer..... please try to call me Nora..... I'm sweet little girl Nora who wrote it to free myself from you. But my mind, me, I, was the book in which you both wrote your private diaries of your hells..... Oh God! How can I escape thinking in this atrophied way? Help me. Teach me! I seem to know..... but it is hard to do it. Maybe I will learn to *think* with my paintings..... through their language of pure images..... and

I must learn to think with my body, of other things. But will I ever be able to do so? Has it been stripped of spontaneity, its soul, forever? Do I delude myself that I can ever be truly free?'

She fell on the grass again, sobbing, but her mother left her there for some time before laying her hand gently on her hair, as black as her own. Nora's real father's hair had been quite blond. Strange how the genes select. So many of Nora's words had been her own..... but if it took a very long time, Nora had to recover for herself. Otherwise it would be no victory. These were truths she could never admit to a man..... any man probably..... even a psycho-analyst! In some things, a woman was needed. Even a mother who had failed. Only mothers now could create a future..... try to avoid another holocaust. The technology for it was building up so fast.....

Nora whispered into the grass..... 'Oh how the body of the earth is shaking and shivering..... its flesh is becoming as arid as mine. As incable of arousing true passion!' She was digging her fingers into the soil, tearing at it, eating it..... burying her face in the clumps of longer grass.

Her mother didn't move a fraction of an inch, not wishing to disturb her. It was better Nora spoke to the earth. It would still be there when she had gone..... she had a dinner appointment in Munich and would have to leave soon..... but she was wondering, maybe Nora had been right not to say the word. The accusation. She had said a better word, by not saying it. Le néant. Nora embodied the truth, despite lacking certainty that she knew how to express it, that the patriarchy had its secrets that it protected, and its guilt, repressed and more powerful than reason, drove it to celebrate them. Women and children had to be abused to keep the wheels turning. It was a fantastic proposterous fact and no-one wanted to believe it, especially women..... wives..... daughters. But the unconscious knew. The collective unconscious knew. The Warsaw Ghetto had never happened. It was indeed, the Christian and Jewish hell, known in the collective unconscious both before the imagined event and after it..... a mere image. A premonition become reflection. An eighteenth and nineteenth century etching. The Warsaw Ghetto was a Piranesi prison drawing. The responsibility went back a long way. The massacre of the innocents..... but hell was hunger too..... people were still starving years after the defeat of the first war, and so it had been easy again to orchestrate - for Hitler to harness the desire of the people to his own ends - All hell let loose again. When people stopped starving, the good-enough image of hell might go away..... but hell never went away when people were starved of love! Had she not tried, in all her work, to dissipate the hate, and afterwards the self-hate, by showing the responsibility was not ours alone..... it was in the step we had all taken out of the sacred wood? Nora was trying to go back there but was it possible? Truly Nora was her daughter. But it was not going to be easy..... it had not been easy for she herself, who had made a successful enough emotional life out of forgiveness, being deprived of the pleasures of knowing blind desire..... and finding an object for it wrapped in human flesh. So much of her life was nothing but theatre. Artifice and props. A lot of what Nora had said, was directed at her, she knew, and it couldn't be otherwise..... but life was compromise and paradox, as was love..... otherwise it became war. Or society sustained with fascism. Nora was merely growing up. Maybe some experience or other at the time of the barricades had pushed her in the right direction. In that sense, it had been useful after all.

Nora turned to look at her. Her mother was gazing into the water, smiling uncomfortably. Nora had expected her to be angry. But now, she seemed almost amused, turning away from Nora onto her stomach, picking grass and playing with it in her fingers and in her teeth..... rocking gently from side to side, as if laughing inwardly. Nora was angry with herself for noticing she still had a beautiful bottom. Then, not looking at Nora at all, she said quietly, releasing the words slowly, carefully. 'How strange we are..... you and I..... how difficult to reveal the truth..... how close are those two words, revelation and revolution! They mean the same. A moment's lapse into revolving, cyclic time. Now it is my turn. I have a very strange truth to reveal. I was privileged to know the truth of the Warsaw Ghetto, a reality impossible to grasp. At least I was there. But is it necessarily truth, just being somewhere? All my life since I have tried to imagine it as a fantasy, twisting and moulding it. I couldn't of course, the one memory I could never erase. Yet I have transformed its energy into something positive..... even fulfilling..... as you said in the book. I had no choice, or die.

You must do the same. It was inseparable from my first experience of sexual desire..... the primitive horror of it deflowered me psychologically, forever. Yet I was privileged to experience sex for the first time, at its most intense moment, at its deepest level..... almost as an animal..... in a primitive rite, and it became my myth. Its remembered image became the source of my pleasure, at the same time, dislocating reality forever. What a terrible way of having to deal with reality, with a truth so unacceptable. And yet now......Anna..... you show me, once again, how we have to respect that delicate flower we call desire..... how beautiful it is, that red rose, how mysterious is its transforming power, how you overcame the terror of that wall around you, and learned to live inside it. Both he and you, and how different are we woman to the men, we who have a real rose to be plucked! And like a rose I start to ramble! You see..... I don't know how to say this. But..... You succeeded where I failed. You were right of course. Your father and I were never lovers, which is why, in the end, it forced us apart. You succeeded by the strength of your not-at-all innocent, evolving desire..... a rose has the power to force itself through the concrete of a garden path to emerge into the sun. Imagine the pressure inside those young roots, and you were pushed and guided by unconscious knowledge too. Unconsciously you knew the truth and you forced it into the open..... and forced me out! You took what was yours, by instinctive right, which was the lonely man you really wanted, who showed you tenderness and consideration, whom I had so miserably failed. And now you have written a book about me and my story with your father and it is beautiful and so moving - deliberately poetic and evasive but highly suggestive - exploring and exchanging each other's bisexual natures, so to speak, and yet it is totally untrue, as I must now prove to you, by telling you my secret, the biggest secret of *my* life! Your book was not merely your story disguised as mine and authentic to itself as words on a page..... a book..... a text, true within those limits. Yes, BUT! Now you will see how wrong truth can be! Why don't you ask me, now, the ultimate..... inevitable question? Why do you hesitate?'

Nora didn't understand what she meant and told her so. Her mother turned round to look at her, pulling her knees up to her chin. She had beautiful legs, sheathed in delicate, expensive black silk stockings. Nora felt certain she was wearing red underwear and almost asked her, but didn't have time, her mother angrily repeating, 'Why don't you ask me the ultimate question?'

'I don't understand! Why..... What?'

'An..... An..... Nora! Shall I repeat myself? As I said, you won where I had failed. Your father and I were never lovers.....'

Nora looked at her, still not understanding.

Her mother straightened her skirt.

Nora seemed to have grasped the situation. 'Ah! But I'm not surprised, after the years of analysis with him! You were being analysed by him for two years or more before you married, so it was inevitable he should have deep repression towards you, all those fears, taboos, because to seduce your patient is a terrible crime, isn't it? The first law of psycho-analysis, you must not show the slightest sign of sexual feeling. You must be a robot..... unless of course you simply can't hold back, like that long-suffering saint Ferenczi. As a father should not seduce his daughter! I can understand the difficulties. His love for you, as the text always revealed, albeit indirectly, was absolute. You were the total Mother to him. He worshipped you. He identified with you. You must forgive him for having failed you sexually, for not being a good lover. You said it. He was so gentle and tender and feminine. He was never aggressive, an obvious male. He gave you something much more important than sex..... he gave you back to yourself. He taught you, under analysis, to accept the difficult, painful truth about yourself. Gave you a means of dealing with your inevitable sado-masochism..... forever doomed to seek men who reminded you of the soldiers in the Ghetto, who alone would be able to arouse you, fully, and as I learnt from the original text, you could only have an orgasm with a man dressed as a German soldier. That was hardly something my father would have found easy to do - a gentle, sensitive, intraverted, rather feminine Jew! Or even to bear to think about, so let's be fair to him. He must have suffered enormously knowing that - didn't he?'

Her mother stood up, apparently really angry now, glaring at Nora. 'Yes yes yes..... yes Anna..... I know all that, but can't you see, he and I were never lovers ..... never, never lovers!' She stood up in front of Nora, her eyes blazing. 'Am I to presume that Elektra, as well as Oedipus, is also totally and absolutely blind? Can't you see ..... we NEVER made love, he and I!'

At last, it dawned on Nora what her mother meant. 'Never!' Like her early drawings, nothing was appearing quite real ..... and she turned away. The flood of ideas and images that surged through her, all at once, drowned her mind. She walked unsteadily toward the edge of the lake. For a moment she almost fell in. She went over to her favourite willow tree and clutched it and stayed there for some time, looking into the water. Some ducks swam by ..... and she wondered if they were residents, or wanderers, just passing through, forever, forever, like the Jew, doomed to wander ..... without a real place in which to dig roots. It was no wonder he dug them upwards into heaven's belly ..... the tree of the Cabbala having its roots in the sky, its branches reaching down to earth.

Her mother came slowly towards her. 'I had to tell you Anna ..... for many reasons. And now was the best time. NOW, especially, I wanted you to know, in case you ever felt guilt or shame, or ever turned from your love of him, to hating him. He was not your real father after all. So when you became lovers, it was ironically, justified. He was in his right, in a way. At least, it wasn't such a crime, being your step-father. No family blood involved! Few men could have done otherwise, left alone with you ..... once YOU had decided I was out of the way, and you wanted him. In a way ..... a terrible way ..... because I had failed him, I secretly, blindly, unconsciously hoped ..... I dreamt about it only ..... but children can listen in to their mother's dreams, and my crime was to dream that you and he would become lovers. I wanted it, don't you see? I would be free, but also I could feel forgiving and generous that I gave him YOU! Also, it was to go against the code, the taboos, which I have never totally believed in, in the world of psycho-analysis. Sublime blasphemy! But it had always been so sad. I could not arouse him with my body. As you say, he was too blocked. He never had a chance. His mind was too full of the images I had projected there like a pornographic film. But I knew he desired you. I sensed it, without seeing it. He was very discrete. But how could I not? These things are quite natural. What was not natural was the predicament we were sharing, a so-called family. A social lie. Forgive me! Because he and I had failed, ironically, I was happy at the idea of you and him. I know you knew it unconsciously..... it was ME who drove you to him! If anyone is guilty, ironically, it is me. I was in collusion.....'

Nora looked at her mother, feeling at last, for the first time, superior to her..... She would never know the truth about her father. She would ironically prefer to believe the lie. Were they not all victims of the church-blessed Fatherland? She stood up, shakily. 'Who then IS my real father, for God's sake? Do you fucking well know? Is he still alive?' She was trying to appear aggressive, but she was tottering on the verge of some kind of hysterical fit..... It was like that time in Paris when every man was every other man..... except at that time it had been Rimbaud. Now she knew, it would be..... it would be..... she'd not know his name. Or someone dressed in uniform. For some unknown reason she heard the word 'wormwood' in her inner ear, repeating itself like a mantra, trying to drive her mad..... trying to steal her two-faced soul..... little girls never knew there were two faces until later..... of Janus.....

Her mother came to her and hugged her and Nora hugged her back, though apprehensively now. It was much more complicated than she had ever dared to imagine, killing ghosts. When you thought you had them in your sights, they disappeared..... or the lens misted over from the tears. You kill ghosts by photographing them, making them real.....

'Let's go back to the house, I want a double brandy,' one of them said weakly..... and slowly they picked their separate ways back through the bushes and trees, Nora's sacred 'jardin des animaux'..... to the back door into the kitchen with its two trap-doors for cats and Nora sat at the table, not daring to imagine what she was about to hear.

'So! Your *real* father. Yes. He is still alive. I had not seen him for three years or so, until recently. He always wanted to see you but always respected the situation. When I told him your so-called father had died, he said, of course, "Then now I am free to see her!" I was thinking about it for some time. Would it upset you too much? Was it better never to tell you the truth? Then the book came out. He thought it was beautiful too

..... understanding it almost too well! You see. In the world I was living in then, he was a colleague of your father ..... I mean your so-called father! Helmut! We can give him his real name back now, now that he is no longer mystical "Daddy"! He and Helmut were friends for some time. Helmut knew that we were lovers, but he assumed I had other lovers, so he was never sure who the father was, but he never asked. He hoped desperately that we might continue to live as a family and for a while we did, very happily. It was paradise for a long time. He always said he wanted a child, and he was delighted and happy when you came into our arid life together ..... as if from nowhere, a gift of the Gods! But still he could never make love to me, even though I wanted him even more. I tried everything. I acted every Greek Play in the book, but he couldn't make love to me. There was the invisible wall between us, that he described in the book, without ever revealing the whole truth. It was the one thing he could never bring himself to admit in the text, that we had never ever made love, that our daughter belonged in the profound, telepathic sense, to someone else. YOU would have known for a start. The irony! He could make love to anyone else ..... everyone else ..... but not me. He was very promiscuous in those early days. If a pretty girl came to him and he fancied her, he recommended her for analysis to someone else in case he might meet her by accident in the street, which he immediately contrived to do! I know from a girl-friend of mine, he was a beautiful, considerate lover, and ......'

'Yes he was!' Nora snapped, surprised at the suddenness of her response. But then she put her head in her hands. 'Oh God. If only I had known. If only! To think ..... I could have escaped feeling guilty ..... never needed to know whether to forget or not .....'

Her mother was taken aback by the sharpness of Nora's interruption. 'Er ..... Well yes ..... You know too! As I was saying. Helmut knew your father. He is coming to Paris soon and I have arranged it already. I too like imagining the next chapter, trying to make it happen - in reality as well as fiction. He was an analyst of course, aren't we all, God bless our split and twisted souls, and God protect our patients! But only for a year or so. He reacted against it very quickly. He became an artist. He does many things, like you, he draws ..... and writes..... and he loves music. He has just written another book recently, a penetrating and brilliant book, about our milieu, which is why he is so especially proud of you and your novel, as you will see. Your novel about your mother, tearing away the veils of her fragile truth! He broke away from Freudian orthodoxy like we all did, and was a Jungian for a while, but that was not enough. More and more he believed that analysis was a total failure. When he gave it up, he started writing plays for the theatre instead, saying, "Better to try and analyse a whole group, all at once!" He believed in the catharsis achieved by art, as the Greeks believed, rather than a pseudo-science like psycho-analysis. As he always said, if only Marx and Freud AND Hitler had been dramatists or novelists or painters or composers, the twentieth century might have been a much better place to grow up in. Reality is far too multi-dimensional to be unravelleled by such a limited situation as analysis, and never by rationality. He believes, as I do, that consciousness is continuously renewed..... invaded if you like..... by other, outside resonances. Most of it on the level of the unconscious, dreams and so on. We MUST expose it. Open it. Otherwise we atrophy and die. Theatre and ritual are what is needed. He had two great successes in Munich. He has written this new book recently. It will come out in two weeks time, simultaneously in Paris and Munich and Vienna. You will love the book, I know. Ironically it is a study of Sandor Ferenczi..... the metaphorical father of us all..... master of our splinter group. Your real father was trained under Ferenczi's direct supervision. He shows that Ferenczi was the great visionary of the whole movement, who tried to develop Freud's methods towards one that included the soul, the spirit..... The book is part new biography - he found some papers and a notebook never published - and part criticism..... showing how much a poet Ferenczi was, how he tried so hard in his life to reach his patients through love and tenderness..... as your fa..... er..... er ..... Helmut, believed later on, too. He is a great admirer of "Thalassa" as I know you are. The book is mostly about why analysis so often fails because the only person who should be standing in front of the patient when they go right back to the primal trauma, is the mother. Not the father at all. I think you know that. Yes! I remember. You say it in the book. Where did you get that idea from? You will love his book, I know, as you will love him. But his theatre plays are fantastic. One will become an opera soon. He is a fine man, of great integrity.'

Nora went to the window. She couldn't understand why the garden seemed so bright. It sparkled with a strange light that seemed to be coming from inside everything..... it was so radiant, so numinous..... she murmured to herself..... 'Just like 'la vie en rose!'.....

She could see her cat coiled up in a cusp of the willow tree. Now she would never dare to guess its name. She'd get a female next time so they could mate. She'd name the kittens after flowers and birds..... Robin, Primrose, Daisy, Peregrine.....

She excused herself for a moment, and went to her studio to bring down a drawing and her copy of 'Thalassa'. She gave the drawing to her mother. 'It is an amazing coincidence but I used this book, and the lines I had underlined, as the starting point for most of the drawings in my exhibition!' She flicked the book open and recited some lines she had underlined..... the first ones that popped up.....

> '..... so that we have represented in the sensation of orgasm not only the repose of the intrauterine state, the tranquil existence in a more friendly environment, but also the *repose of the era before life originated,* in other words, *the deathlike repose of the inorganic world.'*

They both remained silent, until Nora continued. 'I became like that. A stone. The earth, but barren. Until recently, anyway. I had better read the book yet again, yet again, before I read my real father's book. I was never sure why I was using "Thalassa". I just felt I had to!' She stood up and went to the window again, and while looking at the garden, she asked her mother..... 'My father..... what is his name..... and is he Jewish?'

Her mother took some time to reply, 'His name is Karl-Ludwig. We have reason to believe his father might have been Jewish. Or half Jewish. But we can't be sure. He'd died early. He comes from a poor background. Records were destroyed, often deliberately. Look at Hitler! There was such a mess in the war. But he is quite German.'

'Aryan . . . . . as they used to say?' Nora asked, coldly.

'Yes. Very. Of course! He has, as they say, an Aryan eye. Oh Anna . . . . . let me call you Anna just for now . . . . . I might as well tell you the whole truth, now, once and for all. He was a soldier in the war. In the SS. In fact he was THE soldier in the war. It was he who arranged for my father and I to escape. We kept in touch. Later we became lovers again. For real, this time.'

Nora suddenly laughed, despite herself. 'For real! What an expression from you of all people, mother. For real! And . . . . . while I think of it . . . . . while we are on the subject of fathering, how is YOUR father, by the way?'

'Oh him, poor soul! Poor devil! Fine, thankyou. Quite frail in body, but as ever, alert in mind. Doesn't miss a trick. He read your book very carefully, looking for a needle in a haystack, he called it. He rang me up afterwards and said, "She did a good job! Discrete thank God!" You saying it could not be ascertained if the incest was real or imagined.'

Nora turned to her mother, smiling, 'Yes, he liked it because I concealed the truth. Money! Sex didn't matter so much especially as it was vague. We are a strange family Mother. Perhaps we are not the ideal model on which to base theories about love and life and psycho-analysis . . . . . and the world at large, or are we?'

'Never! But it doesn't matter. Forget all that. That is the past now. We must find new ways now, the three of us, to find our peace with ourselves and with our past, our traumatic memories, and our future. We are victims though like everyone else of the all pervading repressions on which the state thrives.'

Nora laid the little wooden object on the table and smiling mischievously, she said, 'You can have it back mother . . . . . I won't be needing it now!'

But the older woman smiled. 'Don't be too sure. Keep it. It has brought you luck so far . . . . . you never know . . . . . you might need it from time to time!' and they both laughed. 'Oh by the way. Some even more amazing news. Your book . . . . . well . . . . . Karl-Ludwig showed it to a friend of his, a well-known film producer. He was bowled over by it and is at this very moment trying to persuade a large film company in Munich to make it as a film. If he manages to arrange it, he will pay you a very large sum for the Film Rights! What do you say to that? At least he is starting on the right track, this new father of yours! The film producer said he would make it a portrait of the young woman ..... cut out a lot of the ideas, and make even the parents less important ..... in fact he would want to call the film just "Nora". Develop the love affair with Anna much more ..... make it a film more about the children of our revolutionary times ..... play down all the psycho-analysis and the references to the Ghetto. Too heavy. People of today would rather forget. Crazy of course but it's a film - not truth - and would make you a lot of money. What do you think?'

..... Nora couldn't think things like that ...... she returned to the window to look at her garden and felt herself fragmenting ..... With long pauses, almost in a trance, she spoke, finding it hard to remain coherent, fighting back the waves of emotion just below a surface.

'Yes, what a good idea!

Let them do what the hell they want with it as long as they pay, mother!

It's my past now and I don't care about it any longer, AND I am looking forward to meeting my new, my real father .....

How strange to suddenly have a father who is all future and nothing of the past ..... only lightly unblemished by fantasy ..... at least no photographs!

The King is Dead. Long Live the King!

I have no image of him in my mind. I always saw him, that soldier of yours, without a face. A blank.

He sounds interesting. He will be more interesting with a face.

Oh and by the way, on the subject of money, thankyou for the house! The mansion! Now I can feel it is really mine .....

I am happy here ..... my Eden. I love the willow trees. They always reminded my of my father's four poster bed ..... or should I say 'his' four poster bed. Like a tent.

You know it's sad, I have only one cat now ..... which will have to be enough, though I still don't know which one. Perhaps I don't want to know which one.

It has been a strange time since the merry months of May and the so-called events! I really went there to stand in front of the SS..... the CRS..... I nearly stripped!

..... to understand what YOU felt and I ended up losing my virginity to an Immunologist! Quite a nice chap, but essentially dull..... a rationalist, lightly coloured by a naive romanticism, all gleaned from his ex-girlfriend. Totally unoriginal, his mind made of layers of photographic emulsion. Mille feuilles.

I wonder if they were right to bring in the soldiers to restore law and order. Men in uniforms performing dark rites, masquerading behind their theatrical 'props' of plastic and steel.

The first night I went into the fray, I wore a red rose on my black outfit, but soon lost it. For that I cursed them. I so wanted to look pretty.

It was frightening seeing the State hell-bent on murdering its own children..... all over again..... On the wall of the Sorbonne they wrote 'It's bleeding!'..... Now, I won't bleed ever again..... not the innocent bleeding of first betrayals.....

The biggest shock of all was discovering my plumb-line was a pendulum, used for divining water. Isn't that silly?

That was the night I abandoned my final barricade, surrendered my virginity..... something as trivial as that, mother. Trivial!

It is going to be hard imagining you making love with another man..... creating me! My primal scene will have to be re-drawn. Can it ever be? A man with an Aryan eye!

Blue like the sky. The Sky God! He who murdered the soul.

I always wondered why I had blue eyes, but thought it was a trick of nature, something remembered in the genes from a former life. An ancestor!

But tell me mother..... before I go to my room for a long period of reflection and a good cry..... what will I do if I don't like my new father? What if I hate his guts?'

Her mother smiled..... 'But you *will* like him my darling, I'm sure! He is tall and blond and very good looking. Very sensitive and creative. He is also very calm. Peaceful. Not like Helmut, so broken, so tormented. All his life the wandering Jew. He has been through his particular hell of guilt and self-doubts, but come through. A nice man. And didn't you always say - "Am I not my father's daughter"?'

Nora thought about it for some time. She was playing with the little pendulum..... 'Yes.....' she said coldly, without emotion at first..... 'The one thing I always clung to, and now I learn it was the biggest lie of all. Strange how the child identifies with the aggressor. But what shall I DO with my time, now? Now that I have discovered a future tense? Get permanently stoned like the daughter of Lot, or was it wife? Take heroin and fuck around like Anna? Pay for another anarchist group? I'll have enough money to buy them all. But no-one ever taught me how to BE, mother..... and just do things..... like poor long suffering lovely screwed up Anna. I love her almost as much as..... as..... Good God! I see it now. I know exactly what I'm going to do!' She turned triumphantly towards her mother. 'Yes I know! I will follow my poor broken heart where it leads me, and it has already spoken. I'm going to breed Abyssinian mountain cats! Hundreds of them. Here in the garden in huge sheds. In walls within walls. Take them back a plane-load at a time..... and let them loose in the Abyssinian mountains, where they're now extinct. Some will survive, won't they? Some will escape without being shot.....? Some will get away and go back to nature, surely, even if we can't?'

Her mother seemed impatient. 'Anna! Why not go back to the Sorbonne and finish your Ph.D.? I know on the grape vine you were doing exceptionally well. I got in touch from time to time..... And your book has brought you much credit even though people are still saying it was your father's work. You have so much to look forward to now.....'

Nora laughed. 'I can't. I burnt all my bridges behind me. I wrote to my Professor and told him he was a patriarchal shit and he could go to hell. That was in March. In May he was in it! And who needs to read another thesis about anarchists, even one revealing they are merely trying to make conscious the sexual wars they have already fought and lost in their own unconscious minds? No, mother. I will breed cats..... and hope in my next incarnation, I will be one of them. Closer to the earth.....

Or, I..... I..........'